Chivalrous

Books by Dina Sleiman

VALIANT HEARTS

Dauntless
Chivalrous

Valiant Hearts ◇ Book Two

Chivalrous

DINA L. SLEIMAN

BETHANYHOUSE
a division of Baker Publishing Group
Minneapolis, Minnesota

Published by Bethany House Publishers
11400 Hampshire Avenue South
Bloomington, Minnesota 55438
www.bethanyhouse.com

Bethany House Publishers is a division of
Baker Publishing Group, Grand Rapids, Michigan

Printed in the United States of America

Library of Congress Cataloging-in-Publication Data
Sleiman, Dina L.
    Chivalrous / Dina L. Sleiman.
        pages cm.—(Valiant hearts ; book two)
    Summary: "In medieval North Brittania, Gwendolyn longs to be a knight
like her brothers but is bound by her parents' treatment of her as only a mar-
riage pawn"—Provided by publisher.
    ISBN 978-0-7642-1313-7 (pbk.)
    [1. Middle Ages—Fiction. 2. Sex role—Fiction. 3. Family life—Fiction. 4.
Nobility—Fiction. 5. Knights and knighthood—Fiction. 6. Great Britain—
History—13th century—Fiction.] I. Title.
PZ7.1.S59Ch 2015
[Fic]—dc23   2015015267

Unless otherwise indicated, Scripture quotations are from the King James Version
of the Bible.

Scripture quotation identified JPS is from the Jewish Publication Society Version.
© 1917 by The Jewish Publication Society

Cover design by Paul Higdon.
Cover model photography by Steve Gardner, PixelWorks Studios, Inc.

Author represented by The Steve Laube Agency.

17 18 19 20 21 22 23   8 7 6 5 4 3 2

To my readers:

My prayer is that you will be strong and courageous. Follow the path God has laid before you, wherever that might lead. Be a doctor, a lawyer, a professional athlete, a wife, a mother, or even a president.

Chase after your dreams, and if a handsome knight in shining armor should happen to come alongside you, headed in the same direction, and you should happen to fall in love . . . then join together and become partners in your quest.

But please remember—you are complete, you are beautiful, and you are dearly loved by God just the way you are.

———— ◇◆◇ ————

A woman of valour who can find? for her price is far above rubies. . . . Strength and dignity are her clothing; and she laugheth at the time to come.

Proverbs 31:10, 25 JPS

———— ◇◆◇ ————

Prologue

I am a knight.
Strong like steel.
Ready to conquer any foe.

Energy surges through me, striving to burst out my skin. The moment is ripe. Above my horse's whipping white mane, I stare into the eyes of my opponent. Though at a distance, I know them well. Bright blue and shimmering with intelligence.

One must always understand one's opponent. Find a way inside said opponent's mind. This one will feint to the right before pressing dead center, but with a flicker of hesitancy just before the end. I shall seize that moment. And victory shall be mine.

Pointing my lance to the sky, I ready myself. In my mind's eye, I picture grandstands made of wood festooned with colorful coats of arms. I can almost see the pennants swaying in the breeze and hear the crowds roaring with anticipation. Just over there, a herald blasts a trumpet. Our names are called. The duke and duchess, arriving just in time, wave to the crowd and take their seats in the ornate chairs prepared for them.

But the picture fades. In truth, our only audience is the tree-lined hillside surrounding this flat patch of grass, the scatter of wild flowers alongside our battle course, and a craggy old mountain looming beyond. Diverting my focus for just a moment, I spy a red bird fluttering past and a squirrel chomping a nut nearby. They alone shall witness my triumph. But it shall be sweet nonetheless. And perhaps someday, against all odds—if dreams come true—I might joust in a real tournament.

I give heed to my opponent once again. With a nod, I lower my lance to the parallel position. The warrior across the field mirrors my every move.

Now!

I slam my heels into my horse's flank and thrust my weight forward with all my might. Locking fist, wrist, elbow, and shoulder into place, I steel my lance against my side. As the wind whips past, time grows oddly slow. From the corner of my eye, I note as the startled squirrel pivots and dashes toward a tree.

My opponent speeds closer one pounding hoofbeat at a time. Blue eyes squint within the slit of the helmet. A loose lock of black hair slaps against the silver armor. Almost there. As I assumed, the lance headed my way shifts subtly to the right. Before my opponent can straighten once again, I lean yet farther forward for the strike.

In an instant lasting an eternity, our weapons clash, tangle, and arc toward the sky. But only I am prepared, and I hold tight. My opponent's lance continues its heavenward flight, looping through the air. The armor-clad figure is thrown backward by the impact, fights for control, and then topples, flipping feet over head before crashing to the ground.

Our horses fly past each other, but only I remain seated with my weapon in hand. I whoop in victory. Waving my blunted lance in triumph, I turn and bow toward the squirrel, who is now hidden in the branches above.

I long to linger and bask in the glory of the cheering crowd. To kneel before the duchess and receive my tribute. Alas, such favor shall not be afforded me this day. Those such as I are not permitted to fight in tournaments. Not even in this supposed Eden where we dwell. Here on the practice field, in secret alone, can I thrill to the excitement of the joust.

My attention turns to my opponent. The armored figure lies crumpled, facedown upon the well-trampled field. My stomach catches in my gut, for my intention had never been to injure. Only to defeat.

Trotting my horse back in that direction, I hop off. "Are you well? Rosalind, answer me, please."

I kneel alongside my beloved servant. Dare I touch her? Might I injure her further?

A few pathetic moans emanate from the too-still figure.

Having little choice, I gently roll her over.

She jerks and spasms, coughing several times, and then flops down again with her arm at an odd angle. Through the slits in her helmet, I detect her tongue lolling from the side of her mouth.

My stomach clenches into a tight knot. "No," I whisper, pressing my hands to my mouth as my heart speeds and my blood chills. I shall never forgive myself if she dies, all for my selfish entertainment.

"Ha, ha! I fooled you." Rosalind bolts to sitting. She pulls off her helmet, revealing gleaming black hair escaping its braid, milky skin, and berry-tinged lips turned into a wicked smile.

I give her a shove as I attempt to breathe normally and untangle my stomach. "That is not funny! You scared the life right out of me."

Rosalind frowns. "You deserved it, Lady Gwendolyn. Besides, 'twas not all an act. You did knock the wind from me. I told you this was a bad idea."

"If I ever wish to improve, I need to test my jousting against a live opponent, not merely the practice quintain." Removing my own helmet, I allow my long blond braid to fall free, and I breathe deep the fresh summertime air.

Rosalind pants as she speaks. "My old mum never thought I'd be in such danger when she sent me to serve a fine lady in a castle."

"Oh, you love it."

"'Do the lady's hair,' she said. 'Dress her in fine gowns,' she said. 'No job like it in the world.' That's what Mum promised when she sent me from home."

Rosalind stands and brushes the dirt away, appearing twice her normal width in her thick padded vest covered with chain mail. "She got the last part right enough. Nowhere else on earth would a handmaiden be set to jousting in a field. I don't mind a sword match now and again, and I admit to enjoying target practice with arrows and daggers. Even a woman must be ready to defend herself and her children when need arises. But I hate this heavy armor. 'Tis hot like Hades!"

"Hush you and take it off, then."

"You like to joust because you know you'll win." Rosalind tugs at her hauberk.

I help Rosalind lift the weighty chain mail over her head, being careful not to catch her hair. "Hugh has been too busy helping the duke to tilt with me. A girl must keep her skills sharp."

"Must she? And for what purpose, might I ask?" Rosalind's blue gaze pierces straight into me. "Have you plans to go on campaign that you have not apprised me of? Perhaps to slay a dragon or a monster along the way?"

The young woman stands nearly my height and can look me in the eye, unlike most females. One of the many reasons I chose her, along with her brash personality and saucy wit. Her astounding beauty almost put me off at the first, but Rosalind has a way with hair and paints that might stand in my favor someday, so I overlook that inconvenience.

Besides, truly, how many maids could be convinced to joust?

Though she is, of course, right that my fighting skills hold little purpose, I do not concede. "I long to protect the weak and the innocent. To defend our just dukedom. Eleanor of Aquitaine led a crusade. One never knows when doors might open for a female warrior."

"One might suppose that if they are not open in the fair and progressive dukedom of North Britannia, they will never open anywhere." Rosalind unfastens the heavy, padded gambeson and removes it.

Her linen tunic clings to a figure far more slender than my own, revealing every curve and cranny until she shakes it loose. "Oh, bother with this heat. Jousting in midsummer. Who ever heard of such nonsense? Shall we try swimming in December next? I hear the water is delightful that time of year."

Ignoring her off-subject tirade, I continue my argument. "One might rather say that if those doors might open anywhere, it would be here. I have met Duchess Adela on a few occasions, and she seems a feisty sort." I cross my arms over my chest, hoping to appear fierce. "The Amazonian women were warriors. I tell you, it could happen."

"You and your Amazons." Rosalind huffs and shuffles to her horse, dragging her armor along the ground. "One legendary group of women in the entire history of the earth, and you must seize to the idea as normal."

Naturally I am fascinated with the Amazons—women who

justify my height and sturdy build. Throughout childhood I played at Amazonian princess and, despite my brothers' teasing, took great pride in my imaginary role. "Let us not forget the prophetess Deborah."

Rosalind swings her armor atop her horse. "Of course we must never," she says with a heaping dose of sarcasm. "But even Deborah did not joust. Perhaps when you foretell the future, I shall hold out hope for your destiny as a knight, but until then, you must be realistic. How long can you avoid marriage?"

Panic rises within me like an icy mountain spring, threatening to take my breath away. "I shall never marry."

"Right then, good luck with that." Rosalind turns her full attention to me. "You never want to plan for the future. But one day soon it will be upon you. Then what shall you do?" she asks with all the wisdom and experience her two additional months upon the earth allot her.

I scowl her way and head back to Andromache, my giant, snow-white mare. I nuzzle the horse, taking comfort in her scent of hay and oats. Andromache never judges me. Never demands that I plan a future or take the practical course. She contents herself to live in the excitement of the moment with me.

At sixteen, I have managed to escape marriage longer than many noble women. With Father ever away and practically in denial about my existence, who is to say I cannot stretch it another three years, or even five? By then I will be past my prime, and perhaps between my advanced age and my ill-suited stature, no one will want me at all.

Perhaps one of my dear brothers, Hugh or Gerald, shall take me in. I could help him train for battle, guard his home when he is off to war, and be a favorite auntie to his children. All might yet be well.

I mount Andromache, and Rosalind pulls alongside upon

a gentler brown mare. "Lady Gwendolyn, do not be cross. I only speak the truth, and only because I care. You are a noble-woman, reared for marriage and breeding. You can't outrun your fate, but perhaps if you are well prepared, you will find happiness within it."

Pressing my heels into Andromache's side, I flick the reins. I shall not argue further with Rosalind. The silly romantic girl does not understand what I know all too well.

There can be no joy in a noble marriage arranged for power and alliance. Only misery.

And so I will live in the moment and milk every bit of pleasure from life while yet I can.

Chapter 1

England, Late Summer 1217

Allen of Ellsworth dismounted and propped his lance against the rails. Victorious as usual these days, he offered a hand to his training opponent and helped his fellow squire from the dirt. The captain of the guard simply nodded his head, but Lord Linden entered the practice field, cheering as he came.

"Excellent job, my boy." The earl, dressed in a regal mantle and cape, gave Allen a good thump on the shoulder despite his chain mail. Allen had come to adore the kindly man with his crinkling eyes and long waving hair that circled a shining bald spot on his head. "Come and walk with me for a while."

Allen turned to the captain, who nodded once again with the same stoic expression upon his face.

"Sir Walter will see to your things, will you not?" Lord Linden gestured to Allen's horse and weapons.

"If you say so, m'lord," the captain answered, for he was ever drilling into his men that their equipment was their life, and they must take care of it at any cost.

How odd it must be to have your every whim granted as Lord Linden did. Since moving to Lindy almost a year ago, Allen still hadn't adjusted to being so closely associated with the local nobility. He pulled off his gloves and helmet, placing them in a stack upon the ground.

"Are you ready, then?" Though well into his middle years, Lord Linden grinned from ear to ear like a small boy. Something must be afoot.

"Yes. Where are we heading?"

"To the village. I have news to share with everyone."

"Excellent." Now that Allen lived with the soldiers in the garrison, he did not spend much time in the village. But he did miss the children of Ellsworth, otherwise known as the Ghosts of Farthingale Forest, his old band of outlaws, and he loved watching them work at creating their new home. Only Red trained with Allen to be a knight at Lord Linden's castle. The rest of the group served nearby as peasant farmers in the village of Lindy.

"I have received word that the king is sending Timothy home to us soon," the earl said.

"I'm sure you'll be happy to have him back." Allen mopped the sweat from his brow and pushed his light brown hair from his eyes.

He had no particular need to see Timothy again, but he would try to be happy for Lord Linden's sake. Not so long ago, Allen had lost his heart to the lovely Lady Merry Ellison. Although he knew she did not belong with a common fellow like him, their joint standing as outlaws struggling to survive in the realm of the evil King John had muddied the situation for a time. In the end she accepted the proposal of Timothy Grey, her childhood sweetheart who was both son and nephew to powerful noblemen.

The baron rubbed his hands together with excitement as they strolled side by side down the wooded lane. "We are all anxious for his return, and we hope a wedding shall soon take place."

Everyone had expected the two noble lovebirds to marry quickly, but no sooner had their intentions been announced than Timothy was summoned to the court of the new young King Henry. It seemed, as a small child, Henry had admired Timothy, and as a newly appointed king at the age of ten, had desired his hero by his side.

"It makes sense that he shall return now that the peace accord has been signed. I'm certain Lady Merry shall be relieved," Allen said.

"Merry, her aunt, and my wife have had the grandest time planning the nuptials and celebration. Once Timothy arrives, we shall set a date and invite all the nobles in the area for the long-awaited event."

Allen looked away, hoping the man beside him never realized that he had tried to thwart Merry and Timothy's romance. Though he had come a long way in letting go of his affection for Merry, the memory still stung, and he had no real desire to watch her and Timothy celebrating their marital bliss.

"A long-awaited wedding, indeed," Allen said, trying to appear pleasant about the situation. "Four years in the making, one might say."

"King John certainly did have a way of mucking up matters, did he not?"

"God rest his soul," Allen mumbled, for he would wish the fires of hell upon no man, not even King John, who had murdered his family and would have seen their entire village dead if he'd had his way.

"You looked good on the jousting field." The shorter man reached up to clasp Allen's shoulder.

"Thank you. I try my best. God has gifted me with height and strength, and you have gifted me beyond my wildest dreams with training. I only hope to someday live up to those gifts and serve my country well."

Though Allen had been raised a peasant, after the Ghosts' two-year ordeal in the forest, Lord Linden had given sanctuary to the young survivors of Ellsworth. Allen had grown several inches in the past year and broadened considerably. At eighteen, he towered over most of the soldiers in the garrison.

Lord Linden nodded thoughtfully. "That someday might come sooner than you think. Sir Walter says you are ready to move from squire to knight. I look forward to conferring the honor upon you, although I assume there is another to which you hope to pledge your fealty."

Allen had not deemed himself ready to head off into the world, but if Sir Walter thought him worthy to be a knight, perhaps he should go now, before Timothy returned and the winter weather arrived. "I still long to head to North Britannia, m'lord. You of all people know that I've felt oddly drawn there ever since I learned about it. Do you truly believe there might be a place there for one such as me?"

"Now that the political situation has stabilized, North Britannia has opened its borders, and as we assumed, it has continued in its quest to become a just and righteous dukedom after the tradition of Arthur's Camelot. They say that any man of valor and pure heart might find his place there."

"As much as things have improved in England as a whole, I still wish to be a part of such a quest. I cannot help but believe that God himself has placed such a strong desire in my heart." Anticipation rushed over Allen.

"I shall send you with a letter of introduction and give you my highest recommendation."

"You are too kind, m'lord, but I would not wish to inconvenience you."

"'Tis no bother. I am proud of you, my boy." Lord Linden led the way around a turn in the path.

The previously abandoned village, which had been a tangle of weeds, bushes, and decrepit huts a year earlier, now appeared neat, tidy, and bustling with life. At a distance he spotted Lady Merry, dressed in a lilac kirtle rather than the boy's clothes she had worn to lead their forest raids. She sat on the steps of the manor home singing to little Wren, who cuddled upon her lap. Merry's waving brown hair had grown from its previous short cut and now tossed in the breeze, accenting her striking features.

"Please do not tell them I plan to leave," Allen said. "I would like to speak to Lady Merry first."

"I am certain your former mistress will support your decision." Lord Linden seemed not to understand how close they had all become in the forest, nor how class divisions had melted away. And he most certainly did not know that Allen, born of the lowest class, had once kissed the noble Lady Merry on a tree branch.

Allen's cheeks warmed at the thought, but he hoped that any ruddiness would blend with the flush of the day's earlier battle. "Yes, but I feel I should tell her before we make the news public."

"You shall stay for the wedding, of course," Lord Linden said.

"I think not. I had best start out as soon as possible. It will take me several weeks to get there, and I should be well on my way before any early snows might block the mountain passages."

"You have ample time, but I understand your eagerness. I had thought to save it as part of the wedding celebration, but I shall arrange for your knighthood ceremony a few days hence. An exciting adventure awaits you!"

"Thank you." Allen hoped that Lord Linden was correct, for he was about to leave everything and everyone he held dear far behind.

◇◇◇

"You shall never win at that pace!" Gwendolyn shouted over her shoulder as she raced Andromache through a rainbow field of wild flowers.

Rosalind's faint, "I'm trying," was muffled against the rush of wind.

Gwen thrilled at the exhilarating moment of freedom as she clutched her horse's mane, leaning forward over her graceful white neck. Hovering weightless with each powerful stride, she felt as if she could fly.

Together they dashed down a rolling hillside and crashed through a trickling stream. Droplets of frigid mountain water splashed against the bare skin of her forearm and speckled her tunic. They raced across her hidden jousting field, through a patch of trees, and up a rocky incline before pulling to a stop next to a small wooden building.

Gwen had already removed her hilt and sword by the time Rosalind joined her, though she left a small jeweled dagger in her boot.

"Not fair," declared Rosalind. "Should I not get some sort of head start? You've been riding all your life."

"Now, where would be the fun in that? You must challenge yourself if you wish to be a warrior worth your armor."

"Who said I wished for that? I'd be happy braiding flowers into your golden hair and fussing over your silken gowns."

Although Gwen had managed to woo Rosalind to her warrior ways, the young woman had not adjusted entirely. Rosalind might have spent a boisterous childhood dancing through fields, climbing trees, and tussling with village lads in the dirt, but weapons of steel and giant horses still tested her limits.

"But admit it." Gwen grinned impishly. "This is so much better."

Rosalind giggled. "I suppose so. I never dreamt of such excitement. If I ever need to look for employment again, I shall have an exhaustive list of skills to my name."

"You see. You might guard a threatened princess."

"Or escort a noblewoman on pilgrimage."

Gwen gathered her armor. "Come, time to head home."

They hung their swords inside the dim little structure next to lances, shields, chain mail, and even a battle ax. Her brothers had helped her build this hidden structure years ago. Though her mother cared little what Gwen did, if word ever reached her father that she trained at the warrior arts, she dared not imagine the consequences.

One of the few times he had deigned to visit home, he had thrashed her bottom merely for riding on horseback. According to Father, true ladies rode in traveling wagons, or better yet, were carried in litters, or best still, did not leave home at all.

Once their weapons were safely stowed, Gwen brushed her mantle of rich burgundy down over her tunic and turned to Rosalind. "How do I look? Ready for inspection?"

Rosalind pulled a twig from Gwen's braid and tucked some flyaway strands behind her ear. "That will have to suffice until I can redo your hair for supper. If one does not peer too closely, you might almost pass for a lady."

"Funny." Both of them wore thick men's leggings and leather boots beneath their women's apparel with slits up the sides for freedom of movement.

They gathered their horses and led them at a walk down the trail, for they did not wish to startle the villagers by thundering through. Gwen picked a green leaf from a bush jutting into the pathway and crunched it between her fingers for the feel of its lush snap. A rich, herbal fragrance wafted to her nose, and she drank deep the smell of the countryside she loved. She gazed into the azure sky, which rippled with white clouds like waves in the sea.

As they reached the village and passed through the huts with their mud-daubed walls and pale thatched roofs, Gwen waved to her father's serfs. These people had been more a family to her over the years than most of those who dwelt in the cold stone castle, always busy with their own affairs. She surveyed this world of browns and tans, so subdued after her afternoon in the bright field yet brimming with vitality.

A young girl named Maggie, wearing naught but a plain tunic with tatters about the hem, dashed across the muddy lane and threw her scrawny arms around Gwen's waist.

Unable to resist the wave of warmth that filled her, she scooped the girl off the ground, feeling her bones beneath coarse fabric. "Maggie, have you been eating your porridge?"

Hugging Gwen tight, the girl wrapped her legs around Gwen's waist and caught her grimy, bare feet together behind her back. "I don't like it so much as I like them apples you bring me."

How Gwen wished she could offer Maggie—not to mention the other village children—trenchers of bread filled with hearty meat stew. But her eldest brother, Reginald, who ruled in her father's absence, would never tolerate such generosity to their serfs. "Well, I have a surprise you might like."

With Maggie dangling from her, Gwen dug through the sack on Andromache's side. Pulling out not one, but three bright red apples, she held them before the wide-eyed little girl. "Now you must promise to share these with your brother and sister."

"Of course, miss." Maggie dropped back to the dirt and jumped about.

"One should call her Lady—" Rosalind began, but Gwen cut her off with a wave of her hand.

She had no need for ceremony with these villagers. Handing

the treats to her small friend, she hustled Maggie to her hut. Then Gwen and Rosalind continued toward the austere stone tower, which she was obliged to call home.

If only Reginald would tend their serfs in the manner recommended by Duke Justus, she should not have to fill her sack with apples. His dukedom, North Britannia, had grown near legendary for its adherence to the law and Christian charity. Chivalry and kindness ruled the day. The very reasons Gwen wished she could fight to protect the dukedom alongside her brothers.

But her eldest brother, Reginald, walked a fine line. While he had little choice but to treat their serfs with a modicum of fairness, being so close to the grand castle of the duke, he also had to please their father, who expected him to rule by the old values.

The only Christian principle her father seemed to stand by was divine order—nobility over peasants, men over the spawn of Eve. Forget the Ten Commandments. Forget the gentler instructions of Jesus's sermon on the mountain, which their duke held so dear. An eye for an eye would suffice for her father. Being sent such conflicting messages from a young age, Gwen had chosen to ignore religion, trusting instead her own inner sense of right and wrong. She could not help but think religion mostly a man-made system for proving one's own preferences correct.

Hoofbeats drew her attention as a horseman in full armor raced in their direction. When the rider drew near, her brother Hugh's jovial features and riot of golden curls came into view.

He pulled his destrier up hard beside them and hopped lithely to the dirt road, tossing up a cloud of dust with the impact.

"Gwennie! My most darling and beloved sister on the entire earth." He caught her head under his arm and tousled her hair in a boisterous display of affection, as he had since childhood.

"Your only sister on the entire earth." She shoved him away with a chuckle. After handing off Andromache's reins to Rosalind, Gwen gestured to Hugh's formal attire. "What is this? And why the dramatic greeting?"

Rosalind cut between them and curtsied. "Afternoon, Sir Hugh. How can we be of service?" Her flirtatious tone revealed far more about the nature of her relationship with Hugh than Gwen wished to acknowledge.

Hugh, always carefree and charming, raked Rosalind's form with his gaze. "Ah, my fair maid Rosalind, I fear there is little you can do for me today but bid me a fond farewell."

"Are you leaving?" The words burst from Gwen in an unexpected shout as her heart sank to her boots. Her brother Gerald was still supporting the king's army in Lincoln where they had defeated the rebels. Must she lose Hugh as well?

"Yes, I am to escort the new king, Henry, on a tour of his recently reacquired northern realms. Father believes my jovial nature might be an asset with the young sovereign. Perhaps I shall pull a gold coin from his royal ear."

Gwen swatted her irreverent brother. "I am just glad England is no longer under the rule of that awful King John."

"As are we all, but that is not why I came," Hugh said. "I must warn you that Father has at long last returned. You best rush back home and into your finest gown."

Gwen's stomach plummeted to meet her heart in her boots, and there proceeded to churn mercilessly as she struggled to catch her breath. Father? Home? Why after all these years? Was there no war to be found anywhere? She gathered her courage to ask the only question that might bring some respite. The words emerged in a breathy whisper. "For how long?"

Chapter 2

Hugh's expression turned as near to serious as she had seen on him in many years. "Father is staying for good, or so he claims. He says he has left his holdings in Reginald's haphazard care far too long. You should have seen him fuming and tossing all manner of items about the great hall."

Tears formed in Gwen's eyes as haunting scenes from her father's brief and infrequent visits flashed through her mind. She blinked them back and pulled herself up tall like a warrior, as Gerald and Hugh had taught her.

Hugh gazed down at her with naked sympathy in his eyes. With a tenderness reserved for these moments of dealing with their father, he tugged her to his chest. The clink of his chain mail beneath her cheek comforted her, as did the soft kiss he placed upon her forehead.

'Twas an old, familiar dance. She, Gerald, and Hugh fancied themselves so strong and valiant—until their father came along to dash their illusions. Of course Gerald and Hugh had grown into men, knights in their own right. But what of her?

Who would stand on her side? Mother? Certainly not. Reginald? Not likely.

Gwen could almost pity Reginald. The youngest three siblings had grown up free and wild in the fields surrounding their castle. Ever outrunning nursemaids, tutors, and when the mood pleased, even the knights who trained the boys at warfare. Their childhoods had been filled with humor, imagination, and adventure.

Only Reginald had lived under the heel of his father's boot, and learned to treat others—most of all his unfortunate bride—likewise. At only twenty-five, her sister-in-law, Katherine, appeared weighed down with a burden none should have to bear. She seemed little more than a specter as she trailed her rambunctious passel of children about their small manor home just to the west. Would such be Gwen's fate as well? She could never allow that to happen.

"Hugh, whatever shall I do?" She hid her face against his chest. Gwen felt small and vulnerable in his arms. Only her mammoth brothers could dwarf her so and make her feel a fragile woman.

He nuzzled her hair with his gruff chin. "First, you shall run home and take a bath. Father shall explode if he finds you smelling of sweat and horseflesh." He bent down to sniff her, then shoved her away again in his playful manner, shaking them both free from their doldrums.

Gwen could not hold back a wry grin. "And whose fault is that?"

"I admit that as lads Gerald and I found it the greatest joke to teach you to fight." Again seriousness overtook him. "But I would not want the joke to be upon you, Gwennie. Perhaps it was a youthful error."

"Never say so!" Gwen protested. "I have become precisely who I wish to be. My nursemaids tried to turn me a lady. It was my choice to defy them."

"You had best remember their training now." He turned to include Rosalind in the conversation.

Gwen had nearly forgotten her presence. At Gwen's encouragement, Rosalind oft defied her prescribed role as lady's maid. But in such a poignant moment, she had apparently chosen to tuck herself between the horses and fade into the background as a proper maid should.

"Rosalind, you must be her ally now. See her groomed and dressed on all occasions. There shall be no more jaunting to the countryside. And no more battle training. You know what is expected of a proper lady, and you must help her appear one."

"As you wish." Rosalind batted her long black lashes at Hugh.

Gwen harrumphed. "Not likely."

Hugh detached his stare from Rosalind and swiveled toward Gwen. "Come now. Despite my best efforts to the contrary, you are a lovely lady when you try."

"Do not be ridiculous." Gwen's own mother had told her how ugly she was. Repeatedly.

"Surely you know 'tis true." Hugh winked her way. "You would blush if I told you the things I have overheard the soldiers say about you."

Rosalind stepped forward. "I have told her as much."

Of course Rosalind must say such things, but Gwen winced every time she observed Rosalind's slim form and fair skin next to her own hulking mass and dun-colored complexion.

Hugh took Gwen's hand in his much larger one. "Please do not make me argue that you are beautiful. There are some things a brother simply should never do. And you can play the pipe, embroider, and dance quite well. Do what you must to keep the peace. Soon enough you shall be married and out of his grasp."

"And what good shall that do me?" Anger welled within Gwen. A reviving sort of anger that helped her find her strength.

"Out of his grasp and into the stranglehold of a husband. Would you resign me to a life like our mother's? To the drudgery Katherine suffers at Reginald's hand? You did not train me for such a dreary existence."

"Oh, Gwennie, you were never mine to train. Of course you must marry and bear children. There are good men in the world. I shall talk to Randel Penigree on my way out and convince him to offer for your hand. He would treat you kindly. Perhaps even let you dally with a sword when you are not expecting a child."

"Randel? That silly boy?" Gwen could not imagine taking him to husband. While she might dread a domineering man, she could never respect a weakling either. In their youth he had oft joined in the fun of training Gwen in the warrior arts, but it had not taken her long to best him.

"Well, you must marry someone. Better a friend since childhood who understands your nature."

Her mouth fell open. "I could never." She knew little of marital intimacies. Only what she had heard whispered amongst the maids. But still, she could not submit to such indignities at Randel's bumbling hand. As she further considered, she could not imagine submitting to that with any man. He might just find her dagger to his throat.

"Have you a better plan?" Hugh stood with his feet wide and crossed his arms over his chest as he awaited her reply.

Perhaps she had lived in the moment too long. She had no plans. No contingencies for her future. She grabbed hold of Hugh's huge arms. "Take me with you!"

He pulled away. "Father would never permit it. 'Tis clear he has plans for you now that he has returned."

"Then I must run away."

"To where?" He tapped his foot impatiently.

"To . . . to . . ." She scanned the sky for ideas. "To a nunnery!"

"A nunnery, you say." His features twisted in disbelief. "Because you have always been a religious sort?"

She could hardly lie to this brother who knew her like his very shadow. She had no wish to dedicate her life to God. She still resented Him for creating her a second-rate woman when she would have rather been a knight. "Fine then, I shall run to the forests and become an outlaw. You will come with me, Rosalind—will you not?"

Rosalind gasped. "I . . . well . . . of . . . it would only be . . ."

Hugh caressed Rosalind's shoulder and put an end to her stammering. "Do not give way to her foolishness. If you wish to serve my sister, convince her that all men are not like my father. As well you know." His gaze turned soft as he ran his hand down Rosalind's arm and up again.

Rosalind shivered under his touch and appeared to lose herself in his tender gaze. Her pale cheeks stained to a pretty shade of pink.

For the briefest moment during their exchange, a touch of longing flared to life in Gwen's breast. No man had yet looked at her in such a way. But she doused that flame just as quickly, for she would never allow herself to be as vulnerable, as powerless, as Rosalind seemed to be.

At last Rosalind rallied herself. "I'm sure I have no idea what you are referring to, good sir."

Hugh tossed back his head and chuckled. "If you insist. Just promise to keep my sister out of trouble."

Rosalind looked to Gwen, and Gwen silently pleaded with her maid. "I will serve Lady Gwendolyn's best interest. That is all I can promise."

"Hmm . . ." Hugh swung onto his giant destrier with ease. "That is not what I asked of you, but as I must away soon, I suppose I have no choice but to accept it."

"How soon?" Gwen's voice sounded small to her own ears.

"In an hour or so, and I still have many tasks to accomplish before I leave. You, my wayward sister, must be there to see me off and appear every inch the young noblewoman. So I suggest you hurry as well."

"Of course."

"Take the back route past the kitchen. And be careful," Hugh said over his shoulder as he trotted off.

Together, Gwen and Rosalind headed toward the stables. So many thoughts swirled through Gwen's mind that she could hardly make sense of them. She had lived in denial of the future for too long, and now it would catch up with her.

◇◇◇

Rosalind hid in the shadows of the upper hallway, waiting for Hugh to emerge from his chamber. The family was already collecting outside to see him off, but he had run upstairs to gather a few last items. Though her distraught mistress would no doubt be needing her soon, she could not pass up her only opportunity to bid Hugh farewell in private.

Her heart ached at the prospect, but surely it was for the best that Hugh should be departing so soon after his father's arrival. While a man like Lord Barnes wouldn't give much thought to a dalliance between his son and a servant girl, if he took note of how attached they had grown over the past months, Rosalind might well be tossed out upon her ear.

Hugh's door crashed open, and he flew down the hallway, but Rosalind was ready for him. She stepped out of her hiding place and caught his arm just as he rushed past.

Hugh pulled to a stop and pressed his hand to his chest. "Gracious, Rosalind! You gave me a fright."

She tugged him into the shadows of a small alcove. "Shh! I

merely wished to say farewell." Now that she had him in her grasp, she felt uncertain what to do with him. "Have you any idea how long you might be gone?"

"I wish I knew, but I do know I shall miss you, my pretty little Rosebud." He gathered her to him and cupped her cheek in his hand, stroking it with his battle-roughened thumb.

Even in such dim light, she could stare at his chiseled face and blue eyes for all eternity and never grow weary. There was so much she wished to say, but truly, she should not. He was a noble, she a serving girl. She had known from the beginning that this could be nothing more than a dalliance.

He pressed his forehead to hers. "You have been . . . quite special to me."

Rosalind's heart fluttered at those words, but she bid it to settle, for surely he would offer no more than that. "You must know I feel the same." She bit her lip as she continued to stare into his eyes.

He glanced down the hall and back again. His thumb slid to her lips, brushing across them before he claimed them with his own. But just as quickly, he pulled back. "I would love nothing more than to hide away kissing you all day, but I can delay no longer. Please tell me you understand."

"I suppose I do." Her head understood, but her heart simply would not be convinced.

"Farewell, Rosalind."

"Farewell, Sir Hugh."

As he backed away a sad little sigh escaped her mouth. She pressed her hand against it.

With one last hungry look, he strode down the hall.

Rosalind attempted to quiet her raspy breathing and still the rapid pounding of her heart, both familiar consequences of kissing Hugh in shadowy corners. She knew that Hugh could never be hers, but she had not expected to talk with him for hours upon end about nothing in particular and to be happy just to hold his hand while watching the clouds roll overhead. Though she could no sooner deny Hugh's impish grins and kisses than she could stop the sun from turning about the earth, she had tried to hold back a part of herself.

'Twas for the best that he was leaving. She must keep telling herself that. She could not afford to displease the baron. Though Rosalind's own father had once been a reasonably prosperous miller, after his death her family had been left in the most terrible position. Rosalind's income had put them back on a steady path. Her mother and younger siblings still depended upon her for their daily bread.

She could not let them down.

After a few moments she managed to gather herself and went in search of her mistress. As she passed by the great hall she noted that Lord and Lady Barnes had already come inside. Rosalind continued through the grand front portal and found Lady Gwendolyn standing forlornly in the courtyard, waving to Hugh's back as he headed down the lane with a small retinue.

Through the shimmer of unshed tears, Rosalind watched her first love depart, but it simply would not do to let Gwendolyn see her crying over her noble brother.

She slipped quietly next to her mistress. As Hugh rounded the corner and disappeared into the rustling green trees, she reminded herself that he was meant to be the first of many men in her life. There would be plenty of love in her future, and she would find a way to endure this parting.

However Gwendolyn, despite her brave stance, appeared upon the verge of shattering. Rosalind had spent the last hour dissuading her from dressing up as a squire and following Sir Hugh, for she would be found out and sent back before the sun set. But she understood Gwendolyn's distress. Hugh and Gerald had always protected her from the harsher realities of life, and now both were gone, leaving her alone to face the father she dreaded.

Rosalind placed a gentle hand upon Gwendolyn's shoulder. "Come, m'lady. We shan't do any good standing here all day."

They linked arms and leaned upon one another for support as they trudged through the courtyard.

"Ugh! I am being such a girl. Enough of these blasted tears." Gwendolyn pressed thumb and forefinger against her eyes. "They will do me no more good than staring at an empty lane."

Despite her heavy heart, Rosalind determined to lighten the moment. "You are right, my lady. Besides which, you look like a swine with the pox when you cry."

"Oh, shut up," Gwendolyn said, but she gave Rosalind a shove and began to chuckle just as she had hoped.

Rosalind pasted a false smile upon her face. "We must appear pleasant for your father. I do hope to please him."

"No one pleases Father. The best you can wish for is anonymity."

Rosalind sucked in a sharp breath. The servants had been telling her horror stories of Lord Barnes ever since she arrived, but she had assumed them to be exaggerated. Gwendolyn rarely spoke of the man, but when she did an edge of fear tinged her voice, which Rosalind would not have thought possible in her mistress had she not heard it with her own ears. "Perhaps now that the war is over, he might be in a better mood."

"Father creates his own wars."

As they made their way up the broad stone steps, a booming voice emerged from the portal. "Gwendolyn! Where is that ungrateful chit? Gwendolyn, join us at once."

Gwendolyn jumped.

Rosalind took Gwendolyn's hands in her own. She inspected the gorgeous concoction of braids and curls she had devised for Gwendolyn's thick, golden hair. The rich green gown with gold edging clung to her mistress's enviable curves to perfection. Its long flowing sleeves nearly swept the floor. She looked every inch the lady.

Pleasure surged through Rosalind at the realization that she had served her mistress well. "You are no longer a little girl. There is nothing to fear."

"You do not know him." Gwendolyn's voice sounded breathy.

Rosalind gave her hands a squeeze. "But I know you. You are strong and courageous. Think of your father as an opponent on the jousting field and face him with all the confidence I know you possess."

Gwendolyn nodded but did not seem convinced.

"And I shall go with you." Rosalind offered an encouraging smile.

Gwendolyn shook her head. "Father will not want extra servants about. You will only put yourself in harm's way."

"Are you certain?"

"Completely."

Perhaps Gwendolyn was correct. Rosalind would not wish to anger the baron upon their very first meeting. Much as she wished to support her mistress, she had her family to consider as well.

At that moment, a lone rider crashed into the courtyard, flinging himself from his horse and dashing up the stairs, thrusting Rosalind aside in the process.

"Hello to you too, Reginald," Gwendolyn muttered to the retreating back of her dark-haired eldest brother. He offered half a wave without turning to look at her.

"I hate to leave you thus, Lady Gwendolyn," Rosalind said, looking from the great hall to her mistress and back again.

Gwendolyn seemed to gather some of her fighting spirit. "I insist. Go."

With a backward glance over her shoulder, Rosalind headed down the passage that skirted the great hall and led up the stairway to the bedchambers. In their hurry this afternoon, they had left Gwendolyn's room looking like a tempest had struck. Gowns in rainbow shades of silk and linen festooned the furniture. Pots of paint sat scattered upon the table. Jewels dripped from a wooden chest.

And Gwendolyn had no use for any of it.

Rosalind picked up a burgundy gown and shook it out.

In the early days Rosalind had resented Gwendolyn over her lack of appreciation for the many blessings she had been afforded, but now Rosalind understood. Her mistress wanted only to be free.

Rosalind was her own woman. She would have her fun, enjoy her life in the castle, live out romantic adventures with a few handsome knights, and someday settle down to her own husband and family. Perhaps she would even marry a wealthy merchant or a castle steward, as her mother hoped.

But Lady Gwendolyn was a commodity to be bought and sold.

Chapter 3

By the time Gwen reached the great hall, Father seemed to have forgotten her entirely. In her stead, he bellowed at Reginald.

" . . . some sort of jest! Surely you have not been off at the duke's castle while my serfs laze about wasting time." Gwendolyn's father—with his dark beard, unruly hair streaked with silver, and mammoth frame—sat ramrod straight in a cushioned chair upon the raised dais.

Mother sat next to him, a delicate golden flower by comparison, shrunken into her own chair with a look of pain marring her pretty face.

Gwen turned a deaf ear to Father's rant and sank into the side of one of the huge purple tapestries featuring the Barnes's white-wolf emblem that hung from the stone walls. She supposed the banners were meant to appear festive, but the wolf's bared teeth had ever reminded her of her father's angry snarl, and she had long preferred to hide behind them rather than face the beast.

How many dinners had she spent invisible behind the tapestries? But she was too old for such nonsense—besides which, her large form would surely make a lump in the fabric.

"Why did I trust you? Worthless fool, I told you, there are ways around Justus's mandates. I taught you better." Father barely raised his voice, but he had a special way of adding a barbed edge to each word, and the bulging blue vein on his temple bespoke his anger.

Reginald kept his gaze to the floor. "Yes, Father. I tried to live up to your esteemed reputation, but I lack your experience and wisdom."

Smart man not to argue with Father. It only fueled his fury. But a part of Gwen wished he would stand up to the tyrant upon the dais rather than pacify him as Mother had taught them all to do.

Father's telltale vein shrunk to half the size at Reginald's compliance. "Good thing I have returned. And none too soon."

"We are thankful to have you back, my noble father."

"Of course you are. I only want what is best for this family. Your inexperience has not served you well. But at least the duke speaks highly of you." Father waved to a servant, and the man hurried forward with a goblet of wine.

Mother, who had up to that point sat motionless next to her husband, sparked to life at the sight of the rich red liquid, but Father squelched any chance of her requesting her own with a sharp glance in her direction.

Mother sank deeper into her chair.

"From this time forward, my wife is to have no wine except at celebrations." Father handed down his mandate without so much as a blink.

Mother's skin turned a sickly shade of grey, but she uttered not a word. She practically subsisted on wine. Some days, it seemed her only reason for waking in the morning. If Father refused her mead and ale as well, heaven help the poor woman.

The servant stood gaping at the extreme command.

"Is that clear?" Father ground out between clenched teeth and shot an icy glare at the man.

"Yes, m'lord." The normally confident servant scurried away like a scared mouse.

"Gwendolyn!" her father hollered. "Where is that girl?"

Gathering the courage Rosalind had assured her she possessed, Gwendolyn took a step away from the wall. Perhaps Rosalind was right. If she pleased her father, they might make a new start. "I am here, Father."

Father nearly choked on his wine. "For heaven's sake, stop skulking about like a rat. Come into the light. I wish to see you."

He had ample opportunity to see her when they had bid farewell to Hugh but obviously had not bothered to take notice. Gwen lifted her chin as she approached the edge of the dais and stood next to Reginald, but she kept her gaze down in a demure fashion, which she thought might please her father. He never suffered arrogance, especially in women.

Peeking through her lashes, Gwen watched as he inspected her head to toe.

"Hmm . . . lovely hair."

Rosalind would be so pleased.

"Comely figure. Pleasing features, at least when she wears such a gentle expression. I do recall her scowl to bring out harsh planes on her cheeks."

Gwen did not appreciate the way her father assessed her like a cow gone to market and would have been happy to demonstrate that scowl, but she held herself in check. She glanced nervously to Reginald, but he offered no support. Merely slid a few feet to the side, happy to leave her the sole object of Father's scrutiny.

"Overall better than expected." As was her father's reaction to her appearance. Rosalind must have worked miracles with her paints, for Gwen knew her face to be plain at best.

Father turned his attention to Mother, who flinched ever so subtly. "But could you not stop her from growing so tall? Good heavens, Evangeline, she must tower over half the men in the dukedom. I thought she might inherit your daintiness."

Mother reached out and patted Father's hand. "There, there, dearest husband. She is your child through and through. You have proven a powerful sire to my brood mare." Her giggle tinkled through the room. Mother had always known how to handle their father. She had a special knack for soothing him that oft worked wonders, but on rare occasion exploded back upon her.

Father's deep chuckle rose to meet Mother's giggle and wafted across the room. "'Tis true. I sow a powerful seed."

"And I do believe I recognize that scowl you mentioned as well," Mother dared to joke.

Gwen braced herself for the possible aftermath, but Father tipped back his head and laughed all the louder.

He leaned over and placed a smacking kiss on her mother's cheek. "At least she has your legendary golden tresses. That will stand in her favor."

Gwen had nearly forgotten that once upon a time her mother had inspired poets and troubadours. She now spent most days hidden in her darkened chamber. And that legendary hair remained covered by wimples and scarves as best befit a married lady.

"But what is wrong with the child's skin?" Her father sounded perplexed, more so than angry. "I thought I told you to keep her indoors where women belong."

"Our Gwennie loves nature as much as her father, and you know what a soft heart I have. I cannot bear to keep her locked in the shadows when she longs to be a child of the sun. I allow her to tend the herb garden and stroll within the courtyard. These are acceptable activities for a young lady, are they not?"

Father huffed but otherwise remained calm. It seemed Mother had managed to dodge that fiery arrow. He peered more closely at Gwen's face. "But she is accomplished in the womanly arts?"

"Naturally," Mother said and shot a warning glance in Gwen's direction. "She embroidered the lovely trim upon that gown. And after dinner she shall play the pipe for you."

Conveniently, Mother did not mention that Gwen had embroidered the trim during a snowstorm that kept her trapped in the house for weeks and nearly drove her batty with boredom. Nor did Mother mention that Gwen most often played her pipe in the highest branches of the yew tree just beyond the castle walls.

Was that a gleam of approval in Father's eye? Gwen was not certain, for she did not remember seeing it before. Something warm blossomed in her chest. All these years she had longed to be a boy so that she might win his favor, yet now that she was grown, he was impressed by braids and silken finery. Should she play a haunting ballad or a spritely tune for him this evening? Which would win his smile?

Father nodded and continued his perusal. This livestock just might pass inspection. "You must keep her indoors for a time. And teach her to stoop. She needs to minimize that height. I will depart for Edendale in a few days, and you will join me for the tournament and festivities to celebrate this new peace in England three weeks hence."

"Wonderful plan," Mother simpered.

"Gwendolyn, my darling daughter." Father had never called her such before. He held out his hand to her.

Gwen stepped forward to feel the strong grasp she had longed for all her life. To bask in the approval she had sought but never won.

As he smiled at her, crinkles formed around his bluish grey eyes. "You shall soon be a bride."

Those words sucked the air right from her lungs. "But . . ." She had only just won his favor. Dare she cross him so soon?

"How wonderful for you, daughter." Mother shot her another warning.

Father's grip tightened on her hand, squeezing her knuckles hard against each other. His sharp calluses dug into her skin. "But do not think that I forget your rebellious nature. I recall well how many lashes it took to break your spirit. More even than your brothers." He sent a cold look of disapproval Reginald's way.

Gwen could not discern if he condemned her brother's own spiritedness or the fact that a girl outranked him in stubbornness. "I am sorry for that, Father. But as you see, I am a lady now."

"A lady on the outside, but well I remember your wild heart." He let go of her hand and Gwen retreated backward from the grasp she no longer desired. She felt as though a bucket of icy water had doused that warm flicker in her heart.

Mother bristled, and then reached to rub Father's tense shoulder. "All shall be well."

"I shall make certain of that. We will find a firm husband to keep her in check. We cannot have her disgracing the family by galloping through the countryside like a hoyden."

The room began to spin about Gwen. She could not find enough air.

Mother sighed. This time she sent Gwen a silent message of compassion and camaraderie. "Come, Gwendolyn. Let us retire until supper, and we shall discuss our battle plans. We shall catch you the fiercest husband in the dukedom. A tough man worthy to be son-in-law to the renowned Lord Reimund

Barnes." Mother's giggle rang false to Gwen's ear, but Father smiled his approval once again.

Mother wrapped her arm around Gwen in a nurturing sort of way, although she only stood to Gwen's chin. She took Gwen's hand in her free one and led her out of the great hall with surprising gentleness.

Gwen traveled from the great hall to her chamber in a haze of confusion, but awoke when the heavy door clicked shut. She blinked and glanced about. Rosalind had tidied the room, and she could now see the rich plum blanket covering the bed and the profusion of cushions once again.

Tugging away from her mother, she stumbled to the bed and sank into the feather mattress. She threw herself backward upon it and moaned.

Mother sat gingerly beside her and patted her knee. "There, there, darling. All shall be well. You can do this. You are a capable woman. Strong, intelligent, even beautiful when you choose."

"You always said I was ugly." Gwen grabbed a cushion and smothered her own face with it to stifle a scream.

Mother removed the pillow, placed it neatly on the bed, and patted it into place. "You were ugly in grooming and mannerism. Why, you spent half your youth covered in mud with a fierce expression on your face. But your features are quite lovely. Just look at you now."

That helpful flame of anger flared in Gwen's chest. She sat up and turned to face her mother square on. "Why do you even care? You never did before."

Her mother stroked a wisp of hair from Gwen's brow. A little girl, hidden deep inside of her, reveled at the soft touch.

"Of course I care," Mother said. "I have always loved you with my whole heart. Be fair, Gwendolyn. You are the one who had little use for me."

Gwen's tense shoulders relaxed. She supposed her mother might see matters that way, especially when her whole heart was generally soused with too much wine. The woman did on occasion try to lure her to the solar for embroidery and tapestries, but Gwen hated to sit idle. Mother showed love by fussing and coddling, for which Gwen had little use. Although in a moment like this, Mother's warm affection did bring her some comfort.

Taking her hand, Mother kissed Gwen's brow. "Now that your father is home, we must join forces. There will be no more running off to the fields for you and no more hiding away in my chamber for me. He is a ruthless taskmaster, but we can find a way to keep him in a pleasant mood. Such is a woman's lot in life."

Gwen did not bother arguing with that point. Mother only spoke what everyone else seemed to believe. "He cannot force me to marry. I must give my verbal consent."

Mother bit her lip. "Your father is a determined man. I would not test him in this. He can go to great lengths to exert his will, and fathers have been finding ways to circumvent that law for as long as it has existed."

"I cannot do it, Mother. I cannot marry a harsh and controlling man. Everyone thinks me so strong, but that I could never survive."

Chapter 4

Mother gave Gwen's hand a squeeze. "Do not be silly. If I can survive such a marriage, so can you."

"But what if I do not want your life?" Gwen persisted.

"I have everything I desire. A home that is large, safe, and warm. Wonderful, accomplished children. Abundant food. I would be a fool to ask for more."

Then call Gwen a fool, for that would never be enough for her. "What of happiness?"

"I am happy enough."

Gwen pulled from her mother's touch and scooched several inches away from her on the bed. "You lie! You are miserable. Why else would you hide away day after day? It is not enough for you, and it will never be enough for me."

Mother bristled and swiped an invisible bit of dirt from her shoulder. She focused on the grey stone wall to the far side of the room. "I had one goal in life. To marry a rich, handsome nobleman. And I accomplished that goal."

Gwen snorted. "Perhaps you should have added charming to that list."

"Everything in life comes at a cost. I have embraced my bitter along with my sweet, and I shall thank you not to belittle my achievements." Mother raised her chin, and steel fell across her features.

A part of Gwen wished to continue arguing, but she could not alienate both of her parents at a time like this. "I am sorry."

"You lived with luxury all your life. You have never known the clawing agony of hunger. You have never trudged a rocky trail with bloodied bare feet, stinging with cold until numbness thankfully overtook them."

Gwen pressed her lips together and stared at her mother with new eyes. When dealing with the beautiful lady, it was easy to forget that she had not been reared in a noble home. Though her grandfather had been a knight, Lady Evangeline had not been born to nobility. When her village was ransacked by invaders, her family had fled to Edendale for refuge. Poor and without prospects, she had used her wit and beauty to claw her way to the top, catching a handsome baron's son in the process.

"I have no regrets," Mother whispered, but tears slipped down her cheeks.

Gwen gathered her much-smaller mother in her arms and allowed her to weep upon her shoulder for a good long while.

What horrors had her mother endured? What costs had she paid that Gwen would never know? In that moment she could almost imagine sacrificing freedom for safety and security. But what of the bruises she had spied on her mother's lovely face and delicate wrists? Were they worthwhile as well?

Rosalind tapped upon the thick wooden door and stuck her head around the corner.

Mother pulled away and swiped at her cheeks.

"I'm so sorry," Rosalind said. "I will bring these back later." She indicated the fresh linens in her hand.

"No, no." Mother waved Rosalind into the room as she straightened her gown and wimple. "Please come in. Perhaps you can help me convince Gwendolyn that she can hold far more power as a married noblewoman than as some sort of renegade warrior."

Angel and Mischief, Gwendolyn's beloved little dogs, trotted in behind Rosalind. Just the sight of the furry little bundles of energy took the edge off her frayed nerves.

Mischief hopped onto the highest pillow upon the bed, for he loved to be above everyone in the room. He sat there regally appraising them all with his soft white curls flopping over his eyes. Meanwhile, Angel snuggled herself into Gwen's long, flowing sleeve, as she so loved to do on any occasion Gwen actually deigned to wear a proper gown. She turned herself in a tiny circle and promptly poked her soft, fuzzy head out so as not to miss the action.

Rosalind shook her head at the dogs' antics and then turned serious once again. "I've tried to help your daughter see reason, m'lady, but she will not believe me. As if these absurd little creatures she keeps about do not scream of a woman who longs for a baby."

Mischief sent a few angry barks in Rosalind's direction as if he understood the slight.

"Oh, hush you!" Gwen said to Rosalind, despite Angel curled upon her lap like an infant. Of course a child would bring her a similar pleasure, but at far too great a cost.

Unwilling to give way to Rosalind's teasing, she said, "Mischief is my dog, and Angel is Mischief's dog. So truly, I only have one."

"Yes, clearly. Warriors keep deadly falcons, you know, not

toy dogs." Rosalind turned her attention to Mischief. "Now, get down from there." With a brush of her hand, she attempted to chase him from the pillow he was rumpling.

But Mischief bared his bitty teeth and growled, releasing his inner wolf, and they all chuckled.

"You see," Gwen said, "I am well protected."

"My daughter's penchant for girlish pets aside, I fear I have been lax in my training, but we shall remedy that before the tournament."

"Tournament!" Rosalind's pale cheeks flushed pink with excitement.

"Yes." Mother smiled. "You see, Gwendolyn, that sort of enthusiasm is how one responds to news of traveling to Edendale for a celebration. And yes, Rosalind, you shall be joining us."

Rosalind's hands trembled, and she clutched them together. No doubt she wished to dance a jig but settled for, "Thank you so very much. Won't it be fun, Lady Gwendolyn?"

"I suppose," Gwen said.

"And if all goes well, your mistress will soon be married." Mother beamed with pride.

Gwendolyn moaned and fell backward onto the bed once more. Angel licked her face in a show of sympathy.

Rosalind's eyes grew wide. "I see. How . . . nice."

"My daughter does not think so. Which is why we must work together to convince her. She has three weeks to learn to be a proper, demure young lady."

"I do believe the nursemaids who preceded me attempted to instruct her. And you have always been a wonderful example, Lady Barnes." Rosalind busied herself with putting the last polishing touches on the room.

"You see." Mother hoisted Gwen to sitting with surprising strength. "It shall not be all bad. We shall work on graceful ways to draw attention from your height. And as Rosalind says, you know how to act a lady, you simply must choose to do so. Your father shall be so pleased."

Did Gwen want to please her father? She had not considered the question in years. But as she did now, a war ensued inside her chest, pulling and pushing her one way and then the other.

Mother offered one last kiss before standing and sweeping from the room with all the elegance a noblewoman should display.

Rosalind took Mother's place on the bed beside Gwen and smiled. "A trip to the grand castle will be fun. Surely you can look forward to that part."

Angel, always the jealous sort, wiggled her way between them.

"Father wants to find me a fierce husband." Gwen scowled, though inside she shook with panic. "One who will not let me ride about on horseback like a hoyden."

"Then 'tis time to sharpen those feminine wiles. As your mother said, there are other ways for women to hold power."

Gwen did not know whether to growl like Mischief or melt into a puddle of tears. But Rosalind did not deserve her temper, and if she started crying, she might never stop. Instead she pulled Angel into her arms once again.

"Plus." Rosalind held up a finger. "There is a tournament involved. Won't that be fun?"

"A tournament, to watch idly, from the stands, stuffed into a silken gown." Gwen shook her head in disgust. "I do not wish to watch a tournament. I wish to fight in one."

As the words poured from her mouth, an idea sparked to life in her head and took hold of her. Before succumbing to a life of drudgery, she would enjoy one glorious hour of triumph!

◇ ◇ ◇

Allen stuffed down a final berry tart as he sat crammed into the long trestle table of the candlelit manor home with all of his old companions. Though he was fed well in the castle, he had missed Jane's exceptional cooking.

His friend Red should make things official and exchange his vows with that girl before someone stole her away. But since matters had settled into some sense of normalcy, Red and Jane no longer seemed as certain of their affection. They now had a whole world of potential mates to choose from, not just their little group of twenty-three members.

Hadn't Merry said something along those lines to him last year in the forest? Allen glanced in her direction, for a brief second taking in her glistening hair and warm doe eyes, noting the faint echo of his old heartache that yet remained.

While he had come to accept that a fellow like him did not belong with the noble Lady Merry Ellison, he was no longer a match for a simple peasant girl either, and had yet to find a new maiden to catch his fancy. Under Merry's tutelage he had learned to read and write and fight like a warrior. Over the past year as he continued to hone his battle skills, he had studied the languages of the nobles, and even learned to craft a love poem.

Perhaps once in the city of Edendale, he might meet a free woman, an educated woman. Perhaps the daughter of a merchant or a clerk. Being so near to Merry made him feel small, somehow beneath the person worthy of honor and respect that he had striven to become.

"Allen!" Abigail, now age seven, managed to squirm her growing frame onto his lap. "You must tell us more stories of your adventures. Shall you truly be a knight soon?"

"It seems so." He tapped her turned-up nose with a finger. "But I have told you quite enough stories for one day."

Sadie tugged at his sleeve from beside him. "But you must come and train us. Teach us the new things you've been learning."

"I thought you were settling into this agrarian life. Young village girls don't train in battle maneuvers."

"This one does." Sadie crossed her arms over her slight chest.

"I agree," Merry said from the head of the table with a wink.

Allen chuckled. "Well then, I suppose I must. On the morrow. Why wait?"

"Huzzah!" Sadie squealed.

"Excellent!" Young Gilbert caught hold of the excitement. "Training with a real knight."

"A squire for now," Cedric, just as scrawny and awkward as ever, corrected. "We wouldn't want his head getting too big for his helmet, would we?"

"Wonderful!" Abigail threw her arms about Allen's neck and squeezed tight. "You shall tell me another story, then."

"Easy there, little one, even a valiant knight must have air to breathe." Allen loosened her stranglehold.

"We would welcome your instruction," Robert said. "But you needn't rush. 'Tis not as if we face imminent threats anymore."

Allen could not yet tell them that he chose tomorrow for he planned to leave soon, and perhaps never return. He would enjoy one last day of training his former troops before he apprised them of his plans and faced the inevitable protests and tears.

"One never knows when we must be ready to fight. We should not grow complacent. This new regent is still an unknown entity." Merry's eyes took on that battle-hardened glint they had before a mission, despite her soft hair and fine kirtle, reminding Allen that she had once swung from trees to rob passing carriages and feed these children.

Little wonder he had admired her so.

"I think we can relax for the moment. England is at peace now." Allen climbed from the bench and stood, lowering the dangling Abigail to the floor. "Lady Merry, I must speak to you before I leave."

"Of course." Merry pushed her chair from the head of the table and stood as well. "Let us go outside for a bit."

The tiny lady barely reached the top of his chest. Without thinking, he placed a too familiar hand on the small of her back but just as quickly snatched it away and scratched his head. Finally, he motioned with his hand for her to lead the way.

Once outside, they settled upon the stairs where she had sat earlier that day. The night was warm and glittering with stars. A generous moon cast its silver light upon the village, allowing Allen to make out each of the small triangular dwellings surrounding the common circle in the center.

Merry gazed up at the sky and sighed. "Sometimes it is still hard for me to believe that we are safe and settled in a new home. And now I have my aunt, and Timothy's family, and the children. It is more than I dared to wish for."

"And . . ." Allen prompted.

"And what?" She twisted toward him with a puzzled expression.

"And you shall be married soon and bear your own children. We both know 'tis true. You needn't spare my feelings."

Merry patted his knee.

He waited for her to speak, but she had always been a woman of few words. And truly, what could she say?

"Merry, I'll be leaving soon. For North Britannia. It has been my dearest dream for nigh on a year now. Probably long before that, except that I never believed such an idyllic place could exist."

"Do not leave on my account. The children will be heartbroken."

"I'm not leaving because of you." Allen pondered his statement. He valued integrity above all virtues, and it did not completely ring of truth. "Well, perhaps in small part. But this is right. This is God's plan for me. 'Tis time for me to head out and find my own place in the world."

"Oh, Allen. I shall miss you!" She looped her hand through his elbow and gave him a squeeze in a motherly manner.

He did not wish to be pacified like a child, but he managed not to bristle. "I shall miss you too."

"Allen." The word was so soft he could barely hear it.

"Yes," he whispered in return.

"In a different . . . " She paused. "If matters had turned out . . . You will make someone the finest husband in the world. I want you to know that."

His heart twisted in his chest.

This was not helping. To think that he might have escaped to France, started a new life there, been the one engaged to Merry. He jerked himself away and stood. "I will be back to train the children tomorrow. I will tell them then."

"As you wish." Merry sounded wistful as she wrapped her arms about her legs and tucked her chin to her knees.

"Good-bye, then," he said.

"Good-bye."

Allen grabbed up his sword and stray pieces of armor. He headed through the village circle and down the lane. Though he would miss his dear friends, he was ready for a new start. Ready to leave his peasant upbringing and the tragedy and heartache it had brought upon him far behind. Pain seared through him at the memory of all he had lost in Ellsworth, but he turned his thoughts to his heavenly Father, always a whispered prayer away, entreating with all his heart that God might lead him to a bright future in North Britannia.

Chapter  5

Though in the stories of King Arthur, he and his esteemed knights never failed to encounter adventure after adventure upon their journeys, Allen's trip north had proven sadly uneventful. Not a single highwayman, nor even a grumpy boar, to thwart his path. Weeks passed idly by as he and his destrier, a gift from Lord Linden along with his armor, made their way across the unending countryside and through the craggy mountain passes.

At last the vast city of Edendale, North Britannia's prize jewel, spread across the valley before him, its pale stone walls glistening against a backdrop of green trees and blue sky in the early fall sunshine. Tall buildings stood at alert all around the soaring castle in the center. A colorful profusion of tents surrounded the city like lesser gems spilling across the verdant lawn.

The road had grown more congested as he approached, and now he understood why. The city teemed with life. From this distance the press of bodies melted into a single writhing serpent flowing through the streets. Although he always enjoyed the company of others, the sight of such crowds pulled him up short not a furlong from his destination.

As he gazed down over the city, a retinue galloped past with banners waving in the breeze. They wound their way down the ribbon of road toward his goal. The Jerusalem to his pilgrimage.

But at this very last moment, he himself paused and knelt. Closing his eyes, he offered up a silent prayer. *Father God, I have done my best to follow your plans in coming to this place. Help me to serve the duke well and to use my skills to protect the weak and the needy. Allow me to find a place here where I truly belong, and—*

"Whatever are you doing?" A high-pitched young voice jolted him from his petition.

Allen turned just as a peasant woman in rough, grimy garb boxed a little boy along the ear and tugged him in her wake. "Now what 'ave I told ye about children keepin' their mouths shut. Botherin' a fine knight, of all people. Lord 'ave mercy upon your soul. Pray, forgive us, good sir."

Allen chuckled. He moved to rumple the lad's blond hair. "No offense taken. But perhaps, if you would be so kind, you might answer a few questions for me."

"Of course." She pulled up from her slumped position and straightened her tunic with a gap-toothed grin. "I'd be 'appy to serve ye."

"Is it always so crowded in the city?" he asked with a bit of trepidation, waving his hand in the direction of Edendale. How could he make a place for himself in such a vast throng of humanity?

"No sir, 'tis the tournament tomorrow that draws so many."

He brightened at that. "A tournament, you say?"

"Indeed. The duke and duchess are fond of tournaments. This one is to celebrate the new peace in England. I 'ear tell before long the young king shall tour in this direction, and no doubt we shall celebrate again."

Tingles washed through Allen. He could not believe his good fortune. "And is this tournament open to all?"

She scratched her head at that. "As far as I know. Though not many 'ave the armor and trainin' to fight."

He sighed. "But alas, I shall never find a team to join on such short notice." Allen's newfound excitement fled him.

Eyeing him up and down, she said, "You're not from around these parts, are ye?"

"No, mistress, I am not."

"The tournaments in North Britannia are fought by single knights. Joustin' mostly."

So not the melee style used throughout the rest of England. Likely he would face many new traditions in this new place. And just that quickly, excitement filled him again. "I am so glad we spoke. Could you offer me any advice if I wish to participate?"

"Ye shan't find accommodations in the city on a day like this, but all are welcome to camp in the valley and make use of the stream to the north, and ye can go through the gates durin' the day to purchase provisions. Ye must enter the tournament right and proper as well. 'Tis why yon knights thundered past in such an ungodly 'urry, I'd wager."

"So it is not too late?"

"Not if ye 'urry as well. Although, do me a favor and don't be scarin' any wee ones out of their wits along the way."

"I wasn't scared!" the child said. "Only surprised."

Allen smiled to him. "I can see you are a strong and brave young man. Perhaps someday you shall be a knight as well."

"Don't be silly." The boy held his belly as he laughed. "Only noblemen are knights. I shall be a farmer like my da. There are those who work, those who fight, and those who pray. Did I get that right, Mum?" He lifted his head to his mother for approval.

"Indeed ye did, my clever boy." She smiled down to him.

It seemed even in North Britannia some things stayed the same. Allen's own father had drilled that mantra into his head. Had taught him again and again of divine order and his lowly place in it.

Yet Allen had defied that place. Perhaps that explained why he felt always adrift of late. He had thought he sensed the good Lord smiling down on this plan. But had it been his own wishful dreaming? Worse yet, his pride?

He did not wish to dwell further on the matter. "I have heard tell that in North Britannia any man of good character might find a place for himself."

"A place, for certain," the woman said. "As a knight . . . not likely. Duke Justus says 'e seeks nobility of 'eart, not of birth. But I've yet to see 'im prove this true."

"Oh." Allen resisted sagging at this news and held himself regally, as befit his new position as a knight. He felt confident that he possessed a noble heart—a heart always after God, one that sought the welfare of others over his own—yet he could not stop that heart from crumpling just a bit in his chest.

"Ye'll do fine," the woman said. "Don't worry yourself. Why, never 'ave I seen such a noble knight as ye."

At that he rallied and lifted his chest. "Thank you. You are so kind."

"I wish ye Godspeed," the woman called as she departed.

Godspeed. Yes, that was precisely what he needed. If God had indeed led him to this place, then it was high time to stop lagging about and speed onward to his destiny and his new home.

◇◇◇

"Name," the scribe behind the table barked.

"Al . . . That is, Sir Allen of Ellsworth." He had somehow managed to squeeze his way through the crowded streets, find the tournament grounds, and endure the long wait to the front of the line.

The man placed his quill upon the splintering tabletop and peered at him with a snarl. "Never heard of you."

Why was this so much harder than staring down a pointed lance or the razor-sharp blade of a sword? "I am new to North Britannia."

"Have you any papers?"

He fumbled through his sack for the only paper he possessed. "I have this letter of recommendation from Lord Linden near Bristol." Perhaps he should have presented himself to the duke at the castle first. But he could not bring himself to take such a presumptuous step. Besides which, he had been itching to fight in a tourney for years.

The man snatched the document from him and examined the official seal. "Humph." He surveyed Allen with a sharp eye. "Says here you are a ward of Lord Linden. I suppose that will do. Newly knighted, though highly recommended." He set down the scroll and turned his full attention to Allen.

As a peasant Allen had been taught subservience to his superiors, but there was no reason for him to cower before this scribe. As the man had just confirmed, he was a knight now, and evidently ward of a nobleman. Dressed in a fine surcoat of that nobleman's red-and-gold colors with a rearing stallion upon his chest.

He held back a grin as the full realization of what Lord Linden had done washed over him. Ward to a nobleman! The unexpected gesture of kindness bolstered his spirits. Yes, he could do this. And well he deserved this opportunity.

"Most of the men you'll be competing against are seasoned knights. Are you certain you don't wish to wait a bit? You wouldn't want to make a fool of yourself." The scribe stared straight into his eyes with a devilish grin.

Allen rankled and stared back, unwilling to waver. "Indeed, I do not. I wish to prove myself worthy to be a knight in the realm of Duke Justus DeMontfort."

The man's wary gaze shifted to one of admiration. He tipped his quill pen to Allen before adding his name to the growing list. "Sir Allen of Ellsworth, in that case, welcome to North Britannia. Return tomorrow morning just as soon as the city gates open." The man offered the letter back to Allen.

Sir Allen of Ellsworth. It was the first time a stranger had spoken his new title aloud. Taking the precious piece of parchment, Allen turned and let the smile that had been itching at his lips for the last few minutes fully emerge. Tomorrow would be his big chance. If all went well, soon he would be a knight of North Britannia.

◇◇◇

As the tall, broad-shouldered knight before Gwen turned, his brilliant smile nearly swept the breath right from her lungs. Joy spilled from his handsome face like sunbeams through the clouds. It surged through her in warm waves. She felt somehow buoyed upon it. For the briefest moment, weakness overtook her knees.

She turned to watch his strong profile and the waving sandy brown hair that grazed his surcoat as he sauntered past. How had she failed to notice him during her long wait? Perhaps she had been too nervous that she might be detected. That some gesture, some tenor of her voice might give her away.

A tug at her sleeve caught her attention. Rosalind, dressed

like a male squire with a hood hiding her hair, shot Gwen a warning look and gestured to the table.

"I said, name." The scribe glowered at her.

Remembering to lower her voice and infuse it with a French lilt so she would sound like a foreign knight, Gwen answered, "Sir Geoffrey Lachapelle."

She had sold a family heirloom and put both herself and Rosalind at considerable risk to acquire her forged patent of nobility. She could not ruin things now. Her blue-and-white nobleman attire was perfect, her long braid well-hidden beneath her cap, and her stance and speech must remain perfect as well.

Rosalind handed the required document to the man.

"Sir Geoffrey. Your reputation precedes you."

Cold fear froze Gwen to her spot. She dared not shoot a glance to Rosalind, but the girl stepped closer in a show of support.

"I'm so glad you finally made your way across the channel to grace us with your presence."

Whew! So the man had never met the knight she impersonated. She managed to shift her stance and lift her chin in acknowledgment of his statement.

"You shall find excellent competition here. Although, for the first round I must warn that you shall be paired by entry position alone. So you'll either be facing the fellow who just left or"—he twisted his face in disdain—"that one behind you."

The man added her purchased name to the bottom of the list.

Gwen studied the entry preceding hers and managed to make out the upside-down script. Sir Allen of Ellsworth. She must remember that title. Although he appeared rather formidable as a potential foe, he seemed a pleasant sort. Perhaps she might look for him at the feast after the tournament.

Shoving aside memories of Allen's heavenly smile, she turned to assess the man behind her—shorter than her by an inch or two, with a slight build for a man and a rather dim-witted look to his dull brown eyes. Yes, that fellow she could take. She nudged Rosalind, who raised her brow in agreement.

Being careful of her voice again, Gwen merely grunted, "My thanks." Maintaining a masculine stride, she hurried from the man who held her fate in his ink-stained hands.

Once she and Rosalind made their way around the corner, she ducked into an alleyway and collapsed against the wall. "We did it." She sighed. "I cannot believe we actually did it."

Rosalind giggled. "I like the way you barely said a word. Smart of you. Or perhaps addlebrained. I haven't yet decided."

"Smart indeed." Gwen smiled, no doubt a smile of exuberance to match the one on the face of the handsome knight.

"Smart perhaps, if you get paired with that scrawny fellow behind you."

"Yes, but did you see the other one? He was glorious." Gwen's hand clapped over her mouth. She had not meant for the statement to come out sounding so dreamy and feminine.

"Oh, good gracious!" Rosalind planted her fists on her hips. "Do not tell me that now, of all times, you have decided to notice a man? Your timing always was utter rot. Thank the good Lord you didn't let this girlish nonsense show in front of the scribe."

Gwen gathered herself together. "I would never! And I did not mean it that way. Only that he seemed a formidable competitor, just as I have always dreamed."

"Ah, so then you didn't notice him at the first." Rosalind studied Gwen for a moment. "Interesting, for he caught my attention straightaway, fine-looking fellow that he is. Why, a man like that could cause a girl to tumble from her tower of virtue."

Rosalind fanned herself with one hand, then placed it firmly on her hip. "But I noticed other things about him as well. His surcoat was frayed about the edges, and he had no servant. And did you hear the scribe speaking with him? The man is newly knighted and merely ward to a nobleman."

A poor, newly knighted ward to a nobleman. Sir Allen of Ellsworth was nothing more. A hope that Gwen had not allowed to fully form in her mind was shot down like a bird from flight with an arrow straight through its chest. Besides which, she had no time for ludicrous thoughts of romance. She had a tournament to fight.

"Good observations, Rosalind. You may now add spying to your ever-growing list of vocational skills."

"And squire to a knight, but do not change the subject."

"I am not changing the subject. The subject is the tournament tomorrow, and as your keen assessment indicates, I now stand a good chance of making it through the first round."

"But to what purpose?" Rosalind huffed. "Sir Hugh will be so disappointed with me. And heaven help us both if your father finds out. I swear, Lady Gwendolyn, if you get me tossed out upon my rump . . ." She did not finish the idle threat, although she shook a finger Gwen's way.

But Gwen's mind remained focused upon Rosalind's question. *To what purpose?* She had asked herself the same question over and again as she had snuck out to train, as she had plotted and connived to get the proper armor and papers, and even today as she had lied to her parents in order to come and enter the tournament.

But deep down she knew.

She did it for more than just one brief moment of joy as she had tried to convince herself and Rosalind. This was not just one final wild romp before she settled into marriage. A small— albeit admittedly foolhardy—part of her yet held out hope that if she won, her father might see her through new eyes. That he might grow to love and appreciate the true Gwen. That he might let her choose her own course in life.

A course that would never, ever include marriage.

But even as the thought went through her mind, another one clashed against it like a lance against a shield. No, not a thought so much as an image. The image of a purehearted, breath-stoppingly handsome knight, beaming with joy like the sunshine.

Chapter  6

Rosalind stared out the hallway window to the bustling city of Edendale. Nearby hawkers cried their wares, and children dashed squealing about the busy streets.

As a small child, like nearly every other girl in her tiny village, she had played at being a duchess in this very city. Of being captured by an evil villain and a handsome knight coming to rescue her. But lady's maid in an elegant townhome would do quite nicely for the real world. She would have more than enough adventure on the morrow if Gwendolyn had her way.

Enough daydreaming. Rosalind desperately needed this position and could not afford to muck it up. Too well she remembered those days after her father's death when disaster and deprivation had struck their family. The hungry whimpers of her younger brothers and sisters yet called out to her. She could never risk losing this position and subjecting them to that again. But Lord Barnes had been dismissing servants one after another since he returned.

Thank the good Lord he had no idea what she and Gwendolyn had been about earlier this day, nor what they planned for the morrow. But Gwendolyn was her best ally in this place, not to mention quite dear to her, and Rosalind did not wish to disappoint her mistress.

As she entered Gwendolyn's bedchamber, the oddest sight met her eyes. Lady Barnes examined her daughter's twisted form much as a physician would a patient.

"Thrust your left leg to the side a little further please. Hmm . . . better." Lady Barnes tapped a finger to her lip and walked a circle around her Amazonian child. Though Rosalind had never considered Gwendolyn overly large, even she must admit that next to her diminutive mother, Gwendolyn appeared a hulking figure.

Tonight Gwendolyn would be officially presented at the duke's court, although she seemed not at all excited. She looked beyond lovely for the occasion in a rare velvet dress of midnight blue with sweeping sleeves inlaid with a gilded fabric and glimmering jewels stitched across the fitted bodice.

Yet her mother frowned. "You must keep your shoulders straight, of course, but try dipping your head demurely to one side—like so." Lady Barnes demonstrated.

Gwendolyn followed suit, bending her neck at an awkward angle so that her ear nearly grazed her shoulder.

"Excellent!" Lady Barnes clasped her hands to her chest. "That takes off a good two inches and adds a soft touch of femininity as well."

By Rosalind's way of thinking, Gwendolyn's ample curves and artfully arranged golden tresses provided quite enough femininity, but it was not her place to say so. Gwendolyn shot Rosalind a silent plea for help.

"Now bend your supporting knee," Gwendolyn's mother said.

Already teetering in her bizarre position, Gwendolyn dipped her knee, completing her transformation from lovely noble-woman to humpbacked troll.

"Perfect! Why, altogether we have reduced your height by nearly half a foot." Lady Barnes pressed her hand to her mouth in delight. "Your father will be so proud."

Gwendolyn grimaced. "Nonsense. I shall get a crick in my neck and a cramp in my leg bent over like such. And however shall I dance?"

Lady Barnes's pretty face twisted in confusion. "I had not thought that far. Rosalind, what do you suggest?"

Dare Rosalind mention the troll? "I do understand your concern to make Lady Gwendolyn appear shorter. But do you not agree that in doing so you have created a silhouette that appears both more withered and rather stout?"

Lady Barnes sighed. "Goodness. This is true. I had not considered that by making her shorter, we would draw attention to her girth."

"Which would be a pity, for she is by no means fat. And she shall not be able to perform that graceful walk we have been practicing if she is hunched over. Perhaps just a slight dip to the knees and bend to the head," Rosalind said.

Gwendolyn shifted her stance.

Her mother resumed her circular path around Gwendolyn. "Do you feel more comfortable now, darling?"

"Yes, Mother. I suppose I could manage this way."

"That puts her beneath the average height of a nobleman. And might I suggest," Rosalind dared to add, "that if she dances or converses with a man taller than herself—which, rest assured, many shall be—she need not worry so much about her height. I fear such concerns shall cause her to grow nervous and awkward in her conversation."

Lady Barnes put a hand on her hip and tilted her head. "I think she shall fare well enough. We have been rehearsing her banter, and she has been instructed to smile and giggle, to flutter her lashes and turn her eyes to the floor as oft as possible. Men are quite susceptible to such tactics."

"Are you all quite finished discussing me as if I am not in the room?" Gwendolyn sneered.

"Tut, tut, tut!" her mother said.

Gwendolyn pasted a syrupy smile in place of the sneer.

"Much better." Lady Barnes raised herself on tiptoes to place a kiss on her daughter's cheek. "Never fear, darling. Once a handsome young man catches your fancy, our efforts will make perfect sense."

"As if Father cares who catches my fancy," Gwendolyn grumbled.

"Now, what have I been telling you?" Lady Barnes stomped her petite foot upon the stone floor. "You must curry your father's favor. Charm him alongside everyone else, and he shall give you your way."

"Like he has given you your way over the wine issue?" Gwendolyn cocked a brow.

Her mother's cheeks flamed bright red. "That is . . . different, and rather unkind of you to mention."

But Gwendolyn's harsh statement did its job in closing the subject. Rosalind still did not know if the baron might relent from finding a domineering husband for Gwendolyn as he had threatened. Rosalind for one could not imagine life trapped with such a man.

Of course these days she could only imagine life with one virile, jovial, and entirely unsuitable man. Despite her strict instructions to herself, her mind wandered to Hugh's attractive face day and night. Rosalind managed to hold back a groan of pain. Why was it that she could offer such excellent advice to Gwendolyn, while in affairs of her own heart, she behaved like a half-witted sot?

At that moment, Gwendolyn's troublesome little pup Angel, who had been drowsing upon the hearth, streaked in a flash of white across the room and stole Gwendolyn's blue silk slipper from where it sat near the bed.

"No! No, you bad little dog!" Rosalind grabbed for her, but Angel took that as an invitation to play. She ducked under the bed and flew out the other side.

Rosalind dove over the mattress but wasn't quick enough. She chased the dog about the bed, slipping as she rounded the corner and nearly crashing into Gwendolyn's mother.

"Good heavens!" Lady Barnes squealed, clutching her hands to her chest.

Mischief, perched on his imperial pillow throne as usual, seemed to think the chase a grand idea and joined in the fun, jumping down to grab the matching slipper and dash about as well.

"Stop that at once, both of you," Gwendolyn demanded in a stern tone of voice. "Bring!"

The absurd little dogs obeyed their mistress like a tiny battalion of well-trained soldiers. Meanwhile, Rosalind held back her huff of frustration.

"Good girl, good boy," Gwendolyn said as they dropped the slippers at her feet, and she gave them each an affectionate pat.

Lady Barnes straightened her mantle. "I cannot believe I let you drag those troublesome creatures along."

No sooner had she said as much, than Angel stood upon her hind legs and commenced to clawing at Gwendolyn's gorgeous gown, all the while whining to be held.

"And now she shall mess your gown!"

"All is well, Mother." Gwendolyn shooed away the dogs and held up her slippers for inspection. "You see. No harm done."

Rosalind marched to the door and opened it. "Out, both of you."

Angel's eyes popped open wide, and she scurried through the door. However Mischief stared at Rosalind, clearly taking her measure.

"Now!" Rosalind pointed to the hall.

After a moment the dog casually trotted away, as if it had been his idea the entire time.

Once the door was safely closed, Lady Barnes performed a check of Gwendolyn's attire. "Everything seems to be in order. You truly are divine, darling. Do not let an obsession with your height destroy your confidence."

"*I* am not the one obsessed with my height. Would it not be better to find a man who does not mind? Surely some might prefer a tall woman to give them large sons. I cannot crouch all night." Gwendolyn stood to her full stature, straight and strong like the female warrior she was.

Lady Barnes's smile stretched across her lovely face. She had not smiled so in weeks, her withdrawal from alcoholic drink causing headache after splitting headache. But then again, this was the first time Gwendolyn had spoken of finding a man without throwing a rebellious fit.

"Do not think of it as crouching. Think of it as being demure," Lady Barnes said, clutching her daughter's arm with affection. "Men like to feel superior, and we must help them maintain that illusion. We are the pedestals upon which they perch, silent beneath their esteemed feet, elevating their masculine strength with our beauty."

Good heavens, pedestals? Rosalind adored a strong man as much as any woman. However, that was taking matters quite too far. No wonder Lady Barnes let her husband trample upon her so.

Though the words threatened to burst from her, she managed to exchange them for more tactful ones. "I prefer to think of a man and woman standing side by side, offering mutual support. But never fear, Lady Gwendolyn, all will be well. Everyone shall love you tonight."

Or so Rosalind hoped. Gwendolyn had a kind heart and a quick wit, but she also had an explosive temper that could easily get her into trouble. Rosalind offered up a silent prayer that this evening might go well.

And on the morrow, Rosalind would play squire to Gwendolyn's Sir Geoffrey Lachapelle. If Gwendolyn could somehow survive the next day with her health, dignity, and identity intact, all might yet turn out well.

Tension clamped upon Rosalind's shoulders as she considered the price she might pay if caught as a participant in this addlebrained scheme. Gwendolyn did not fully understand how desperately Rosalind needed this employment. However, as Gwendolyn took the biggest risk—and seemed to somehow require this experience to soothe a wound deep in her soul—Rosalind could fathom no option but to support her.

◇◇◇

Allen patted the firm flank of his horse—bedecked in red and gold, much like Allen himself—as they awaited in the jostle of knights and steeds outside the gate to the tournament arena. Together he and Thunder could do this thing. They had little choice, other than running home to Lord Linden in failure and an awkward existence next door to Merry and Timothy.

Barely able to sleep last night due to his nervous excitement, Allen had spent hours in prayer, communing with the Divine until the wee hours of the morning. In God's presence alone he had found peace and rest. But it would not hurt to whisper up one last petition. He pressed his face into the shiny brown coat of Thunder's neck for a moment of private contemplation.

Lord, not my will but thine be done today. Let me move by your power and your spirit. Give me courage, strength, speed, and agility. But most of all, give me wisdom and peace to accept if your plans are not the same as mine. . . .

A chorus of trumpets sounded, snatching his attention. Allen's head snapped up. The time had come. He mounted his horse and filed into line with the rest of the knights, festooned in a rainbow of colors and branded with crests of hawks, lions, horses, and the like. Many of them were followed by squires carrying banners and pennants.

A pretty serving girl offering a cup to a particularly hulking knight on horseback caught Allen's gaze, but the awful fellow backhanded her across the cheek just as quickly and sent her sprawling backward. "I have no time for silly refreshments."

She hid her face in her hands.

The procession moved forward before Allen could say a word in the maiden's defense, but he hoped he might have a chance to put the abusive fellow in his place today. He supposed not every knight could be chivalrous, even in a place called Edendale.

They entered the tournament arena, surrounded on each side by tiered galleries, their walls festooned with colorful coats of arms. As the knights paraded past the crowd, common folk cheered and waved kerchiefs, hollering and stamping. Children hopped up and down and climbed upon their parents' shoulders for a better view.

A better view of him. Sir Allen of Ellsworth. Son of a peasant farmer. Now a hero of the realm. He would say he had dreamed of this moment his whole life, except that he had never dared to until a few years ago. Until fate had turned him an outlaw, and an exceptional woman named Merry Ellison had turned his life topside-turvy.

He had never even seen a tournament until he was twelve and his father had taken him to the nearby town of Farthingale. Pain sliced through Allen at the memory. How he missed his father and his brother, who had been so cruelly butchered by King John, and his mother, who had died years earlier of a fever. How he wished they could see him now. But he must do this thing without them.

His pulse pounded in his ears. As his eyes scanned the frenzied crowd, his head grew light and swishy. For a moment he thought he might waver upon his horse, but he managed to gather himself together. He had trained long and hard for this moment.

After passing three-quarters of the way around the field, he fell into line alongside the horse that had been in front of him and faced the grandstand. Its more formal galleries, like open-air rooms, featured gatherings of noble men and women dressed in bright silks and furs.

Exquisite young ladies draped themselves over the ledges to wave and throw kisses to their favorites. One tossed a kerchief to the ground, which a fine-looking knight lifted with his lance. He flicked it into the air and caught it as the crowd went wild once again.

Over the din came the cry of the herald. "Hear ye! Hear ye!"

The noise settled to a quiet roar.

The herald continued. "I give you our beloved duke, His Grace, Justus DeMontfort of North Britannia."

A hush fell over the crowd.

Then a man in understated clothing stepped forward. He wore his golden brown hair and beard trimmed short. The duke lifted his chin and surveyed the arena. Allen liked the look of him. Old enough to exude wisdom and experience, yet young enough to offer an air of vitality. Kind, yet in perfect command.

"My dear and faithful servants of North Britannia." The duke swept a hand from his right side to his left. "My esteemed guests." He nodded to the noblemen on either side of him. "And most importantly, our valiant knights who shall fight today." He actually bowed to the knights before him, lowborn Allen of Ellsworth included.

Pride and humility, confidence and insecurity waged an epic battle inside Allen's chest. He could hardly fathom he was here. Before the duke. A handsome knight on a fine steed.

The duke reached back to squeeze the hand of a striking woman with dark hair wearing a burgundy gown. "My fair duchess and I welcome you all to this celebration of a new and—with all hope—lasting peace in the realm of England. Long live King Henry."

The crowd echoed the words, and Allen spoke them with gusto. "Long live King Henry."

While hiding away in the forests, running for his life along with the many children of their group, he had feared this day when England was ruled by a just king might never come.

The duke directed his attention to the knights once again. "Brave warriors, as we commence the games today, be honorable, be courageous, be chivalrous, and be strong. But most of all, go hand in hand with the God of all creation."

Tears sprang to Allen's eyes. So it was true. This was a righteous, God-honoring region. He had feared it might not be possible after living under the ruthless and evil King John for so long. How Duke Justus had maintained this bastion of goodness and truth, he desired to discover.

"Let the games begin!" the duke said.

The herald raised his hand and called over the crowd, which

again had commenced its cheering. "The rules of today's tournament shall be as such. Each set of competitors shall begin with a joust. If both competitors keep their seat, they shall continue jousting until at least one falls. If only one falls to the ground, his opponent shall be declared the victor."

A year ago, although he was a well-trained warrior with a sword, Allen would have never dared to engage in a joust, but so much had changed in that short time. Confidence won the battle in his chest, for he could unseat any man in Lord Linden's service.

"If both should fall to the ground and only one rises to his feet, that man shall win. If both stand to their feet within the allotted time, a sword fight will commence."

He glanced to the nervous-looking knight at his left in green and gold and to the one in blue and white at his right, with a youngish face peeking through his open visor. No problem there, but tomorrow, as Allen rose through the ranks, matters might prove more challenging, for he had noticed some fearsome competitors among the group.

"If one man should be pinned, lose his sword, or surrender, the other shall be victorious. If the battle reaches a stalemate, Duke Justus shall decide the winner."

All sounded fair to Allen. This tournament would proceed much as his training rounds in Lindy.

"After all competitors have battled, the winners shall move to the next round until a single champion is declared and a prize of gold coins awarded." The herald raised a fist overhead. "Prepare to fight."

Allen sighed as he turned his horse back toward the gate. Having registered his entry late in the day, he would have a long wait before him. But he simply must win that prize, both because he needed to curry the duke's favor and because his small savings would not last long in this wealthy city.

For a moment he wished he had a squire—or better yet, an entire retinue—with which to while away the time. He was naught but a stranger in a strange land. But he had his faithful steed, Thunder, and God, his constant companion.

They would see him through this day.

◇ ◇ ◇

If Warner DeMontfort had to endure one more minute of this chaotic caterwauling, he might just lose his morning meal on the hood of the man who stood—or more accurately bounced—in front of him. He pushed his way through the crowd and out of the arena for a brief respite. His reconnaissance mission had proven quite successful already. The duke had little enough security around him. That pompous fool clearly expected to be loved and doted upon by his people, but not everyone wished him well. If only he knew his banished cousin freely roamed the arena, scheming his demise.

Over the past year, the resistance had grown to a sizeable force. Many in North Britannia longed to return to the old ways, to the classic feudal system in which the nobility ruled with an iron fist as God intended. Under Duke Justus, their peasants had become too cocksure, too entitled, and far too educated for anyone's good. This ridiculous council and rule of law was simply not to be tolerated any further.

As Warner had watched Justus presiding over his adoring fans, he had thought his head might explode from sheer hatred. Of course they loved him. He treated them like equals, leaving this region weak and ripe for invasion. Already Warner had won a few council members to his side. If only he could recruit the newly returned military leader, Reimund Barnes, his plan would be complete. From all he had heard, the man had grown weary of the duke's progressive ways as well.

Now that matters in England had stabilized, North Britannia needed to join forces with the rest of the nation. To do so, someone must put this ludicrous Arthurian rot to rest once and for all. And he was just the man to do it. Was not his grandfather once the duke of a strong and traditional North Britannia? Did not DeMontfort blood run just as rich through his veins as through Justus's?

Another round of cheering welled from the spoiled commoners in the stands. But they would not be cheering for long. Not if he had his way.

Chapter 7

Gwen took deep whiffs of Andromache's warm and welcoming scent to soothe herself as the crowd cheered in the background. Much like Gwen, the mare was large for a female, and disguised in blue-and-white finery it would have to pass for a destrier this day. She had schemed to great lengths to get the horse to town, but was thankful to have this familiar piece of home with her for the momentous occasion.

Not long now. Gwen scuffed her boot impatiently into the dirt. She had suffered through hours of waiting, a tedious midday break, and yet more waiting. This entire day and the evening before had been naught but torture upon torture, what with her father showing her off like a broodmare during the reception at Duke Justus's court.

She glanced about for Sir Allen, whom she had been matched against this day, but did not find him. Of course she had seen him this morning at the opening ceremony. A smile tickled her lips at the memory. She had at long last felt included in the grand tradition of tournament and knight. The duke had welcomed and honored her right along with all the others.

But she knew not if she truly deserved her place in these ranks. Her chances of winning were slim, especially paired against Sir Allen, but if she could survive a round or two, all would be worthwhile. She continued to take deep breaths to calm herself, wringing her hands together and stomping off her nervous energy.

Rosalind, dressed as a squire in a similar hooded blue-and-white costume, ran through the crowd toward her. "Only this round and one more. We should prepare."

Gwen stretched her neck against the strain. "I thought this moment might never come. I thought I would be found out for certain."

"You put on quite a convincing performance this morning with your fake vomiting. When you dashed from the morning meal with a finger pressed to your lips and cheeks swelling, I would have sworn you turned green as well. However did you manage that?"

Gwen chuckled. "Sheer power of the will. I should have tried it last night. Perhaps I will this evening."

"Your parents would take their chances and drag you along nonetheless. They might not have relented today, except that tomorrow is the main event and many skip the early rounds." Rosalind handed Gwen her helmet.

As she donned it, her maid—rather, squire—did a last check of her saddle. The tournament officials had already tested her lances and sword to make sure that they were all sound and dulled to the proper degree for safety. Gwen put her shaking foot into the stirrup and mounted Andromache. She must pull herself together. She would not ruin this one rare chance over nerves.

Rosalind offered her the blue-and-white shield, then gathered the lances and walked alongside Gwen and Andromache. "'Tis too bad they did not match you against that scrawny fellow. You could have taken him easily."

"It is as it is. Besides, what sort of victory would that have been?"

"A sure one," Rosalind said. "But if you wish to put your skill to the test, then you shall have your chance with that Sir Allen. It seems a fair match. He's much larger, but you are quick and have faced fierce competition in your brothers."

"I can best him."

"'Tis possible. Not that I would want to face Sir Allen across the field. . . . Although I might not mind meeting him in one— say, late at night under the full moon." Rosalind feigned a swoon. "Perhaps you should wait for that opportunity instead. All the competitors shall be at the feast this evening. You never know what might happen."

"Do not be ridiculous. Have I not made it abundantly clear that I have no interest in romance?"

"On the contrary, your demeanor yesterday made it clear that you *are* interested in romance with one specific man." Rosalind adjusted the heavy lances and continued walking.

Gwen chose not to acknowledge that comment with a response, yet she could not deny the heat that filled her cheeks. At least her embarrassment served as a welcome respite from the nerves of the day. She would send this Allen sprawling to the ground just to prove he held no power over her.

The crowds erupted again.

"Only one more round," Rosalind said as they stopped to the right of the gate.

Sir Allen of Ellsworth stood to the left side, alone, his lances propped against the rail. Gwen watched with undue fascination as he worked his gloves of metal and thick leather over his hands. She could not remove her gaze as he covered his handsome features and waving hair with his helmet.

She simply must unseat him, for she feared she could not beat him with a sword. He looked quite fit and agile despite his size. She wished she had seen him fight before. Watching him now, she detected no obvious weaknesses. He appeared bright and focused, courageous and calm. She must face him head on from the start and pray they not be unseated at the same time.

Her gaze remained locked upon her foe until cheering burst forth once again.

"Well, that was quick." Rosalind checked Gwen's harness one last time. "Are you ready?"

Gwen swallowed down a lump of fear, yet excitement tingled through her at the same time. She had dreamed of this opportunity her entire life, and she must relish every moment. "As ready as I shall ever be."

"Godspeed, good sir." Rosalind winked and handed her a lance.

An official-looking man crossed to her. "Sir Geoffrey Lachapelle?"

"Yes. At the ready."

"Good. And this is your squire?"

"Indeed," Rosalind said.

"You shall joust from the far side of the field." He turned to Rosalind. "Run ahead and prepare your weapons."

Rosalind did as bid. Gwen continued to drag soothing breaths into her lungs. She gripped tightly to the reins and pressed deeper into her saddle, sensing Andromache's strength against her thighs. Yes, she was ready.

She and Sir Allen lined up side by side once again. He nodded to her, and she returned the gesture.

"Best wishes," he said.

It seemed in addition to the virtues she had already noted, he was kind and generous too—for not many would bid an opponent well. But she feared her voice might quaver if she answered, so she did not return the felicitations, only nodded again and shot a stern look in his direction, which she hoped might convey that she was a foe to be feared.

"Sir Allen of Ellsworth to face Sir Geoffrey Lachapelle," the herald announced.

They rode out in tandem, bearing their lances before them. In the center, they faced the duke and bowed before turning to the crowd on either side to present themselves. Finally, they parted and headed to their assigned starting points.

Along the way, Gwen caught a glimpse of her parents in the grandstand. Her helmet would keep her hidden, but what if it fell off in battle and they recognized her? The smallest part of her almost wished they would, and that they would be forced to face the truth about their daughter. But a much larger portion was grateful for her anonymity, especially as she had little chance of winning.

Rosalind waited for her with a cheerful grin. "You can do this, Sir Geoffrey," she said. "I believe in you."

Did Gwen believe in herself? Not quite, but she would try with all her might. As she turned to face her opponent and lowered her visor, like she had a hundred times before, that familiar energy surged through her, striving to burst from her skin. She forgot her nervousness as instinct and training took over.

Leveling her lance, she stared into the slit of the helmet across the field. She recalled the bright and focused gleam in her opponent's eye, and determined to equal his intensity.

As always, time slowed as she thrust her horse into action.

Hoofbeat after hoofbeat to match the thumping beats of her heart. She squinted and honed in on Sir Allen's broad chest covered in a red surcoat, like a giant target. She aimed for the spot just beyond his shield. A strike there would be sure to knock him down. From the edges of her vision, she watched his horse and his lance, searching for any weakness, any flaw, any stutter—but nothing.

The crowd seemed to cheer in an odd sort of slow motion. The horses drew closer and closer. She must keep her seat. She must do something to protect herself from the threatening lance headed straight for her with unerring accuracy. She would never have the strength to hold her shield steady against such a thunderous blow.

In that last heartbeat before they clashed, she shifted her own aim to deflect his strike.

The long poles tangled, and his alone went sailing through the sky, only to crash down a breath later. By that time Gwen was far past him, but unless he was the worst knight in the realm, he must have kept his seat, for she never touched him at all.

She slowed Andromache and turned the mighty steed. Indeed her opponent was still astride his horse. An attendant returned Allen's weapon to him. As neither lance had broken, they faced off from opposite sides of the list as the herald declared, "Pass number two for Sir Allen and Sir Geoffrey."

Once again they squared off. But time did not slow this round. Instead, Allen rushed toward her before she felt quite prepared. She must unseat him, and quickly. His lance appeared just to the right of where it should be. She aimed dead center for his chest, but at the last he adjusted his aim and both lances splintered, as the force of a battering ram slammed into her shield. Gwen fought for control, clinging to her reins with all her might, but to no avail.

The next thing she knew, she found herself slipping, and then landing facedown in the dirt. A part of her wished to stay there, but she felt certain he had fallen as well. She wheezed in an attempt to find her breath. Her chest burned with searing pain, and the world spun around her. But she would not be defeated so easily.

"Eight, nine, ten, eleven," the herald cried.

She had only until the count of twenty. Calling upon every ounce of strength and stubbornness she possessed, she struggled to her feet and drew her sword.

As she scanned the field, her last hopes scattered into the breeze, for Sir Allen of Ellsworth already stood tall and proud, his weapon prepared for battle.

"Let the swordplay commence," the herald practically shrieked in his excitement.

"Do you need a moment?" Sir Allen whispered beneath the roar of the crowd. "I wish this to be a fair contest."

Gathering her fighting spirit, Gwen said, "I need nothing from you." Not his handsome face, nor least of all his pity.

"In that case . . ." Allen circled around her, looking for his opportunity to strike.

But Gwen lunged first, catching the big man off guard, and delivering a hard blow to his ribs.

It seemed Allen would not make such a mistake again. He swung at her, and she dodged his strike.

And so it began. For the next minute, they dodged and parried, struck and spun. Gwen managed to meet him at every blow. Just when he stumbled to the ground and she thought she had him beat, he performed a surprising tumbling maneuver, flinging his feet back over his head and springing out of her reach. As she still reeled in surprise, he slashed a blow to her back. Pain exploded once again, now radiating from her back to her chest in pounding waves.

She pulled away a few steps, struggling to find her breath

and to gather her wits. This man possessed considerable skill. Not just strength, but as she had suspected, cunning and agility.

The battle raged on.

Gwen grew tired and fiery hot. Sweat dripped down her face and into her eyes, but she had no way of wiping it through the helmet. The crowd went hazy and sharpened back into focus again, seeming to grow closer and then retreat farther away. She could not keep up this pace much longer. But at the moment they each had one good blow upon the other. She must not give up.

Strike after strike they continued. Just when she thought she might collapse, Allen pulled back. He whipped his helmet from his head and wiped his brow with the leather part of his glove. Oh, how Gwen wished she could do the same. In a show of bravado, Allen tossed his helmet aside and poised his sword in front of him with two hands.

With a fearsome bellow, he surged toward Gwen. She tried to fend off his blows, but they came one after another with staggering speed and force. Just when she thought she might survive the onslaught, he dove low and swept her feet from beneath her with the swing of his leg. As she crashed to the ground, he flipped to standing and pressed his sword to her neck.

She had lost her own weapon at some point during her tumble to the dirt. No chance remained. She held up her hands in surrender as the crowd roared.

Sir Allen withdrew his sword several inches, but continued staring at her. Only then did she realize that her visor had flipped open from the impact of her fall. As she gazed into his deep hazel eyes, the world grew swishy and hazy to even a greater degree than it had during the battle. Odd tingles ran through her, seeming to coalesce in the vicinity of her lips.

She must be injured. Perhaps she'd hit her head without realizing. Surely this was no normal sort of reaction. Shaking off the strange sensations, she snapped her visor shut and pushed to standing. No, other than the throbbing in her chest and back, she felt well enough.

Might he have noticed she was a female? Not likely, for her hair and form both remained well hidden. And if by some chance he suspected, surely he would never confess to nearly being bested by a girl.

Allen reached out to shake her hand. Through the double layer of gloves, she could feel nothing but a slight pressure, although her heart warmed at the gesture.

"Good effort," he said. "You surprised me."

She had surprised herself as well. She had managed her nerves, found her spirit, fought her hardest, and performed her very best. Yet she had been found lacking. Her illustrious career as a tournament knight, over so soon. Over before it ever really began.

"The victor is," the herald called, "Sir Allen of Ellsworth."

And now what was left for her? A life locked away in a castle. Marriage. Children.

Yet gazing at Sir Allen, somehow those prospects did not seem as horrible as they had a day earlier.

Chapter 8

Gwendolyn stifled a yawn as her parents chatted with the duke and duchess in the resplendent hall of Edendale Castle. Though she had little use for all the gilt and frippery, or the fancy marble pillars, she had to confess it was pretty enough. And tonight's festivities were far jollier than the stately affair the previous evening.

Minstrels strolled about the room, playing a lively tune within the glow of the torches lining the walls. Couples danced in the center of the floor, while a collection of knights bedecked in the North Britannian crimson-and-black regalia enjoyed a rowdy game of dice beneath the hugest tapestry she had ever laid eyes upon.

The whole place smelled of the fresh meadowsweet and sage strewn throughout the rushes on the floor. She might almost enjoy this evening, were it not for her exhaustion from the day along with her aching muscles and bruises.

A while back she had tuned out the discussion of politics

surrounding her, but now the name Allen of Ellsworth caught her attention.

"Yes, he gave us the finest fight of the day." The duke nodded his approval. "Were wagering not a vice, he would be my choice."

Father guffawed a bit too loudly. "Well, I have no such scruples. Perhaps I shall take your suggestion."

"And his opponent, that Lachapelle fellow, put up a valiant fight. I wonder if either of them is here?" The duchess scanned the crowd. "It is difficult to recognize the combatants when they are out of their armor. But I should like to congratulate both of them."

Gwen froze in place before she did something that might give her away. Warmth welled within her. It seemed that despite her defeat, she had performed better than she realized.

"I, too, was impressed by Lachapelle," Father said, "especially for such a young man."

"Young?" The duke's imposing face twisted in confusion. "Whatever gave you that impression? Lachapelle has been well-known in the continent tournament circle for nigh on a decade."

"That is odd." Father scratched his head through his wild mane of black and silver. "I would have sworn I spied a youth, but perhaps the shadows were deceptive."

"Or perhaps he is young in spirit." Mother finally spoke, but as usual, only a passing comment in general support of her husband, and not any clear opinion of her own.

"What think you, Lady Gwendolyn?" the duke prompted.

"I think I wish I had been there and not at home with a . . ." Gwen's mind sought for a delicate way to phrase the matter. "Not at home with a fickle constitution."

"Ah, I did not realize," the duke said. "We are glad, however, that you made it this evening. I hope you are feeling well. You appear quite lovely and fully recovered."

"I am much better, thank you. And I look forward to attending the tournament on the morrow."

"We shall look for you." The duchess gave Gwen's arm a squeeze. "I should love for you to join us and share your commentary. You must be quite the expert, what with your renowned brothers training at your castle."

"I am afraid not," Mother said before Gwen could answer. "Our daughter mostly stays indoors weaving and embroidering."

"And playing the pipe." Father smiled from ear to ear. "You should hear how lovely she is upon the pipe."

"Perhaps tomorrow you will play for us." The duke gestured to the grand dais at the front of the room.

"Oh, I could never." Gwen pressed a hand to her cheek, not needing to feign demureness for once.

Father's chest puffed with pride. "I am afraid our Gwendolyn does not enjoy so much attention. She is rather meek at heart. Perhaps at a more intimate gathering."

"Excellent." The duchess pressed her hands together. "We shall arrange for one soon."

Mother shot Gwen an appreciative glance. She and Father were always looking for ways to curry favor with the duke and duchess. Although Gwen did not share their interest for social maneuvering, she was happy to have brought them some small joy.

The duke and duchess excused themselves to continue mingling among their guests.

"Yes, you should mingle as well, Gwendolyn. Reestablish old acquaintances. Make some new friends," her father said. "Later, there is a fellow I would like to introduce you to, but I have not seen him yet. Find someone to dance with. Nothing makes a woman more desirable than the attention of one's rivals."

Though she did not mind dancing, as it was both a physical and a musical sort of activity, the thought of facing the huge gathering alone horrified Gwen. "But . . . I . . . truly, Father. Might we stay together?"

"Do not be silly, darling." Despite her simpering smile, Mother gave Gwen a rather forceful shove out of their concealing corner. "We have been preparing for this. Now is your chance to shine. No man will ask you to dance while your frightening father glowers over your shoulder."

Her mother and father departed in the opposite direction and were soon engaged in animated conversation with another couple.

Gwen took a few hesitant steps, attempting to sway her hips, bend her knees, and tilt her head all at once. She searched out any friendly female face, but her family had been quite reclusive in their craggy tower castle, and Gwen had not gotten along well with the few girls who had visited. She spotted several familiar matrons but had no desire to spend her evening with them.

And of course she recognized her brothers' friends, Randel Penigree included. She knew not whether Hugh had spoken to Randel about courting her as he mentioned, but she would not wish to give Randel the wrong idea. Especially not in this ridiculous gown of girlish pink silk, which showed off far too much of her feminine assets. Gwen pressed a hand to her exposed chest. She had preferred last night's elegant blue concoction.

With a lift of his chin, Randel smiled and caught her gaze. It seemed Hugh had indeed spoken to him, but she managed to blend into the crowd and make an escape. After burrowing her way to the far side of the room, she paused for a moment, and a welcome sight met her eye. A padded bench nestled into an alcove. Perfect.

She ducked her head low and dashed directly for the place of refuge, only to smack into a broad chest that seemingly came from nowhere.

The man grabbed her elbows to steady her. "My goodness, aren't you in a hurry."

Gwen dreaded looking into his face, but she had little choice, for he seemed unwilling to let her go until she answered him. As she lifted her head, much to her shock, she stared directly into the sunshine smile of Sir Allen of Ellsworth.

"Sir Allen!" she uttered before she could catch herself.

His smile turned to one of bemusement. "I am sorry. Have we met?"

"I . . . uh . . . no . . . rather, I saw you in the tournament today." Instantly she regretted her words, which so contradicted the ones she had spoken only moments earlier to the duke. But there was no turning back now.

"Of course," Allen said. "I am not accustomed to such notoriety."

"You were quite impressive. One could hardly forget."

Sir Allen yet held fast to her arms, causing strange bursts of energy to course through her and making it difficult for her to think straight. She looked pointedly to her arm.

He released her and stepped back. "I'm sorry about our little crash. Are you well?"

"Yes, do not fear. I have survived far worse." Gwen noticed her father glaring her way. Not wishing to incite his anger, she adjusted her position, giggled, and fluttered her lashes, allowing her gaze to fall to Allen's leather boots. Goodness, even his feet were handsome.

"And where did I stop you from rushing to?"

"I was just headed for yon bench. I fear my head grew light in this crowd, and I wished to rest for a while."

"Then allow me to escort you." Sir Allen gallantly took her arm, sending a confusing blend of warmth and chills shooting through her. What bizarre sort of malady did he inflict upon her? She was not certain that she liked the many odd sensations he evoked in her.

She did not concern herself with swaying her hips, as she did not wish to bump his, but she twisted herself as small as possible as they moved toward the bench. Once there, she sat and tilted her head while he settled himself beside her, grazing her thigh with his own due to the small space.

Her thoughts set off in erratic directions at his nearness as her mouth grew tongue-tied. Her heartbeat sped, though she remained at rest. She must strengthen her resolve against the strange reactions she seemed to suffer at his nearness.

"Actually, do I know you from somewhere? The more I think of it, the more you look familiar to me." Allen seemed not to suffer from her affliction of the tongue, although something in his eyes and that playful grin made her think he might enjoy gazing upon her.

At first Gwen could not find the words to reply, but she needed to come up with something before he associated her with his battle from the afternoon. She asked herself what her mother might bid her say. "I wager you say that to all the ladies."

Proud of her answer, she smiled, a true and natural smile. Sir Allen seemed a safe enough fellow to practice her new skills of flirtation upon. Her parents would never consider him a marriage prospect, so she need not fear a prospective romance, but they might be pleased that she made some attempt to follow their instructions.

He tipped back his head and chuckled. "I deserved that. But truly, I feel I know you."

Her tongue finally loosened. "Perhaps you have met one of

my brothers. My surname is Barnes. Have you encountered a Reginald or a Gerald or perhaps a Hugh?"

"I do not think so, m'lady. But if you might grace me with your own name, I would be forever grateful."

She stopped a sigh just in time. No one had ever spoken to her in such a lovely manner, but she was not sure she liked the way it left her feeling weak-kneed and vulnerable. "Gwendolyn. My name is Lady Gwendolyn Barnes, daughter of the baron Lord Reimund Barnes."

He lifted her hand and kissed it, sending pleasant shivers to dance across her skin, up her arm, and down her spine. Again he stared deeply into her eyes. Though she must steel her heart against any romantic silliness, something told her that she could happily lose herself in the swirling hazel pool of his gaze.

◇◇◇

"And are these brothers of yours here tonight?" Allen asked, the taste of her silken skin still heady upon his lips. Perhaps the kiss, though proper and chivalrous, had been a mistake.

"Alas, only Reginald, the one I like the least. And my parents."

She indicated to a dark-haired young man with a somewhat shriveled and mousy woman hovering in his shadow, and then to an older gentleman with a fierce demeanor flanked by a diminutive blond.

"And they have left you to fend for yourself in this throng? How cruel!" He only half jested, for he himself wished his parents might be beside him for support this night.

The lovely Lady Gwendolyn laughed. A hearty laugh, not the false giggle of moments earlier, and she sat straight now, no longer hunched. "You understand me well, Sir Allen. In fact, if I had my way, I would not be here at all."

"And where would you be?"

"Perhaps strolling the woods outside the city gate."

"So you love the outdoors. Would you believe me if I told you that I lived as an outlaw in a forest hideaway for nearly two years?"

With a quick intake of breath, she gave him a little shove on the arm. "You did not!"

Perhaps he should have weighed his words more carefully. Though the evil King John was long dead and never well loved, he had no idea where this woman's loyalties might lie.

But after a moment Gwendolyn sighed and gazed at Allen with a wistful expression upon her beautiful features. "I have only dreamed of such adventures. You have no idea how jealous I am."

Relief coursed through him. "'Twas not all fun and games."

"I assume not, but how I long for a great adventure."

He twisted his head and stared at her curiously. From the moment he walked through the grand archway, this confusing young woman had caught his attention, standing taller than the females around her. One second he had noted the confident tilt of her chin, then she had crouched over and stared at the floor.

He'd watched as she oddly shuffled amid the crowd one moment, and agilely ducked through it with the grace of a huntress the next. Until, of course, he moved just enough to send her crashing into him. He held back a chuckle at the memory. She was a puzzle he simply must solve.

Only one woman had ever surprised and delighted him like this. And unbelievably, Gwendolyn Barnes with her golden tresses and curving figure was even more beautiful than Merry Ellison—at least when she relaxed.

However, he would never make the foolish mistake of losing his heart to a noblewoman again. Facing that sort of humiliation once in a lifetime was quite enough. He planned only to pass a few entertaining moments in Gwendolyn's charming presence. Something about her suggested a kindred spirit. A person he might befriend in this sea of strangers.

Gwendolyn glanced about, her gaze settling on the burly fellow she had indicated was her father. She tilted her head awkwardly to the side and stared at the bench between them. "Well, thank you for rescuing me, Sir Allen, but I suppose I should let you go now."

Chapter 9

Let him go? Allen could not lose her so soon. He knew not a single soul in this place, and had yet to solve the mystery of Lady Gwendolyn Barnes. "Perhaps I could convince you to dance."

Gwendolyn's aqua blue eyes, which contrasted so stunningly with her tan skin, set to sparkling, and her soft rosy lips lifted into that breathtaking smile once again. "Yes, a dance would be perfect."

He offered his hand, and her smaller one fit nicely in it. Unfortunately, that surge of warm energy he had experienced when they first touched pulsed through him again, but he attempted to ignore it. She continued smiling up at him for the duration of several heartbeats but then dropped her eyes and crouched into that strange position he had seen earlier.

Had someone bid her to disguise her height? Why on earth? She was Venus. She was Aphrodite. A goddess in all her statuesque glory. But as they completed their bow and curtsey and took their first patterned steps, she remained in her awkward position.

How could he right this travesty? He took her fingers lightly in his as they began their stilted progression across the floor. "You seem . . . rather uncomfortable, Lady Gwendolyn. I confess to being rather new to courtly dancing, but my teacher always insisted I stand straight and tall for ease of movement."

"Oh!" Her cheeks turned pink. "'Tis . . . only . . . just that." She dared to glance up at him. "Well, it is just that I am so very tall."

"Not next to me." He chuckled.

"True." She appeared to relax. "How kind of you to mention it rather than avoid the subject. Although I have been told it is not a maidenly virtue, I appreciate directness."

He wrapped his arm around her slender but firm waist and turned her in the other direction. "As do I. Clear communication saves so much time and energy. Do you not think?" It had been a trait he had always admired in Merry.

"Absolutely." She laughed and stood to her full elegant height, still a good bit shorter than him. They moved well together, and she danced with surprising grace once she was freed from her bizarre crouch.

"Ah, much better. Now I can look into your eyes." And look he did, attempting to unlock the secrets of her soul. He had never been able to gaze at Merry like this whilst standing, as her eye level hit somewhere in the vicinity of his chest. He rather liked Gwendolyn's height. It made her seem somehow an equal with him, as he believed a woman should be. Especially a woman one might consider as a wife.

Dangerous territory, that! He steered his mind away from it.

"So tell me something about yourself," Allen said as they continued through the genteel shapes and patterns of a dance he had learned at Linden Castle.

"I have never been an outlaw, although I have wished to be.

And I wish I could say I have gone on a crusade or a pilgrimage, something grand and exciting, but I have not."

"Something else, then. Something simple and everyday." He yet needed clues to decipher this enigmatic lady.

She pondered for a moment as she twirled beneath his raised arm. "I play the pipe. There is something quite magical about turning one's breath into such enchanting tones."

"Do you now? How wonderful." Music, dancing, beauty, honesty, a sharp wit, a daring spirit—what other fine qualities might this young lady possess?

"Alas, I feel I owe you the full truth," she said.

As they moved in unison, her lips turned into a mischievous smile. They joined hands overhead, and she stood a mere whisper away from him. "And what is the full truth?" he asked.

"I play my pipe in the highest boughs of the yew tree beyond our castle walls."

He chuckled again. "Perfect. I can think of no better place. You must promise to play for me there someday."

Her step stuttered momentarily, and her eyes grew wide. "Truly?"

"Truly." But the thought of Gwendolyn upon a bough brought to mind the kiss he had shared with Merry in a tree. *Foolish man!* If he could not rein his thoughts, perhaps he should get away from this entrancing noblewoman. . . . Except that he had no real desire to leave her.

They found their stride and proceeded with the dance.

"And I ride and shoot a bow as well. What think you of that?"

"I love it." She was so like Merry. Little wonder he felt drawn to her.

She shook her head in disbelief. "Forgive me for being so forthright," she said, "but I have spent the last weeks being inundated with instruction to play the addlebrained coquette. I

have been told again and again that I must suppress my boisterous nature. That men desire weak, demure women. Is this not
so? Please tell me your opinion, Sir Allen, for I am desperate
to hear it."

Ah, so finally, the mystery unraveled! This was but an act
she'd been bid to play.

They joined the line of dancers and tunneled their hands as
other couples rushed through. Caught up in the tide of movement, they took their turn running through as well, and he
tucked her close to his side. This poor girl, no wonder the con-
tradictions in her behavior. Yet he was pleased he had noticed
her true nature longing to break free.

Once they could converse again he said, "I have always admired a strong and courageous woman. A woman with spirit
and conviction. Even one with ability to lead. Perhaps I am the
exception, but I appreciate a woman I can respect."

"Ability to lead?" The dance sent them spinning away from
each other for a moment and then back again. "Is not such
a woman an abomination to God and nature? Does God not
wish for women to be subservient to their husbands and mas-
ters?" Her eyes pleaded with him to tell her she was wrong
once again.

He caught her taut torso within his grip and tugged her close
as all breath whooshed from his body. Allen fought off a wave
of dizziness as he held her near. Surely the young lady could
not affect him so much upon their very first meeting. Yet now
that he was beginning to understand her, his determination to
resist her draw was wavering.

He did, however, manage to focus his thoughts upon her
question about a woman's role. "I am not the expert on the holy
Scriptures that I wish to be. I know there are passages about
wives submitting, but I also recall a section about all believers

submitting one to another, as well as one about the husband treating the wife with care."

Her mouth formed a pretty little O shape. "Would you show these to me?"

"I will try. My Latin is not the best."

"Nor is mine. Still, I long to learn more about this. You seem such a purehearted sort, yet what you say is opposed to all I have been told."

The music stopped, and his eyes locked to hers as they stood still before each other. This was the true Gwendolyn Barnes. Her soul naked before him and desperate for truth. Though he must somehow resist her pull, he longed to help her, to shield her tender heart. "You mentioned you watched my battle this day."

She nodded.

"Then you must have noticed the way Lachapelle matched me strike for strike. That man brought out the best in me. I have never fought so in my life. Only with an equal was I able to rise to my full potential."

Gwendolyn looked for a moment as if she might faint, but then pulled herself up straight and tall again.

What must be going through her head at his ridiculous rant? "Do not misunderstand, I do not mean to equate marriage with a battle. 'Tis more like a dance. Like the way our well-matched heights allow us to move so comfortably together. Forgive me, I have spent too much time on the training field this year."

"Do not dare apologize. Your analogy was perfect." Wonder shimmered in her expression to match the wonder in his heart.

Suddenly, she was jerked away from him. He felt cold and alone, and ready to punch whomever had done it. But her father held tight to her arm, and Allen dared not offend the man.

Without so much as an apologetic word to Allen, her father bellowed, "Gwendolyn, there is someone I would like you to meet."

Allen could not unglue himself from his spot, and so was forced to watch the awful scene unfold.

"Lady Gwendolyn Barnes, meet Sir Gawain Ethelbaum. He was one of my most trusted soldiers when I assisted in the rebellion against King John."

Gawain, what sort of pompous and ridiculous name was that? The meaty man who approached Gwendolyn had a ruthless, predatory look in his eye despite his long waving black hair, elegant clothing, and preening walk. He might have been on the right side in the rebellion, but he appeared a villain nonetheless.

"So this is the young lady. She is rather . . . hearty, is she not?" The man raked her up and down with his gaze. "But overall comely as you described."

Lord Barnes nudged his daughter, and Gwendolyn slowly shifted back to her hunched position. She fluttered her lashes to Sir Gawain, who was even larger than Allen and had no need to gripe about the height of this exquisite woman.

"Do not be mistaken," Lord Barnes said. "She is a lady through and through."

"Indeed, she has some generous attributes." Sir Gawain leered at the cleavage revealed by Gwendolyn's low-cut gown, which Allen had noticed only in passing as a part of her overall feminine beauty. She pressed a concealing hand to her chest as her cheeks turned pink to match her dress.

Gawain laughed, a meanspirited sort of laugh that set Allen on edge. He remembered the oaf from the tournament now. The very fellow who had so callously struck the serving maid. Despite his disdain for the man, Allen had quickly assessed him as a force to be reckoned with. Perhaps the fiercest competitor there. Certainly one of the wealthiest, judging by the fine cut of his surcoat and his huge retinue. But beyond that, Allen had deemed him an unscrupulous villain.

The man reached out to take Gwendolyn's arm, and Allen wanted nothing more than to rip it away from him. Instead he attempted to step between the two. "So sorry to interrupt, but the Lady Gwendolyn promised me one more dance."

Gwendolyn's father sneered at him. "I am sure you are mistaken. The lady is finished with you for the evening. Come Gwendolyn, Sir Gawain, let us find some refreshments."

And with that he ushered the lovely woman away from Allen.

He found the bench where Gwendolyn had sought refuge and collapsed upon it, feeling as though he'd shrunk to miniscule proportions and nearly out of sight completely. He was naught but dust beneath their esteemed feet. There were plenty of women in the world, and this noble lady was out of his grasp. At the end of the day, knighted or not, he was a peasant born and bred.

He must accept that fact, and merely be thankful that his heart had healed to the point that he might develop new attractions. Right now, he did not need a woman anyway. What he needed was to win the tournament and begin carving out a place for himself, for he had nothing to offer any woman yet. Despite his new status as knight, he clearly remained a man of little account. Somehow, he must change that.

And if along the way he found an opportunity to teach the arrogant Sir Gawain a lesson or two, all the better.

Chapter 10

Gwendolyn's heart fluttered like a bird in flight as she thrilled to the sight of Sir Allen preparing to battle yet another opponent in the joust.

"Red and gold, red and gold, red and gold," the spectators shouted over and again in his honor.

Throughout the long day, he had grown to be a crowd favorite, and she could not have felt more pride in this new and dear friend if he had been a member of her own family. Only one more round and Sir Allen would face that awful Sir Gawain for the championship.

Ugh! Gawain. With his ridiculous silken black hair. Perhaps it was that girlish hair that had confused him into thinking he could strike his maidservant so heartlessly yesterday. Gwen had no desire to even consider how such a man would treat a wife.

Surely Father would never expect her to marry the churlish dolt. As much as Allen had won favor through his courage and honor, Gawain had gained the crowd's disdain through his pompous displays and unchivalrous behavior. 'Twas a wonder the duke suffered the fellow at all, except that Gawain's father was a powerful nobleman in his own right.

Allen leveled his lance, and Gwen's heart thumped as if she were about to joust herself. The horses thundered toward one another. How quick it all happened when she observed rather than participated. In one neat move, Allen thrust his lance and sent his opponent crashing to the ground with a loud *thump*.

"He unseated him in just one pass!" she said in wonder. It was true, she had fought well yesterday, merely had the misfortune of being matched with the best man on the field in her first round. Thus far, not a single competitor had survived against Sir Allen as long as she had.

"Not surprising," Gwen's brother Reginald said with a grunt. "He has done so several times now, but I dare say Gawain shall put this upstart in his place." Tournaments always put Reginald in a foul mood, since Father had never permitted him to participate in one. According to their father, he was the heir and must be protected. Hugh and Gerald were the knights. And Gwen the marriage pawn to be sold to the highest bidder.

Life was disturbingly simple in the mind of Lord Reimund Barnes.

Too bad Gawain's father had not kept his son hidden away at home as the coddled heir—otherwise Father might never have met the oaf.

Mother fanned herself. "Sir Allen is quite a contender, but he would never stand a chance against either of our boys. The fact that Gawain beat Hugh in their last tournament was naught but a fluke."

"Gawain is a beast of a man, and that serves him well." Admiration tinged her father's voice. "But I agree. He has not Hugh's agility."

Rosalind looked to Gwen and rolled her eyes. No one but Father would think being a beast was a good thing.

"Let us be forthright," Reginald said. "Gawain is a ghastly brute, but at least he is a North Britannian citizen of noble birth. I hear rumors that this Sir Allen is of questionable stock."

"As I suspected." Father glared at Gwen. "I had best not see you wasting more time on that lowly fellow."

Gwen inclined her head to acknowledge her father, but she had no intention of obeying the command. Allen had been the only bright spot in her dreary evening, and she would not insult him by ignoring him tonight.

As the attendants prepared the field for the final battle of the day, Gwen caught sight of a hand waving at them from the center of the grandstand. She leaned out the opening and found the duchess, who was dressed in a lovely gown of fern green, calling to her. "Lady Gwendolyn! Oh, Gwendolyn, there you are. Come and join me for the final round. It shall be so exciting."

Gwen turned to her parents to ask permission.

Mother waved her away before Gwen could utter a word. "Go, and hurry with you. One does not decline an invitation from the duchess."

"Of course." Still a bit flustered by the request, Gwen called out to the duchess. "I am coming. Just one moment please."

She gestured to Rosalind, and the two of them ducked through the exit from their box and into the bright sunshine behind the stands.

"Thanks be to God!" Rosalind caught Gwen back. "I thought we'd never escape them. What happened last night? That Allen fellow has had his eye on you all day. And do not think I missed that kiss you blew to him when you thought no one observed. Why did you not tell me when you came home?"

Gwen felt a flush rise to her cheeks. Of course she could

hide nothing from her handmaiden. "We did spend some time together last night. He is an admirable man, very kind and encouraging. But he is only a friend. As I have told you time and again, I have no need of romance."

She nearly said, *nor of a husband to hold me under his thumb*, yet she knew such would never be the case with a fellow like Sir Allen.

"Surely you do not expect me to believe that." Rosalind pressed a hand to Gwen's forehead. "Fetch the healer—this one has got it bad."

"I do not!" But even as she protested, Gwen feared Rosalind might be correct.

"Of course you must say that." Sympathy shone in Rosalind's eyes as she offered Gwen a half smile. "I'm happy that you have found a new *friend*, Lady Gwendolyn, and I will not mention any obstacles this *friendship* might present. Only be thankful it has brought you such joy."

"Oh hush, you." Gwen gave her maid a playful shove. "Come. We must hurry. The duchess awaits."

This was an odd turn of events for certain. Gwen had never expected to win the woman's favor. They nodded to the guards at the entrance to the duke's gallery and entered just as the trumpets blasted to announce the final event of the day.

"Oh good! You made it in time." The duchess held out a hand to Gwen, and Gwen gave it a squeeze.

She settled herself in the empty cushioned chair next to her grace, the Duchess DeMontfort, and Rosalind stood attendance behind them.

"This should be the best match of the tournament," the duke said.

"I could not agree more." Gwen's tongue felt free in such a welcoming environment. "Sir Allen has fought gallantly all day."

The duchess leaned forward as the herald finished the announcements preceding the battle. "Yes, and Sir Gawain has fought to win and for naught else. Let us not pretty up the truth. I know who I shall be cheering for. Red and gold, red and gold, red and gold."

The delicate duchess punched the air in rhythm with her chant, and soon Gwen and Rosalind, not to mention much of the crowd, joined in. Gwen had reckoned correctly that the duchess was a feisty sort.

Allen in his red and gold squared off against the mammoth Gawain bedecked in blue and green. But as they had all expected, this was not an easy win for either competitor. After four passes and at least as many broken lances, the joust continued.

"Oh, this is just too exciting." The duchess pressed her kerchief to her mouth. "I can barely stand it."

"Imagine how they must feel," came from Gwendolyn's mouth before she thought to stop the words.

The duchess raised a knowing brow her way. "Ah, so you do know a thing or two of battle."

Gwen smiled. "Perhaps."

As the knights prepared for another pass, an odd sight caught Gwendolyn's gaze. Just beyond Allen, at the far side of the arena, a young child stood and balanced himself atop the high railing along the side of the stands. He teetered right and left, then straightened himself and quickly sat upon it. Goodness, where were the child's parents? Although he looked to be no older than six or seven, no one seemed to notice him.

But all thoughts of the child were swept from Gwen's mind as the horses rushed toward each other once again. She recognized that determined set to Allen's shoulders. "Look at his form. Someone is going down."

With a resounding clash, both lances splintered as the riders flipped in tandem to the ground at the tremendous impact of their joint blows.

The duchess squealed in delight. "You are a genius, my girl." She patted Gwen's leg. "This is your permanent seat from this day hence."

"Five, six, seven . . ." the herald shouted.

"But will they rise?" asked the duke, as both men yet sprawled upon the ground.

Gwen had noticed slight twitches from both of them. Neither had been knocked out cold, and both were fiercely determined. "Absolutely. Just give them a moment."

A secret part of her struggled along with Allen, gathering air and courage as he hoisted himself from the ground. Gwen let out a breath she had not realized she had been holding. "Thank goodness!"

"Fifteen, sixteen . . ." called the herald, just as Sir Gawain also managed to rise.

"And let the swordplay begin."

But both men paused for a moment before approaching one another.

"This should be splendid." The duke propped his elbows upon the waist-high wall of the gallery.

"Gawain far outranks in size and strength, but Allen is amazingly agile. I could not believe those tumbling maneuvers he performed y . . ." Gwen nearly faltered but caught herself in time, remembering she was supposed to have been ill yesterday. "Against his opponents."

"You should have seen him yesterday when he faced Sir Geoffrey," the duke said. "Now that was magnificent indeed."

"Yes, whatever happened to Lachapelle?" asked the duchess. "I did not find him at the feast."

"Perhaps he slunk back to France with his tail between his legs at our superior English might." The duke chuckled.

"Oh, stop that." The duchess slapped his arm. "Men! Whatever shall we do with them?"

"I have no idea, Your Grace." Gwen could hardly believe she was jesting with the duke and duchess.

"You shall figure it out soon enough." The duchess laughed.

Gwen winced at the reminder, but the two men now approached each other, and the final battle began.

They were a sight to behold, their swords clashing with a volume to raise the dead. Again and again they slashed at each other. Gwen wondered how their shields survived. Allen spun and ducked and performed several evasive tumbling maneuvers, while Gawain was all aggression and brute force. At last, after several minutes, Gawain took a step back to find his breath, and Allen likewise retreated for a respite.

"Should you call a winner?" the duchess asked her husband.

"Not yet. They are still too evenly matched. This round might be decided by stamina alone."

Gwen smiled. "Then Sir Allen should win. For he was only recently knighted and is surely at the peak of his training."

The duke turned to her. "You seem to know much about this young man. I hope you are right."

Gwen looked away before the duke might read anything upon her face.

In that instant, the odd sight caught her attention again. The child teetered now on one foot, perched precariously upon the rail a good eighteen feet from the ground. If he slipped off to the side, no one would see him. No one would hear. Before she could do a thing, before she could even scream, his foot flew out from beneath him. In the last second before he fell to sure destruction, he caught himself by his fingertips along the ledge.

"Heavens, no!" Gwen shrieked. "The child!"

The duchess turned to seek the trouble—the dangling child was barely visible from their angle across the field, but she followed Gwen's finger and found his form peeking out from the side of the stand.

"Do something!" yelled the duchess.

The duke, caught in the throes of battle, did not hear a word. An attentive guard disappeared out the rear door, but he would never make it to the far side of the arena in time. Gwen debated jumping onto the field, but she would never make it either, and would risk being skewered in the process.

Staring straight at Allen, who was mere yards from the lad, and willing him with all her might to look at her, she pointed and screamed, "The child. Save the child!"

◇◇◇

Allen scanned the grandstands once again. Where had she gone? Her strength and support had gotten him through this day, making him feel a part of something greater than himself, offering him a sense of friendship and belonging that fueled him to fight.

"Red and gold, red and gold . . ." the crowd bellowed once again. In support of him. He could hardly fathom it. If he had felt miniscule last night, he loomed mammoth today.

From the far side of the field near the grandstand, Gawain wavered with weariness, but came at Allen nonetheless. Allen saw his chance. His heart soared. He would defeat this foe.

And that was when Allen noticed her. Standing and shrieking in the center gallery. Pointing beyond his shoulder. What on earth did she shout? Then he understood.

"Save the child!"

He swiveled and saw a child hanging by one hand from the rail along the stands, a deadly height above the ground. Even as he watched, a tiny finger slipped away, but the child's screams were swallowed by the roar of the crowd.

Gawain rushed directly at Allen now, but Allen could not allow the young lad to perish. With no time to think, Allen tossed his sword to the ground and ran with every ounce of his strength toward the dangling child. He dove over the chest-high enclosure with one neat move, tumbled along the ground, and back to standing. The boy's fingers lost their grip, and the child began his agonizing descent. Just before he crashed to the hard-packed ground, Allen surged forward and caught the boy in his arms.

The crowd grew deathly still.

What had Allen just done? Had he thrown it all away? But as he clutched the warm bundle to his chest, he knew he could never have chosen otherwise.

"My baby! My baby!" a woman shrieked, clambering down the stairs toward him.

Allen walked around to meet her, and the crowd finally seemed to put the pieces together and began cheering once again.

"Oh, thank you! Thank you, kind sir. You are truly the most chivalrous knight in the land." The crying woman kissed Allen's hand.

Gawain, grinning his evil, arrogant smile, held Allen's sword high over his head. "Did you lose something?"

Allen's stomach sank as his dreams crashed to the earth, just as surely and violently as the boy might have crashed to his death. If Allen had sheathed his sword, the match would have continued. But in that fraction of a second, the child could have perished, or at the least been maimed. Any honorable knight would return the sword to Allen, but Gawain had no honor in him.

The victory might belong to Gawain, but at least Allen had

won the spirit of the day. He would not give up all hope yet. The duke remained a just man.

"I was thinking that rather I had found something." Allen held the boy high over his head and the crowd went wild once again.

Gawain sneered at Allen with deadly hatred in his eyes. Once the woman gathered her son, Allen climbed back into the arena, and the crowd settled, Gawain spat upon the ground. "You are mistaken, Sir Allen. For we all know that in forfeiting this sword, you lost the round to me."

Silence now reigned in this place that had been thundering with noise all day.

Allen would give Gawain the benefit of the doubt and assume the man did not understand that the child could have died without his help. He glanced about, unsure of what came next. The herald should declare Gawain the winner now, yet he stepped back and said not a word.

The duke stood and raised a hand. "Is this truly how you wish to play the game, Sir Gawain?"

"I have won fairly, and I have won most assuredly. That is precisely how I wish to play. The child was naught but a convenient excuse, for Sir Allen knew he could not beat me."

A few boos and hisses emerged from the observers, but mostly they remained as stunned and still as Allen himself at this man's outlandish audacity. For a moment nothing happened. No one moved. Allen approached the grandstand, hoping that might prompt the duke to end this lingering torture.

He might not win, but he would yet hold fast to his honor. Standing side by side with Gawain, Allen spoke. "I concede. Gawain has won. I know the rules, and I relinquished my sword. There is nothing else to be said."

"Understand that I have taken the measure of the both of you today. I shall not soon forget this outcome." The duke nodded slowly to the herald.

With disdain thick in his voice, the man announced, "The victory goes to Sir Gawain."

"Yes!" the pompous fool shouted. "Yes! Yes!"

But no one joined him in celebration.

The duke tossed a bag of coins to the man, the likes of which might have supported Allen for years. Might have allowed him to look forward to marriage and family. His stomach clenched.

But then Gwendolyn stood, resplendent in a gorgeous amber gown, tall and elegant and drawing the attention of the entire crowd. "Sir Allen! Your prize for your valiant deed this day." She tossed down her kerchief to him.

Then the duchess stood and did the same. And the comely dark-haired lass next to Gwendolyn. And then a shower of fabric drifted from the sky toward him like a soft spring rain. Every color imaginable. Embroidered silks and satins next to rough scraps of beige flaxen fabrics.

Gawain turned a slow circle, shaking his bag of coins and his triumphant sword over his head as if the attention were all for him. Allen chuckled at the absurdity of it all, and at the glory of it all. He might not hold a bag of gold, but he held the esteem of these people. Just as he had always hoped he deserved.

Gwendolyn cheered and clapped with a huge grin upon her face.

The duke just smiled and nodded at Allen.

Perhaps all was not yet lost.

Chapter 11

Allen entered the elaborate great hall of Edendale Castle with its soaring ceilings and colorful banners and braced himself for an uncomfortable evening. A part of him had wanted to stay home and pout over his loss that day, but since home yet consisted of a bedroll next to a stream, and as he still needed to win the favor of the duke, he had hastened himself to the celebration.

He smoothed down the dark blue linen of his finest tunic, unfortunately the same one he had worn last night. Then again, no one but Gwendolyn had given him much heed, and he didn't think her the type to care about fashion.

There she was.

His evening took a sudden turn for the better as Gwendolyn rushed to him and took his hands in her own. A sense of coming home washed over him. She was a vision of loveliness in a gown of turquoise and silver with silver ribbons twisted through her golden tresses. As he leaned close to kiss her hand, he noted she smelled not of traditional roses or lavender, but of a wilder herbal scent, which better suited her feisty nature.

He hesitated for the briefest moment, pausing over her hand like a honeybee hovering before taking its first taste of sweet nectar. The room seemed to hush as he fleetingly touched his lips to her skin. Truly, he must cease this silliness and think of her only as a dear friend.

"Sir Allen." The admiration in her voice warmed him and bolstered his confidence.

"Lady Gwendolyn."

Despite his resolve, tiny charges like lightning crackled from her hands to his and back again. He breathed up a quick word of thanks that she was not yet a married lady who must hide that glorious mane of hair.

Thoughts of prayer caused him to recall her request for the first time this day. He gave her hands a squeeze. "I am so sorry, but I just realized that I did not have the opportunity to search out the Scriptures for you as I promised."

"You were rather busy." She grinned up at him. "And quite amazing. Congratulations on a fine tournament."

"But I did not win." He lowered his head as his bliss diminished by half.

She tipped it up with her finger. "You won favor and respect and proved yourself the more honorable knight. Duke Justus was none too pleased with that awful Gawain."

Perhaps all was not lost. If the duke was pleased with Allen's character, then he might still apply for service as a knight of the region. Although he was as yet unsure if that would put him in close proximity to—as Gwendolyn called him—that awful Gawain. "I take it you like him no more than I do."

"He is a coward and a bully."

"I couldn't agree more."

Gwendolyn looked as if she would like to spit the foul taste of the man from her mouth. "And if my father tries to force me to marry him, I might try my chances as a forest outlaw after all. Would you consider joining my band?"

Allen's stomach clutched as he recalled the oaf Gawain backhanding his maidservant. Such behavior was sadly tolerated in England, but he knew not the statutes here. Either way, it was churlish and unchivalrous in the extreme, and he would never wish to see Gwendolyn with such a man. "Surely your father would never. Does he not realize that the man is a brute?"

Gwendolyn frowned. "My father knows exactly what Gawain is, and loves him all the more for it."

And Allen's stomach churned all the more over it. Though he dare not think of Gwendolyn in a romantic light, he would not stand by idly and see her wed to that fiend.

"Excuse me, please." A deep voice interrupted them.

Allen turned to see Duke Justus himself at his side.

"Your Grace!" Allen bowed, before stopping to think if that was the correct response.

The duke lifted him with a brush to his shoulder. "No need, Sir Allen, though I appreciate the sentiment. My Lady Gwendolyn, would you forgive me if I steal this chivalrous young knight from your company?"

"Of course. I dare not keep the man of the evening all to myself." Gwendolyn offered a smile of reassurance his way. "I think Sir Allen is a person you should get to know better."

"Ah, precisely as I was thinking. Come, my good man." The duke pressed a friendly hand to Allen's back and led him to a table where a group of auspicious-looking men gathered. "Sir Allen of Ellsworth, may I introduce you to some of my council members."

Allen's head swirled as the duke called them each by name, title, and role. He would never remember it all. For the next ten minutes these men shot questions at him about his training and background as Allen fought to maintain his composure. He had not been reared for such interviews, although his time with Lord Linden had helped to prepare him. He only hoped he would not make an utter fool of himself. But by the looks on their faces, he seemed to be managing adequately.

"Outlawed by King John—you don't say!" An ostentatious-looking council member in a plumed hat chuckled. "That alone is enough to win you favor in these parts." He slapped Allen heartily upon the back.

"And you stayed with those children to protect them all that time." The duke nodded with admiration. "Little wonder you put the child's welfare above your own today."

"But ward to a nobleman?" A voice came from Allen's left. Allen searched out the skeptical-looking older man in a simple russet tunic—a historian, if Allen recalled correctly—but he saw no malice in the man's eyes, only concern. "Are you certain you have no noble blood at all?"

Allen sought out Gwendolyn, who hovered nearby watching the exchange. She sent him a nod of support. Allen scanned his mind, and surely enough, an answer came to him.

He had not thought of it in years, but . . . "My old grand-father used to tell tales of an ancient Breton king in our family, but I always considered them fanciful stories."

"Merciful God in heaven," whispered the man with the long black beard beside his interrogator with awe in his voice. "This one might be a descendant of the legendary Arthur himself."

Allen laughed at the ridiculous extrapolation. "I never made any claims like that."

"But it all makes sense now," the old historian said. "You showed such nobility upon the field today."

Allen clenched the edge of the table as anger flickered in his chest. He was not at all sure that he liked the way the conversation was heading. "I was told that Duke Justus honored nobility of heart above nobility of birth."

The duke sent the historian a pointed look. "Sir Allen has the right of it, Lord Fulton."

"But such nobility does not merely appear out of the ether." The historian, evidently named Lord Fulton, held his ground.

"Sir Allen," called a man dressed in red bishop's robes with a tall pointed hat. "Do you consider yourself a religious man?"

Allen held in a sigh of relief. He felt more comfortable with this line of questioning. "I was blessed to be instructed by the finest priest during my childhood. Although to hear him speak of the matter, it seemed to be more about a relationship between a man and his God than religion per se."

"I see." Interest sparked in the clergyman's deep brown eyes. "Do explain."

"I spend much time communing with God through prayer, and I long to please Him with every choice I make."

"And do you please God by coming to North Britannia?" asked the duke.

"I hope you will not think it arrogant of me to say so, but I believe I sensed God leading me in this direction."

It seemed the duke and bishop sent several silent messages back and forth between them, but Allen could not discern a single one.

Finally the bishop spoke again. "Do you spend time in the Scriptures as well?"

"I confess that I only learned to read Latin during this past year. But I have spent many a free moment in the evenings studying the Scriptures, and nearly every penny I earn on candles to do so."

That provoked a round of laughter from the men at the table.

"Tell me the most surprising thing you have found in the Scriptures," the priest challenged, he alone maintaining a serious expression.

With Gwendolyn fresh upon Allen's mind, the answer came easily. "The prophetess Deborah. Although I was never one to think women inferior to men, I had always heard that God ordained men to do the leading. I was intrigued to learn in reading of Deborah that this was not always the case. And I served under the most amazing noblewoman during my time in the forest."

A moment too late, Allen wondered if he had spoken too transparently.

"Excellent answer, my boy." The bishop offered his first smile of the evening. "We like to think of this as a progressive dukedom, which is open to new places that God might lead us through the study of His Word. Although I imagine we are still more mired in English traditions than we might hope."

Allen sat forward with excitement. "How has North Britannia managed to hold to such high ideals despite the depravity all around?"

The duke tapped the tabletop. "It has not been easy. My father had a vision of a fair and honorable region after the fashion of Arthur's Camelot. We managed to break in most practical ways from the reprobate Prince John when he stirred up so much trouble during Richard's absence, and then completely when he was at odds with the pope a decade ago."

His eyes glowed with pleasure as he spoke. "From that time until the coronation of our new king, Henry, we functioned as an independent dukedom. Our laws have long contained the sort of freedoms sought by the English rebels in their recent Charter of Liberties. It took much prayer, much determination, and much education to bring us to this place."

"Precisely," the old historian said. "Over time people realized it was for the best."

"Most people," said the bishop with a raised eyebrow.

"There will always be dissidents." Fulton spoke directly to Allen. "A few selfish noblemen would rather keep everything for themselves, but they are not worthy of our notice. The common people have embraced the new ways, and we must continue this forward momentum."

"Well." The duke leaned back in his chair and nodded to Allen. "Intelligent, kind, humble, honorable, and spiritual. What more can we ask?"

Evidently he needed not ask any more at all, for every man at the table nodded.

"Absolutely," Lord Fulton said.

"Without a doubt." The bishop smiled to Allen again.

"Indubitably!" The man with the plumed hat affirmed his assent so heartily that he nearly lost said hat.

Allen alone sat mystified concerning their meaning.

"Sir Allen, my good man, what do you say to joining our ranks?" The duke put an end to Allen's bafflement, yet left him stuttering nonetheless.

"As a knight? I would . . . I mean . . . that is to say . . ." Wonder overtook Allen and set his head to spinning all over again. This had been far easier than he expected, particularly after today's farce at the tournament. Truly God stood on his side. "That is what I wished for all along."

The group of councilors began to laugh again. Allen hoped his answer had not seemed too pathetic.

"As a knight, certainly," the duke said. "You are welcome to move into my garrison this very evening. But we need godly men like you to help lead this region. Besides which, I wish to send a strong message about the occurrences at the tournament."

Again he paused to survey the men at the table. "Sir Allen of Ellsworth, would you consider joining our council?"

Allen could no longer think straight, nor could he keep his jaw from dropping open. From the side of his eye, he noticed a flash of turquoise as Gwendolyn moved closer with a questioning look upon her lovely face. Only one thought fought its way through the sea of confusion to the forefront of his consciousness.

Perhaps the fair Lady Gwendolyn was not out of his reach after all.

"Yes," he mouthed silently to her, meaning so much more than that simple word could convey.

She clasped her hands to her bosom and grinned her support. How forever grateful he would be that she had shared this miraculous moment with him. He could hardly wait to escape this interrogation and spend more time with Gwendolyn.

But he must not run away too quickly. A member of the council! Allen could hardly fathom it. He must put first matters first and secure his place in the dukedom. Once that was settled, perhaps he might win the favor of some young lady—dare he dream even of the Lady Gwendolyn?—for good.

For what was all the success in the world without a loving family by one's side?

◇ ◇ ◇

From behind a marble pillar, Warner glared in the direction of Justus and his passel of squawking imbeciles. Let them laugh now, for they would not be laughing long.

And what was this nonsense? Why did they consult with that lowborn knight as if he were one of the magi from the east? Matters at court had clearly gone from bad to worse during the five years since he last spied upon them, and they would soon reach a critical crossroad. He had returned none too soon, it seemed. If Justus had his way, before long the peasants would be running the country entirely.

Two men headed in his direction down the shadowy corridor that ran along the side of the great hall. At last, the moment he had been waiting for.

"Hello, friend." Sir Gaillard, the slight and grizzled knight from the border area, wisely did not mention Warner's name.

He hid deeper in his concealing cloak nonetheless.

Sir Gaillard was a member of the council, though not one of the favored fellows who had been dining upon the dais this evening. "I have brought the man, as you requested."

"Ah, Lord Barnes." Warner eyed the hulking fellow up and down. A military genius, or so many claimed. Yes, he would do quite nicely. With the baron at his side, Warner could move forward with his plans in full confidence. "I hear we have much in common."

"I am not yet convinced of that," the man snapped.

"Truly? Well, then. Tell me what you think of the goings-on upon the dais."

The baron grumbled. "'Tis ridiculous. Who is that fellow? Some lowborn knight from central England. Why do they seek his opinion? Bah!" He swiped his hand through the air in disgust.

"You see! Precisely as I feel," Warner said. "I believe you are as weary with the duke's progressive nonsense as I am. What is the point of being endowed with nobility by God in heaven if one intends to hand over power to lesser humans? Those created for nothing more than to work the earth and procreate? They have not the intelligence, nor the discernment, to be involved in decision-making. Education only serves to twist their minds and confuse them."

The baron considered Warner. "I cannot argue any of that,

but I am not sure we see eye to eye on how to bring about change. Whether or not Justus and his council like the fact, North Britannia is yet part of England. In time things shall come back around. The regent shall not tolerate such nonsense."

Indeed, Warner knew William Marshall well, had fought alongside him, in fact. That was precisely why he needed to seize power now, while his ally might support him. But this Barnes fellow was yet an unknown entity, and Warner's gut told him he should not trust him too far. He had risked much merely approaching him to gauge his opinions. He would certainly not trust the man with his plans, not at a pivotal time such as this.

"Well"—Warner extended his hand to shake Lord Barnes's meatier one—"it is always a pleasure to meet a kindred spirit. I hope that if at some point in the future . . . shall we say . . . matters change, I will have your support."

"Do not count on that. The duke is well loved. I yet feel a good degree of faithfulness to the man, although I agree we are in dire need of change. I must take time to consider this. Now if you will excuse me, I should get back to my family."

With that, Lord Barnes took his leave.

"So what do you think?" Sir Gaillard asked.

"I think we had best stick with our original plan. Perhaps once it is under way, the good baron shall join us. But either way, we must move forward."

"I am still not certain. We would benefit from more support. If we give the baron some time, he might come 'round . . ."

At that moment, Duke Justus stood and tapped his goblet with his knife. Good heavens, what inanity would the man come up with now? If only Justus knew his banished cousin stood watching him from the shadows, conspiring with his own nobles, the fact might wipe that insipid smile from his face.

"Good people of North Britannia and esteemed guests, I am

pleased to announce that Sir Allen of Ellsworth, most honorable knight in all the land, has consented to join my council."

The lowborn fellow stood beside the duke with false humility pasted across his face.

Warner slapped a hand over his mouth to stop his protest from spewing out. That was it. The final straw. He would proceed with his plan without an ounce of regret.

"Surely he must jest!" Sir Gaillard dug his fingers through his hair. "Does his idiocy know no bounds? He did not even bring this to the full council for approval."

"Do you see now? Do you understand why we can no longer delay?" Warner fought hard to keep desperation from leaking into his voice. He had waited a lifetime to be afforded the title and power he so deserved. He had no wish to wait any longer.

The man sighed. "Yes. This has gone on long enough. I shall speak with my colleagues and it shall take place a week hence, precisely as you requested."

"And I shall be able to do it with my own hand?"

"Absolutely," the man said with a wicked grin. "We would not have it otherwise. You are the only person who can do this thing with impunity."

Warner rubbed his hands together. He could almost taste victory. How fortuitous the timing of his cousin's addlebrained announcement had been.

Before long, North Britannia would be his.

Chapter 12

Back home at Castle Barnes, Gwen snuggled deeper into the pillows on her bed as she studied the weighty words of the book Allen had recommended to her during their extended time together over the days following the tournament. Mischief perched near Gwen's head, and Angel, tucked into her side, commenced to snore. Meanwhile, Rosalind bustled about unpacking Gwen's trunk.

"Tell me again of your glorious evening." Rosalind scooped up the turquoise gown she had been attending. She held it against her chest, taking one long sleeve into her hand, and spun around Gwen's chamber with its plain grey stone walls as if she herself were dancing at the grand Edendale Castle.

All along their trip home Rosalind had asked to hear the story of Gwen's magical evening with Allen. Heat filled Gwen's cheeks. "Do not be ridiculous. We need not relive it again and again."

Rosalind laid the gown over a chair. Then she sat upon Gwen's bed beside her. Rosalind tugged the leather-bound manuscript out of Gwen's hand. "Of course we must. Tell me a tale of romance!"

"Give me back my book!" Gwen reached for it, but Rosalind swept it high over her head.

"Not until you relent."

"Fine." Gwen pushed against the mattress and sat up straighter to begin her tale. "But you must stop making such a silly fuss over it. After being introduced to the entire assemblage as the newest member of the council, Allen came straight to me for a dance, and all eyes were upon us. I swear we were the couple of the evening, and a fine couple we made, towering above everyone in our turquoise and blue. I have never felt so beautiful."

Allen evoked a new softness within Gwen, the likes of which she had not suspected she was capable. And since he was now on the council . . . and since she had to marry someone . . . she had begun to think perhaps she should not resist these feelings after all. "No one has ever looked at me like that before."

Rosalind gave a little click of her tongue. "I know that is not true, for I have seen men rake you with their eyes as if you were the main course at a feast."

"I hate that sort of attention." Gwen hugged her arms over her chest. "Allen looks at me with a tender, pure sort of longing, and 'tis quite different when it comes from a man you admire. There, so I have poured out my heart. Is that quite enough?"

"No, no! Tell me more." Rosalind patted the mattress in her excitement.

"I suppose, if you insist."

"I do."

Gwen sighed. "We danced several dances, and then were forced to switch partners. Father looked perturbed, but he had told me to make myself visible and be certain to dance, for nothing makes a woman more appealing than the attention of one's foes."

Gwen giggled, and then clapped a hand over her mouth to stop the silly, girlish sound before continuing. "When Gawain asked me to dance, I thought the evening ruined, but it was a lively tune, and even he could not bring down my high spirits."

"And then . . ." Rosalind wiggled her brows, for she knew the story well.

"And then Allen asked if we might take a stroll through the moonlit gardens. I looked about for Father, but he had been sent on the urgent mission that yet keeps him away, and Mother gave me her permission without hesitation." Gwen quieted for a moment, recalling the feel of Allen's strong arm beneath her fingers, the brush of his hand along her back, the way she sank into the depths of his eyes as they glimmered with moonlight.

At last, she spoke again. "We just walked and talked for what seemed an eternity. About everything in the world and nothing at all. Then we sat upon a bench together. He told me tales of his adventures in the forest and stories from the Scriptures as well. And then over the following days . . . Oh, Rosalind!"

"I am glad your mother agreed to stay awhile," Rosalind said.

Gwen smiled as those marvelous sensations washed over her once more. "There is truly not another like him in the world. Neither so good-hearted nor so brave. He gives me hope that all men might not be brutes."

"And I dare say Sir Allen gives you a new view on the subject of marriage."

"Perhaps." Gwen bit her lip. Fear nibbled away at her wonder and awe, as it had so many times since that night. "Although I have still not adjusted entirely to the idea. And I am still afraid Father might not find him suitable."

"Don't be silly. He is to be a council member."

"Yes, but Father was none too happy about the decision. I heard him grumbling about peasant upstarts before Allen caught me away."

Rosalind frowned. "I warrant he shall get past it."

"But he might not get past the fact that Allen treats me as an equal. He wants a husband who will tame me." Gwen's stomach wrenched at the thought.

"Allen, is it?" Rosalind shot Gwen a pointed look at the familiar use of his first name.

Gwen batted her with a small pillow. "Stop it!"

At once, both Angel and Mischief perked up and dove for the pillow. Angel caught it first, and began flailing it about, as if it were a squirrel and she would wring its neck in a manner not at all true to her name. But Mischief snatched it away and jumped to the floor with his tail wagging. Angel followed him and they commenced a tugging war.

"Shall I rescue the pillow from the troublesome pups?" Rosalind asked.

"Let them have their fun." Gwen was thankful for the distraction from their conversation.

"But I am dismayed he did not mention marriage or at least courtship." Alas, it seemed Rosalind would not let the subject go so easily.

"'Tis too early for any of that. But he did say that once he was settled in his new position we would have much to discuss."

◇ ◇ ◇

"That does indeed sound promising. And do not forget that he kissed your hands for much longer than good manners allow. I love that part." A pang of jealousy surged through Rosalind, for although she and Hugh were closer than Gwendolyn and Allen in many practical ways, they had never made even the vaguest plans for future meetings. Only lived in the moment when circumstances allowed.

Hugh's moods ran wild like a tempest, and she never quite knew what to expect from him. Though she hated to admit it, he could behave quite poorly at times.

But she swept aside any envy. Gwendolyn deserved this moment of happiness, and Rosalind loved seeing the new tenderness and femininity that had come over her mistress.

While Rosalind enjoyed hearing Gwendolyn's tales of romance, she herself needed to find a new man to catch her fancy. She had spent too much time dreaming of the unattainable Sir Hugh Barnes, and now had begun to despair. If she could not meet a new fellow in the teeming city of Edendale, there was no hope for her.

"Now, have I earned my book back?" Gwendolyn snapped Rosalind from her reverie.

Rosalind held the book in one hand and tapped it upon the palm of the other. "I can't help but wonder what is so fascinating about it. You've never bothered much with pleasure reading before."

"Al . . . rather Sir Allen"—a smug look crossed Gwendolyn's face as she corrected herself—"mentioned this book of sermons to me, and I found it in our library, but Father would not like the book if he bothered to read it."

"That explains everything. Sir Allen is the source of your sudden interest." Rosalind flipped through the crinkling pages. Though she had learned the fundamentals of reading, wishing to stand out as a candidate for lady's maid, most of these words were not familiar. "And is it any good?"

"I like the perspective, and it is written in French, which is much easier for me than Latin."

That explained why little seemed familiar. "Would you read a passage to me?" Rosalind asked.

Gwendolyn flipped to a section she had marked with a ribbon and kindly translated into English, for though the Norman nobles could float easily between French and English, Rosalind knew only the basics of French required for her station.

"'Christ gave His life as a ransom for us and restored us to right relationship with God. Thus we become children of the living, all-encompassing creator of the universe. Love incarnate indwells our very beings, and from our sense of deep gratitude, we are spurred to keep His law and live a holy life worthy of His sacrifice.'"

As Gwendolyn continued reading the powerful words, a sense of awe and humility rushed over Rosalind. Although she regularly attended mass, she had never heard anything quite like this. She had never considered herself indwelt by God, though perhaps she should have. Her chest tightened as she realized that though she believed in God, she had been rather thoughtless about His commands.

Wasn't it human nature to yield to one's passions and desires? Only the clergy were called to holy lives, as their station required. Yet this book caused her to wonder. They sat quietly for a few moments, as Rosalind recounted her many sins with a degree of regret she had never experienced before. "What do you think of the passage?"

Gwendolyn held the book away from her body, as if putting some distance between herself and the powerful words. "I am not certain. This is so different from what I have heard at mass."

"It occurs to me," Rosalind whispered in reverence of their holy conversation, "that if these ideas are true, one cannot simply go on one's way and ignore them. They require a change in how we live."

"Agreed. *If* they are true—which I am not convinced of at this point." Gwendolyn snapped the book shut. "But I am disappointed that I have found nothing on the issue that concerns me most."

"Which is?"

"How God views women. I do not desire to serve a God who would create me only to serve and pander to men. To suffer their whims and abuses."

Rosalind believed that God created her to serve her betters, and the idea had never caused her a crisis of faith, but she kept her mouth closed on the matter. "Our job is to trust that God knows best on these issues."

"Perhaps you are right."

"And perhaps your experience with your father has clouded your views." Lord Barnes could make any woman dread marriage. Knowing Hugh was raised by such a man was the only fact that brought Rosalind some consolation in the knowledge that they could never be together. And truthfully, she should keep reminding herself that she had spied some cruelty lurking behind Hugh's charming smile. Gwen might not recognize it, but Rosalind had.

Gwendolyn pursed her lips. "Allen thinks I might have it wrong entirely. He told me stories of other strong women from the Bible, not merely Deborah. And he believes the New Testament calls a husband to serve his wife and treat her with care."

"This *Allen*, as you persist in calling him, truly sounds like a gem."

"That he is." A vulnerable smile transformed Gwendolyn's face.

"Lady Gwendolyn, you know that as your maid I try not to presume upon you too much."

"Although you tease me like the dickens."

"True." Rosalind chuckled. "But I was wondering if you might consider reading this book to me in the evenings before we retire."

"I like the idea. We can discuss it together, for it is much to digest on one's own."

"Thank you so much. I will treasure every moment." For if the book was true, Rosalind had much to consider. She longed to have the relationship with God that it described, but in order for that to happen, some aspects of her life might need to change. And she would require more than one brief recitation to find the strength and determination to make such changes.

Chapter 13

"The law is not just," declared the duke. "Therefore it begs reconsideration."

Ensconced in his first official council meeting, Allen studied the reactions of the men surrounding the huge round table, reminiscent of King Arthur's legendary one. He longed to understand his place on this council and contribute in a meaningful manner.

The bishop stood. "But it has been the law for nigh on twenty years. Surely this alone proves that it is a just and worthy statute."

"A law is just because it is the law? That is no sort of logic at all." Lord Fulton, the historian, launched into a long tirade on the philosophy of law making, but Allen could not bring himself to focus any longer.

The past five days had proven a whirlwind of excitement. Becoming better acquainted with Gwendolyn, moving into his new quarters in the garrison, adjusting to the training regimen of the knights of Duke Justus, and now acclimating himself to his new duties on the council, which met weekly to review laws, budgets, and judicial decisions.

During the rest of the week, each man was free to commence with his individual duties, be he merchant, nobleman, or priest. Most of them lived in homes throughout the city or in nearby castles. To Allen's knowledge, he was the only council member other than the clergy who did not hold land, as well as the only member new to the area. He still could not quite fathom the honor that had been bestowed upon the lowly Allen of Ellsworth.

His next goal would be to find a permanent home for himself, although he did not yet know how he might accomplish it. His salary as a knight would be generous, but it might take him years to earn enough for a house befitting . . . He could hardly believe he was even considering the thought, but now that he had joined the council he felt that he could. He dreamed of acquiring a house befitting a lady. He could only hope to win the duke's favor yet again and be granted his own holdings.

The Lady Gwendolyn's lovely face floated through his thoughts, as tended to happen these days when he considered future or marriage. She had found her way into his heart during their days together. He could no longer consider her merely a friend.

But his more rational mind maintained huge concerns about his relationship with Gwendolyn. As they spoke at length, he began to wonder if she was a Christian believer at all. He could never tie himself to a woman who did not share his love for God. It seemed Duke Justus's grand system for religious education had somehow bypassed—or rather been intentionally routed from—the Castle Barnes. Gwendolyn had a strong sense of justice, and the version of God she had been offered did not fit with her high ideals.

A shift in the conversation caught Allen's attention. Something about children. "I am so sorry, Your Grace, but could you please repeat that?"

"I am glad to know I was not the only one to nod off during Fulton's lecture." The duke chuckled.

Lord Fulton huffed and crossed his arms over his chest.

"We are discussing some rather new business concerning the children of a village called Seaside," the duke said. "A pox swept through that area in the early summer and wiped out primarily adults, leaving an unprecedented number of orphans. Nigh on thirty. Their neighbors have been caring for them as best they can, but we need a lasting solution."

Allen's heart clenched for those children. He had been such a child.

"If we spread them about the region, it would only add a child or two to each church orphanage," said the nobleman with the plumed hat, whom Allen was beginning to understand had a strong opinion about everything. Today he wore a particularly outrageous outfit of bright blue, green, and purple, which taken along with his hat, gave the impression of a preening peacock. Swap the hat for a jester's cap with tinkling bells, and the outfit would be complete.

"Our orphanages are overtaxed as matters stand." The bishop's eyes bespoke compassion. "But I suppose we would do our best."

"Perhaps we can send extra funds from the city coffers," the duke offered.

"Your Grace, we cannot simply throw money at every problem," said the black-bearded minister of finance.

The bishop waved a hand to dismiss the idea. "The Lord will provide. I just hate to see so many children growing up that way. It is not the same as a loving home."

No, it would not be at all the same. How Allen wished he

could bring them into his home, but he was naught but an unwed knight. At that thought, an idea sparked to life in his mind. He sat forward to speak, but Fulton and the bishop had commenced bickering once again.

The duke raised a single hand, and everyone fell silent. "I believe Sir Allen wishes to contribute to the conversation. This is rather an area of expertise for you. Is it not, Sir Allen?"

A grizzled, grey-haired knight pushed out his chair and rose to his feet, his face so mottled and twisted that it looked as though he might have a fit of apoplexy. "I object! This man was brought on to the council without a full vote. Some of us were never consulted at all. I thought he was to be but a statement against Ethelbaum's outlandish behavior. And now you ask his advice?"

Allen's nerves pulled taut. Of course this had been too good to be possible. He should have suspected, but he never thought it might all come crashing down quite so quickly.

The duke likewise stood and stared down the man, but he remained calm. "I see. I was not aware that you objected so strongly, Sir Gaillard. But let us put it to a vote, right here and right now." The duke swept the table with a cool, imperious gaze. "All those in favor of adding Sir Allen of Ellsworth as a member of our council—a full and active member of our council—please raise your right hand."

Immediately five hands, the hands of those men Allen had noted to be close to the duke, including Fulton and the bishop, lifted into the air.

But that would not be nearly enough.

Allen's stomach plummeted.

Many of the men studied Allen, seeming to take his measure.

He gulped down a huge lump from his throat and wiped drops of newly formed sweat from his brow. Then one by one, more hands lifted, until only three dissenters remained.

Still, Allen did not know the rules of the vote in this place.

"That is more than the two-thirds majority needed," said the duke. "Sir Gaillard, have you further objection?"

"I . . . but . . ." the man stuttered. Clearly he had objections aplenty, but he had lost this match. "I have had it with the lot of you and your progressive nonsense. You have taken matters too far this time!"

"Then you are free to take your leave." The duke waved to the door.

After another stuttering fit, the man stormed out.

The two other dissenters kept their peace, each nodding to the duke. Allen took a deep breath, as the knots in his shoulders and twist in his gut unwound.

"As you were saying, Sir Allen."

What had he been saying? Something important surely. *Father God, please give me your words.* As they came back to him, he managed to push them past the lump that yet blocked his throat. "When the bishop mentioned loving homes, it gave me an idea. Lord Linden and his wife had no children, and so they found great delight in helping the orphans of our former village. In fact, as some of you are aware, they claimed me as their own ward."

"That is all well and good once you have met a child and grown to care about him," the bishop said, "but we cannot expect our noblemen to take in a passel of peasants out of the sheer goodness of their hearts."

"Many childless couples would do anything to have a family. I realize that adopting an orphan as one's own has not been accepted in England, but the Scriptures speak favorably of it." A little shiver shot through Allen.

He felt he spoke not only his own words, but words inspired from above. "According to the book of Romans, God himself has adopted us as His heirs. Can His followers not do the same?"

Every man in the room stared directly at him, and not a one seemed inclined to interrupt.

So Allen continued. "We could separate the children into small family groups and find couples to adopt them. Perhaps nobles, or if that presents too many impediments, then well-to-do freemen with much love to give."

The duke considered the proposition for a moment. "That is precisely the sort of forward thinking I was hoping to hear from you, Sir Allen."

"It is interesting," said the bishop. "Although, as he pointed out, adoption has not been practiced in England for . . . well, perhaps ever."

"We would not wish to stir up trouble with the new king," the minister of finance said.

"There is precedent against adoption, due mainly to inheritance issues, but I do not know if there is any written statute prohibiting it." The old historian rubbed his chin as he considered the matter. "I must check the laws. The newly reissued Great Charter has changed matters."

"For now we shall take it under advisement." The duke leaned back and crossed one leg over the other. "If there are no specific religious or legal impediments, I am in favor of carrying out this plan according to Sir Allen's recommendations."

"Hear, hear!" the bishop hollered, and several others followed suit.

"But I hope I can assume there will be a proper vote this time," grumbled one of the dissenters.

"Of course there shall be, and I do apologize for rushing into matters with Sir Allen. Hopefully now we can continue in full agreement on the issue. I believe that concludes our business for the day." The duke stood to his feet and stretched. "I for one am ready for my supper."

Allen stood as well, and to his surprise, several of the council members approached to thump him on the back and offer congratulations for his fine idea. He had not expected to perform so well on his very first day, especially not after that fiasco with Sir Gaillard.

It seemed once again that God smiled upon him. And did he not deserve God's favor? He had studied the Scriptures and lived a holy life. He had fought admirably against the finest knights in the land. Merry might not have taken note of his skills, but they were finally being acknowledged properly.

As the men filtered out, the duke still stood by his cushioned chair. "Sir Allen, will you sit by me at supper? I should like to discuss this issue with you further, and get to know you better, of course."

And why not? Allen—just as he had again and again during his time in the forest—had saved the day. "Of course, Your Grace. It would be a pleasure."

The duke looped his arm around Allen's shoulder. "For starters, tell me what it was like living in the forest. However did you manage to hide for two full years?"

As they walked through the shadowy corridor, Allen switched to storyteller, a role that well suited him. He was beginning to feel a part of this land already. They wanted him here, and more than that, they needed him. He would do his best to bring his wisdom and experience to North Britannia—perhaps be the voice of God to these people who, though indeed admirable, were not quite as righteous nor as holy as he might have imagined.

His chest puffed as he spoke, but surely it could not be pride. Just intense satisfaction and great joy. He could hardly wait to see where God might lead him next. Perhaps even into the arms of the lovely Lady Gwendolyn.

Chapter 14

"Gwendolyn!" Father's angry bellow preceded crashing footsteps up the stairs.

Suffocating fear caught in Gwen's chest. She watched as Rosalind froze midstroke with the brush poised over Gwen's blond hair.

"Oh dear! Perhaps you should leave," Gwen offered. How she wished she could escape Father's temper. He had a special way of making her feel trapped, like a deer staring down an arrow in a deadly bow. But they had been getting along so well of late. Perhaps she could pacify him.

The pounding footsteps grew closer and louder. On second thought, she did not truly wish to be left alone with him.

"I . . . perhaps. . . ." Rosalind's gaze darted from Gwen to the door and back again.

Father thrust the door open with a bang. "Out!" he shouted at Rosalind, pointing to the hallway.

The normally confident Rosalind scurried away like Angel had at a similar command not long before.

Gathering every ounce of her courage, Gwen forced a smile and a light giggle. "Father, do be kind to her. Rosalind so wishes to please you. She has not yet grown accustomed to your surly ways and does not understand that beneath it all you are a wonderful man who loves his family and only wants the best for them."

Her father's face lightened in shade from bright red to a pinkish flush, and that telltale vein she dreaded shrunk to half the size. "I have no complaint with your maid. *She* did a commendable job in Edendale. I am glad that *someone* wishes to please me."

Gwen walked to him with her hands outstretched, as Mother would do in such an instance. "Goodness, whatever has gotten you into such a dither?" She took her father's hands and led him to sit on the bed. "Let us talk about this. Surely we can find a solution. If I have offended you in some way, I deeply apologize."

There. That did not hurt so much. Perhaps she could handle this feminine manipulation act. And in truth, she never did anything out of spite toward her father, although she often managed to displease him in the general being of herself.

"Perhaps I misunderstood," Father said. "To see you now, so gracious and so kind . . . But I thought you realized that it was Gawain I wished you to woo. Sir Allen is entirely unacceptable. And I hear that after I was sent away, you spent extensive time with that peasant upstart."

Gwen stuffed down her anger. She managed such an excellent beginning to this conversation. She must not muck up matters now.

Swallowing the biting tone she wished to use, she employed a gentle one instead. "Father, I am confused. I know you introduced me to Sir Gawain, but the situation has changed. Sir Allen has been chosen to the council. He showed such chivalry

upon the battlefield, and earned great favor in the eyes of the
duke. I thought that by winning his attention, I would bring
honor to you. Was I wrong?"

Gwen topped off her ludicrous performance by looking demurely down at their joined hands and batting her lashes.

Father patted her hand. "Oh, my naïve little Gwendolyn. You
do not yet understand the ways of the world. This Allen has
no property. No connections. It is your duty to bring not only
honor to our family, but wealth and power as well."

"Would not being wed to a member of the council bring
power?"

Father gripped her hand too tight, and she winced against
the pain.

"Do not speak of wedding that whelp ever again. This Sir
Allen is nothing but a passing fancy of the duke's. Sir Gawain
is from a strong family with roots and tradition and several
fine holdings. Centuries from now the Ethelbaums will remain
important in this region. What shall Sir Allen of Ellsworth be?"

Father spit on the floor in a rather unchivalrous display.
"Nothing but dust in the ground."

Her anger flared now. The world seeped to red all about her
as her heart pounded hard in her chest, but still she maintained
a civil tongue. "I do see your point, but matters could change.
Sir Allen could grow in favor and holdings."

"I doubt it." Father sneered. "He is a nobody, and he is likely
to remain such."

Gwen could no longer keep the pleading desperation from
her voice. "He is not a nobody to me. Do my opinions count for
nothing? I have no points of common interest with Sir Gawain.
He has yet to speak a civil sentence to me, but with Sir Allen I
felt at home and conversed with ease. This is my life, my future
we are discussing."

"Your family is your life. I am your life, and soon your husband shall be! I have chosen Gawain for you, and now 'tis your job to charm him into desiring you." Father's face turned red again, and the throbbing vein protruded from his temple.

Gwen's own anger built inside her head, like a steaming kettle threatening to explode. Through gritted teeth, she said, "I will not marry Gawain. He is a beast. Anyone but him."

Father thrust her hands away and stood to his feet. His arms flailed about him as he yelled, "You will marry whom I tell you to marry! I will not stand for your rebellious fits. I was right to pick Gawain. He alone can tame your wild ways. You are a child—a girl child, no less. Weak and stupid. You are not fit to run your life!"

"Weak! Stupid!" Gwen stood as well, too furious to be afraid. "You did not find me weak nor stupid when I faced Sir Allen in the tournament."

Too late Gwen clapped her hands over her gaping mouth. She did not just say that. Surely she had imagined the words but never spoken them. Except that Father's stunned stillness told her she had.

Dear God in heaven, please wipe the last ten seconds away. Nausea overtook her stomach. Perhaps if she threw herself from her window, death would come swiftly. But with her luck, she would land like a cat without a scratch.

She cowered away from her father and hid her face in her hands.

He sank back to the bed. "It all makes sense now. Your stomach ailment. How young Lachapelle appeared for his supposed experience. I felt certain I knew him from somewhere. But . . . but . . . you would not . . . You could not . . ." Confusion gripped his face and turned it deathly pale.

Gwen seized to that small hope. She let out a nervous, garbled giggle and tugged inanely at her curls. "Of course I could not.

I have no idea why I said that. I am just a foolish girl, as you mentioned. Such silly notions overtake me at times. Of course it was not true. Will you please forgive me?"

"No." Father shook his head slowly. "No. It was you. I am sure it was." His hands began to quake. The vein looked as though it might burst at any moment. He stood and growled, "Do not ever lie to me again."

He reached for her and grabbed her shoulders.

She squealed.

"I cannot believe you would commit such outrages." He shook her violently, but she was too numb with fear to feel the pain. "Dressing like a man! Committing perjury to fight in a tournament! Does your rebellion know no bounds? I . . . I do not even know what to say."

Father pushed her away. She stumbled back several feet before crouching low to the floor. Her fighting instincts welled up within her. If he attacked again, she would not idly play the victim.

His eyes turned hard and cold. "You disgust me. I cannot imagine the shame, the humiliation you nearly brought upon this family. You are not to leave this chamber for a week. Rosalind may visit once a day to bring you water and a single crust of bread. I shall send the priest daily as well. You had best pray, and pray hard. If I cannot find a suitable husband for you, I might just throttle you yet."

Dear God in heaven, what had she done?

Father walked out the door and turned the key in the lock. She sank to the floor and cried as she had not cried since she was a child, hoping against hope that somehow Allen and his God might save her from this desolation.

◇ ◇ ◇

Warner ran his finger along the blade of his jeweled dagger and could not hold back a chuckle. The time had finally come. For nearly two decades he had fantasized about this moment. The dukedom would be his, as it always should have been.

His father should have been heir to his grandfather, Gregory DeMontfort, for the old duke did not trust his eldest son, Christian, to rule the region with the iron fist he expected. Duke Gregory had written his wishes into an official edict, but his councilors had deemed him senile in his old age. With the support of the dowager duchess and the people, the title had been given to Warner's uncle, Christian DeMontfort, after all.

Christian, with his ridiculous precepts of law and justice for all. Of equality and joint leadership. Such rubbish! Warner's father had rebelled, had tried to seize what should have been his, but he failed and was banished as a mere knight to his wife's dower lands outside of North Britannia for good.

And so Warner had been born barely a nobleman at all, rather than a future duke, as he rightfully should have been. Instead, Christian DeMontfort grew in favor and in madness, passing his ludicrous government on to his son, Justus, when he died. Warner's idiot cousin had expanded on his father's absurd ideals for the past fifteen years.

Meanwhile, Warner remained a poor and vanquished knight. But enough was enough! Many noblemen on the outskirts of the region now sided with him against Duke Justus the Imbecile and longed to return to the old ways. With the new king and regent headed their direction, the time for change was nigh. They must supplant the supplanter now!

The fact that the duke had not yet produced an heir would secure the title for Warner. And while William Marshall might not overthrow the duke outright to put Warner in his place, surely he would support Warner if he held the title when the king's contingent arrived. Perhaps Warner might take the striking duchess as his wife just for the added pleasure of stealing yet another prize from his hated cousin.

He smiled with satisfaction and tucked the dagger into his boot. Entering the castle kitchen, he took the tray that had been arranged for him to deliver to the duke as the idiot took his private afternoon rest. Dressed in livery of ivory, crimson, and black, Warner blended with the other servants of the castle. And because he had spent his life banished from this dukedom, he needed not even hide his face.

With full confidence he strode from the kitchen, across the courtyard, and past several of the duke's strong knights. One nodded him through the portal.

He glided across the great hall smooth as could be.

As he rounded the corner a nobleman came flying at him from nowhere and nearly tumbled his tray, but Warner performed an evasive maneuver worthy of a swordsman and rescued the wine and bread with nary a slosh.

"I'm so sorry." The preening fellow with his foppish plumed hat and peacock attire straightened the stack of parchments he had nearly dropped. "Please excuse me. My mind was elsewhere."

"No trouble, all is well," Warner said with an easy smile.

This was almost too simple.

Almost.

But he would take his victory any way it came.

◇ ◇ ◇

Gwendolyn's belly clenched from emptiness. She had never before experienced these awful sensations. Father had always just whipped her with a leather strap and been done with it. Such ostracism and hunger were worse punishments by far.

The red welts she'd endured as a child had been easier to ignore than the ravenous bird claws scratching mercilessly at the pit of her abdomen now.

During her five days of imprisonment, she had been left with little to do other than pray and read the book of sermons Father had thankfully failed to confiscate. Sitting next to the window for what slivers of sunshine she could gather into herself through the small opening was the only thing that kept her from complete despair.

A part of her was tempted to climb down the side of the castle and over the wall to her favorite tree. But she dared not risk increasing her father's wrath. Instead she created a world in her mind where she might escape to battles and glory. A bright, colorful world where she would protect the weak and the innocent. A world full of stories she had escaped to all of her life.

Yet there were new stories as well. Stories of kisses and embraces. Of a little manor home with Sir Allen and a passel of children who sported his warm hazel eyes.

One way or the other, she needed to be far, far away from here.

If only she had been thrown in the dungeon like a proper prisoner, she could easily escape. She and her brothers had always suspected Father was capable of imprisoning them, and had made a game of planning several escape routes. But if she ran away now, it would have to be for good, and she was not that desperate . . . yet.

These past days she had been left with far too much time to think, and to regret. But while she regretted losing control with her father, she still felt she was right in her stance to refuse Gawain. And her prayers and reading of the sermons only solidified her conviction.

A tap upon her door jolted her from her thoughts. She had

not expected Rosalind until the evening. But any company—other than Father—would bring a welcome respite. "Come in."

Mother swept regally through the door, followed by Rosalind, who carried a heaping tray of bread, fruit, cheese, and even a huge roasted goose leg. Angel and Mischief trotted into the room at their heels. Spotting Gwen, the dogs ran to her and whined as she petted and kissed them in greeting.

"Set the tray on the bedside table." Mother took charge before Gwen had fully processed the situation. "Gwendolyn, you must eat slowly at first. You do not wish to shock your stomach."

"But . . . but what about Father? My week is not yet finished." Gwen fought confusion. Perhaps this was not real. Perhaps her hunger-clouded mind had conjured them from her imagination.

"Your father had an urgent summons to the castle." Mother's hand upon Gwen's shoulder felt so warm and real. This could not be mere daydreaming. "But never fear. We shall keep this a secret so that he does not add to your sentence. Be sure to feign hunger and weakness when he returns."

Gwen reached for a handful of berries. Those would be light and fresh to start her first real meal in over five days. Angel stared up longingly at the food. "Not today, you little beggar."

The tart sweetness burst in Gwen's mouth as she bit into the fruit. She sighed in delight. "Oh, Mother, I cannot thank you enough. I thought I might lose my mind. And I vow I shall never see a single peasant go hungry if I can do anything to help it."

Mother pulled over a chair and sat beside her, while Rosalind stood attendance nearby. "I tried to tell you. There are worse things in life than being bullied into a noble marriage by a father who, in his own way, loves you and wishes the best for you. And who chose a rather handsome young man for you, might I add."

"Ha!" Gwen would have argued that Gawain was no such thing, except that she would rather eat. She tried to start slowly, but her very marrow cried out for sustenance. She quickly devoured a piece of warm, soft bread and took several gulps of wine. Angel jumped onto the bed and sidled up next to her as if to cuddle. But as Gwen reached to pat her head, she ducked under Gwen's arm and stole a berry.

"Cease!" Gwen said. "That is my food, you thief."

Mischief eyed her warily from the hearth.

"So now you want one too? 'Tis only fair, I suppose." She tossed a berry to him.

He sniffed it, then turned up his nose in disdain and walked back to the hearth. Angel, the consummate opportunist, jumped from the bed, snatched it up, and joined him by the warm fire.

Rosalind just shook her head as she always did when Gwen spoiled her pups so.

"Foolish creatures," Mother said, but she smiled at them nonetheless.

Gwen sighed. Despite the distraction of the dogs, she could not put off this conversation any longer. "I suppose Father told you everything."

Mother shook her head and smirked. "Indeed he did, *Sir Geoffrey*. I know not whether to burst out laughing, bow in awe, or throttle you."

"Father seemed fairly clear that throttling was the preferred course of action."

That evoked the laughter Mother had fought to hold back, but it was short-lived. "Truly, Gwendolyn, 'tis not seemly for a young lady to function in a man's role. I confess to knowing that you have often romped about the countryside playing with swords and bows. But truly, I never for one moment suspected you had intentions to fight in a tournament. This is not pleasing in God's sight."

Mother sighed. "But you know all of this."

"I do. And yet I do not. Oh, Mother, I wish I could convey to you how wonderful it is staring down an opponent over the tip of a lance. The rush of exhilaration that comes in battle. 'Tis nothing short of heavenly."

Mother tapped her chin with her finger. "And what has your role been in all of this, Rosalind?"

Rosalind lifted her gaze to the ceiling and rocked back and forth upon her heels.

Gwen gripped her mother's arm. "Leave Rosalind out of this. She has only ever obeyed me as a proper lady's maid should. This is my fault alone."

Mother sat pondering for a moment. A bemused smile turned her pretty pink lips. "You were amazing in that arena. There is no denying that. Why, you might have come in third or fourth had you not been pitted against Sir Allen from the start."

"She is indeed a sight to behold." Rosalind finally dared to speak. "Strong and determined, like the goddess Athena."

"Like the famed Amazon warriors of old," Mother said.

"So you understand, then? A little?" Gwen prayed it might be true.

"Only a little." Mother shot her a hard glare. "You could have disgraced our family. And I have no idea how offensive a sin this might be."

"According to Father Michael, I have committed the sins of deception, pride, covetousness, and disobedience, not to mention the more repulsive sin of dressing outside my gender. But I put little faith in his opinions. After much searching of my motives, the only part I truly feel remorseful about is the deception. Although I long to be obedient, 'tis difficult when one's father is a tyrant with moods like a tempest."

A subtle sadness swept Mother's features. "Yes, but you could obey me. I do my best to soften Father's moods and protect you from the worst of his temper."

Gwen had always suspected her mother's bruises had more to do with standing up for her children than anything else. Otherwise, she would just charm or relent as always.

"I am sorry. I will do my best to obey you from now on, and to not let bitterness keep me from obeying Father in the areas that I can. But I must also stand up for myself when it comes to issues that affect my entire future. Like marriage."

Mother beseeched Gwen with open palms. "We have told you again and again. You must marry. There is no way around it."

Gwen set aside her half-empty plate as a wave of nausea swept over her. Her mother had been right about not eating too fast. In fact, Mother was right about a surprising number of issues. "I am adjusting to the idea of marriage. But I wish to marry a kind man, a man like Sir Allen of Ellsworth. Not a brute like Sir Gawain."

Mother smiled. "We shall work on your father together. I have already heard rumors that Sir Allen is growing in favor. And truth be told, I prefer him for you as well."

"Thank you, Mother. Oh thank you!" Gwen fell to her knees upon the floor and threw her arms around her mother's neck, hugging her smaller frame tight to her own hulking one.

Mother kissed her atop her head and held her far enough away to look her in the eye. "I said I would try. But I make no promises."

"That is all I could ever ask." Gwen returned to her chair. The food caught her attention again, and she stared at the goose longingly as its scent wafted toward her, tempting her against her better judgment.

"I will leave you to eat. Keep the tray until this evening. There is no chance of your father returning until nightfall, and more likely it will be in a day or two."

"Thank you again."

Her mother left and closed the door behind her. Gwen wondered how she had dealt with the guard beyond it, but Mother had her own way of maneuvering people.

"I am so relieved to see you happy!" Rosalind said.

"Perhaps after I have finished dinner, I can read you my book, as I promised."

"Of course, and after that we might sneak through the window and out to your favorite tree. Most of the guards have left with your father, and not a one of them is pleased with the way he has been treating you. And I've brought your pipe."

Gwen marveled at how well her maid knew her thoughts. "That is precisely the thing to cheer me. Oh, Rosalind, I know I should not say it, but you are the best friend I have ever had."

Rosalind sat in the open chair and took Gwen's hand. "You are mine as well, but you must promise never to let your father know."

Gwen winced. "Yet another secret we shall keep safe from him. Although I wish I could trust him and tell him all."

"Of course you do, but it is a child's wish. A man as selfish and cruel as your father cannot be trusted. Forgiven, yes, for the good of your own soul. But not trusted."

Gwen would have thought she had cried out a year's worth of tears during the past days, and yet a few more found their way to her eyes. "I wish he did not hold my fate in his hands."

"He does not." Rosalind gripped tighter to her hands. "God holds your fate in His hands. You need only to trust and follow God's leading in your heart. Is that not what your book says?"

How Gwen wished it might be true. Deep within, she suspected that Allen of Ellsworth might be the only man for her. She would spend the rest of her imprisonment praying—nay, crying her heart out to God—that somehow, someway, matters might work out for the good.

Chapter 15

After one final reverberating clash, the blood-encrusted man crouching before Allen sidled backward and took Allen's measure.

Within the setting rays of the sun, a lifetime of emotions flashed through the man's eyes. Then his foe shouted to his comrades, "Retreat!" and made a mad dash for his horse. Several men followed, rushing into the trees, shadows in the grey haze of smoke against a backdrop of blood-red sky.

Allen's focus narrowed back to the space before him—the split second ahead of him. In battle, there was only here, only now. He turned a circle and slashed his sword but at long last met no resistance. The past fifteen minutes had been a constant onslaught of blades, slow-moving weeks of time—yet none at all.

Sweat poured down his soot-covered face as he sucked in huge gulps of acrid air. Looking down, he noted his chain mail splashed with crimson. His own blood or that of his foes, he could not yet say. Fierce energy yet surged through his body, blocking out all pain.

He scanned the area surrounding him and distinguished a nearby shriek of fear from the ruckus. Dashing toward the noise, he found a huge bandit with his sword raised over the head of a young peasant who had not quite grown to manhood.

Without a second thought, Allen threw his sword like a javelin through the back of the marauder. The man slumped to the ground with a groan. Paying little heed to the fallen villain, Allen withdrew his sword and helped the young villager to his feet. He did not relish killing, as every life mattered in light of eternity, but he would never apologize for stopping evil and protecting the innocent.

He checked the vicinity one more time. "I think it is over."

"Thank you, sir. I feared I was about to meet my Maker."

Allen nodded. His senses remained sharpened to high alert. His heart pounded with an odd exhilaration he had never before experienced. His first real battle.

Truly, this was what he had been designed for. As he fought, he had sensed God's pleasure despite the sadness of the occasion. He had sensed an affinity with David, with Joshua, with Samson and Gideon. Mighty men of God throughout the ages.

All sounds of battle had finally ceased. His men had prevailed. They gathered about him in the open circle at the center of the village, strong knights all, in the duke's crimson-and-black colors.

Allen surveyed the smoking ruins. With the battle now over, horrid memories of his own flattened village threatened to overtake him. Sharp pain gouged at him from the edges of his consciousness, but he must push that all aside. He could not wallow in the past at a time like this, for he had a duty to complete.

The duke had sent him out with all haste to lead his first mission. Though the central portion of small North Britannia was held safe by the duke's army, villages along the outskirts often fell prey to bandits or invading Scotsmen from farther north—even greedy noblemen from England at times.

Allen rubbed a hand over his face. At once pride in his accomplishment this day buoyed him and sadness at the depravity of mankind weighed him down. He stared at the charred ruins of what had once been someone's home, their sanctuary. It might have been far worse had the duke not been tipped off to the raid by one of his many supporters.

As that fierce energy subsided, a deep ache poured through the muscles of Allen's entire body and a clear stinging sensation overtook his upper left arm. Glancing down, he deemed it a mere flesh wound, but several of the knights had injuries that required immediate attention. And one seemed to be missing. Allen prayed he would join them soon and not be found dead amidst the rubble.

His troop had arrived just as the violence broke forth. Yes, the night could have been much worse. He whispered up his thanks that God had given him the courage and clarity to act decisively and wisely.

The door of the church cracked open, and a lone, old man stepped forth. "Is it over?" he called.

"It is over. You are safe." Relief washed over Allen as joy lit the man's face.

"'Tis over!" he hollered to the others, and they streamed from the church in a flood.

Allen pulled off his helmet, put his sword in its sheath, and prepared to meet them. Crying women hugged him. Old men thumped him on the back. Soon enough they would realize that several of their houses had been destroyed and that some of their sons, husbands, and fathers were dead, but he would let them enjoy the moment.

A young boy tugged at Allen's fine surcoat featuring the

duke's ivory falcon crest. "Thank you, sir knight! You have saved us all."

Unable to resist, Allen swept him from the ground and into his arms. He felt compelled to speak true. "I wish I could have saved every single person, but I'm afraid a few men died in the fighting."

The freckle-faced lad with his gap-toothed grin smiled up at him.

Allen wondered if someday he might have such an adorable child himself, and he could not help but picture Gwendolyn as the child's mother. Together they would breed lovely daughters and fine strong sons who would be champions, for certain. Heat crept up his face at the thought of how such children might come to be, but he pushed such notions aside and focused on the boy.

The lad ran his grubby hand over the rough planes of Allen's face. "But you saved me. You saved all of us who could not save ourselves."

A tide of warmth crashed over Allen and nearly swept him from his feet. He held tightly to the child to keep his bearings. His protective instincts had never felt so keen, so sharp. This was all he had ever dreamed of doing with his life. Protecting the weak. Using his God-given skill and strength to make a difference in this world.

A woman he assumed to be the child's mother scooped him away. "Thank you, sir. Thank you so much. Leave the fine knight be now, Charles, for he has much yet to do."

His duty now was to clean up, bury the dead, and perhaps help with building some temporary shelters and patching cottages that might yet be salvaged. But before he could start determining the details of his plan, a lone rider in the duke's colors galloped down the lane straight toward him.

The fellow dismounted and removed his helmet. Allen re-called him from one of his later battles in the tournament as well as from the garrison. Sir Randel Penigree. A fine, chivalrous knight from everything Allen could surmise.

Sir Randel approached. "Sir Allen, I have an urgent message for you from the council. You must return to the castle at once."

"But my mission here . . . ?" Allen's gaze swept the smok-ing village and the peasants, many of whom now wept as they assessed their losses.

Sir Randel clasped Allen's arm. "Never fear. I shall take over matters. I might not stand a chance against you with a sword or lance, but I am quite adept at logistical issues."

Allen detected intelligence and compassion swirling behind the man's eyes. "I thank you, then. These people will need much assistance and encouragement. But I have a feeling you can handle that."

Randel nodded. "I can. As I have too many times in the past." He glanced about the village. "I have seen worse."

"I only wish we had arrived sooner. We might have routed the whole incident."

"You did well. But you must make haste. Lord Fulton was in quite a dither when he sent me to find you."

"Then I bid you farewell." Allen hurried to his horse and cantered off in the direction of the castle.

What important mission might the duke have for him now? Allen had managed to make himself quite indispensable in a mere fortnight. Before long he just might attain a position that would allow him to offer for Gwendolyn's hand and protect her from Gawain. Allen rode away from the smoking ruins and into the bright future that stretched ahead.

◇◇◇

Shortly after dawn the next morning, an exhausted Allen stared at the council gathered about the large round table.

Bizarre words, impossible words filled the room and swirled around him. The duke. Dead. Murdered in cold blood. Killer roamed free. It was not possible. He could not bring himself to believe it.

Yet the pale faces and shaking hands of the normally robust council members attested to the truth of the matter. As did the duchess weeping quietly in the corner upon the shoulder of her maidservant.

Lord Fulton brought the group to order once again. "I realize we are grieving, but now that we are all here, we must settle the issue of succession quickly. Before matters are taken from our hands."

"Hold!" Sir Gaillard stood. "There is yet one person who should be consulted. And since no one here is thinking rationally, I have invited the man myself."

He strode to the door, anger fairly seeping from him, and swung it open.

In swaggered a man perhaps in his forties, of middling size and height with dark hair and a face that some might consider appealing—though Allen found him too charming, and his instincts put him immediately upon his guard.

"I am sorry," Fulton, the senior advisor of the council said. "I do not believe we have met."

"Allow me to introduce Sir Warner DeMontfort." Sir Gaillard led the man to the table. "Or, as we all know should be the case, the new Duke Warner DeMontfort, for the line of succession is quite clear."

"How dare you show yourself here!" Fulton's face mottled red, although he was a cerebral sort, and Allen had never seen him so angry before.

"I have come to claim what is rightfully mine. I can hardly do so from outside the borders." Warner's lips tipped in a lazy grin, but the council did not seem to be accepting his act.

Several of the knights among the group now stood with their hands to their sword hilts. Allen wondered if he should follow suit, but not understanding the details of the situation, decided to await further instruction.

"I believe I speak for the council when I say we do not see it that way." Fulton glared at the man. "In fact, we shall be investigating your part in this murder."

"Do not be ridiculous." DeMontfort maintained his relaxed demeanor.

"You do not speak for me, Lord Fulton!" Sir Gaillard cried even as DeMontfort spoke.

"Nor me!" Another nobleman rose to his feet.

"Nor me!" A third man crossed his arms over his chest.

"Then let me hasten matters and proceed as I know our dearly departed duke would in this case." Fulton gripped the table and raised his voice. "Those in favor of considering Warner DeMontfort as successor to the Duke of North Britannia, please raise your right hands."

Only the three dissenters did so.

"Then we have our answer."

"But wait," Warner protested. "You have not given me an opportunity to speak on my own behalf. You call this place a fair and just dukedom. Do not punish me for my father's sin."

"You have committed plenty of your own, by my reckoning. All in favor of throwing Warner DeMontfort out of the dukedom immediately and casting him into prison if he attempts to enter again, raise your right hands." Fulton began to shake, and fire seared from his eyes.

This time every hand except for Sir Gaillard and the other

two dissenters, including Allen's, went into the air. If Fulton felt so passionately on this issue, that was good enough for him.

"If he is leaving, I am leaving with him!" Sir Gaillard shouted.

"With my blessings, for you are now on my list of murder suspects as well. Sir Cedric, Sir Percivale," Fulton called to the guards by the door, "please see Sir Warner beyond the borders. Sir Gaillard may accompany him if he likes, as he is still a member of this council, although we shall take that matter under reconsideration as well."

Warner surveyed the room with deadly silence, then huffed and moved toward the door. The guards flanked him on both sides, grasping his arms and leading him out as Sir Gaillard followed in defeat.

The place went wild with grumbling and accusations, but Fulton managed to bring them back into order. "I am glad we are in agreement on this DeMontfort issue, but now we must move forward and plan for the future."

The man who generally wore the plumed hat, whom Allen now knew to be a merchant named Hemsley, was dressed soberly this day. "We may not have proof that Sir Warner was behind the murder, but he has likely stirred up much of the trouble at the borders. If our suspicions hold true, we do not wish to reward him with the title. Besides which, he is out of touch with our policies and our way of life."

"But I am afraid the DeMontforts have not been as hearty or fruitful as they have been wise," Fulton added. The other men grumbled their assent to this sad truth.

"Perhaps we have been rash," said the black-bearded minister of finance. "I was as angry as anyone that he showed up unannounced, but we have no other prospects. If we do not follow our own laws on this issue, the people will lose trust in us. We must maintain stability in the region above all else."

The bishop stood. "I say the duchess is the obvious choice. As the duke's third cousin and a DeMontfort in her own right, she is from the family next in line for the title after Sir Warner, and the people already adore her. His family has been vanquished for many decades. No one will trust him. But the duchess has shown strength, wisdom, and dedication during her time in power. She is the one we need to keep North Britannia strong."

The duchess turned to them and swiped her tears, giving them her full attention now. Could they truly do such a thing? Surely it was the perfect solution.

Hemsley shook his head. "While I agree that she would make an excellent ruler, she would quickly be reduced to a pawn of William Marshall and the new king. The regent would claim guardianship over her and force her to marry whomever he favored. We cannot take that risk. Our region would never be the same. No offense to you, Your Grace."

"None taken." The striking lady sniffed.

Disappointment washed over Allen. As he observed her, he realized for the first time that she had truly loved her husband. These were actual widow's tears, not merely those of a woman who had lost her ally and access to power. He had never stopped to assess her before. A beautiful lady, perhaps in her early thirties, full of elegance and grace, even in a moment such as this.

"Everything we have worked for would be undermined," the minister of finance said. "It simply is not an option." He turned to the duchess. "But do you not have an elder brother, Your Grace? He would also be close in the succession."

The duchess stood and approached the table. "We rarely speak of it, but he is rather dim-witted. His mind is that of a child. And my younger brother has been off on crusade for years. He could be dead, for all we know."

"But this older brother . . . " Hemsley said. "Perhaps with the help of the council . . ."

"No." The bishop shook his head sadly. "With a weak leader the people could not trust, North Britannia would be ripe for the picking. And if we go further in the line of succession, we shall never get away with bypassing Sir Warner. His father might have been banished, but we have no firm proof he himself has ever acted against North Britannia."

The bishop sat back down, bowing his tonsured head and looking hopeless.

Allen's stomach churned. He had only just come to this region. Only just begun to rise in favor. He had such faith in this system of justice and equality. It could not fall apart so soon. How he wished he could do something to help, but he felt powerless.

Fulton took a breath so loud, he drew every gaze in the room. Slowly he rose, but then stood silent.

"Lord Fulton?" the bishop prompted the old historian.

"I am hesitant to bring it up, but I can think of no other recourse. Many years ago, late in the reign of Duke Gregory, an advisor to the duke who many thought to be an oracle of God decreed a prophecy over this region."

A hush overtook the place. Might there yet be hope?

"Please, Lord Fulton, do tell us!" Hemsley cried.

Lord Fulton cleared his throat. "He claimed that someday the dukedom would face great peril and that a man of lowly birth would save them by marrying a duchess and thwarting a deadly foe."

"I heard tell of this in my youth," whispered a white-haired council member. "I had nearly forgotten."

"Duke Christian did not wish for it to cast a pall over the people," Lord Fulton said. "And so he passed a law forbidding anyone to speak of it. But I wager that most of the older generation will remember and support it."

"The Duchess Adela could rule us, and she could be safely married to this man before the king arrives." Hemsley smiled.

"Who would dare naysay such a prophecy?" Hope lit the face of the bishop and brimmed in Allen's heart as well. "And no one would begrudge only a short period of mourning in this situation."

"We cannot trust such a *prophecy*," said one of the dissenters who had supported DeMontfort. "God no longer speaks through rogue prophets like He did in the days of Jeremiah and Isaiah. The church speaks on His behalf, and I have no doubt the pope would support Sir Warner's stronger claim if we but bother to ask."

"We cannot wait months to pass messages to and fro!" Hemsley grew agitated now.

Allen had already surmised that the devout Christians of North Britannia had little patience with the politics of Rome.

"I agree," the bishop said. "I can speak for the church in this area, and I say that it is still possible for God to send messages through ordinary men. The Scripture says He is the same yesterday, today, and forever."

"But can we trust this so-called prophet?" asked the minister of finance. "Did he genuinely speak for God, or was he some sort of pagan sage?"

"Precisely!" Warner's defender shouted.

"I recall that Duke Christian did not trust this source as truly divine," said the white-haired gentleman. "And we all know that while he strived for Arthurian principles, he did not believe witchcraft nor sorcery had any place in a holy realm."

"Perhaps we need not question this matter too deeply." Hemsley entreated them with open palms. "True or not, this prophecy is just what we need to rally the people and save the day."

"I for one believe it to be true." The bishop stood again, exuding a confidence and leadership that stirred Allen to the core. "And I have the perfect candidate for our purehearted man of lowly birth."

Allen glanced about the room.

"God has brought him to us just in time. He himself recently shared with us that he sensed the Lord guiding him to North Britannia," the bishop continued. "I nominate Sir Allen of Ellsworth."

Allen's mouth gaped. Surely he had not heard correctly, but all eyes in the room focused upon him. Even the duchess stared his way, appearing as shocked as he was. Might the Lord have led him here for such a time as this?

"What say you, Your Grace?" Lord Fulton asked.

The duchess gulped. "It is much to process, but you know I would do anything to maintain this region as my beloved husband wished it to be."

"Sir Allen?" Fulton, along with every other person in the room, turned to him.

So much anticipation and expectation surged Allen's way. So much pressure. What of his beloved Gwendolyn? But perhaps this was God's way of saving him from a woman who did not share his devotion.

And had he not just a moment earlier wished there was some way, any way, he might help? This might be the very reason God had called him to this place.

That now-familiar sensation—which he was certain could not be pride—welled within him. They needed him. He alone could save the day. He could protect this grand dukedom and every person who dwelled within it. Oh how he had dreamed of a moment like this his entire lowly life.

Again he looked at the duchess. A stately, godly woman.

Older than him, of course, yet still beautiful by any man's standards. How could he ever dream of a greater honor than taking her to wife to sustain the well-being of North Britannia?

As he could think of only one answer, he need not even pause and pray. "I will do anything in my power to protect this dukedom."

He pushed aside thoughts of Gwendolyn as the council members gathered round to congratulate him yet again.

Him.

Allen of Ellsworth, born a peasant, now the savior of North Britannia.

On the ninth day of Gwen's confinement, a tap sounded upon the door of her chamber. Although Mother had lightened her restrictions, Father had bid her to keep Gwen locked up until he returned and could assess her attitude.

Mother peeked her pretty face around the doorframe. "Is this a good time to talk?"

Gwen waved to the chair next to where she sat in the streaming sunlight of her open window with her pup Angel curled by her feet. "I have nothing but time at my disposal, at least until Father comes home."

"Where is Rosalind?" Mother glanced about the room.

"Still determined to get a stubborn berry stain out of that ridiculous pink concoction you made me wear to the feast."

"Ridiculous?" Mother sat with a huff. "I love that gown. You looked like a fairy princess."

"I looked like an overripe rose, especially the way I fairly dripped from that bodice. Truly, Mother, whatever were you thinking?"

Mother held up her hands in surrender and laughed along

with Gwen. "Fine. You need not wear it again if you feel that strongly. Throw it in the rubbish heap."

"I need not wear anything so fancy ever again if I do not leave this chamber."

"Well . . . " Mother picked at her own burgundy gown now. "On that issue I have both good and bad news to share with you."

Gwen stilled her mother's fidgeting hands with a soft touch. "Tell me straightaway, Mother. There is no use in mincing words." She had spent the last nine days as a prisoner. Her father planned to marry her to a brute. What news could possibly be worse than that?

"The good news is that Father has returned and soon you will be free to roam the castle." Her smile faltered.

"But . . . " Gwen prompted.

Mother took a bracing breath. "But I am afraid a tragedy has struck our region. Duke Justus has been murdered—God rest his soul. The duke's outcast cousin, Warner DeMontfort, is the primary suspect, but he has not claimed responsibility, and no one seems to know for certain."

Gwen struggled to decode the words her mother had just spoken. Duke Justus? Murdered? "It cannot be. Everybody loved him so."

"Not everyone, I am afraid." The silent tears gathering in her mother's eyes convinced Gwen more than words ever could.

"Dear God, no!" Gwen felt as if a swift kick had struck her ribs, as if all the breath had been sucked out of her. It was too awful to be true, but when she looked again into her mother's eyes, she realized that she must accept the situation.

The kind, fair, cheerful ruler she had conversed with less than two weeks ago was gone. "What of the dukedom? What of the duchess? Whatever shall we all do?" How Gwen wished she could hunt down this evildoer and protect the region.

Mother's hands took to fidgeting again, as she wrung them together. "A plan has been proposed, and once you have adjusted to the idea, I think you of all people might approve."

"What do you mean, 'me of all people'?" A dark dread spiraled about Gwen and coalesced to drive a hole through the pit of her stomach. Surely this could not get worse.

"You see, there was a prophecy delivered many years ago during the reign of the old duke, Gregory DeMontfort. It said that someday the dukedom would face great peril, and a man of lowly birth would thwart a deadly foe."

Hope struck bright in Gwen's heart. "Allen?"

"Yes. But there is more. The prophecy claimed he would marry a duchess and thwart a deadly foe. It has been decided that if Allen of Ellsworth marries the Duchess Adela, the dukedom will be saved and all will be well."

Gwen's mind shattered as she digested these last words. Her hope snuffed away as quickly as it had flamed. As her mother continued speaking, Gwen felt as though she listened from beneath a pool of thick, murky liquid.

"The plan has given the people much hope. They have rallied around Allen and the duchess in a way I would never have believed possible. The common folk are aiding in guarding the region until the wedding a month hence."

"Wedding. A month hence." Gwen feared she might choke on the awful words. But as she pushed them out, anger welled within her. "But it is just a foolish old prophecy! Who believes such nonsense?"

"I suppose if anyone would, it would be the people of North Britannia. Not only have we been taught to believe in a God who is alive and active in the issues of men, but we have put great stock in those Arthurian legends as well."

"But do the leaders believe? Does the duchess?" The room

spun around Gwen. She still could not accept that it was true. "Does Allen?"

"I cannot say, darling." Mother took Gwen's hands, and Gwen clung to them as if they alone could pull her from the depths of that pool that drew her ever deeper and deeper. "True or not, the people believe it. And as hard as I know this will be for you, you must accept it. You cannot stand in the way of destiny."

Tears slipped down Gwen's cheeks, but she dared not swipe at the warm trails, for if she let go of Mother's hands, she feared she might slip into a dark abyss and never escape. "But I love him!"

She had not quite realized it until she spoke the words, but they rang true deep in her heart.

"Love comes in many forms. You barely know this man, and you shall find love again."

"Never!" Gwen spat the word. "Not with that awful Gawain."

"Not with Gawain. But with someone. Perhaps with Randel Penigree. I saw him speaking with your father at the banquet, and he walked away quite disappointed. I felt sure he requested to court you."

"But he is so . . . so . . . Randel! How could I ever get past those big feet and that gangly neck?"

Mother patted Gwen's cheek. "He outgrew those years ago, silly girl. He is quite nice to look at now. Not as handsome as Sir Allen, perhaps, but kind and considerate. Keep in mind that he knows of your dalliance with swords and lances, yet shows interest anyway. He would treat you well, and you could build love together."

Gwen had no words left. Her last hope had been dashed as a ship against the rocks. She gathered Angel into her arms and rocked back and forth in her chair, attempting to hold back tears that would do her no good.

◇◇◇

Warner picked up the earthenware goblet, turned it over for inspection, then flung it against the stone wall of his small castle fortress with a crash. Satisfaction filled him as the goblet smashed into fragments and rained across the floor, but the sensation lasted only a moment.

His plan should have worked. He had justice—not to mention a goodly number of North Britannian nobles and his own army of backers—on his side. Even now he should be riding through the dukedom to declare it his own. But matters had gone completely awry.

Sir Gaillard had been right. They should have garnered more support before making their move, particularly in the council. He still could not fathom that they had turned him away so coldly. With such utter humiliation. Now more than ever he wished he had the region's top military leader on his side, but perhaps Lord Barnes would yet come around. One way or another they would pay for this. Every last one of them.

Just this morning he had received the incredulous report that the duchess was to marry that lowborn Allen of Ellsworth. The people were all caught in the frenzy of some old prophecy, and no one seemed to have given Warner's right to the title more than a passing thought.

He wished that he could have five minutes alone with that fellow Allen. He would gladly wrap his hands around the usurper's neck and finish him off for good. But it seemed the army of North Britannia had strengthened its watch about both the borders and the city. Even the peasant folk were rising up to help during this vulnerable time before the noble wedding.

Unfathomable!

And so Warner had finally done what he should have done

months ago, though the decision rankled at his conscience—he had summoned Morgaine.

He longed to think himself a better and more traditional Christian than his progressive cousin, Justus, notwithstanding the fact that he had recently committed murder—

No, not murder. Warfare. Punishment! He sought to convince himself, despite the echo of slick blood he yet felt dripping down his palms.

Was he not the one who scrupulously followed the rule of the king in England and the pope in Rome? While Warner knew that the black arts were not permitted, there came a time when a man had no choice but to seize every resource at his disposal.

If he had consulted his half sister, Morgaine, from the start, surely he would have seen this coming. He might have dispatched with the despicable Allen before the trouble started. Had not even Justus's precious King Arthur consulted with enchantresses and sorcerers? The next time Warner rode into North Britannia, he would not do so blindly.

At that moment Morgaine swept into his chamber with that same haunting quiet that always seemed to trail in her wake, as if the stone floor retreated to let her pass. Were he to engage his imagination, he could almost picture wisps of fog spreading from the bottom of her jet-black gown.

Her dark hair bound tight in braids and stacked upon her head in a serpentine manner shone brightly in the firelight and added to the eerie impression. She rarely left her reclusive tower room, and he hardly recalled the last time they had spoken.

"Finally," was all the greeting Warner offered his younger and less-legitimate sibling. At their widowed mother's request, he had allowed Morgaine to continue residing in his home despite her wayward interests. Helping him now was the least she could do. "Did you bring the supplies?"

"No proper hello for your sister? Perhaps a kiss?" Her voice rang low and hypnotic as always. She followed the statement with a wicked laugh and a flick of her wrist that showed she desired no such niceties from him. "Of course I did. Why else would I have left my sanctuary?"

Morgaine pulled out a basin from beneath her arm, where it had been concealed by her long billowing sleeves. "Just have your man bring us some fresh water."

Warner waved his trusted manservant away. "Will it take long?"

Her yellowish-green cat eyes caught the reflection of the torch upon the wall and burned like fire. "That is hard to say. The future is a fickle mistress. And like the water in which we shall view it, it is always shifting and swirling. 'Tis not set in stone, as some might think."

"But you shall be able to advise me?" In desperation, Warner clutched the edge of the table where she set the basin.

"I shall do my best."

Warner studied his sister as she removed a satchel from her waist and opened it, sniffing the contents. An odd herbal scent wafted toward him. Better than the toads and spiders he had feared. She put a finger in the satchel and stirred the contents about, while he held back a nervous chuckle.

The servant returned with a pitcher of water and poured it into the basin, as Morgaine indicated. Warner dismissed the man, for he did not want the innocent servant to be held culpable for what they were about to do. The man sighed with relief as he hurried out the door and clicked it closed behind him.

Morgaine tossed a handful of herbs into the water. Then she approached Warner and reached for him, running her fingers sensuously through his hair. He felt drawn into her hypnotic eyes and sensed her evil presence wrapping about him like a snake. But he could not back down now.

A memory of Saul in the Bible consorting with the witch of Endor flashed through his mind. Matters had not gone well with Saul from that time forward. But following the church's commands had gotten Warner nowhere so far. He had to give this less-orthodox course of action a try.

With a swift jerk, Morgaine plucked a single dark hair from Warner's head.

As he rubbed his stinging scalp, she dropped it into the basin with the herbs. Then she stirred the concoction with her finger as she had done to the herbs in the satchel. With her thick, raspy voice she mumbled words he did not understand in some ancient tongue, and that dark presence in the room increased tenfold. It threatened to choke him and nearly snuffed out the torch before it fanned back to life.

"What do you see?" He pushed the words through his tight throat in a whisper.

"All is not lost. There is yet a chance."

His throat seemed to unclench at that. Surely he was being silly, and it was only his own fear, not some evil presence, holding him bound.

Morgaine continued to study the water, her glowing, all-seeing eyes taking her to some different sphere. "Right now you have little land, no power, and no title of consequence. You are a man dispossessed. There is a way to acquire all this and more, but it shall take daring and courage, the likes of which I do not think you have."

"Did I not dispose of the duke? Yet you doubt me."

"That is what sisters are for." She cackled and peered yet deeper into the basin. "I see a woman, alone, with power and land. You must seize her. Marry her, and claim them for yourself. If you can accomplish this, I believe you will stand a chance of claiming North Britannia."

"A chance? Is that the best you can do?" Had he come this far, risked so much, for nothing more than a chance?

"As I mentioned, the future is fickle."

"Who is this lady I must seize?" Warner fought the urge to grab his sister and shake the information out of her. He grew weary of her enigmatic speech, but one did not dare anger a woman such as Morgaine.

"That is for you to discover. But I believe her to be an English noblewoman. Perhaps once you have gained possession of her holdings, Marshall will desire you as an ally and help you defeat Duchess Adela and her young whelp. I cannot say for certain, but this is your best hope."

Warner ran through a number of calculations in his head. If he were to find such a noblewoman and kidnap her, once he had cohabited with her, they would be wed by default. If he hurried, it could yet be accomplished before the noble wedding.

Of course such actions were frowned upon, yet they happened from time to time. It would be an opportunity to demonstrate his determination and his might. And since he already counted William Marshall a friend, it just might work. If nothing else, as Morgaine had said, it was his best hope and well worth the gamble.

Swiping against the thick presence in the room, he planted his feet firm upon the stone floor. "I will do it."

And at that moment the darkness seemed to enter him—filling him, choking and strengthening him all at once until he gave way and accepted it as his own.

Chapter  17

Allen sat in his newly appointed chamber and stared out the window at the setting sun that streaked the sky with shades of turquoise and pink. The same colors as Gwendolyn's gowns. Why must everything remind him of her? As if God had designed the very nature surrounding him to conjure the lady. Or perhaps it was his own mind playing such tricks upon him.

He shuffled about the papers he had been staring at for the past hour, thankful for the privacy of his personal sanctuary, the luxury of which he had never known before. As a lad he had lived in a one-room cottage, and then with all the boys of the survivors of Ellsworth, and finally in a large communal room as a soldier in Lord Linden's garrison. He must accustom himself to such niceties and more, as he would soon be the duke of North Britannia. His brain still could not quite process such a ridiculous notion.

But one thing he had discovered during this last week, privacy allowed one a troublesome amount of time with one's thoughts.

He glanced down at the ten pillars of chivalrous conduct he had copied from the official annals of North Britannia in order to memorize.

Love God and love His church
Protect the weak
Show respect and honor to women
Display courage at all times
Seek peace but battle evil
Stand for right
Promote justice
Serve your region
Be truthful above all
Demonstrate generosity

He must continue to focus on his duties and not allow his errant heart to sway him. He must love God and the bishop's instruction more than himself. He must be courageous to serve and protect the dukedom. He must honor the duchess by accepting her, even if he must deny his heart to do so. He must seek the peace that this marriage would bring and battle his own selfish desires that might stand in the way. He must be generous with his love and his very life.

The dukedom needed him. Him! Lowborn Allen of Ellsworth had arrived just in time to save the day, and he would not shirk from this awesome responsibility.

With the duke's grand funeral finally behind them, tonight Allen would meet the duchess for a meal alone in her solar. The first of several planned for them to become better acquainted, although the poor woman remained in the throes of mourning for her husband.

Allen picked up the second sheet of expensive paper before him. He had wished to write a courtly love poem to the duchess in hopes of cheering her. Surely the exceptional woman deserved, nay expected, such a fine and chivalrous gesture. But images of Gwendolyn's soft golden form continued to push past those of the duchess's sterner, darker variety of beauty, and he had at long last admitted defeat.

The time had come. Gazing into his very own mirror, Allen straightened his new burgundy silken tunic over fine black woolen leggings. He had never dreamed of such luxuries. Nor of the fancy window seat, the paned glass, nor the bizarre indoor privy that his chamber boasted.

As he passed a brush made of fine metals inlaid with colorful stones through his wavy brown hair, he couldn't help but picture Gwendolyn's thick silky tresses of spun gold. He slammed the brush down on his table and sighed. Gripping the back of the chair for strength, he attempted to banish her from his thoughts once again.

The irony of the situation did not escape him. He had come to this modern-day Camelot in search of legendary glory, but he had never expected to play Guinevere to Gwendolyn's Lancelot. However, unlike the weak Queen Guinevere in the story—who cheated on her husband, Arthur, with Lancelot, the knight she dearly loved—he would not betray the duchess. He would not allow his heart to bring his downfall.

No, he would choose duty, the good of the whole dukedom, over some romantic notion of love. He would marry the beautiful Duchess Adela and be patient as love grew between them.

Allen offered up a brief prayer, as he so often did—but ever since he had arrived to Edendale Castle, his prayers seemed to bounce off the strong stone ceilings. Perhaps he should get out of doors again to experience God's presence. Or perhaps it was the cloud of conflicting desires and motivations in his own mind keeping God's direction at bay.

He braced himself and tugged at the gilded laces of his tunic. He could do this thing.

During his trip across the inner bailey he continued mumbling prayers. As he crossed through the outdoors, the sun took its final rays of light and hid behind the horizon for good, but he would not accept it as an omen of night falling in his own heart. Once to the tower, the steward led him up a mammoth marble stairway and into the duchess's private solar.

There the graceful woman awaited him. She looked stunning as usual in a gown of the finest black wool with a gilded circlet holding her matching veil in place over her dark hair. A huge fire roared in the hearth, chasing away the chill on this fall evening. Torches and candlelight set the room aglow. A centerpiece of late blooms festooned the table, creating the perfect environment for a man and a woman to discover one another.

The duchess smiled up through watery eyes. Allen couldn't begin to understand how hard this must be for her. Yet the duchess had been reared a noble, reared to put duty and honor before personal desires. Meanwhile Allen had always expected he would choose a simple peasant girl whom he loved and desired. So in some ways his situation was no easier.

The duchess stood and offered her hand. "Welcome, Sir Allen."

He lifted her hand to his lips and kissed it with compassion and admiration, but with none of the fervor, none of the longing, with which he had kissed Gwendolyn's. Perhaps this was better. Perhaps this more logical, prescribed sort of relationship could last long after the flames of romance might have been extinguished.

"Your Grace," was all Allen could choke out.

She took his hand in hers now and patted it in a motherly sort of way. "I am relieved to see this is no easier for you than it is for me. Perhaps in such circumstances, we shall be able to navigate this unexpected path together."

Allen took a fortifying breath. "I am honored to be your espoused husband. Nothing could please me more."

A small laugh escaped her. "While I suspect that is not true, I thank you for saying so. This decision has taken us both by surprise." She indicated to a chair and sat across from him.

"Of course it is true." Allen smiled ruefully. "'Tis simply complicated. And unexpected, as you mentioned. And far too fast."

The duchess blinked back a few tears. "Yes, far too fast."

She gazed deep into Allen's eyes. "But there is something about you I like. A goodness of heart. On that issue at least, the council is correct. And a forthrightness as well. I think we shall deal well together."

Gwendolyn had also liked his forthrightness, but he could never say as much. "I do not wish you to feel rushed, Your Grace. I realize we must marry soon, but know that I will allow you as much time as needed before . . ." He sensed heat rising up his cheeks but needed to say this for both of their peace of mind. "Before we must express our love physically to one another."

"Yes, you are as thoughtful as I had hoped." The duchess gestured for the servant to begin serving the meal.

As the man heaped the ornate table with pheasant, meat pies, fish, and roasted vegetables, Allen struggled to think of what else he might say. He fiddled nervously with his goblet of wine, swishing it about in the cup and then taking a few fortifying sips. Perhaps rather than talking he should ask questions and listen. "So, did you grow up in Edendale, Your Grace?"

The duchess daintily chewed and swallowed a piece of warm

crusty bread before answering. "Not far from here. I was a third cousin of the duke. DeMontforts have always liked to keep matters in the family. I had a charmed childhood in a pleasant castle, but always I was so scared of the imposing man I knew would someday be my husband. He seemed too big, too serious."

At the memory she giggled, the first truly joyful sound she had made that evening. "Then he came to visit when I was seventeen years old. And suddenly the ten years between us melted away. He was handsome, gallant, and charming. He wooed me as any other suitor might, and I fell deeply, intoxicatingly in love."

"You were truly blessed." Allen speared a fish with his dagger and moved it to his trencher, although he knew not if his roiling stomach might hold down the food. How could he deal with the ghost of this woman's one true love, not to mention his own confusing feelings for Gwendolyn?

"But it gives me hope for us as well."

Something about her quiet assurance spread that hope to Allen like a contagion, and he did indeed manage his way through the fresh roasted fish. He even managed to enjoy the toppings of rich butter and savory herbs.

After a few quiet moments the duchess spoke again. "We have much to do over these next weeks. Planning the ceremony and the celebration, and even a tournament, if possible. The council wishes this marriage to appear real and not merely tossed together. And you must, of course, meet the rest of my nobles. I am planning a feast for that purpose a week hence."

"A most excellent idea. But do you think they shall like me?" Allen could not believe he'd let the childish question slip from his mouth, but the concern had been niggling at him.

What if they discovered he was naught but a sham? A lowborn pretender. Or worse yet, what if they took him for a conniving usurper? How would he battle such allegations? He barely believed he belonged here himself.

"Sir Allen, they shall see what the council has seen, and they shall love you. I agree with the bishop. God has brought you here for such a time as this. It has been amazing how the people, common and noble alike, have rallied around this idea. Whether the prophecy was true and reputable or not, it seems God has used it for His purpose to save this dukedom."

Now came Allen's turn to blink back a few tears. He could hardly believe God had chosen him for such an honor. But hadn't he always put God first? Hadn't he lived a holy life and studied the Scriptures fervently at his first opportunity? Lowborn or not, he deserved this chance. He had earned it. If not him, who else could fulfill this prophecy?

"You honor me with your words." Allen focused again on his food as the duchess chatted about some of the noble men and women he would soon meet.

"Oh, and I nearly forgot Gwendolyn!"

He choked on his pheasant and took a moment to cough up the offending bit.

The duchess reached across the table to pat his back. "Are you well?"

Surely he would not be forced to face Gwendolyn now. "I will be," he managed to say, though his voice sounded rough.

She watched him with concern for a moment until he took another swig of wine and a few clear breaths.

"Anyway, yes, Lady Gwendolyn. She is utterly delightful. I still cannot place my finger upon precisely why I like her so much. In some ways she is a mystery, yet there is a freshness and an honesty beneath the persona she so often puts on. I long to discover it. I dare say I might bring her here to serve as one of my ladies if her parents approve."

Allen knew not what to say. As much as his heart longed to see Gwendolyn on a daily basis, he knew not if he could withstand such temptation. He was strong, yes, righteous, yes. He desired to do right, and in this circumstance surely doing right would include fleeing such proximity from the young woman he found himself increasingly drawn to.

Yet he did not wish to concern the duchess. She had trouble enough of her own. Finally the answer came to him. "I believe I met her, but I think she is to be married soon."

"Oh, I was not aware. But of course she is the right age. Do you know to whom?"

"Her father seemed set on that Sir Gawain fellow."

"Dear me, I hope not. Although the match is certainly suitable. Well, if they do end up married, all the more reason to bring her here."

Allen's appetite fled him completely now, but he continued to chew and swallow food that tasted of shoe leather in his mouth. *Duty. Honor. Service.* He must keep these words in his mind. The duchess was a good and admirable lady. He would be the betrothed, and soon the husband, that she deserved, and he would let nothing, not even his mounting feelings for the Lady Gwendolyn, stand in his way.

◇◇◇

Early the next evening, Allen entered the hushed and shadowy chapel of Edendale Castle. Just a hint of sunlight filtered through the bold glass window with its picture of Eve considering the forbidden fruit.

So red, so juicy, so tempting in Eve's outstretched palm. No, he could not—would never—allow himself to betray this dukedom over the sweet, delectable temptation of Gwendolyn Barnes. But neither could he bear to leave her empty-handed after he had hinted to the possibility of marriage in their future. Thus he had come to this sacred place today.

Might the painting be a warning? Should he stay far away from Gwendolyn? Yet how could he when her eternal soul already lay in peril, and his marriage to the duchess might be the event that would push it over the edge to destruction.

"Do you plan on standing about staring at yon artwork, or can I help you with something?" A good-natured voice tugged Allen from his reverie.

He jolted and pivoted toward the man.

A doddering but jovial-looking priest dressed in simple black robes chuckled. White hair tufted about his tonsured scalp. "You are not the first to wrestle with temptation, my lad, nor shall you be the last. 'Tis not the temptation that is the sin, but rather what you do with it."

Allen had seen the man before, as the castle held services several times daily. Father Marcus, if Allen recalled correctly. The priest only ever seemed to linger about, never lead the services himself. Perhaps those days were long past for him. Allen had previously wondered if the odd old fellow was a bit addled in his mind, although he seemed a good-hearted sort.

The priest came closer and scrutinized him, peering in one direction and then the other. Seeming to stare deep into Allen's soul. "Although on closer inspection, I detect a special light in you. Hazed perhaps by only the smallest touch of pride. Beware—for the devil will use even the slightest of weaknesses to bring one down."

Allen sucked in a gasp. Exactly the fault he had feared.

"But do not dismay. In truth, you possess one of the purest souls I have ever witnessed. Perhaps it is not sin you wrestle with so much as confusion."

Something about the man's intense probing shook Allen to

his core, yet the overall positive assessment soothed his fraying nerves. "I hope you are right, good father."

"So what can I help you with today? I hope it is not the confessional, for if so, you are bearing a false guilt."

How could the man be so certain? But something about his calm demeanor told Allen he spoke true.

"No, I did not come to make confession, although yon picture caused me pause." Allen took a deep breath. "I would, however, appreciate your help. I need to search out what the Scripture has to say about the place of a woman, in both marriage and in life. A female friend of mine is quite vexed over the issue."

"Ah, interesting you should bring that up. 'Tis one of the many areas that our progressive dukedom has found cause to reconsider. I personally have theories about the afterlife of animals—particularly dogs and horses—but those never seem to catch favor."

The priest brushed away his own digression. "I imagine the official church position on women might be closer to what your friend expects."

"So do you not consider the pope to be the final authority on such issues?"

"Tricky, tricky, my boy. As a group, the clergy here in North Britannia have hesitated to stir up trouble by declaring that we do not." The priest fingered the cross hanging from a long rope over his round belly. "But we have seen too much corruption in the church. It has become just another branch of politics and has lost its spiritual center."

Allen rubbed his chin as he considered that too true statement. "Then how is one to know the will of God?"

"Well, I suppose we must cling to the unchanging Word of God, as well as to the revelation of the Holy Spirit in our own hearts."

Allen sank onto the stairway leading to the altar. Again, all words he knew to be true, yet much to consider. Especially in light of his decision to follow the guidance of the bishop and the council concerning his upcoming marriage.

The priest busied himself lighting candles along a wooden railing and allowed Allen a moment with his thoughts.

Although he had always followed that inner guide, somehow he had never quite paused to consider what might happen if that guide led him in a different direction than the authority of the church. "So might you have suggestions on Scripture references for my friend?"

"I have some rather telling ones, in fact. I think you will begin to see a whole new picture about God's design for the sexes." The priest led Allen toward a large tome on a table to the rear of the altar.

A part of Allen wished he might find a whole new picture about God's design for him and Gwendolyn as well.

No. The people of North Britannia had spoken, and he had accepted this chivalrous sacrifice he must make. But at least he might be able to provide Gwendolyn with a peace offering of truth and perhaps even of a relationship with the God who could sustain her through whatever heartache life might bring.

Chapter 18

Once again ensconced in her mistress's chamber at the smaller Edendale townhome, Rosalind shook out the deep blue velvet gown that she admired above all the others. She laid it flat over the bed and brushed any stray ripples from the fabric. Thankfully, due to the brief nature of this trip, they had left Gwendolyn's troublesome pups at home, and they would not be mussing it this time.

Perhaps someday Rosalind might own a gown like this. One never knew. She had worked hard to better herself. She could read and write a bit, spoke a dash of French, knew her way around manners and fashions. Hadn't Sir Allen of Ellsworth begun his life as a country villager much as Rosalind herself? Yet he would soon be a duke. A duke! Life was a mountain stream, full of the most amazing twists, turns, and plunges into the unknown.

But the thought of plunges pulled her attention toward Lady Gwendolyn, who was still caught in her deep abyss. Although her imprisonment had ended more than a week ago, one would never know it from the look of her.

She sat hunched over a small writing desk with her features hanging low. Crumpling a piece of paper in her hand, she let out a moan and tossed it over her shoulder.

Rosalind picked up the paper and held it toward her mistress. "Are you quite finished with this, then?"

"I have written nothing that might help."

"I told you the list was worthless." Rosalind did not need to read it to know what it said, for they had discussed the issue over and again throughout the last days. "You would never survive the sedate lifestyle of a nun, forest outlaws end up hanging from the gallows, and I shall not suffer you to dive headlong from the tower."

"But what is left for me, Rosalind? Wherever shall I go from here?"

"For tonight you thank the good Lord that you are free from your imprisonment and of the proper class to enjoy a dinner at the grand castle. The duchess seems to like you. Perhaps you shall find an ally there."

"I am certain Duchess Adela has bigger concerns than my future. Like her deceased husband and her upcoming nuptials." Gwendolyn moaned again and buried her face against her knees.

"I know your heart is broken. But look at it from a different angle. For the first time in your life your heart is also awakened. Go, eat, socialize. All the nobles of the region shall be there. Perhaps you will meet someone new."

"Do you truly think so?" Gwendolyn's eyes pleaded with Rosalind for reassurance.

"Of course. Allen was your first infatuation. We all must have one. And we all must cleanse that first girlish impulse from our hearts to search for something more lasting and true. Now that you've experienced attraction, you will most assuredly be more open to it in the future." Rosalind would do well to take her own advice.

Gwendolyn cocked an eyebrow. "I notice how neatly you dance about the word we both know to be true. Love. Before word of his engagement reached us, I was deep in the throes of falling in love with Sir Allen."

Rosalind nodded to the gown. "Come and dress. It shan't be long now."

"Do not avoid this issue." Gwendolyn stood and approached nonetheless.

"'Tis just that I do not in fact know that you're in love." Rosalind tugged off Gwendolyn's casual kirtle over her head. "Love does not happen in an instant. That sort of love is the stuff of fairy stories. If you ask my opinion, you do not know him well enough to be in love with him."

Gwendolyn glared at Rosalind as she prepared the blue velvet.

"Arms," Rosalind ordered and tossed the gown overtop Gwendolyn.

From beneath the thick fabric emerged Gwen's retort. "Well, 'tis a good thing I did not ask your opinion." Then her head poked through the hole.

"Turn around."

Gwendolyn did as instructed and leaned against the bedpost. Rosalind pulled the laces down the back much tighter than she recalled doing previously. Her mistress had lost weight between her imprisonment and her melancholy mood, but she still appeared lovely with her well-toned curves.

Finally secured tightly in the dress, Gwendolyn turned back to Rosalind, her eyes beseeching once again. "I do know Sir Allen. I know that he is honest and forthright. I know that he is virtuous and kind. I know that he is the only man, besides my brothers, who has ever treated me like an equal worthy of respect. What else would you have me know?"

Rosalind had no answer to that. Romantic fancy aside, Gwendolyn's reasoning was quite sound. No need to point out he was no longer available, for Gwendolyn knew that all too well. Instead Rosalind made a few small adjustments to the gown and added a low-hanging belt of gold around her mistress's hips. "Perfect. And this color is ideal for a castle still in mourning."

Gwendolyn brushed her hand over the costly velvet. "This is my favorite gown. I almost do not hate it." She gave a wry smile.

"Go and show your mother. See what she thinks of the belt. I wanted to give the gown a different look this time. Too bad we did not have the opportunity to make a new one."

Gwendolyn waved the notion away as she headed toward the door. "Neither nuns nor outlaws have need of more gowns."

"Nor dead women splattered upon the courtyard." Rosalind wiggled her brows.

At that Gwendolyn laughed outright and turned down the hall.

Only then did Rosalind allow her mind to verbalize the thought that had been screaming from the edges of her consciousness for the past hour.

Sick!

Her stomach ached and her limbs felt weighted with lead. How she longed to lie upon Gwendolyn's feather mattress and sink into oblivion. Why could she not shake this annoying ailment? At least she had managed not to pass it along to Gwendolyn. She could not let her mistress, nor more importantly Lord or Lady Barnes, know how ill she had been this past week. Servants were not allowed such luxuries as sickness, and she could never hurt her mother and siblings by losing this much-needed income.

She spied under the bed to make sure the chamber pot remained nearby in case she lost the contents of her stomach.

Rallying herself, she straightened the jars and pins upon the table in preparation for Gwendolyn's hair and face. Just another hour and the family would be gone for the evening. Then Rosalind could rest.

By some small miracle she had managed to escape indictment over the tournament incident. It seemed Lord and Lady Barnes had been too upset with Gwendolyn to give much thought to a mere maid, and if anything, seemed to consider her a steadying force.

However, Rosalind might well bring destruction down upon herself.

She could not go home to her mother in defeat. She would not lose her position in this family. She would hold tight to her future, to the bright path she had chosen. Beyond all that, she would not give up the chance to see Sir Hugh and snuggle into his strong arms and press her lips to his once again.

◇◇◇

Gwen glanced nervously about the ornate room with its tall pillars. This one was smaller than the great hall, where the feasts had been held, yet far more elaborately bedecked. Enormous tapestries in deep earthy tones hung from ceiling to floor, covering most of the walls, and a roaring fire blazed in a mammoth hearth. But none of that could warm her chill-cold soul.

Tonight she would see Allen for the first time since his engagement, and she knew not how she would bear it.

"Do not just stand there like a ninny." Her father gave her a shove from behind. She stumbled through the giant archway onto the polished marble floor.

She turned and frowned at him. "I was collecting myself."

"The only thing you need to worry about collecting is a powerful son-in-law for me."

How was everything always about Father? As if he were the earth about which the sun and moon spun. Gwen stopped herself from shaking her head. Perhaps a lesson on the mythical Narcissus was in order, but she would not be the one to deliver it.

"We are in no rush, my love." Mother rubbed Father's arm and attempted to smooth his mood.

"Please excuse us. I need to speak with Lord Fulton." Reginald led his mousy wife, Katherine, even more a shadow of herself than usual, away.

But Gwen ceased to pay attention to them. There he was. Across the room. With his hand pressed to the small of the duchess's back. Dipping his head close to the lovely lady to better heed her.

Gwen's stomach seized into a tight knot. She managed not to clutch her belly. Instead she merely winced and took a deep breath.

When first she met Allen and he had such a strange effect upon her, she had feared some sort of sickness had struck her. Now she knew for certain. She was indeed sick. Love was the most soul-crushing malady of them all. What a fool she had been to fall under its spell. She blinked back tears and pulled herself up straight and tall.

Father smiled her way. It seemed that since choosing the hulking Gawain for her, he had abandoned his quest to shrink her into oblivion. As if he had read her mind, he said, "Where is that Gawain tonight? I am anxious for you to renew your acquaintance. Be sure to sit by him at dinner. That shall allow you ample time to converse. You will like him, I am sure. He and I are much alike."

Exactly as Gwen dreaded.

At that moment a flash of black headed in her direction. A subdued but still gracious Duchess Adela held out her hands as she approached Gwen.

Gwen moved to meet her and took her hands with a squeeze. "Your Grace."

"There you are," the duchess said. "Sir Allen, I believe you have met my friend Lady Gwendolyn."

"Indeed." Coming up behind her, Allen offered a tight smile that seemed to hide a pained expression.

"Nice to s-see you again, Sir Allen," Gwen stuttered. Pain sliced through her head to match the look on his face and complement the growing ache in her stomach.

"I have been hoping to speak with you." The duchess shifted to include Gwen's parents in the conversation. "Good evening, Lord Barnes, Lady Barnes. I am so glad you could make it. Your daughter is quite the breath of fresh air about this place. I have been thinking ever since the tournament, and I would appreciate it if you would consider lending her to me for a while as an attendant. Right now, of all times, I could use a cheerful companion."

What was that small flicker in Gwen's heart? Hope? She could not dare to hope, so she snuffed it out. And none too soon, based on her father's countenance.

His face flushed bright red. "I . . . well . . . of course. . . ."

"What my husband means to say," Mother interrupted with easy charm, "is that Gwendolyn is already past marriageable age. I am afraid with him being gone so oft, we neglected her in this area, and would not wish to do her any further injustice."

"Oh, I see." Disappointment tinged the duchess's voice, but Allen seemed to relax a bit.

During that brief moment of hope, Gwen had not thought

so far as to realize that being the duchess's companion would put her in close proximity to Allen on a regular basis as well. But it would still have been better than marriage to Gawain.

"Do not misunderstand." Mother reached out to touch the duchess's arm. "You are welcome to her through the time of her engagement, and if her husband approves, perhaps after that as well."

The duchess smiled. "That would be lovely. Gwendolyn, do you ride? I realize many ladies do not, or at least do not confess to it, but I have been desperate for a gallop through the woods since my husband's death and require a companion to do so. I had a feeling you might not be a stranger to horses."

Father's vein pulsed, but Gwendolyn answered nonetheless. "Since you asked, my brothers took me out riding a time or two."

"Or two hundred?" The duchess's merry laugh reached out to Gwen. "Yes, I am well versed in such stories."

What a cheerful lady the duchess was, even now in her grief. To Gwen's dismay, she realized that Allen would be blessed to marry this woman.

"And she plays the pipe," Father added in desperation. "Do not forget she plays the pipe."

"Indeed, I remember. Would you play for us tonight?" the duchess asked.

Gwen looked around the room. This selective gathering was still fairly large, but a performance would soothe her father. Not to mention sweep her away to that magical place, as her music always did. "I could do that, I suppose, if time allows."

"It shall." The duchess smiled her assurance.

"You should have told me you wished to ride," Allen said to the duchess. "I could have taken you."

"Well, it might not be proper until we are wed." The duchess had to tip up her head to meet Allen's gaze. "But perhaps the three of us might all go together on the morrow. What say you to that, Gwendolyn?"

Gwendolyn's throat grew dry and tight. "A ride. Tomorrow. How . . . how lovely. Perhaps I shall bring my maid along as well." For she would desperately need the moral support.

"Perhaps we shall take our bows and try a little hunting while we are out there." The duchess winked.

"And she embroiders. Trim!" Father pointed to the embellishments sewn upon Gwen's collar somewhat pathetically.

Just then Gawain came crashing into the room with his too-bold energy and his too-loud voice. "Your Grace." He flung the words to the duchess, and just as quickly turned his attention to Gwen.

"So there is the lovely lady." He snatched her hand up for a kiss, his glossy black hair falling across it, and she wished to spit upon him in return. "I hope you will be dining with me tonight."

"I assume so," was the most polite response she could conjure.

"Dear me." Duchess Adela pressed a hand to her cheek. "I am afraid you must forgive me, for I made other arrangements. Lady Gwendolyn, I wish for you to sit at our table, and I prepared for my knight, Sir Randel Penigree, to escort you. I hope that will not cause any trouble."

"Of course not," Father ground out from between clenched teeth.

Gawain simply glowered.

"How kind of you," Mother said. "What an honor you do our daughter."

The duchess wrapped an arm around Gwen's waist and hustled her away from the uncomfortable scene. She whispered up to Gwen's ear, "I assumed you might wish to be rescued from that oaf, but if I am wrong, it is not too late to correct the situation."

Relief flooded Gwen. "No, you are absolutely correct."

"Then allow me to introduce you to Sir Randel. He is the most good-hearted knight in my employ, and I suspect perfect for you."

"Oh, we have known each other since . . . " But as they approached the pleasant man leaning against the long ornate table, Gwen was not sure she knew him at all.

Where were the big feet? The gangly neck? The awkward nose? Though of course the face was familiar, it seemed Randel had grown into his features to a degree she had not anticipated. And although he had a more slender build than Allen, he stood to nearly the same height. He wore his dark brown hair cropped close, as always, but his skin was now smooth rather than spotted. In one aspect he remained entirely familiar though; his warm brown eyes still glowed with kindness and intelligence.

How had she not noted these changes before? She had seen him several times over the past year. And of course at the recent tournament and feast, but she had been intent only on outrunning him.

"Sir Randel," the duchess said, "may I present your dinner companion, Lady Gwendolyn Barnes."

Randel swiveled from the duchess to Gwen and back, and then a smile burst forth upon his face to rival Allen's grin of pure sunshine. "What a wonderful surprise. And this meets with your approval, Lady Gwendolyn?"

"Absolutely." Gwendolyn offered a warm smile in return. Indeed, how could she resist?

"We shall leave you two to get acquainted while we greet more of our guests." The duchess bustled off with Allen. He offered one backward glance of support before they melted into the crowd.

Randel scratched his head. "You need not feel stuck with me, you know."

"And you need not feel obliged to offer for my hand just because my brother asked you to, you know," Gwen retorted with a saucy quirk of her brow.

The hollows of Randel's cheeks turned an attractive shade of plum, quite different than Father's ugly red flush of anger. Randel's face might not be as strongly chiseled as Allen's, but Mother had been correct. He was quite nice to look at.

"Um . . . I am not sure what to say to that. Are you not supposed to feign oblivion to such issues?" He chuckled and shuffled his foot like a young lad, reminding Gwen that he was only two years her senior. The same age as Allen.

Maintaining a steady gaze, she awaited his answer. She would not play the coquette with Randel. Either he would like her for her true self or not at all.

He met her gaze. "I confess your brother spoke with me, but I did not approach your father out of obligation."

"Then why?"

Randel glanced away, but then focused on her again. "Gwennie . . ."

His use of her childhood name softened her, and without forethought she melted from her determined stance into a decidedly more feminine silhouette.

"Gwennie, I have always admired you, always adored you as a sister. Surely you know that. But over the last few years, those feelings have shifted. I might have approached you sooner had I not felt certain you would laugh in my face."

Though tickled by his statement, she restrained herself from laughing now. "Smart of you."

He shook his head. "But when Hugh came to me and told me your father was determined to see you wed, I realized how important it would be to you to find a man who would allow you to remain your real self and not attempt to domesticate you."

Gwen gulped down a lump in her throat. She had not expected any of this. "Smart indeed." And direct. So very direct—precisely as she preferred.

"I've always thought you something of a hero, and I would not see you changed."

Now she had no idea what to say. Perhaps she had underestimated Randel on every account.

"I know you do not feel for me in that way." He reached out and took her hand. "I know you have always thought me silly and weak, but I have grown up as well. Let us start anew and see where this relationship might take us. What say you to that?" He bowed and offered a gallant kiss upon the back of her hand.

Although the kiss did not overwhelm her with a shower of tingles, gentle warmth flowed through her at his touch. The warmth of lasting friendship and heartfelt appreciation. Perhaps Rosalind had been right. She barely knew Sir Allen. But she did know Randel—at least his heart, if not this new more handsome form. Perhaps she should give him a chance.

Chapter 19

The haunting melody that floated from Gwendolyn's pipe wrapped around Allen's heart and squeezed tight. Only a pure soul could produce such perfect praise.

Throughout the evening he had sworn to himself that his impending marriage was for the best. Not only for the dukedom. Not only for the duchess. But for him as well. He strove to convince himself that Gwendolyn did not share his passion for God. Yet he sensed through the stirring strands that filled the room—that somehow she did.

Perhaps she did not yet know it. But she longed for the Divine. Needed only to meet God in a tangible way. A high trill of Gwen's pipe soared to the heavenlies, yet managed to stab him straight through the gut.

He could no longer hide the truth from himself. Though he must fulfill his duty to all these precious people surrounding him, must protect this amazing dukedom from an unscrupulous usurper, marrying the duchess would not be the best course for his own heart.

Then again . . . he must trust that God knows the future far beyond the present affliction of his frail human emotions.

Did Gwendolyn look a bit too thin and wan this evening, or was he imagining it? He tried to brush the thought aside. Truly, he had no right thinking about the specifics of her figure and face.

The song melted into silence, and cheering and pounding thundered throughout the room. Gwendolyn offered a quick, bashful curtsey, then returned to Sir Randel's side, where she had been stuck like a burr throughout the evening. Perhaps she did not share Allen's deep affection. Or perhaps she clung to Randel only to protect herself from the similar sight of Allen dancing attendance to the duchess.

He took a deep breath and resisted the temptation to sigh. What a messy situation his heart had gotten him into this time. Why must he continue plaguing himself so? He needed a new perspective on this issue. And so he squinted his eyes ever so slightly and attempted to see her in a different light. From the heavenly sphere.

That is when it came to him. This was his chance to share those Scriptures with her.

Thankfully, the duchess waved Gwendolyn their way. "Darling Gwendolyn, do come and visit with me."

Gwendolyn managed to detach herself from Randel, although Allen fancied he could hear the ripping sound over the distance of the long gilded table.

"That was beyond lovely," the duchess said. "Your song shall echo in my ears for days to come. I shall hear it in the whisper of the wind and the call of the birds."

Gwendolyn ducked her head. "'Tis just a silly pastime. Music brings me pleasure, and I am honored to share it with you."

Allen recalled her confession that she oft played her pipe high in the trees. How he wished to witness such a spectacle.

"I can hardly fathom that you have kept your gift hidden all these years. It is a crime. Sir Allen, remind me to bring this up at the next council meeting," the duchess teased.

Gwendolyn's cheeks turned pink, and she glanced about as if seeking an escape. From down the table, Sir Randel offered her a grin that seemed to soothe her.

Allen longed to offer reassurance as well, but she would not so much as meet his gaze. "Lady Gwendolyn, as you played I was reminded of your questions from a few weeks ago. I have been studying the Holy Book in my free time, and I have some Scriptures I would like to share with you when opportunity allows."

"Well, she is free right now." The duchess gestured to Gwendolyn. "In my opinion, when it comes to matters of the spirit, one should never delay."

"I . . . would love to see them, but . . ." Gwendolyn warily eyed her father.

"I understand, my dear." The duchess gave Gwen's arm a squeeze. "I can handle this."

She retreated for a moment to whisper to a nearby servant.

Allen and Gwen stood in awkward silence until the duchess returned.

"Just a few moments and my brilliant scheme shall be enacted." The duchess nudged Gwendolyn with her shoulder.

Allen had not seen this mischievous side of his future bride before, and he rather liked it. Truly, despite their age difference, they could make a good match if only it were not for . . . He cut off his errant thoughts.

"Did you hear of Sir Allen's latest triumph with the council?" the duchess asked Gwendolyn.

"No, I did not." Gwendolyn's fathomless blue eyes sparkled with interest. "Do tell."

"'Tis nothing." Allen shrugged.

"Do not be modest, my dear." The duchess looped her arm through his. "He devised the grand idea to find childless couples to adopt the orphans from Seaside."

"Adopt?" Gwen pressed a hand to her lips. "Is that even legal?"

"Not typically," Allen said. "But it is mentioned in a positive manner in Scripture. And Lord Fulton spent time researching any specific prohibitions against it."

"It seems that according to English common law, adoption is not allowed." The duchess nearly bounced in her excitement. "But Fulton was assured that we would not be required to adjust fully to their system for several years, and that any decisions we make now will stand in the future."

Allen smiled, catching her excitement despite his discomfort with Gwendolyn.

"So the children will have homes," the duchess said, her voice tinged with wonder. "Real homes, with real parents. I could not be more delighted."

"I am so happy to hear that." Something new lit Gwendolyn's eyes. Might she be proud of his accomplishments?

He could not decide if that pleased him or made him more miserable than ever.

The servant returned with a small parchment, a quill, and a bottle of ink. The duchess made quick work of scratching out a note as Allen and Gwendolyn stood awkwardly once again.

"There you go." The duchess waved the note in triumph.

Gwendolyn looked to Allen in confusion.

"Come," the duchess offered by way of explanation.

They followed her across the room to a nearby table where Gwendolyn's parents sat.

"Lord Barnes," the duchess said with urgency to her tone, "I have an important mission for you. I need you to take this message to the guards at the outer wall immediately."

"Immediately? Me?" For a moment he looked perplexed. He glanced around the room at the many soldiers of lesser rank who might carry out the mundane chore.

"I would appreciate if you would deliver it personally."

Lord Barnes swiped a look of ruffled pride from his face and replaced it with one that depicted the respect due the duchess. "Of course, Your Grace. I am at your service." He offered a small bow and headed off with the note as Allen fought to stifle a chuckle. Once the baron was safely through the archway and around the corner, Allen could hold it back no longer.

The duchess and Gwendolyn joined his laughter over their private amusement.

"What is this?" Lady Barnes asked with humor in her eyes.

"Sir Allen would like to show your daughter some Scripture passages concerning an issue they discussed previously, and we thought *you* might be agreeable to the idea," the duchess said.

"Of course, as long as you do not mind lending your handsome fiancé for such a purpose." Lady Barnes offered him a smile. Unlike her husband, Gwendolyn's mother appeared to be kindly disposed toward Allen.

"Not at all. Sir Allen has a keen mind for theology, and he should put it to good use."

"Naturally they shall take a chaperone." Lady Barnes offered the suggestion in the most diplomatic sort of way.

"Yes, that is a good idea." The duchess scanned the room. "Perhaps Sir Randel would accompany you."

On any normal day, Allen would be thankful for Sir Randel's company. He had grown to appreciate the man more and more over the past weeks, but he was the last person Allen wanted along right now.

Yet Gwendolyn brightened at the idea. "Yes, I am certain he would." With a simple flick of her wrist, Sir Randel—who must have been watching the entire exchange—hurried to her side once again. "Randel, would you please accompany Sir Allen and me to the chapel? He would like to show me some Scriptures we discussed the other week."

Just plain Randel, was it? They must have been friends for a very long time.

"I would be happy to. Sir Allen has a keen mind for spiritual matters, I have noticed."

True enough, Allen and Sir Randel had shared several discussions of a religious nature. Allen sought to consider Gwendolyn only as a lost sheep in need of rescuing, and realized that Sir Randel would be the perfect person to assist him in convincing her of God's goodness and love.

Allen must somehow manage to put aside any ulterior motives that might simmer beneath the surface. If he could not marry Gwendolyn, then Sir Randel would be the best choice for her by far. He simply must wrap his mind around this new turn of events and stop torturing himself with what might have been.

◇◇◇

Gwen was still not quite certain how she had gotten herself into this predicament. Flanked by Allen on one side and Randel on the other, she bent over the large tome of Scripture and attempted to read the passage again. On her last time through, Allen had brushed against her arm and sent her concentration flittering into the wind.

Even without such distraction, her mind swirled with the new thoughts of believers submitting themselves one to another. Of

God creating both male and female in His image. Of there being no male nor female in Christ. Of the husband loving the wife like Christ loved the church. It was almost too much to process.

"So what do you think of all this?" Allen turned to look her in the eye.

But he was far too close, and she shifted her gaze to the much safer features of Randel to her other side.

"It need not be as it was in your home," Randel assured her with a gentle squeeze to her shoulder, and then left his arm draped over her. "And look at what comes next."

He seemed completely engrossed in their study. "'So ought men to love their wives as their own bodies. He that loveth his wife loveth himself. For no man ever yet hated his own flesh; but nourisheth and cherisheth it . . .'"

Gwen should not have been surprised at the ease with which Randel translated the passage from Latin to English. She had never thought him stupid, only weak. Yet she found herself impressed nonetheless.

"Would a man bully or abuse himself?" Randel asked.

Gwen quirked a brow Randel's way. "Have you met my father?"

They all chuckled at that.

Randel nodded. "True enough. He is quite a tough old goat, and as hard on himself as he is on his soldiers."

"Perhaps therein lies the problem," Allen said.

Gwen sighed. "And in the fact that he clearly loves himself more than anyone else in heaven or on earth."

"Yes, I could see how that would make a marriage difficult." Randel pulled her yet an inch closer and rested his head against hers. "But I promise you, Gwennie, 'twas not so in my home."

Gwen could not help peeking to see Allen's reaction to the pet name, and thus caught his wince.

But Randel did not and continued. "My father doted upon my mother."

Gwen certainly felt cherished, tucked safely as she was beneath Randel's arm.

"The same was true of my father, God rest his soul." Allen crossed himself. "But we are almost finished. 'For this cause shall a man leave his father and mother, and shall be joined unto his wife, and they two shall be one flesh.'" Allen paused as if to consider that. But no one offered comment.

Gwen's cheeks flushed hot. She did not wish to think of such matters while pressed close to Randel with Allen nearby. Yet the situation offered ample opportunity for comparison. While Randel did not set her blood aflame like Allen, she realized more and more the similarities between the two.

How odd, truly. A few weeks ago her future had been clear. Allen the obvious choice for her. But now she wondered if the future might be far more fluid than she ever suspected. Perhaps now that Allen had been swept from her grasp, Randel might offer a new and promising prospect.

And although she was not quite ready to contemplate marital intimacies with Randel, she had to admit that Allen had awakened something in her that allowed her to understand how a woman might enjoy such touches. Of course she would rather experience the full awakening of her femininity with Allen, but as Allen was no longer a possibility . . .

Such thoughts put her mind in a dither. Right now, she just wished to conclude this conversation.

"So you see," Allen said, "if the husband shows true love to the wife, it all falls nicely into place. It becomes a relationship of mutual give-and-take, like that dance of equals we discussed."

Gwen's mind shot back to their last dance. To their bodies tucked closely together, but she shooed the memory away.

She extricated herself from Randel's grasp and stood up straight. Turning to Allen she said, "Thank you so much for all you have done for me. I sensed that you had come into my life for a special purpose, and I suppose this must have been it."

Perhaps those words would somehow put their tension to rest. A simple acknowledgment that he had meant so much to her, but that they could never be together. Then she backed up against Randel, missing his reassuring touch so soon.

Allen watched them as they stood together. He eyed them up and down, and resolution settled over his features. "Sir Randel, the duchess, Gwendolyn, and I shall be riding into the woods on the morrow. Would you like to join us?"

"Certainly."

Gwendolyn need not see his face to detect Randel's joy over the invitation. He rested his hand upon her shoulder again.

A new path. A new direction. Perhaps it just might work.

Chapter 20

She looked just as Allen always imagined she would.

Gwendolyn sat confidently astride a mare of chestnut brown. Her long burgundy tunic, slit up the side, allowed her brown leggings to peek through. She kicked the horse into motion and giggled merrily as she took off with her maid alongside upon her own mount. The two galloped in a circle about the practice field. Gwendolyn moved in perfect rhythm, creating a picture so noble, so free, that it nearly stole the breath from his lungs.

Until Sir Randel Penigree trotted up to join them. Gwendolyn greeted him in a warm, relaxed manner. In the weeks he'd known her, Allen had seen her behave awkwardly in a number of social situations, but with Randel she seemed entirely herself. Open and alluring, confident and strong.

"I chose well, do you not think?" The duchess's voice caught him off guard. Clearly she had been watching as he observed Gwendolyn. "Both to bring her here and to match them together. We need such vibrant young energy to bring this castle back to life."

"Indeed," Allen said, barely able to take his gaze off Gwendolyn to offer the duchess due attention.

When finally he turned to her, she was studying him with her keen, dark eyes. "But it seems there might be one complication I did not take into consideration."

Allen shook himself from his trance. "'Tis nothing. Only the two ladies look so lovely upon their horses. They belong on a tapestry. Why would anyone desire to keep women locked away in castles?"

The duchess laughed. "I am not sure I believe that is all, but I shall let it go for now. You mentioned you had met Gwendolyn before, but I did not suspect . . . Well, we all have a past. If you would rather not have her about, please let me know."

"She should stay. I love the way she cheers you and brings out your mischievous side."

The duchess offered an impish grin to prove him right. "I feel so youthful when she is about. And her maidservant is charming as well."

A groom brought the duchess's horse to her, and she swept into the saddle without assistance. Her long green kirtle was ingeniously split down the middle and sewn into two loose legs, allowing her to perch astride with ease. She looked as lovely on horseback as Gwendolyn, and even more regal.

Allen likewise mounted his faithful steed, Thunder. He must train his focus to the duchess alone. "You look beautiful today. And every bit as young as yon maidens."

"You and your golden tongue. While I know you to be a man of integrity, sometimes I wonder if the truth of your words lies in your perceived obligation rather than in the depths of your heart."

After pausing to consider his answer, Allen said, "The heart is a fickle organ. And the truth wears many faces. I try to let sober thinking and sound judgment rule both my speech and my

actions—and the guidance of God, of course." He would keep
his duty to the region in the forefront of his mind. Never would
he allow himself to be lured into destruction like Guinevere,
who had destroyed her kingdom over Lancelot.

He was too important, too pivotal to this dukedom, and he
could not let them down. "I am committed to you and to our
coming nuptials. In the truth that is the truest of all truths, I
am deeply honored and humbled by this opportunity. You are
an amazing woman. I consider it a gift from God that I have
been chosen to rule at your side."

"I am honored as well. Although I would never have chosen
to remarry so quickly, I can think of no man I would rather
commit my life to." The duchess brought her horse close to his
and leaned in to offer a kiss upon his cheek. She had never done
so before, and he marveled at the featherlight stroke of her lips.

Yes, the truth wore many faces. Perhaps he had fallen in love
with Gwendolyn. Or perhaps it had merely been infatuation,
and this deep admiration and camaraderie he felt with the duchess was the beginning of something more real.

They trotted in the direction of the others. Gwendolyn
reached out to swat Sir Randel for something he had said. He
ducked away and chuckled. Perhaps the familiar affection and
playful exchange between Gwendolyn and Randel might allow
them to establish something lasting.

Except that a place deep inside of his heart—that same place
that had assured him Merry was never his—still cried out that
he and Gwendolyn belonged together forever.

◇ ◇ ◇

Sitting upon the back of a fine borrowed mare, Rosalind
pulled her bowstring and notched her arrow into place. Her
turn had arrived; the shot was hers.

She focused on the hearty hare against a backdrop of lush green foliage. It would make someone a fine supper. The shadows from the surrounding patch of trees kept her hidden from its view, but the hare perked its ears and twitched its nose as if sensing something amiss.

"Hurry!" Gwendolyn whispered.

Rosalind took aim straight for its heart. The muscles of its haunches pulled tight, but before it could spring into action, she let the arrow fly. It shot like lightning through the air, but just at the last, the hare leapt forward, and the arrow struck its hip instead of landing the merciful death blow.

The animal squealed and hopped frantically in a circle. Poor thing. Rosalind hated this part of hunting. Wishing to put it out of its misery as quickly as possible, she trotted her horse closer, pulled her dagger from her boot, and tossed it straight and sure. That projectile found its mark, and tonight's main course finally lay at rest upon a bed of damp leaves.

When Rosalind looked up, all eyes were fixed upon her, and only Gwendolyn's mouth did not gape.

"Where did you learn to do that?" Allen asked.

Randel chuckled. "Ah, I see you have not known the Lady Gwendolyn for long."

The duchess arched an eyebrow. "Gwendolyn?" she said in the tone of a mother to a naughty child.

Gwendolyn twisted her face in a wry expression and lifted her hands in mock surrender. "We had to do something to keep us occupied in that drafty old castle."

"She is adept with sword and lance as well," Randel said. "Has she taught you those, Maid Rosalind?"

"Indeed she has. And I have suffered the sore bottom to prove it," Rosalind said, though in truth she had enjoyed their afternoons together out in nature. Had, in fact, missed them this past month.

"But I am no match for Rosalind with the dagger." Gwendolyn nodded toward the hare.

"It seems you two might prove more useful than I ever expected. Who needs a guard when Lady Gwendolyn is near?"

Gwendolyn blushed. "Or Rosalind. I told her these skills could come in handy someday."

"Yes, Your Grace, if you ever go on pilgrimage, I would be happy to accompany you." Rosalind giggled.

"Excellent plan. But first we must get through these impending nuptials," the duchess said.

That seemed to put a damper on their humor. Glances darted about. Allen slumped forward a bit over his horse at the reminder. Poor fellow. Too bad there was no way to put him out of his misery as she had the hare.

In contrast, Gwendolyn seemed in better spirits next to Sir Randel than she had been since the wedding was first announced. He must give her hope that things might turn out well.

Needing to break the tension, Rosalind trotted to the hare and hoisted it up by its hind legs. Her stomach roiled in protest of the dead carcass, but she had learned to ignore it over these last weeks. "He's a plump one. And tender, I'll warrant."

"And I have the finest cook in the land. I shall send you some, Rosalind," the duchess said.

"How kind, Your Grace." Rosalind tossed the hare into the huntsman's sack, along with the other game they had captured that day.

In that instant she was struck hard by the fact that she had been joking and laughing with a duchess all afternoon and had barely given their difference in stations a thought. Were they truly so different? All her life she had been taught to treat the nobility as a separate sort of species. Something akin to a demigod. As if their blood did not flow red the same as hers.

But on some core level, were not all people the same? Were they not all made in the image of the same God, and as the book she read with Gwendolyn proclaimed, were they not all His adopted children?

Lady Gwendolyn had become her closest companion. Sir Allen had risen from obscurity and would soon lead the region. Perhaps she and Hugh were not so different either. There might yet exist some way for them to overcome their disparity in stations and find true love, though she had never dared to consider the possibility before.

Surely she could handle his moods and tame him into a fine husband. He had always been an admirable brother to Gwendolyn. And just think what she could do for her family as wife to a nobleman! They would most assuredly never go hungry again.

There might yet be a future for Hugh and Rosalind.

◇◇◇

Gwen and Rosalind entered the townhouse laughing and in high spirits. Late afternoon chill nipped at Gwen's cheeks, but she did not mind. She had not had so much fun since before Father came home.

As she spotted him glowering at her from across the large common room, she pulled up short.

"There you are. Finally. And whatever in God's name are you wearing?"

Gwen glanced down at her split tunic and leggings and then to Rosalind's matching outfit. She took a bracing breath and steadied her temper. "Father, could you please let this go for once? The duchess was dressed in similar attire. One cannot ride astride a horse in a gown."

"Which is precisely why ladies should not be riding horses," he grumbled.

Mother rose from her chair and soothed his ruffled temper with calming strokes to his arm as she so often did. "But of course we would not wish to disparage our gracious duchess in even the slightest way."

Father collected himself. "Of course not."

Truly it was a wonder Father had not turned against the progressive duke and duchess years ago. But she did not wish to rile him against the duchess now. Gwen turned to head up the stairs. "I shall go change."

"Thank goodness this will not last long. I imagine Sir Gawain shall not tolerate such behavior and will find some way to prevent it." Father's statement caught her up short.

She clutched the railing and blinked hard as she processed the horrible statement. "Gawain? Nothing has been settled with Gawain."

"Indeed it has." An evil grin spread across Father's face. "All the attention you garnered last night proved just the trick. Sir Gawain wishes to pursue negotiations before someone else snatches you up. His father invited us to dine at their castle a week hence."

Rosalind slunk quietly into the shadows, even as Gwen took a step toward her parents. "But the duchess wishes me to stay here. I am to move into the castle when you leave for home."

"No bother." Father flicked away the inconvenient detail. "We shall work out something."

"Mother?" Gwen outstretched her hands.

"This is news to me as well, darling." Mother's incessant rubbing of Father's arm grew frantic in its speed.

"Oh." Gwen's shoulders sagged. She had hoped Mother might advocate for her, but she had been denied even that chance.

"Oh, what? What is the problem now? Did we not agree she must marry?" Father's vein popped to attendance.

"Of course she must marry." Mother appeared to brace herself. "But Gwendolyn and I have been discussing other options. Like Sir Randel. The duchess seemed to favor that match, and of course we wish to please our ruler."

"Randel Penigree is no suitable match for her." Father's vein commenced to throbbing. "He is a fourth son for mercy's sake."

"Fourth son of an earl," Gwen dared to retort. She could not give up now. This battle was too important. Her heart, her very life was on the line. "I think the match is quite reasonable."

Father pulled away from Mother and began to stomp about the room like a raging bull. "Gawain is heir to a barony! He is by far the superior choice. Beyond which, I do not trust the Penigrees. I would much rather align myself with the Ethelbaums."

He turned his storming rampage in Gwen's direction.

She pulled back into the corner near Rosalind.

Mother blocked his path and pressed her hands against his chest. "Please! Let us calm ourselves. Perhaps you and I should discuss this in private, dear." The surprisingly brave woman took him gently by the shoulders.

"I will not change my mind!" Father hollered.

"I understand. Just allow Gwendolyn and Rosalind to go change out of the clothes that offended you so much, and we can continue this conversation peacefully."

Gwen did not need to be told twice. She hurried with Rosalind up the stairs. After changing, her next stop would most assuredly be the huge cathedral down the street. She craved the soothing balm of prayer. She was beginning to believe that only God could help her now.

◇◇◇

The sun had barely moved in the sky when Gwen settled to her knees next to Rosalind upon the polished tile floor of the grand Cathedral of Edendale. A wonder of modern architecture, people called it, with its towering arches and elaborate carved ceilings that seemed to graze the sky.

But as the chants of the holy brothers cascaded over her, as the spicy incense wafted through the air about her, it seemed a marvel of a completely different sort. A marvel of heaven come to earth in a cloud of comfort and peace. The sensation cuddled about her like a cozy blanket.

Light flooded the room from the stained-glass windows and shattered into a rainbow of color as it burst across the sanctuary. Comforting scenes from the Scriptures graced the walls for the less literate to better enjoy the Bible stories. One painting of Jesus tenderly embracing a lamb caught her eye.

She nudged Rosalind and gestured to it with a glance. "It is so beautiful," she said in a hushed whisper. "How did I never notice it before?"

Rosalind, more accustomed to churches, just smiled and folded her hands. She closed her eyes in prayer, leaving Gwen to relish the moment alone. She had never experienced anything like this in the stark, dim chapel on their family lands. And though she had visited this cathedral before, she had never fully engaged in encountering God as she did today.

In that moment she could almost fancy herself running into the arms of a heavenly Father, just as she had always dreamed of running into the loving embrace of her natural father. She imagined Him sweeping her high over His head and gazing into her eyes with a paternal delight she had never witnessed here on earth.

The scene shifted, and she pictured herself curling into His lap within a cushioned chair next to the hearth, and she poured out all her hurts and fears to Him. She petitioned Him about her future, and felt His peace and love flow over her like heated honey.

Was it merely dreaming, or something far, far more? Although she could not be certain, Gwen suspected the latter. Time slipped away as she basked in such a sweet presence.

She was so close to committing her life to Christ and accepting God as her Father once and for all. So very, very close. If only she could rid herself of those last doubts that had been ingrained so deeply within her.

At last, Rosalind touched her shoulder. Gwen opened her eyes and noted the sun now streaming low through the windows. In tandem, they made the sign of the cross and stood to head home for their evening meal.

Once on the street, Rosalind said, "You appeared quite lost for a time there."

"Mmm, 'twas glorious. I begin to understand Sir Allen's passionate longing for God." Although now out of that holy place, Gwen could not entirely discount her own tendency to slip into a fantasy world.

"It has been a while since you read your book to me. Shall we proceed again?"

"Of course." Gwen would not spoil the fun by telling Rosalind she had read through to the end during her confinement, for she wished to experience it anew through her friend's perspective.

She took a deep breath of autumn air. The world was a beautiful place, and after her incredible afternoon, she dared to hope that her future might be beautiful as well.

◇◇◇

Warner rubbed his hands together in anticipation and stared out the window of his craggy castle to the horizon beyond. Not long now. Though he had not risked being anywhere in the vicinity when the girl was captured, today he received a dispatch confirming that the mission had been a success and she would be delivered to him soon.

Would she be fair-haired or a raven beauty? Tall or short?

He had not heard, only that she had been living in seclusion for years. She was young, that he had ascertained, and presumably a maiden—for the regent, William Marshall, had denied her marriage to the man chosen for her. He planned to offer her as a prize to one of his favored earls instead.

But he and Marshall were close enough friends. Once Marshall understood Warner's purpose, understood he would be Duke of North Britannia and a strong ally, Marshall would be sure to forgive him this small indiscretion.

His mind wandered back to his soon-to-be bride. Not that she knew that, of course. She must be frightened out of her wits, but he would put her mind to rest soon enough. Warner had always had a way with women. He knew himself to be handsome, if a bit of a rogue and slightly past his prime.

In his position as a vanquished knight, he had never bothered to marry—did not want to be saddled with someone beneath his true standing. But the idea of marrying the heiress to a barony quite appealed to him. A woman worthy of him at long last. Again he wondered over her appearance and temperament. The woman might not be pretty at all.

Indeed she might be a complete shrew. He might not wish to be close to her as a husband should a wife. But that mattered little.

From this girl he needed only her title and her lands. And an heir to secure his future.

He had a dream. Nay, a goal. To take back the dukedom that was rightfully his. And if Morgaine's prophecy proved true, he would have it soon enough.

That dark, choking sensation rose up in his throat and overtook him again, as it always did when he considered his dalliance with magic. But such slight vexation would be well worth it once North Britannia was in his grasp.

Chapter 21

Wearing naught but a simple white chemise, Gwen sat before her looking glass, a luxury that had been bought by her father years ago to encourage her to take interest in her appearance. She observed the way her golden hair glowed in the firelight and brushed through it a few more strokes to watch it pool into gentle waves about her shoulders. Finally she believed it to be true.

She was pretty.

She must be if both Sir Allen and Sir Randel found her so. All her life she had thought herself ugly, had hardened her heart to keep from growing jealous of beauties such as Rosalind and the Duchess Adela. She had told herself she wanted nothing of that sort of silliness, that any attention to appearance was foolish.

Weak.

Drawn to the corner of the room like a moth to a flame, she floated in that direction. From beneath a loose floorboard, she pulled out a doll she had placed there nearly a decade ago. She returned to her seat with it and cuddled it to her chest.

Years earlier she had hidden the poppet her mother had bought for her. A gorgeous wooden doll dressed in a gown of silk. Her brothers had mocked it. Her father disdained it. And so she had buried it away, wanting to be strong and tough like them. Never wishing to be a victim like her mother.

But . . . she had taken it out when no one watched. She had loved it, admired it, stroked its polished, curving hair. Now with hesitant motions, she ran her fingers along its tresses, carved to perfection and painted a pale flaxen shade.

Then she returned her gaze to the mirror. The girl staring back at her did not look so different than that doll. She had a fine bowed mouth. Large wide-set blue eyes. A pert nose and a graceful slope to her cheeks. Smooth skin rose from the top of her chemise, and she protruded nicely where a woman should.

Yet she remained strong. Strong enough to thrive in a tournament. She could be both strong and feminine, could open her heart and be vulnerable without losing her passion and her fighting spirit.

She hugged the doll closer. How Gwen wished to care for a child of her own body like she once cared for this toy. Not merely nieces and nephews or village children, not only her little dogs as she had resigned herself to doing.

Perhaps a child with her blond hair and Al . . . or rather Randel's warm brown eyes. Soon enough she would adjust to this idea. Surely Mother would convince Father of their plan. Gwen must believe her prayers would be answered.

Cradling the doll in her arms, she rocked back and forth several times. Until a tap sounded at her door. On long-established instinct, she slid the doll across the wooden floor toward her bed.

It slid beneath just as Mother tiptoed in without awaiting an invitation. "He is asleep at last. I thought his foul temper might never end, but he usually wakes cheerful in the morning."

"I am sorry, Mother. I realized dinner was tense, but I did not know you continued to fight over my impending marriage."

Mother sagged into a chair beside Gwen. "Yes, mostly while you were at the cathedral. But he lectured me about my errant opinions well into the night."

"And?"

"He will not budge. Nothing I say can convince him."

Gwen tensed and attempted to conjure that hard shield that had protected her heart all these years. Why had she ever let it down? Why had she ever dared to hope?

"I am so sorry, daughter." Mother raked her fingers through her disheveled hair.

And that is when Gwen saw it. A bruise in blaring blue and purple sneaking out from the sleeve of Mother's gown.

She jumped up and grabbed Mother's wrist, pushing up her flowing sleeve and holding the injury to the firelight. "What is this? Did he hurt you?"

Mother snatched her wrist away and pulled the sleeve down again. She cuddled her arm to her chest and rubbed her thumb over the back of her hand. "'Tis nothing. Do not concern your-self. I only tried to escape his tirade and he grabbed me."

"I do not believe you!"

Then Gwen noticed a slight redness and swelling around Mother's right eye. She might have attributed it to crying, but that should affect both eyes equally, and given the evidence of the wrist . . . Gwen had seen such injuries before. "What else did he do to you?"

"Please, Gwendolyn, let it go. He has never hurt me in any permanent sort of way. It is my fault. I should submit to him. But I do not think straight when it comes to protecting you children." Mother began to sniffle.

Anger roiled inside of Gwendolyn. "Nonsense! This is abuse,

pure and simple. One must be an equal before one can submit. Yet he treats you like a scullery maid. This is your family too. You have a right to your own opinions."

"But he is the head of this home, not to mention the lord of our barony."

"Why do you let him treat you thus? Why do you take the blame for his brutality?"

"What option do I have? I am a weak woman from a poor family. I knew what he was when I married him, but I wanted the life he could offer. I made a choice and gave my pledge. I must accept it."

"I will not!" A red haze filled the room. Fury gathered in Gwen's head to the point that she feared it might explode. There it was. The fierceness. The strength. The armor about her heart. She found it again in her anger over this injustice, in her driving need to protect her mother.

Gwen marched to the leather chest at the foot of her bed. She grabbed out her leggings and boots and tugged them on. She tossed her split tunic over her head and thrust her arms into the openings. Next she tucked her dagger into her boot . . . just in case. She would not face the man unprepared.

"What on earth are you doing?" Mother pressed a hand to her mouth.

"What someone should have done long ago." Why had Hugh, why had Gerald, never stood up for their mother? She simply could not fathom.

Mother waved her hands before her. "Please, wait!"

"The time for waiting has passed."

Gwen stormed down the hallway and shoved open the door to her parents' bedchamber with a crash.

Father bolted upright upon his bed, tangled in blankets with his hair sticking straight toward the ceiling. "Who . . . what . . . ?"

Anger seethed within Gwen, pressing to be released through her fists. She balled said fists at her sides and planted her feet wide. "Do not ever hit my mother again. If you do, you shall answer to me."

A sleepy haze of confusion clouded his face. "What is the meaning of this?"

"'Tis about the bruises on my mother's arm. Do not ever touch her again, or I swear I shall thrash you. You horrible brute! You wish me to marry a man like you, but I shall never."

"Do not be ridiculous! You shall marry whomever I say."

"I swear that I will not. Just try and make me."

Father rolled out of bed. He pointed an accusing finger at her. "To whom do you think you address such impertinent words? Unclench those fists, you devil spawn."

"Never!" she shouted, pulling them up closer to her chest and shifting her feet to a lunge out of instinct.

"I mean it." He clenched his own fists at his sides.

In the dying light of the embers from the hearth, she watched his vein throb. Her own heart similarly pounded, but she did not relent.

"Fine," he said. "You think yourself a warrior, then prove it." He readied his fists for battle.

Gwen had not truly meant to fight him. Only to confront him over his shabby treatment of her mother. She faltered for a second as she considered her next move, but in that brief moment he snatched her right wrist and twisted her arm behind her back.

"Now we shall see who is the man." Then he shoved her away.

She fell hard upon her hands and knees but ignored the sting and sprung up to a crouched fighting position in a flash.

Though well into his middle years, Father towered over her, and his hard-muscled, mammoth girth stretched to twice her width. No doubt he expected her to tremble at his mere presence. But she was done cowering to this bully. Gwen was quick and agile, and now boiling with fury as well. She would not back down until she had inflicted a score of bruises upon him, as he had done to her mother over and again.

Feinting high and right, she slammed a blow into his gut. Her fist burst with searing pain as if she struck a stone. But his grunt of shock was all she needed to continue. She jabbed his jaw from the underside and followed it with another blow to his face.

Father stumbled backward, clutching his face. Blood dribbled from his mouth. His next words emerged garbled by his injury. "That is enough! I shall squash you like the pesky gnat that you are."

He roared toward her now. A sharp backhand across her face sent her sprawling toward the hard timber wall. Her shoulder hit first, then her head cracked upon it. Pain radiated through her in surging waves. Bright white spots flashed before her eyes, and a thickness filled her body, as if she moved through syrup, but still she would not give up.

Diving straight toward his middle, she slammed her head into his gut like a battering ram.

He tumbled backward onto the bed, but he rolled off just as quickly. "You disgust me. You hoyden. You maggot."

Stepping closer, he said, "I knew a girl child would bring nothing but trouble."

He glared down at her now with pure hatred. "I knew I could never love you."

Then through clenched teeth he ground out, "I should have snuffed out your life in the cradle."

Those words stretched out and struck Gwen with more force than his hand could ever muster. She felt them like a blow to the stomach. All air exploded from her in a pained gasp. She knew it. She'd always believed he had never loved her. But to hear him say it . . .

Gwen's fight drained from her like water from a broken cistern. Seeping out about her feet and puddling upon the floor. As her shoulders drooped and her arms fell to her sides, her father took that opportunity to punch her in the gut.

She flew backward and landed with a sick thud. He kicked her hard in the ribs and face over and again for good measure. But none of his assaults could hurt her, could wound her deep to her core, the way his words had.

"Get out!" He hauled her to her feet and threw her out the door. "And do not ever forget who is the man in this house."

Gwen stumbled in the direction of her room. Her vision failed her completely for the moment. She groped with her hands along the walls and around the corner until she came to the opening she knew to be hers. She made out the shape of her mother kneeling next to the blazing fire.

Wiping away her tears, her tangled hair, the blood pouring from a cut that throbbed over her brow, Gwen saw her mother's hands feverishly clicking beads upon a string. Mother's eyes clenched tight as her lips muttered Hail Marys.

Worthless words. Useless prayers.

"It is over," Gwen whispered.

"Gwennie!" Mother ran to her and caught her in an embrace.

Gwen groaned and grabbed her ribs.

"What has he done to you?"

"As you like to say, nothing permanent." He had only broken Gwen's heart.

"No." Mother choked out the word. "I cannot let this happen. Gwendolyn, I promise that I shall do something to help you."

Gwen could not imagine what. Neither of them had a shred

of power against the fiend who ruled over them. Rosalind had been mistaken. God did not hold her future in His hands. Father did, and he would snuff out all hope as he had just snuffed out her very reason for living. A hollow, aching dread filled the void left when her father broke her spirit.

He did not love her. He'd never wanted her. If one's own father wished one dead, why exist at all?

◇◇◇

"This is ridiculous." Allen gripped the rounded edge of the table in his frustration as he stared down the council. "I am to rule this dukedom soon, but you will not allow me to defend it?"

"Our best defense is to see you safely wed to the duchess." The old historian, Lord Fulton, pinched the bridge of his nose.

"But if Warner DeMontfort and his dissidents try to invade, we shall need every last warrior." Allen's hand itched to draw his sword even now. He had been wrapped up in tutoring and mundane legal obligations this past week. Other than their hunting trip, he had barely been outdoors to see the sun lighting the sky.

"If we are so worried about an invasion, then perhaps we should move up the wedding date," said Hemsley, dressed in a garish ensemble of red, gold, and purple this day. "That is our best guarantee for a secure dukedom."

"I would not advise that," the bishop said. "We are rushing matters as it is."

"Absolutely not!" Duchess Adela slapped her delicate hand atop the table. "It is too fast already. We have a feast to prepare. A tournament to organize. Surely you jest."

Hemsley's ostentatious purple plume flopped over his eye. "We can have the nuptials first and then celebrate."

Tears slipped down the duchess's cheeks.

"No!" Allen stood to his feet. "I refuse. It shall be eighteen days hence as planned or not at all."

"Let us all calm ourselves." Fulton pressed his hands in a downward motion against the air. "The wedding date shall remain as planned. And Sir Allen shall remain safe in the castle until it occurs. All those who agree, raise your right hand."

Hands shot up all around the table, sealing Allen's fate.

Allen dropped to his seat with resignation. "What about after the wedding?"

"Sir Allen, you must understand." The bishop offered him an apologetic grin. "As a duke you might someday lead a grand campaign, but you shall be the protected, no longer the protector."

The subject turned to a new issue. Clearly the matter was closed. Allen wished to bury his head in his arms and sulk, but of course he could not.

He would soon be a duke. Only the king would rank above him in this land. And yet he would trade the unbelievable honor in a heartbeat for an hour upon the practice field.

Dread filled him, threatened to suffocate him. Had he made a terrible mistake? This was not the life he wanted. Not the tediousness, nor the title, nor the weight of responsibility, and most assuredly—despite how lovely she might be—not the wife.

Chapter 22

"Please lean forward for me," Rosalind bid her mistress.

Gwendolyn obeyed, but with no life, no spark of recognition in her eyes.

Rosalind fluffed Gwendolyn's pillow and then laid her back upon it. She placed a cool cloth upon Gwendolyn's brow. Several days had passed, and the cut above her eye had scabbed over. The purple bruises on her face and ribs had faded to greenish-yellow, but Rosalind had no idea what wounds had been inflicted upon Gwendolyn's heart.

A wave of nausea struck Rosalind, and she retched into the chamber pot right in front of Gwendolyn. But the broken shell of a woman upon the bed did not bat an eye. Rosalind did not recognize this person anymore.

She cast the contents of the pot out the window onto the lawn below, then rinsed it with water from a basin, tossing that out as well. It was highly unlikely the baron and his wife suspected what she was coming to believe was a certainty—and she must keep matters so.

Gwendolyn stared at the wall across from her, as if all her life had drained out. If not even her protective nature, her concern for a friend's well-being, could draw Gwendolyn out, then there was nothing left to try.

This went far beyond her gloominess during her imprisonment, past her melancholy over losing Allen. Now Gwendolyn was a ghost, but in reverse. Surely somewhere her spirit lurked these halls, while her body remained naught but an animated corpse upon her bed. Rosalind would have never suspected her strong, resilient mistress could be reduced to this, but beneath it all she must have hid a fragile soul. It had chosen to flee rather than face life at the hands of that monster Gawain.

Rosalind left the desolate room and hurried in search of the Lady Barnes. She found her similarly staring at a wall in her own chamber with a goblet of wine clutched tight in her hands. But she rallied as she heard Rosalind approach.

"M'lady, what would your husband say?" Rosalind attempted to tug the goblet from the Lady Barnes.

The woman tugged it back and pressed it to her chest. "He is not here, and I no longer care." Her speech emerged slow and slurred.

"Have you received word from any of your sons?"

"Reginald will not help. He claims his father is within his rights to discipline Gwendolyn. Gerald's regiment has moved to Wales to deal with some rabble-rousers, so he is out of reach, and Hugh has not responded. But I warrant he will not leave the king at a time like this. He will not risk losing favor for our region over some minor domestic dispute."

"Minor? You call this minor?" Rosalind said with hands upon her hips. Truly, she should not treat the lady so. But no matter what direction she took these days, Rosalind was bound to rile someone, whether Lady Barnes, Lord Barnes, or Gwendolyn.

At some point she must simply do what she believed to be right and trust God to see her through.

"I promised Gwendolyn I would help, but I was rash," the lady said. "She brought this on herself, marching into his room in the dead of night like a firebrand. What did she expect?"

"I know well her temper, but clearly something is wrong beyond her physical injuries. And she shall not rouse from her stupor until she has good reason. 'Tis our job to supply her with that reason." Rosalind huffed in her frustration with the weak woman before her.

Lady Barnes drained her goblet. "I am tired. I wish to return to my bed."

"No! I will not allow it." Rosalind blocked her path. "Someone must fight for what is right."

"Why? We will not win. And I have no ideas left." The lady stumbled past Rosalind toward her bed and collapsed upon it.

Inspiration flared to life in Rosalind's mind. "I do!"

◇◇◇

Some part of Gwen registered the knock upon her chamber door, but she had no desire to deal with the real world. The real world was ugly. It was devoid of hope, of color, of love. So she would remain tucked within the cocoon of her own mind, where all was safe and beautiful and happy.

Voices wove around her, tickling at her senses, threatening to break the spell. But she did not wish to join them in the clattering, vicious land of reality. Instead she wished to gallop upon Andromache through a cool mountain stream as she had done not long ago.

Back in the real world, warm skin pressed against hers. Someone tugged upon her arm.

But she lifted her lance and faced off against her opponent.

She would win this time, as she always did in this wondrous land. No one could defeat her, no one could break her. In today's fantasy a child clapped from the sidelines. A familiar child. Her child. Allen's child. The girl now perched upon his hip, and he smiled to Gwen with pure sunshine flowing from his face.

Someone in that other realm whispered they were sorry.

And then that cool mountain stream rose up and crashed over her head in a torrent of ice, sucking her back into her bed. Freezing water coursed down her face. She blinked and sputtered against it, swiping frantically at her eyes even as frigid fingers dug deep into her torso and ran down her chemise to soak her bottom.

For the first time in days, she found her voice and squealed. "Ack!"

The room about Gwen came into focus. The faces of Mother and Rosalind hovered nearby, which she might have expected. What she did not expect was the duchess standing over her, looking annoyed, with a water basin resting upon her hip.

The duchess stretched out her arm to stop the other women from running to Gwen. "She will be fine." She leaned down to speak directly to Gwen's face. "But if you wish to don dry clothes and warm by the fire, then I am afraid you shall have to get out of that bed."

"I . . . but . . . you do not . . ." Gwendolyn did not know what to say. She could hardly scold the duchess.

"I do not what? I do not know how to rally a self-indulgent female who has lost her fight? I would rather say I do! Now get up."

The duchess hauled Gwen from the bed.

"Ouch!"

"Please be gentle with her," Mother said.

"The physician assures me nothing is broken. Sometimes

being kind is more important than being gentle, Lady Barnes.
We must take whatever action necessary to help Gwendolyn
in the long run."

"I suspect her father crushed her spirit more than her body,"
Rosalind said in her defense.

"I understand that. But this wallowing is quite unacceptable.
I am disappointed in you, Gwendolyn."

The duchess herself stripped Gwen's soggy shift. Rosalind
wrapped a warm blanket about her, and Mother helped her
into a chair.

"My apologies, Your Grace. 'Tis only that . . ." Gwen stopped
short.

"Only what, Gwendolyn?"

"You do not understand."

"I do not understand?" The duchess tapped her toe impatiently. "My husband has been murdered. My dukedom is in
disarray. I am being forced to marry a man little more than half
my age and after barely being given a month to mourn. Do you
see me wallowing about in bed?" She swept her hand toward
said bed. "No. I find my strength, and I do what I must."

Gwen choked back her shame. The duchess had survived so
much. Yet still she did not fully comprehend. "It is not the injuries.
I knew the risk I took when I confronted him. 'Tis just . . . he . . .
he said such awful things to me," she croaked out in a whisper.

"What sorts of things?" The duchess's demeanor softened.
She laid a soothing hand upon Gwen's shoulder and looked
deep into her eyes.

But Gwen had no desire to relive that awful night. She squeezed
her eyes closed and shook her head.

The duchess tipped up Gwen's chin and waited until she
looked at her. "You must cleanse this poison from your soul,
my dear. I know it will hurt. But it is the only way."

"He said . . ." The words caught in Gwen's throat, strangled about her. Ugly, horrible words. Far worse than punches and kicks could ever be.

"Go on," The duchess urged with a nurturing caress of Gwen's cheek.

Mother perched on one arm of her chair and took her hand. Rosalind cuddled in from the other side. "You can tell us."

"He said . . ." The words turned her stomach, rose up like bile in her throat. She had no choice but to expel them. "I am nothing but trouble." Her volume increased. "He never loved me." She bit her hand to stifle a cry. "He wished he had killed me in my cradle." Her voice cracked into a sob on that last awful word.

The three women surrounded her like a battalion as she cried out her soul. They covered her like a shield. Their love slipped deep into the dead places of her heart.

After a long while, her weeping died down to a sniffle.

"Gwendolyn." The duchess took her hands. "We love you. We need you. We want you. More than that, God made you as His own dear child. He has a calling and purpose for your life. Never let your earthly father convince you otherwise."

Allen and Randel had almost persuaded her that God loved her. But in light of all that had transpired in the past days, Gwen no longer felt certain. Yet the duchess of the entire region was here now beside her. Caring for her. Helping her to heal. Might not this be the intervention of God?

Gwen clasped her hands together. "But my father holds my fate. He will marry me to that brute Gawain. Please, just let me go back to the place where I was. There is no life, there is no happiness for me here."

"There must be a way." The duchess stood up straight and crossed her arms over her chest.

"If we defy him outright, he will hurt us again." Mother sounded so pathetic.

"And I realize you have authority in this region, but your position is tenuous right now," Rosalind said. "Would you truly wish to anger a powerful military leader like Lord Barnes?"

"His loyalty has been wavering ever since he returned. Sir Allen being appointed to the council, and now to be duke . . ." Mother's head drooped low. "If you deny my husband his right to choose a mate for his own daughter, I fear he will turn on you."

"He is a proud man." Rosalind trembled against Gwen's side. "If you humiliate him, there will be a high price to pay. The law yet allows him to discipline his own wife and child."

"I hate that law. We could never garner the support to overturn it. But never fear, I have known Lord Barnes and his ilk for a long time," the duchess said. "Such men must be handled delicately, but they can be handled."

"How?" Gwen asked, nearing desperation. She longed to retreat back to the sanctuary of her bed, but it would be soaked for hours at the least. Instead she focused her gaze upon a bird in flight outside her window. Perhaps she could drift away right here where she sat. Follow that bird into the clouds. Melt away from this awful place.

"Gwendolyn!" the duchess shouted and gave Gwen's shoulder a hard jerk. "Do not dare! I have an idea. It is coming to me. Just give me a moment."

All three of them watched the duchess as she paced the room. She alternately tapped her forehead and stroked her chin as she strode back and forth. Just when Gwen thought she might wear a dent into the wooden floor, stomps thudded toward them.

Father burst into the room, sporting his own array of bruises upon his face. "What is going on here?"

"The duchess has come to cheer our Gwendolyn." Mother shot a pointed look the duchess's way.

Father took a deep breath and settled himself. He swept a small bow in the direction of the duchess. "Your Grace. You honor us with your esteemed presence. But we should not take your time so. Allow me to escort you back to the castle."

"In a little while, but Gwendolyn and Rosalind shall be joining me. I did so enjoy their company upon their last visit. I have decided they shall come and stay with me immediately, rather than waiting for you to leave for Castle Barnes."

"But . . . but . . . of course. That makes sense." Father strung his words together with a degree of caution he rarely used. "And you might as well enjoy her now, for she will soon be wed."

The duchess lifted her chin and approached Father with understated authority. "I had hoped to speak with you about that. You have not yet finalized negotiations with the Ethelbaums, have you?"

"Well . . . not quite."

"Excellent!" The duchess grinned and clapped her hands together. "Then it will still work."

"What will work?" Father asked, concern etched upon his harsh features.

"My plan. Oh, you shall love it. I had wished for a way to honor you for your faithful service during the rebellion against King John, and this is just the thing. You shall be so pleased."

"So pleased? I shall?" Father eyed the duchess with suspicion.

"Indeed. Lord Barnes, faithful servant of North Britannia, I am about to bestow upon you the highest honor in the land."

"Honor? The council, perhaps?" A touch of hope now tinged his voice.

"Oh no! Much higher than that. For my upcoming nuptials we are to hold a tournament. And listen to this. Oh rapture! Oh joy!"

The duchess was pouring her performance out thick now.

Gwen hoped her father would not see through it, but he appeared entirely perplexed.

"Your own daughter, the famed Lady Gwendolyn the fair, shall be the prize. Can you believe it?" The duchess clapped again and bounced on her toes for good measure. "She shall wed the winner."

"I . . . oh . . . but what of the Ethelbaums? I would not wish to offend them." Father looked as though he might be sick.

The duchess swept away his concern with a delicate flick of her wrist. "Never fear, I shall speak with Lord Ethelbaum. Besides which, we all know Gawain is likely to win. So the conclusion of the matter shall be the same either way, but the process ever more fun."

Father scratched his head, causing his wiry greying hair to stand to attention. "I suppose you are right. I can hardly say no."

"No, you cannot." The duchess's simpering tone turned more firm.

"Right, then. I shall let you ladies return to your planning." Father slipped through the door and down the hall, mumbling under his breath the entire way.

"I do not understand." Rosalind spoke the words they must all have been thinking. "How will this help if Gawain is the reigning champion?"

"It was all I could come up with on short notice." The duchess sank to the dry edge of the bed. "Either this or a nunnery. The church has always provided sanctuary for young women such as yourself."

"Please, not a nunnery," Gwen begged.

"Then at least this plan gives us a chance," the duchess said. "It buys us some time and opens the door for more options."

"I do not wish to hope again." Gwen squeezed her eyes closed against the gnawing pang in her belly. "It hurts too much."

"You must not give up, darling." Mother pulled her close. "All is not lost."

"Without hope the heart will shrivel and die," the duchess said, "as your recent behavior attests. Gawain is a fool, and there must be a way to defeat him."

Mother leaned forward. "You know, we should not discount Sir Randel. He performed quite well in the last tournament, and this time he will have a stronger motive."

"Perhaps, but it would take a miracle." Gwen rested her cheek upon her knees and looped her arms about her shins, locking herself into that infantile position.

"Our God is a God of miracles," the duchess said. "We must not despair."

While the three ladies around her contemplated the issue, Gwen felt herself being pulled toward that other place. She pictured a little cottage deep in the woods. As she tended her babes, Allen entered the door with a huge poached deer across his shoulder.

"Hugh!" Rosalind shouted, pulling Gwen from her reverie once again. "We must get Sir Hugh back. He can fight on Lady Gwendolyn's behalf and choose a husband for her. He will choose Sir Randel for certain. 'Twas his idea to pair them in the first place."

"Hugh is with the king." Mother sighed, sounding defeated once again. "We have already discussed this."

"But I could request that he return for my wedding," the duchess said. "It is my right to request whomever I wish, is it not? I shall send Reginald in his stead for a time, for he seems to side with your father ever since the man returned. We would not want your eldest brother interfering."

"Excellent plan." Mother clutched her hands together.

"And how convenient that the tournament will be just one day prior to the wedding." The duchess wiggled her brow.

Then Gwen finally let herself feel it. That warmth burgeoning from deep within her chest. She could no longer hold it at bay. Hope washed over her. She would not retreat into her fantasy world again. No, she would do what Lady Gwendolyn Barnes did best.

She would fight.

Chapter  23

Allen riffled through the pages of the giant tome yet again. Fulton had given him until tomorrow to learn the extensive legal codes of North Britannia. Yet he had still been forced to spend the morning poring over castle accounts with the chief scribe.

He raked his fingers through his hair. Able to endure no more of that book, he allowed himself to take in the lovely scene surrounding him instead. The duchess and Rosalind stitched quietly in the corner of the solar, while Gwendolyn, who had no patience for needlework, stood playing a melancholy—albeit mesmerizing—tune on her pipe.

If only she might play something more cheerful, perhaps he could pull himself out of this gloom. Since Gwendolyn had arrived a week ago, he had not been able to rouse himself from his thunderous mood. The girl drove him near to daft with her very presence.

He tried to focus on the documents before him, but he had

stared at them so long that the words merely swayed in front of his eyes. Was it only weeks ago that he had been so fascinated by the procedures of North Britannia?

But he had had no idea that the dukedom had devised such a cumbersome legal code.

Such tedium made him long for the simple life he had enjoyed in Ellsworth.

"Here are my favorite people!" Sir Randel entered the room like a fresh breeze to chase away the thunderclouds.

"Greetings, Sir Randel," the duchess called with a smile.

Gwendolyn paused from her piping to wave at Randel.

"Do not stop on my account," Randel said. "I love to hear you play."

He pulled a chair backward before Allen's table and straddled it like a horse. "Good grief, Sir Allen, you look as though you will be hanged at sunrise. Whatever could be so bad?"

Allen would not mention his growing love for Gwendolyn, nor his heart sickness at being denied his dreams of battle. Instead he settled on the problem close at hand. "I am required to learn this entire code by tomorrow."

"Ridiculous! That load of bunk that Fulton has contrived? That man is far too generous with his words."

Allen smiled at that, for he had been thinking the same thing. "Then what do you suggest?"

"Most of it is common sense and Christian principles. If he asks you a question, base your answers upon those, and you shall do fine."

Allen flipped a page. "But is it not my duty as future duke to learn them by heart?"

Randel slammed the mammoth book closed and shoved it to the end of the table. "'Tis your duty to let me thrash you at chess." He slid the neglected board in front of them.

The duchess giggled from her corner. "Do take a break, Sir Allen. The council pushes you too hard. You shall go cross-eyed."

"You see." Randel began arranging the pieces. "Even your betrothed agrees."

"Fine." Allen set up his own side of the board. "I could use a change of pace."

As Randel studied the pieces and strategized his first move, Allen did some studying of his own. This congenial fellow would make the perfect husband for Gwendolyn. Much as it pained Allen to admit it, he had no doubt. Somehow, he must help Randel to win the upcoming tournament and secure Gwendolyn's hand, so that she might stay safe for good.

When Gwendolyn first arrived at Edendale Castle in her injured state, it had wounded Allen like a stake to his heart. She had assured him that her father looked no better and that she had provoked the man, yet he had noted a haunted glint in her eye. He must protect her—from both her father and that abusive Gawain—no matter the cost to his heart.

Randel made his first move, and Allen followed with his own.

He studied Randel's slender shoulders. Randel's only chance for beating the brute Gawain was to unseat him in the joust. Allen thought back over the last tournament. If he remembered correctly, Randel had unseated two opponents, but made a tragic error in his third run, which Allen had seized.

Allen paused with his piece in the air. "Sir Randel, have you had much training in the joust?"

Randel grimaced. "Is it so obvious that I have not? My parents wished me to enter the church, but I never desired such a life. Most of the training I received was in secret with Lady Gwendolyn and her brothers."

Allen nodded. "In that case, you manage quite well. But I

think with a few tips and a bit of practice, you could do even better. What say you to forgetting about chess and heading out to the field?"

The duchess cleared her throat and raised her brows.

Allen pushed away from the table. "I know. The council will not like it. I am sick near to death of the council."

"They might lock you up in the dungeon for safekeeping." She smiled.

"Let them try." Allen put a hand to his hilt.

"Yes, let them try." Sir Randel mirrored his stance with a wink. "Allen is going to teach me to win my ladylove. Let no man stand in our way."

Gwendolyn stuttered upon her pipe. She dropped it from her mouth and blushed prettily. "Thank you, Sir Allen. That is very kind of you."

Allen's heartbeat sped in that annoying way it always did at the sound of her voice. Her smile seemed to reach across the room and stroke his cheek, sending tingles through him that he must again ignore. Allen turned his gaze to the floor before he lost his wits entirely. "I wish only to see you happy, my lady."

"You have been fairly warned," the duchess said. "Do not expect me to deliver victuals to the dungeon."

Allen smiled wryly her way. "They might lock me up, but never fear—they will see their prize bull well fed." The expectations of the council wrapped around his neck like a noose. He must escape this solar and make his way outdoors at once.

Just as he and Randel turned to leave, a servant appeared in the doorway.

"Sir Allen, an important missive has come for you."

"For me?" Allen asked. Although he would be a duke soon, he was no one of any real consequence yet and had never before received a missive in his life.

"Yes, sir, it is addressed directly to you, and requires an immediate response."

Allen took the curious piece of paper from the servant. He did not recognize the seal, so he broke it and scanned down the page looking for a name. The letter was signed by Timothy Grey.

Only then did he realize that he had not even thought to thank the servant. Had he truly grown so entitled already? Wonderful! Just what he needed to make this day perfect.

Although, as he summoned his memories of Timothy Grey—dragging in their wake the surrounding ones of Merry Ellison—he realized that all vestiges of her hold over him had finally been broken. Now if he could only reach such a stage with Gwendolyn.

Although his eyes ached from so much reading this day, he forced himself to give the missive due attention.

My Dear Friend Sir Allen of Ellsworth,

It is my sad duty to inform you that Merry Ellison has been kidnapped by a brute to the north named Sir Warner DeMontfort. But allow me to go back for the sake of explanation.

Merry's title and lands were recently returned to her, thus significantly changing her status. She is now the wealthiest heiress in the land. Despite my new favor at court, the regent deemed me an unfit mate for her and promised her to the powerful Earl of Weathersby instead. While I understood his reasoning in not giving her to a lesser son of a baron such as myself, I am sure you will realize how heartbroken this left both of us.

Then matters changed yet again. This DeMontfort fellow, who is said to be after the dukedom in your own

North Britannia, sent a contingency of troops who kidnapped Merry. We believe he intends to force a marriage, and thereby claim Merry's title and lands for himself.

I assumed William Marshall would be livid, but he is acquainted with this DeMontfort. While a bit disgruntled at having his hand forced in the matter, he did not deem the situation worthy of sending troops for a rescue.

Thankfully, the young king spoke up on my behalf, and here is where the matter now stands: if I can muster my own troops and rescue Merry, she shall be mine. I realize it must pain you to read this, but I know you would want to help her.

I, together with the Ghosts of Farthingale Forest and some of my uncle's men, are rushing to DeMontfort's holdings with all the speed we can manage. Time will not allow me to stop by my father's home for more support, and even if I sent word, they would never arrive in time. In fact, I can only hope this missive will reach you before it is too late. We must save her before any marriage is official, or matters will become far more complicated.

And so, my friend, I must implore you. Gather whatever troops you can and meet me for this rescue. I hope to arrive in the village of Bixby on the 29th day of this month October.

Please, if you cannot bring yourself to do this for me, then do it for Merry. Her future and her happiness depend upon it. And I daresay the future of North Britannia might as well.

Your servant and friend,
Timothy Grey

Allen gripped tight to the missive with both hands. Realizing he had not taken a breath in several paragraphs, he drew a sharp one into his lungs. But the air did little to steady him nor to dull the ache in his stomach.

He stumbled backward into his chair.

"Sir Allen, what is it? Please tell us," Sir Randel said.

But Allen was still attempting to sort the words out in his own head. Merry kidnapped. In the clutches of that villain Warner DeMontfort. She had meant the world to him during their time in the forest. He yet loved her as a sister. Such could not be her fate.

◇◇◇

The occupants of the room all looked as confused as Gwen felt. The Duchess Adela should have been the natural person to comfort her espoused husband over this clearly tragic news, but she only shrugged her shoulders as if the moment were too private to interfere.

Gwen took the initiative, for she could not bear to watch him suffer alone. She placed her wooden pipe on the table beside the abandoned chessboard and laid a gentle hand upon his shoulder. "Please, allow me to read it, Sir Allen."

He nodded dumbly and handed the letter to her.

She scanned through the missive, and her heart clutched. "His good friend, Merry Ellison, has been kidnapped. He has told me of her on many occasions."

"I have heard his stories as well," the duchess said. "How horrible."

"It gets worse." Gwen swallowed down a thick lump in her throat. How she hated to continue. "She has been kidnapped by Warner DeMontfort." She went on to explain Merry's new status and Warner's evil plot. "This affects all of us. We must send troops at once."

"I will go with you!" Randel clapped a hand over Allen's forearm.

How Gwen's heart bled for this woman. How she commiserated with her horrible plight. She wished to jump on a horse and go save Merry herself.

The duchess stood and moved to the window. She stared out it a moment before speaking. "We cannot make this decision alone. As you said, Lady Gwendolyn, it affects all of us. The council will meet on the morrow. They must decide what course we will take."

That seemed to wake Allen from his stupor. He leapt to his feet. "But they will not permit me to fight for my dear friend. I must leave, now! If the council wishes to send reinforcements, they are welcome."

The duchess turned to Allen with a regal stare that would put even the fiercest warrior in his place. "We still have a day to make this decision. You will do nothing rash. You are soon to be a duke, and it is time for you to start thinking like a duke."

Allen deflated like an empty wineskin. Gwen ached for him. She understood his plight—to be denied one's dreams and passions. Why not just bury him in the grave? Yet she suspected Allen would do the honorable thing, even if it killed him. Just as he had chosen to deny his heart concerning her.

"Please, Sir Allen, do not be so dejected." The duchess gazed at something a far way in the distance. "You will survive this, just as I have survived years of being denied the opportunity to lead a campaign to the Holy Land. Someday, they say, when I have produced an heir."

The duchess's words caught Gwen's attention, despite the gravity of the moment. "A campaign? Like that of Eleanor of Aquitaine?"

"Yes, only more successful, I hope. My cousin Honoria and I have dreamed of taking a troop of women on crusade our whole lives. We could inspire and support the soldiers. Work as healers. Serve as an added line of defense during warfare. Though it might surprise some, I have quite a mind for battle plans. Perhaps I could even find my long-lost brother. But alas, it shall never be. Not with our current council." The duchess lowered her head.

"But *this* injustice is right in our own backyard." Randel stood firm behind Allen in a show of support. "We must save Merry Ellison. And Allen must be involved. Allow me to speak to the council on his behalf. They cannot deny him such a basic right, such a fundamental drive. A man must fight for those he loves."

"Do not concern yourself with this, Sir Randel." The duchess pinned her regal stare on him.

Randel bristled for a moment, but then conceded with a bow.

Dear sweet Randel.

Allen might deny Gwen. Might deny his own heart, yet it seemed some gracious deity in heaven would not see Gwen abandoned. The future was such a mutable and astonishing thing. Good, strong, reliable Randel. The gentlest knight in the realm. If she could not marry Allen, then she must pray with all her strength that somehow she might wed Randel.

Chapter 24

The following day as Allen concluded reading his letter from Timothy, members of the council shifted about in their chairs surrounding the huge round table. Not one offered him direct eye contact.

But he had rehearsed his arguments again and again and would not be thwarted. He rolled the crinkling parchment.

Then an echoing silence filled the place.

Finally, Lord Fulton spoke. "No, Sir Allen. Although I have compassion for your situation, it is not possible."

Allen had known he would not easily gain the council's permission, but he had not anticipated being dismissed summarily.

"Now on to the matter of . . ."

Before Fulton could move to the next subject, Allen rallied himself. "Hold, Lord Fulton. On which issue would you so quickly deny me? Sending troops to rescue Merry, or allowing me to go myself?"

"Both. As we have discussed, you and this city must be

protected at all costs right now. We cannot spare troops for superfluous missions."

Hot indignation flowed through Allen's veins. "Superfluous! Warner DeMontfort wishes to steal Merry Ellison's power and wealth to come against us. This is at the very core of what we fight. I am a member of this council too. Soon I will be your leader, and at the very least I demand a full debate on this issue!"

By the end of his impassioned speech his pulse pounded in his ears and his breath had grown quick, but he managed to stand firm rather than thump the table—or better yet kick it—as a part of him wished to.

The duchess calmed him with the lightest touch to his arm. "I agree with Sir Allen. We cannot brush this aside."

The bishop stood and cleared his throat. "And I agree with Lord Fulton. At this time nothing matters more than seeing the prophecy fulfilled. People are calling you the One True Heir of Arthur. All their hope, all their faith is tied to you."

The bishop's words reverberated through Allen, causing him to waver. They had placed their faith and hope in him, lowborn Allen of Ellsworth. Pride crested within his chest, a towering wave that might toss him from his purpose, but he shoved it down.

This Arthur nonsense had gotten out of hand. "The people of North Britannia should put their faith in God, not in a single man. I never claimed to be Arthur's heir."

The bishop folded his hands over his abdomen. "North Britannia will settle for no one but you, and DeMontfort is a fool if he thinks kidnapping an heiress will change that."

"But if William Marshall supports his bid, that could ruin everything." Allen raked his fingers into his hair. He must make them see reason. "We should put our efforts into proving DeMontfort a murderer and thwarting his plots."

"No evidence has been found," said Hemsley, bedecked this day in an outfit that would put a rainbow to shame. "We must stay our course. Once the prophecy is fulfilled, all will be well."

"You do not understand." Tears pricked at Allen's eyes now, but he would not suffer these pompous fools to see him cry. "This woman is like a sister to me. Would you allow your sister, your daughter to remain in such jeopardy?"

"I am sorry, Sir Allen. I do understand your desire to protect your friend." Hemsley fiddled with his striped hat and turned his gaze down to the table.

"I will require only enough guards to travel safely, and we shall rely on cunning, not might, to rescue her."

Fulton shook his head. "It is not possible."

Allen had only one more strategy to try. "'Tis not right that you place your hope in me. The Duchess Adela is the one the people trust. She is the one with the experience to lead. You said the king would respect our current legal decisions, so make a law allowing her to rule alone and choose her own husband."

At that pandemonium broke out. Several men shouted at once. Words like *nonsense, fool,* and *upstart* flew about the room.

The bishop lifted his hands and hollered, "Silence."

They settled and took their seats once again.

"Let us not disparage our soon-to-be leader," the bishop said. "He is young, he is new to our ways, and his heart is broken for his friend. But Sir Allen, the matter is closed. If and when Warner DeMontfort attacks, we shall be prepared. But we have the assurance of the prophecy that all will be well."

Allen scanned the table for any supporter, for a single sympathetic glance. Only the duchess smiled at him with compassion. By a slight dip of her head, she gestured for him to sit.

He wanted to shout, to fight, to draw his sword and dash for the door, but no true noble would do such things. No chivalrous knight would shirk his duty to his dukedom. He had wanted to live in a place where law and the council of many ruled the day. Yet he could not accept their decision as right. It sank into his chest with a hollow ache.

Somehow he must find a way to help Merry. In the deepest part of him, that conviction still burned.

◇◇◇

As Rosalind and Lady Gwendolyn concluded their daily walk, Edendale rose on either side of them, indeed a jewel of a city. Not that Rosalind had ever visited another, but she knew beauty when she beheld it. She doubted even the famed city of London could match this place. Here on the well-protected streets, two young women could stroll alone at leisure, needing not fear thieves or ruffians.

Passing through the row of vendors hawking wares from their stalls in the marketplace, Rosalind drank in the wondrous sight of her mistress wearing a soft and relaxed expression for once. The mood was right.

She must find the courage to seize this moment and approach Gwendolyn with her request before disaster struck. "My lady, you look well today."

Gwendolyn drew in a deep whiff of the fresh mountain air. "I never suspected city life would suit me so well, but we are allowed such freedom in this place. A freedom that, sadly, does not reach to Castle Barnes."

"But we made our own fun there."

Gwendolyn smiled. "We did indeed. But we were always risking trouble as well. This new life with the duchess brings me much joy. And were you there when she mentioned arranging another hunt?"

"I recall something to that effect."

Gwendolyn must have caught the wistful hint in Rosalind's voice, for she frowned. "Are you happy here, Rosalind?"

"I love living in the grand castle. But . . . actually, your question brings up a matter about which I have been wishing to speak to you."

"Speak plain. Surely we have no need to mince words after all we have been through together."

"'Tis just that I have not visited my mother in over a year. And we are so close to my village. Do you suppose I could take a few days off from your service? The castle is full of maids who might attend you. And . . . and . . . I miss her so."

Gwendolyn ceased her progress and turned to grip Rosalind's shoulder. "Of course! You need not list your reasons so carefully. In fact, I apologize. I should have thought of this, although missing one's mother is admittedly a sensation I am not familiar with."

Relief washed over Rosalind. How she needed her mother's wisdom and insight right now. She could not afford to lose her employment. She recalled that awful year after her father's death when her siblings had sobbed with hunger. When she herself had been gripped by the gnawing pains. She could never allow that to happen again.

And time was running out. "Thank you! Thank you so much, Lady Gwendolyn. I shall go quickly, and I promise not to cause you any trouble."

"Stop that! Why must you continually draw attention to the gap between our statuses? We are in Edendale, a place where such differences melt away."

"Diminish. Not melt away entirely." Although, had not Rosalind thought the same thing as she played games and did embroidery in the duchess's own solar? As she danced with knights and conversed with ladies over supper in the evenings?

But such thoughts always brought her back to Hugh and gave her hope. Far too much hope for her own good. Especially in her present circumstance, which would not be ignored much longer. "But again I thank you for your kindness. I have been near desperate to see my mother. I shall leave this very afternoon, if that is acceptable."

"I shall arrange an escort."

"Absolutely not. My village is less than an hour from here, and the roads are well traveled. I took the trip many times alone before coming to live with you and always found a traveling companion with ease." Besides which, Rosalind needed to do this thing by herself.

Gwendolyn's features twisted into a look of concern. "I do not like it. Sir Randel is probably free. I know he would not mind taking you."

Rosalind laughed. "You are being silly now. Not all of us can be pampered noblewomen." Although for the first time such a statement caused a stab of pain to her gut. Perhaps this place was not as good for her as it was for Gwendolyn. "I will be fine. I promise."

"You must take a sword. And a dagger." Gwendolyn wagged a finger in Rosalind's direction. "And a bow!"

"Yes, Lady Gwendolyn," Rosalind agreed happily, ever so thankful for this chance. Her mother would know just what to do. She would fix everything. She always did.

◇◇◇

Gwen still did not love the idea, but she supposed Rosalind could defend herself as well as anyone. She turned to continue down the lane toward the castle. "And if I learn that you did not find a traveling companion, I shall throttle you."

Rosalind smiled and looped her arm through Gwen's. "Fair enough. But let us hurry. I must pack."

Gwen smiled in return, glad to see Rosalind so bright and cheerful. Though she had not mentioned the issue, realizing that Rosalind would perceive it as criticism, she had been worried about her maid this past week. The vivacious girl had not been herself, lacking her normal energy and glow.

Perhaps the problem had started longer ago, and Gwen had merely failed to notice due to the tension with her own family and all the trouble she had managed to get into. Now that they spent much of their time in the peaceful company of Duchess Adela, Gwen could not ignore Rosalind's distress. She had feared Rosalind might be ill or troubled in her spirit.

But homesickness—that would be easily remedied.

As they passed through the huge castle archway to the inner bailey, a strange sight caught Gwendolyn's attention. In the corner near the stables, Sir Allen slumped upon a hay bale with his chin nestled in his fists. She had never seen him melancholy before, had not thought such a mood possible in a man so strong, so capable, so focused upon heavenly matters. Today was full of surprises.

But then she recalled his meeting with the council over his dear friend Merry. She glanced about for someone who might cheer him, but saw no prospect in sight. Perhaps she should go find the duchess, as wisdom would suggest. But she could not bear to leave him alone like this for so long.

She nudged Rosalind and inclined her head in Allen's direction. "I shall catch up with you straightaway."

"Poor fellow. I suppose he shan't be helping Lady Merry after all. Take whatever time you need."

As Rosalind headed across the sunny courtyard to the castle, Gwendolyn took hesitant steps toward the shadows that enveloped Sir Allen. Only when she sank down on the hay bale beside him did he even glance her way.

She had no platitudes to offer him, and knew a direct fellow like Allen would not appreciate them anyway. After a few moments, she simply rested a hand on his taut, muscled back and said, "I am here for you."

"Thank you, Gwendolyn. You alone in this place seem to understand me."

"I am happy to listen, if you wish to share your troubles."

He kicked at the dirt and took a few deep breaths before responding. "I know I should be thankful. I know they offer me honor and privilege I by no means deserve. A part of me loves it. It certainly swells my pride. But somewhere deep inside it does not sit well with me."

Gwen understood that feeling all too well, for somewhere deep in her heart it did not sit well with her for Allen to marry the duchess. But she kept her thoughts to herself and merely rubbed his back in gentle circles, offering her support without pointless words.

"When Merry Ellison taught me to fight, to protect, I knew I had found my purpose in life. But now the council has stripped me of that. I cannot even help the woman who once saved me."

She thought long and hard before she voiced her next words. Gwen did not wish to encourage treason, but well she knew that sometimes the authorities in one's life bullied rather than ruling with wisdom and respect.

Beyond which, she felt such kinship with Merry, who would soon be wed against her will. "Are you certain you cannot help her? Should you not follow your own heart in such a weighty matter?"

"They refused me outright. This is not like when I rebelled

against the evil King John. I cannot defy such a God-fearing council. I must live up to my duty."

"I understand your concern about duty. And I admire your willingness to put the good of the dukedom before yourself." Much as his decisions along that line had caused her pain. "However, this is a different situation. The council is acting foolishly by putting superstition over sound logic, and you have a duty to Merry that precedes your duty to North Britannia. There are two opposing duties, two opposing rights. And I say in such a case you must follow God's leading in your own heart."

Allen shook his head and buried it deeper into his hands. "But is it God's leading? Or is it my own impulse?"

"Only you can say for certain. But I have never known you to be impulsive or selfish, and I doubt you would start now."

For a moment, Allen stared into the distance. "You are right. I do feel led to assist Timothy. And as you say, I know in my heart this is right."

"Excellent!" His sense of peace over the decision drifted toward Gwen and engulfed her as well. "And I shall go with you. I can sneak into DeMontfort's castle. No one will suspect a woman."

"Don't be silly. You must stay here."

Her pulse quickened. "Am I not to follow my own convictions as you shall follow yours? Would you bind me to this place as the council attempted to bind you?"

"I cannot be responsible for you at a time like this. I shall be in enough trouble as it stands."

She leapt to her feet, as her temper flared fully to life. "Who said I was your responsibility? I can take care of myself. Have you not deduced that by now?"

"'Tis just that I shall be distracted by worrying about your safety if you're along."

"Men! You are all the same." She stomped her foot and turned her back on him.

He stood now as well and took her by the shoulders. "I am sorry to disappoint you. But this situation is hard enough for me."

Gwen's heart melted at that. She did understand how difficult it would be for him to defy the council. She turned in his grasp to face him. "I only meant to help."

"Thank you." He rested his forehead briefly against hers, causing her pulse to race for a different reason now.

He must have experienced the same rush of feelings, for he shoved her roughly away. "Thank you for your wise counsel and for your cooperation," he said in a more stilted, formal manner. "I must go and prepare."

Gwen stood with her hands on her hips as he walked away. She would not trouble him with more arguments, but he had misunderstood entirely if he assumed she would cooperate and sit idly at the castle while Merry Ellison needed rescuing.

"Adventure awaits," she whispered to herself and headed to her chambers to prepare for her own journey.

Chapter 25

Long after the sun had set, Gwendolyn stalked through the patch of trees surrounding the camp of Allen and his men. She pushed through the underbrush and crept as close as she dared to better assess the situation and their moods.

The group sat about a crackling fire, teasing and laughing—except for Allen, who stared pensively into the flames. She spied Randel along with several of his cohorts from among the castle guards—trustworthy and skilled knights, all of them.

After seeing Rosalind off, Gwen had made short work of "sequestering" the necessary supplies for her journey. Along the way, she had stayed a goodly distance from the men, always at least one turn in the trail to their rear. In a moment she would reveal herself and deal with the lectures that she by all means deserved.

An insect tickled her cheek, and instinct bid her to swat it away.

One of the guards leapt to his feet and grabbed his sword. "Halt, who goes there?"

Good for him. She had been surprised to have gotten so far.

Lifting her hands over her head, she stepped out of the concealing shadows into the flickers of firelight. "'Tis only I, Lady Gwendolyn Barnes, attendant to Duchess Adela."

The man appeared confused. "Have you brought us a message?"

Randel stood and jogged to her with his typical relaxed grin spread across his face. "Ho, Gwendolyn! Perfect. I do not know why I never thought to bring you along. You are just the person to assist us."

But Allen stood as well and shoved Randel aside. Holding up a stern finger to warn the man off, he grumbled, "Stay out of this, Sir Randel. I shall deal with the lady."

Thunderclouds seemed to gather over Allen's normal sunshine expression as he stormed in Gwen's direction. Randel, not so easily thwarted, followed a few feet behind.

Allen took Gwen by the arm and pulled her into the thicket. "I thought we had an agreement!"

Gwen had never seen him angry before. It seemed this idyllic man contained a full gamut of emotions after all.

Yet his anger lacked the bitter disdain of her father's, and so she pressed on. "I dropped the subject but made no promises."

"This is unacceptable! Where does the duchess think you are?"

Gwendolyn waved away his troublesome question. "Called to Castle Barnes by my mother for a time."

He dug his fingers into his forehead and rubbed it in frustration. "I am disappointed in you, Gwendolyn."

"Why do you insist I cannot help when you followed this Lady Merry into raids and forays?" Her temper flared to life now, but she did not intend to lose her control and this battle along with it.

He huffed. "Lady Merry was well-trained, and the circumstances were highly unusual."

Randel pushed into the thicket beside them. "Sir Allen, my apologies, but I believe you greatly underestimate Gwendolyn's abilities. And I shall take personal responsibility for her."

Allen swung toward him with a ferocity she had not thought him capable of. "*You* would answer to the council, to her brute of a father, if any harm came to her?"

Randel did not so much as flinch. "I would. For I know, and her brothers know, and I dare say even her mother knows that she is every bit as capable of protecting herself as half the fellows we brought along. Beyond which, her gender might stand in our favor if we must sneak into Warner's castle."

"You see." Gwen batted Allen in the arm. She was growing impatient with his stubbornness. "I said as much."

Allen turned back to her and cocked a brow. "You wish to use 'I said as much' as your brilliant defense?"

"Oh, hush! Are you going to let me come or not?"

He huffed again and kicked at the dirt like a young boy throwing a tantrum. So much for her perfect Allen of Ellsworth, yet she longed to reach out and smooth his furrowed brow nonetheless.

He pressed his fists into his hips and stood with his feet wide. "You have left me little choice. But if Timothy bids you stay at camp, you will obey, and you will not cause a bit of disturbance. Do I make myself clear?"

"Abundantly." Gwen conceded, although she was careful to agree to nothing else.

Randel winked to her from behind Allen's back.

Her old friend knew her well. Come tomorrow, she was not about to miss this one last grand exploit before she wed and resigned herself to a life of wretched needlework and board games.

Lady Merry Ellison needed her, and she would not let this kinswoman of the heart down.

◇◇◇

"So what now?" asked Sir Randel as they surveyed the valley just outside their prearranged meeting village of Bixby.

Allen scanned the foliage surrounding them. "Give them a minute. I suspect they will come to us."

Gwendolyn sat still and straight upon her horse. She had done nothing along their route that might draw undue attention to herself. Nonetheless Allen's senses remained highly attuned to her every step of the way.

As she stretched her back in an appealing manner against the strain of their long day's ride, his awareness of her soared to such a precarious height that he nearly missed the call of the crested lark.

"Hold!" He held out a hand to silence them all.

Then it came again. He returned the call.

A moment later his old cohort Cedric came crashing through the bushes with a comic grin stretched so wide across his slender face that it nearly grazed his overly large ears. "Allen! It really is you. I could hardly recognize you in that fine surcoat."

He ran to Allen, and Allen hopped from Thunder to meet Cedric with a manly hug and several thumps on the back. Cedric pulled away and swiped at his eyes. "Stupid dust. Can't escape it in this dry northern climate."

But tears pricked Allen's eyes as well. "I never dreamed I might see you again so soon."

"Come, Timothy is anxious to see you."

As Cedric led Allen's horse by the reins, the rest of the troop, Gwendolyn included, fell into step behind them.

"So have you had a chance to scout the area?" Allen asked.

"We have. Lady Merry's being held in DeMontfort's small fort of a castle. He looks to have ample soldiers, but they mostly laze about down the hill. We presume he must be preparing for an attack on North Britannia but not expecting a strike upon his own holdings."

"Excellent. So stealth will be our best ally."

Cedric eyed him and cocked a brow. Together they chanted, "'Stealth. Anonymity. Restraint. These are our allies. These three we shall never betray,'" then chuckled at the pleasant memory.

"What is this?" Randel pulled up beside them.

"So sorry, Randel. I should have introduced you to my friend Cedric, a fellow Ghost of Farthingale Forest."

"That mantra you just heard served us well for two years. Until Merry stole that chest of gold headed for the king." Cedric gestured with his chin. "We're nearly there."

"Goodness, Sir Allen," Randel said. "Sounds as if you have some stories to share tonight. I shall not suffer you to sit in silence again."

Allen smiled, but the thought of retelling his tales to Gwendolyn made his stomach twist in a knot. Why did the girl not understand that he could never focus properly with her about looking so charming in her men's leggings and boots?

They continued skirting the village and then headed into a copse of trees. Allen quickly spotted Timothy. He felt none of his old jealousy nor discomfort as he gripped Timothy Grey's arm in greeting. Only the affinity of two men determined to save one man's love and the other's friend.

"I am so relieved you have come." Timothy sighed.

"Nothing, and I do mean nothing, could have stopped me." Allen reached over and tousled Timothy's hair, both because he knew that Timothy hated it, and because that smooth, white-blond thatch begged to be mussed.

Timothy ducked away and playfully delivered a punch to

Allen's firm stomach. "Ouch!" Timothy chuckled as he shook out his hand. "Seems as though I have called upon the right man."

"I am so glad to help." This time Allen made proper introductions, including Lady Gwendolyn, whom the men all eyed with curiosity. Once everyone settled in, they gathered together in a planning council.

"Robert, I think you have the best handle on the situation," Timothy said.

Shrewd Robert had served as their tactical advisor back in Farthingale Forest. "We noted that a number of village women enter the castle in the morning. Some apparently to bake bread, and others to stay and—we suppose—to serve as maids and cooks and the like. The guards paid them little heed."

"So we were thinking we could dress as women and sneak in." Cedric cackled, slapping his bony knee. "We haven't done that in years."

Allen shook his head. "But we were all much smaller at the time."

"Which is why I suggested I go alone." Robert, shorter and slighter than the rest, shot a glare at Cedric.

"Aww, I never get to have any fun." Cedric's shoulders slumped.

"Your foray as a traveling tumbler into Castle Wyndemere will have to suffice," Gwendolyn said with a light giggle and a sympathetic smile.

At that comment, all the Ghosts sent pointed glances Allen's way. Allen's air whooshed from his chest. Gwendolyn must have paid close heed to his stories to remember such details. But had he not memorized every word she said, every note she played, every crook of her finger as well?

"Why risk detection?" asked Randel, striding to the center of the gathering. "Lady Gwendolyn is a skilled fighter and excellent at subterfuge, not to mention an actual woman. I can attest to her abilities."

"Perfect!" Cedric shouted, pumping his fist in the air.

"No!" Allen shouted louder. "We cannot risk the Lady Gwendolyn on such a dangerous mission."

"Then why did you bring her along?" Cedric asked, scratching his head of short cropped hair.

"In fact, I did not." Allen ground out the words. "It is out of the question."

"You said Timothy could decide," Gwendolyn reminded him in a gentle tone.

Robert frowned. "Our young women proved quite helpful on missions in the past. I don't understand your resistance, Allen."

Allen glanced about, but could think of no reasonable answer, other than his absurd level of attachment to Gwendolyn, which he could hardly confess.

"What say you, Lady Gwendolyn?" asked Timothy, crossing his arms over his chest and tilting his head as he awaited her reply.

Gwendolyn lifted her chin and stood firm. "No one understands the plight of Lady Merry Ellison as much as I do. To be forced to marry a brute against your will . . . That is the most horrid fate a woman could endure. If you allow me to lead this mission, I swear to you, I will not fail."

A hush fell over the clearing.

"Allen?" Timothy pinned him with a gaze. "Have you any further complaint? For I am quite convinced."

"As am I." Red spoke up for the first time during the meeting. "The rest of us will be at the ready to offer support."

Allen's thoughts swirled in his head. Of course they were right, but still he could not bring himself to speak the words that would put Gwendolyn in jeopardy.

Timothy crossed to Allen and wrapped an arm about his shoulder. "Perhaps Allen and I should speak in private for a moment." He led Allen away from the others to a shadowy spot just beyond their view.

But Allen knew nothing he might confess to Timothy would change the man's mind. It seemed Gwendolyn would have her way, and somehow Allen would have to cope.

◇◇◇

Gwen sat before the fire between Cedric and Red as they told her more tales of the Ghosts of Farthingale Forest. She felt as if she knew the cheerful fellows already.

In the orange and gold dance of light, she studied them closely. Cedric, who was even more comical than she had dared imagine. Red, whom she could perfectly picture in his masked knight costume. A piece of her wished she could tell them about her own experience as a disguised knight, but as she had not yet confessed to Allen, she held her tongue.

"And that is the story of the day the catlike Lady Merry Ellison tumbled from a tree." Cedric concluded his most recent tale.

"You have all lived the most astounding adventures." Gwen could hear the hint of awe in her own voice. "So what advice can you give me for my mission tomorrow?"

"Robert, James, come and join us." Red called over more of the former Ghosts.

The two hunkered down on either side of their group before the fire.

"What advice have we for our comrade-in-arms?" Red asked them.

Robert narrowed his eyes until he looked like a hawk honing in upon his prey. "For an undercover mission, success is always in the small, random details."

"So true," James said.

Cedric hopped to his feet. "Like when we snuck into the castle as traveling players, we insisted we were from Leeds, only not the main village, the part to the north. For my old grandmother lived in the main section, and she hated my mum ever since they fought about that blasted parsnip recipe." The lump in Cedric's gangly throat bobbed up and down as he laughed at the memory.

"Or when I was the masked knight, I mentioned that in my last tournament I nearly forfeited because someone had run over my left big toe with a cart." Red chuckled.

"Precisely," Robert said. "If you pour on the details, they'll be too intrigued, or confused, or in some cases too bored"—he shot a look to Cedric—"to question you."

"When you sneak in with the village women," James said, "you'll need a good reason why you're in town."

They huddled together to consider the possibilities.

In that moment Gwen truly wished she could be part of a band of forest outlaws. But at least tomorrow she would get to experience the adventure of a lifetime. She would not let the Lady Merry down. Yet her own future still loomed bleak before her. A future in which—if she were completely honest with herself—only a miracle from a God she was not sure how she felt about could save her from misery with that awful Gawain.

A new idea began to brew in her mind. Perhaps she should not return home at all. She wondered if Lady Merry Ellison might have need of an attendant.

One never knew what the future might hold.

Chapter 26

Warner carried a tray of steaming food down the shadowy corridor to his new lady's bedchamber. In addition to the fact that not a single one of his maids could be convinced to serve the beautiful young hellion, he yet needed time to win her to his side.

A guard in full armor eyed him warily and placed his hand upon the door latch. "Are you certain?"

"As certain as I shall ever be," Warner said.

The guard unlocked the door, cracked it open, and peered around. With a shrug, he gestured Warner into the room.

Lady Merry Ellison sat stiff upon a chair in the corner of this dim chamber hidden deep in the interior of the castle fort. The room's only window bolted shut from outside.

She did not so much as twitch upon his entrance. Thank goodness, for his former bites and scratches had yet to heal.

Though Warner was a well-trained fighter, this tiny lady with her dark brooding good looks had done some significant damage upon their first encounter. But for his last two visits, she had ignored him entirely. He knew not how to convince her that he was not a villain. Merely a dispossessed duke desperate to regain his rightful place in the world.

Warner flashed her his most winning grin. "I had the cook prepare you something special. My favorite roasted pheasant along with some apple tarts."

"I hate apples." She grumbled her first semi-civil words at him without deigning to make eye contact.

Hiding his shock, he continued in a pleasant tone. "I warrant that is not true. Everyone loves apples." He chanced moving a few feet closer and lowering the tray onto her table. "Come, you must keep up your strength, no matter what the future might bring."

"Actually, I find withering away preferable to any fate you have planned for me."

"Unfair," he said. "For you have not been willing to discuss my plans."

"I care not about your plans." She turned her head farther away from him. "Not a single person has ever given a care for mine. Why on earth am I constantly being kidnapped?"

He chuckled. Warner would not have guessed that she had experience with such situations. Nor had he guessed how tough she might be. Truly, he wished someone had warned him.

"Since you asked," he continued as if she had, "I plan to make you my lawful wife. And once you are, we shall attack North Britannia, of which, by all rights, I should be duke. A bright future awaits you, my pretty. You have no reason to sulk."

Just as he thought to reach for her petite hand to offer a kiss, the glare she shot him brought to mind the teeth marks deep in his arm, and he left her be.

Did the girl give him no credit for remaining a gentleman? If his treacherous sister, Morgaine, had her way, he would have forced Merry into marital intimacies on her very first night here, thus ensuring his plan. But he was determined to play the hero in this saga. He would remain a righteous man, despite his brief entanglement with his sister's magic. His new bride would come to understand this soon enough.

He did not wish to begin their relationship in an ugly and forcible manner, but she had made matters difficult these past days by her refusal to concede to his charm. He had arranged for them to be left alone all night on the morrow, in a small cottage. By the following morning, they would be considered wed, with or without her consent. And once she was legally his, Warner would take great pleasure in consummating their marriage.

He could not put it off any longer than that, as he must make her safely his before any forces might be rallied to rescue her.

Lady Merry had proven far more enticing than he had dreamed. More attractive than he had dared to imagine, even when—or perhaps especially when—she glared at him so. Never before had he made a noblewoman his own, and well he deserved such a long delayed pleasure. Like it or not, Merry would accept him.

But being the congenial sort of fellow that he was, Warner yet wished she might enjoy their union. "Tell me something about yourself, Lady Merry. For I so wish to become better acquainted. What did you do to occupy your days before coming here?"

She arched a brow with scorching disdain. "If you must know, I was an outlaw. I spent my days training to skewer arrogant noblemen upon the point of my sword."

Warner must keep a close watch on this one. He had heard rumors that her father committed treason against King John. Indeed, she might have been outlawed for a time. But as half the country rose up in treason two years later, Warner would not hold that against her.

Once she was settled as duchess in the resplendent Edendale Castle, he dared say she would have no complaints. By the time the sun rose twice in the sky, she would be his.

◇ ◇ ◇

The next morning, Gwen fell in step with the village women as they gathered in the main clearing. Together, they headed up the road toward a stern-looking castle made of nearly black stone. She shivered at the sight of the decrepit tower rising high over the rest of the structure. It appeared the perfect setting for a scary story, and she sent up a quick prayer that she should not have to enter it.

Buried deep in the folds of her hood, she attempted to blend with the group.

"I say!" The old woman in front of Gwen turned on her heel to confront her. "Who are you? I've never seen the likes of you around 'ere before. Speak up at once, for we'll not be tolerating any mischief."

Ten more women quickly drew ranks around the elder spokeswoman with her greying hair and crinkling eyes.

Thankful that Timothy had sent her and not Robert, Gwen pushed back her hood and did her best to put on a rough accent. "I am sorry to 'ave disturbed you. 'Tis just that me brother, me wee Timmy, 'e's so sick with the ague. We was travelin' through, but I feared 'e weren't gonna make it much farther. Stopped by your 'ealer, I did. A Dame 'iggins, you know."

"Of course we do." The women all seemed to relax.

Gwen scanned her mind for the details she had prepared. "Just about scared me out of me wits, she did, what with that wart and all. I thought at first she might be a witch, but she assured me she's just a plain old herbalist. I sure 'ope she spoke true. Wouldn't want to get me brother caught up in no black magic."

The women all chuckled at that. "Never fear," their leader said. "In this case, appearances are deceivin'. If there be any witch in these parts, she's not in the village."

She shot a pointed glance toward the eerie tower that had previously drawn Gwen's attention. Then she said, "My name is Millicent, and these 'ere are my friends."

"I'm Gwen." She saw no need in choosing a false name, for she would have enough details to keep straight.

"Shall you be with us long?" asked a different woman with blond braids.

"That depends, I s'pose. Me brother could use lots of tendin', but I don't 'ave no funds. Dame 'iggins said I might find a bit of payin' work at the castle."

"Come along with ye." The elder spokeswoman, Millicent, herded them all in the direction of the castle. "As fate would 'ave it, our Ermina is down with the nursing fever. You can take 'er place just as long as you need."

"O thank ye! Thank ye! I never dreamed of such fortune."

Old Millicent reached out to give Gwen's shoulder a pat. "Never ye fear, 'ere in Bixby we take care of our own. Lord knows yon tyrant shan't."

Gwen took a moment to study the women. Although peasants in general wore rough clothing and aged more quickly than their noble counterparts, this group appeared particularly downtrodden.

She sent up another prayer that Warner DeMontfort would not take out his anger on these innocent bystanders. For one way or another, she would be rescuing Merry from his castle today.

◇◇◇

Allen, dressed once again in his obscuring outlaw attire of rough flaxen fabric, peeked from behind an oak tree and scanned the castle walls for the thousandth time. Gwendolyn had been inside that dark and eerie place for nigh on two hours.

If ever he truly convinced himself that he did not love the girl, he now realized it had been a lie. For he felt as if his very heart, vulnerable and stripped from his chest, had gone into Warner DeMontfort's dangerous lair.

Although he knew Randel hid close by to his left, Allen could spy none of his comrades, who were likewise dressed to blend with the fall foliage. Each of them had been equipped with swords, a bow, arrows, and ropes.

So far Allen had counted two of DeMontfort's men standing watch at the gate, and three more upon the wall. Perhaps another one or two walked the courtyard, but he could not say for certain.

On their side were Allen, Timothy, four Ghosts, and—between the men from Edendale and Lord Linden's castle—ten other well-trained soldiers. Allen no longer knew which group to count himself among, as he had once been a part of each. They likely outnumbered any nearby guards two to one. But an entire squadron of soldiers lazed less than a furlong away.

How Allen wished he could just dispatch with that troublesome DeMontfort here and now, but he was taking a great risk by helping with this mission at all. Besides which, they had no proof that he was guilty of murdering the duke, a crime punishable by death. Only that he had kidnapped a noblewoman.

Allen clenched his fists and jaw in frustration. To be so close yet unable to do anything! If the North Britannian council had focused on seeking justice rather than some foolish superstition, matters might be very different right now.

This waiting was so much worse than actual combat could ever be.

He should pray. For some reason he had drifted from his

spiritual center these past weeks. Always God had dwelt within easy access, floating just in the back of his awareness. A whispered prayer away. Now his weighty duties and his dreaded nuptials seemed to have pushed God aside.

Allen did not understand what had created the huge gap between them. But as God was never changing, no doubt Allen had been the one to move. He had to dig deeper than ever before for that sweet fragrance, that divine presence. God meant everything to Allen, and he did not know how to live without Him.

Focusing both spirit and mind, he found that inward place where God dwelt, and he poured out his heart.

Father God, how I miss you. Do not depart from me, for I need you more than ever. Lead me. Help me to know your voice and your plan. Protect us. Send your angels to fight beside us. Most importantly, Lord, I pray for peace and for strength. Please comfort my heart while Gwendolyn is at risk. And help me to let her go when the time comes.

Something deep in Allen's chest tensed at that last line. It felt not right, yet his mind could not begin to fathom why. He only sought to do his duty.

That was when the most priceless sound he had ever heard caressed his ears. Gwendolyn's voice mimicking the call of the wood warbler. He sagged against the tree. All was yet well. He must not give up hope.

◇◇◇

Gwen peered down at her raw and chafing hands through a haze of steam. Aching claws dug into her back and beads of sweat trickled down her face. Though she had thought she trained hard at the warrior arts, she had never worked like this in all her life.

She stuck her long stick in the huge boiling laundry cauldron and stirred some more. Already she had scrubbed cookware, served a meal of which she received only a crust of bread, taken a brush to a soot-covered hearth, and even thrown slops to the pigs. At least while outdoors she had been able to send the bird-like signal she had learned last night. The answering whistles had brought her much comfort.

Yet such reassurance did nothing to save her from these tedious chores. Gwen wondered how much more she could take, and just when she might find the perfect opportunity to sneak off to Merry. Though she had peppered the women with friendly questions throughout the day, she still had no clue where Merry was being held.

And she had only briefly spotted the knavishly handsome Warner DeMontfort. How her hand had twitched to run him through with her sword then and there, but she must remain focused on her mission.

"Gwen, I do wish you'd take off that infernal cloak. You'll never survive laundry duty in that blasted thing. 'Tis like a blacksmith's forge in 'ere." Millicent had brought up the cloak several times throughout the day.

While Gwen realized the woman only wished to be helpful, she clung tight to her outerwear.

Of course Millicent did not realize that Gwen hid two swords, several daggers, and a leather hauberk for protection within her clothing.

"No, please, Miss Millicent," Gwen said. "As I mentioned, my dress 'tis quite foul. I would not want to be tossed out on my first day."

"Ain't none of us are dressed like princesses, luv. 'ow bad can it be?" Millicent grabbed a handful of Gwen's cloak, but Gwen maintained her firm hold.

She bit her lip and scrunched her face, creating a sort of

pressure that she hoped would turn it red. Based on the look of compassion that crossed Millicent's features, Gwen surmised she had succeeded in appearing embarrassed.

"That bad, is it?" Millicent clucked her tongue. "I'll tell you what. Why don't you take a break from this 'eat and run that stack of fresh linens upstairs for me?"

"Eeek!" squealed the woman with the blond braids. "Don't you be goin' up there. There's a witch and a 'ellcat up those stairs. 'Tis not right for you to send the new girl."

"Would you rather I be sendin' you?"

Hellcat? Could she mean Lady Merry? Perhaps a clue, finally.

"Morgaine is in the tower as usual. She barely graces her bedchamber anymore. And the guest is well-guarded. You shall be fine," Millicent said.

"I'm not easily frightened. Just tell me where to go."

"At the opposite end of the great 'all, turn to the right and up the stairway. Follow the long corridor to the end, and ye shall find a chest for the linens against the far wall."

"Of course. I'll do anythin' for me wee brother Timmy."

"You're a good girl, ye are, Gwen." Millicent smiled to her as Gwen gathered the linens.

Anticipation surged through Gwen as she headed toward the stairs. Her heartbeat sped and her breathing quickened, but she was careful to remain calm in appearance. She clutched tightly to the bedsheets to keep her fingers from trembling and carefully placed one leather-clad foot in front of the other.

At least she was dressed in simple peasant garb that allowed for ease of movement and not some ridiculous gown and flimsy slippers, but how she longed for her chain mail and helmet at a moment like this.

She felt so vulnerable. So exposed. So . . . she hated to admit it, but so female.

Yet it was her gentler gender that had gotten her this far. She must cling to it as her best asset. While she walked down the hall and past the guard, she attempted to sway her hips as Rosalind had taught her. Though the cloak would conceal much, she hoped that its subtle motion might pique the man's imagination.

As she brushed past him in the narrow corridor, she lowered her chin and glanced up through her lashes, fluttering them a few times, a tactic she had noticed Rosalind attempt with Hugh to great success. A tactic that Robert fellow would never succeed at.

The man offered a low-toned "Mmm" along with a mischievous grin.

She continued down the hall with a few backward glances and a light giggle. At the end she fiddled with the linens as she discreetly adjusted her weapons with her free hand. With a toss of her hair, she turned and sauntered toward him, still holding a single cloth for washing.

"What have we here? A pretty new maid for me?" the guard asked.

"Yes, I've come just for ye." Gwen sidled up next to him and smiled.

"Truly?"

"In truth, I've brought a fresh cloth for your charge. Might I take it in to 'er?"

"Now, now. You don't want to be going in there. Trust me, miss." He patted his belt, which held the key.

"Is she a 'ellcat as I've 'eard? Surely you can show 'er to me. I would feel safe if a strong fellow like you went along." She grazed her finger over the man's large arm. Gwen shocked herself with her own easy performance, but Merry's future was at risk.

"I suppose if you put it that way . . ." The man smiled at her and took the keys from his belt.

Gwen stepped back as he searched for the correct one.

He leaned over in the shadowy hallway to find the hole and insert the key.

In a flash, Gwen pulled her sword and struck him over the back of his head with the flat side of it. The man crumpled at her feet.

She grinned in triumph. Her timing had been impeccable, for the latch opened easily, and she slid into the chamber.

"Who are you?" A small, dark-haired woman stood to her feet in the corner of the dim room.

"Allen and Timothy sent me. There is no time to waste." She tossed Merry a sword, and the nimble lady snatched it from the air. Then she offered her a dagger.

Merry crouched low and surveyed the area. "What is your plan?"

"Here, put this on." Gwen tugged off her blasted cloak and gave it to Merry. "Cover up well and hide your weapons."

As Merry followed her instructions, Gwen checked her own weapons again. She grasped a small dagger and cradled it against her wrist beneath the sleeve of her tunic. Then she peeked around the doorway. The guard still lay in a crumpled heap. "Come. If we move swiftly, perhaps we can escape through the back way near the stables before anyone notices."

"I am ready." Though tough looking, the tiny lady barely reached Gwen's chin, and the rough brown wool cloak pooled on the floor around her. For the first time, Gwen doubted they could do this. But they must.

Neither of them could bear the consequences otherwise.

Chapter 27

From his perch upon a small stark bed, Warner stared at his half sister as she scribbled in her book of spells by the light of a single candle. He knotted and unknotted the kerchief in his hands.

More and more these days, he found himself drawn to Morgaine's eerie, entangling company in this tower room. It somehow comforted him, despite her constant disdain, but he grew tired of the incessant darkness.

"For the love of all that is holy, Morgaine, let me throw open the shutters. 'Tis a beautiful day outside."

She crooked a brow but never looked up. "I do not love the holy, and well you know it, you dolt."

"But I grow bored."

"That is not my problem. Go taste that noble morsel you keep trapped next to your chamber. She shall be yours on the morrow anyway. I do not understand why you wait."

"Nor do I expect you to. But never fear. It shall be accomplished this night."

Morgaine ran her finger through a pile of herbs and paid him little heed. Then of a sudden, her ashen face turned straight to him. Her mouth gaped and her inky eyes popped wide open. "No!"

He hopped to his feet. "What is it?"

"Something is wrong. You have waited too long."

Warner dashed to the window and threw it open without awaiting permission. He glanced about the courtyard but saw nothing amiss.

"Hurry, you fool," Morgaine said. "Do something!"

He ran down the spiraling stairs of the tower as fast as his feet could carry him. His heart pounded wildly in his chest. He could not lose Merry now. Too much was at stake. Surely Morgaine only toyed with him, as she loved to do, but he could not risk ignoring her warning.

As he hurried through the great hall to the stairs beyond, he shoved past two serving maids. "Sorry," he muttered but continued to make haste.

When he reached the top of the stairs, the crumpled form of the guard upon the floor confirmed his worst fears. Merry's door gaped wide open, much as Morgaine's mouth had. Yet he could not quite process the information.

He shook the guard, ran into the room, but nothing. The furniture in the chamber seemed to swirl about him like a whirl-wind. He clasped his head and stumbled toward the window, but it was bolted tight. Rushing next door to his own chamber, he ran to the window and successfully threw it open.

That was when he saw them. The same two serving maids. One tall, and the other tiny, with her woolen cloak dragging upon the ground.

"Guards, seize them!" he screamed with all of his might.

◇◇◇

Just when Gwen had begun to believe they might escape without a hindrance, the man's voice bellowed over the courtyard.

She and Merry shot each other a look, and they both dashed in the direction of the stable, but it was too late. Soldiers in black-and-green regalia came at them from several directions. Merry and Gwen both drew their swords and squared off with their attackers, and Merry sent out the piercing call of the blackbird.

"Aw look," one of the guards said. "The pretty little ladies think to fight us." He tipped back his head and laughed.

"She thinks whistling will help," mocked another.

Gwen felt no fear, only the surge of battle coursing through her. Steeling her. Strengthening her. She had trained for this moment. Waited her whole life for this opportunity. And she was ready.

Gwen and Merry circled back to back.

Gwen longed to toss a dagger through the mocker's haughty throat, but if they could buy some time, perhaps the Ghosts might come to even out the odds. Besides which, these men were likely innocent fellows seeking only to earn a living for their families.

"I wouldn't laugh if I were you. Yon tiny one inflicted serious damage on his lordship," a second guard said.

"We can take them." Yet another guard drew his sword and stepped forward. "Drop your weapons now, and we shall not hurt you."

Merry made the low-pitched *whoo* of a barn owl, purposely chosen to sound like a heavy sigh, for Gwen's ears only—rightly assuming that the men would have taught Gwen the signals.

The guards all closed in upon them now.

Gwen counted out *Seven, six, five* . . . in her head.

The one before her smirked and took another step her way.

Three, two . . .

At the appointed moment, both Gwen and Merry hurtled toward their foes.

Gwen drove straight into the belly of the chortling buffoon. Catching him by surprise, she knocked him to the ground and flung his sword far away. She walloped the hilt of her own sword against his temple, and rendered him senseless. But another soldier already headed her way, and she jumped into a lunge to face him.

From the corner of her eye she caught Merry gracefully tumbling through the air toward her opponent and sending him sprawling in the process. She, too, took his sword and disarmed him.

Gwen met her attacker strike for strike, but more soldiers now hurried their way. Just when she thought all might be lost, streaks of brown and tan rushed at them from the walls.

◇◇◇

"Watch out! There are more!" Warner screamed from his perch high over the courtyard, but his men did not seem to hear.

Though the tough ladies fought valiantly, Warner had felt confident that his men would overtake them.

Until he saw their band of forest ruffians descending from both nowhere at all and everywhere at once. Floating down from the sky like autumn leaves upon ropes with a flurry of arrows flying before them. Several careened directly at his men and knocked them from their feet.

He could no longer stand idly by and watch. Grabbing his own sword from its place against the wall, he dashed down the hallway with his steps thundering in his head.

This could not be happening. *Why, God, oh why?* He crashed down the stairs. He had done everything right this time. Merry

Ellison must be his and North Britannia along with her. He flew through the great hall. He could not fail again.

◇◇◇

Allen surveyed the action-filled courtyard, wanting nothing more than to make his way to Gwendolyn and protect her.

But a guard stood in his path. And over the fellow's shoulder, Allen noted that Gwendolyn was holding her own. His opponent struck hard, straight for his head, which due to Allen's disguise was not covered with a helmet. Allen ducked and maneuvered. Spun and struck, but he was at a huge disadvantage. Not only did he lack armor, but he had no real desire to hurt this man who was only doing his job. Allen was the invader today.

But he must rescue Merry. Must protect Gwendolyn. Must defeat that villain DeMontfort. The situation was messy indeed. Finally he managed to stab the man's shoulder, and while the fellow grabbed at the pain, Allen whacked him in the head with the flat side of his sword. His foe toppled to the ground and did not rise again.

As Allen turned to rush toward Gwendolyn, a bellowing man dressed in black leather ran through the grand portal of the castle and caught his notice.

Warner DeMontfort himself.

Though Allen's heart tugged him to Gwendolyn, she had matters well under control. She slashed at a guard with expert technique, and the guard's sword streaked from his hand. Allen's head won his internal battle and sent him racing toward DeMontfort, the source of their trouble. Now was Allen's chance to dispatch of him once and for all.

As he headed that way, another guard dashed around the corner and blocked Allen's path. This fellow appeared young and inexperienced. Allen could take his life in an instant and rush onward to his true target, but something about the combination of fear and determination in the lad's eye would not suffer Allen to kill him. He had no choice but to bandy swords until he could neutralize the man.

Meanwhile one of Allen's knights, a Sir Durand, reached DeMontfort and began clashing swords with him.

Allen's foe tumbled on the ground in an evasive maneuver, forcing Allen to spin about and lose sight of DeMontfort. But he now saw Sir Randel hurrying the ladies through the small back gate. Finally, he managed to knock the sword from the lad's hand, and sent the fellow scurrying away.

He pivoted to again find DeMontfort, but the villain now lay unconscious upon the ground. *Drat!* He could not run a defenseless man through with a sword. Not even the vile DeMontfort.

"Come!" Sir Durand caught him by the arm. "The ladies are safe and the path is clear."

True enough, nothing blocked Allen's escape. But he yet wished to end the threat of DeMontfort for good. Though they had discussed doing as little harm as possible, Allen had assumed that if faced with Warner himself, it would go unsaid that one might finish him off.

Durand tugged at him again.

Of course Durand had no way of knowing what Warner DeMontfort looked like. And he was right. They must go. The squadron down the hill might be alerted at any moment. Much as it pained him, Allen had no choice but to leave justice and DeMontfort in the hands of God.

◇◇◇

As Warner pried his eyes open, the hazy world spun around him. His head throbbed like the dickens. He pressed a hand to it as he fought to remember how he had come to be lying in the courtyard. Then it came to him in a flash. *Lady Merry!*

He stumbled toward the front gate. He must rally the troops beyond to catch the invaders.

As if fate had finally smiled upon him, his hundred-man contingency moved in his direction. Just as he was about to call to them, the lead knight spoke. "Sir Warner, troops from North Britannia are headed this way. Stay inside. We shall protect you. Keep your sister and mother close."

Warner felt as if he was seeing the man through a shimmer of water. The image undulated before his eyes. His head felt about to explode into fragments.

Blast it all! He could not go after them now.

He must regroup yet again.

But what he could not do, what he would never do, was relinquish his plan to defeat North Britannia. It was beyond belief that it had slipped through his fingers once more. Someone would pay for this travesty. He would no longer be content to take back the region peacefully.

Someway, somehow, hopefully in a manner involving much pain and humiliation, the dukedom would be his.

◇◇◇

Once hidden in their dense copse of trees, the entire group celebrated with hugs, hushed cheers, and plenty of slaps on the back. No one seemed to share Allen's intense disappointment that DeMontfort yet lived to vex the dukedom another day.

Allen pulled Gwendolyn tight to his side even as Timothy swung Merry in a circle. The ladies, the Ghosts, and Allen's fellow guards had all fought admirably.

"I am so glad you are safe," Allen whispered in Gwendolyn's ear.

Unable to resist, he dropped a kiss on her golden hair, which he hoped would seem only the proper chivalrous gesture in the situation.

He had been amazed to see Gwendolyn in the throes of battle—although as he revisited the memory, something about her technique struck him as oddly familiar. . . .

But he was not allowed time to further consider that thought, for the guard they had left at camp rushed toward them.

"A troop of North Britannian soldiers is heading this way."

Allen let go of Gwendolyn and grabbed at the hilt of his sword. His mind scanned through the possibilities. "Most likely they are here to take me home. Those who came with me." He beckoned them with a lift of his chin. "We shall not resist, as our mission is complete."

"Or it could be dissenters en route to join DeMontfort," Durand said.

Sir Randel gathered their group. "Let us don our surcoats and be ready for either contingency."

"Timothy," Allen said, "take Merry and your men and return to the king. Tell Marshall what has been going on here, and that North Britannia needs his help."

Merry took Allen's hand. The gesture warmed his heart but nothing more. "How can I ever thank you enough?"

"No thanks is necessary. Just marry Timothy quickly and make him a happy man." He winked her way as the Ghosts, along with Lord Linden's men, prepared for a quick departure.

Finally he turned to Gwen. "It would do no good for the troops to recognize you. You must fend for yourself, I'm afraid, and get back home as fast as you can."

"Of course." She stood straight and tall at his side.

How he longed to pull her into his embrace and shield her

from the world forever. Instead he offered her the only gift he could. "You fought well today. I was a fool to doubt you."

She melted from her warrior stance into a gentler, more feminine shape and blushed prettily. "You did not know, and you only wished to protect me. But I must hurry away."

Standing to her toes, she pressed a quick, soft kiss to his cheek. It sizzled there like lightning.

However, he could not stand around dreaming of lovely maidens who could not be his.

He pulled on his surcoat and prepared to meet the contingent from North Britannia. Along with the rest of the guards who had supported him, he mounted his horse and trotted toward them along the road.

"There you are, you traitorous whelp! I have been sent to fetch you home." The words came from a rough, scowling face surrounded by wild grey-and-black hair. Lord Reimund Barnes.

Why the baron of all people? The troops surrounded him and his small group of soldiers.

"We shall not fight you," Allen said, lifting his hands over his head. "We have completed our mission, and we are ready to return home." He scanned the surrounding terrain to ensure that Gwendolyn remained well hidden from her ruthless father, and was relieved when he caught not a single glance of her.

"Do you think you shall get away with defying the council so easily? I believe a night in my dungeon along the way back will teach you all a much-needed lesson."

As the troop led them toward home, Allen groaned. How he hated to be in the clutches of this man, and in the clutches of the tyrannical council he represented. But a night in the dungeon would be a small price to pay for saving Merry from a dreaded marriage. Now if only he could save himself from a similar fate.

But he knew he would not. He must do his duty. He must

honor his commitment. And so he trotted his horse back home toward North Britannia with his head held high.

◇◇◇

Gwen peered through the trees as her father led Allen and the men away. Now was her chance. She might slip off to the central part of England and thus escape her tyrant father's grasp. Lady Merry had proven as valiant and honorable as Gwen had dreamed. No doubt she and Timothy would understand and take Gwen along.

Yet Allen and the men needed her help now more than ever. She had no idea what awful plans her father might have in mind to punish them.

If she followed Merry, not only would she give up her chance to help Allen, she would relinquish her home, Rosalind, and her mother, even Mischief and Angel, whom she missed so already. She had never meant to leave them this long. Perhaps even her brothers would be lost to her. But if she went back now, she might yet be wed to a fiend.

She glanced in one direction and then the other, her heart pulled in two. What she did in the next few moments would set the course of her life for many years to come.

Chapter  28

The stench proved not as awful as Allen had expected. He had noted not a single skeleton nor ghost, nor so far even a rat in Lord Barnes's dungeon. The place reeked of disuse more than human suffering. The five of them had been tossed in roughly, but were not secured to cuffs or chains.

All in all, Allen would have been a bit disappointed by his first trip to the dungeon, did it not offer a welcome respite from all the wedding preparations and incessant tutoring at Edendale Castle.

In the sparse beams of moonlight that streamed down from the small barred windows near the ceiling, Allen spotted Randel lounging to his right with his head resting on his balled surcoat. "You look surprisingly comfortable over there." Allen chuckled.

Randel groaned and shifted positions. "I doubt I shall be able to sleep in this place, but we should get what rest we can."

"Perhaps you can help me with something that might pass the time."

"What is that?" Randel propped himself on his elbow.

"I need to write a blasted love poem to read to the duchess at the feast before our wedding. The council desires that our love ring true. And 'tis only proper and chivalrous that I do so. Do you not think?"

"Hmm . . ." Randel paused. "I suppose it is. Except that I do not believe you are in love with the duchess."

"But she is an exceptional lady, and she deserves such a gesture."

"Agreed."

"Could we not compose it together?"

"I will try and help."

"Good." Allen moved to a comfortable cross-legged position. "All I have come up with so far is this. *Your curves call out like a wave in the sea. Your hair as a waterfall beckons to me.*"

Randel pursed his lips and nodded his head from side to side as if weighing the words on a scale. "Very pretty sentiment. You surprise me, Sir Allen. I thought you more a man of action than of words."

"So it is good?" Hope surged within Allen.

"I did not say that." Randel sat up to face him. "For the duchess is not a particularly curving woman, and her hair is ever caught beneath a wimple. Have you even seen it down?"

"No, although I can tell it is dark, for not all of her wimples hide it well."

"Well, I've seen it. It falls quite straight, not at all frothy like a waterfall, or—for example only of course—the Lady Gwendolyn's waving hair. And now that I think of it, the Lady Gwendolyn's curving figure."

Sir Durand chuckled at that from across the room.

"Mind your own business!" Allen picked up the closest projectile he could find, a leather glove, and threw it at the fellow's head.

"It seems you've made your love life all of our business." Durand slid closer. "Why not make the waterfall sparkling with golden sunlight and be done with it?"

Sir Agravain, an older married knight, joined their little party. "Since you're speaking of waves and water how about *Your aqua eyes do quench, do intoxicate my soul.*"

Everyone but Allen laughed now. God help him, was his infatuation with Gwendolyn so obvious to them all?

"*And your bowed pink lips do beseech my kiss,*" Durand added.

Allen's cheeks flamed. "Enough!" he shouted. "This is not funny. Would you so disrespect your duchess?"

They fell silent.

"Besides," Allen said to Randel, "I thought you wished to marry Gwendolyn."

Randel blew out a slow breath. "I admire Gwennie, care for her deeply, and desperately wish to save her from Gawain. She would make a good match for me, and I believe we would be happy together. But I have never yet loved any woman with the passion I see in your eyes when you gaze at her."

Allen slapped the ground beside him. "This conversation has gone too far."

"I am sorry," Randel said. "But you asked. Besides which, though I did not wish to mention it, my right arm has been pounding like thunder and lightning ever since I dropped from that rope. I fear 'tis broken, and I shall not be able to fight for her now. We shall have to find a different champion for our Gwendolyn. What of you, Durand?"

"And risk the wrath of Sir Allen? Thank you, but no."

"Cease this!" Allen raked at his hair.

"Oh, do not be a bad sport, Allen," Durand said. "Your sulking over Gwendolyn was hard to miss. We know you would not dishonor the duchess. But admiration of ladies in general is well entrenched in the chivalrous ideal."

"Just because such admiration is chivalrous does not mean it honors God," Allen said. "Look at Lancelot and Guinevere and the destruction they wrought. The duchess is to be my wife, and I am determined to be faithful to her in both thought and deed."

"Good luck with that." Durand ducked before Allen could send another glove sailing his direction.

Just then, an odd scratching sound met their ears and they all jolted to attention.

"What is it?" Randel whispered.

Allen cocked his head and peered at the outside wall, from whence the sound came. "I know not."

A moment later, in the dim light he detected a large stone moving slowly outward, smoothly, almost magically, as if on wheels or some sort of conveyance. Then moonbeams broke through the hole, and a figure burst into their dungeon along with a thick cloud of dust from the misplaced stone. In silhouette against the milky haze stood a tall curving figure with her feet placed wide, hands on her hips, and a braid cascading down one shoulder. *Gwendolyn!*

As she approached, he noted her chain mail and the sword hanging from a belt about her hips. "Come, we must hurry," said the voice he had come to cherish.

No one moved.

She waved them toward the hole. "Now! What are you waiting for?"

"Gwennie," Randel spoke first. "We appreciate your efforts, but we should not anger your father nor the council any further."

Allen stood and stepped forward. "They only plan to keep us here this one night."

"Do you think you can trust my father? Return to Edendale while you can. The council will be happy enough once you have arrived." Gwendolyn huffed and tugged him toward the hole.

But Allen stood firm and crossed his arms over his chest. "No. I insist. I have shirked my duties long enough. "

"You and your insipid duties!" She pressed her fists into her hips again.

That pride Allen still did not wish to acknowledge rankled at her statement. "I will thank you not to insult me in front of my comrades."

"Then come outside and speak with me in private."

Allen took a step, then hesitated.

"Please, Allen," she said, her tone now pleading and feminine. "There is a yew tree I once promised to show you, and we might never have this chance again."

His heart melted at her soft entreaty. "Are you certain it is safe?"

"Trust me." Gwendolyn reached her hand to him. "This is my home."

Of its own accord, Allen's hand met hers, and they wrapped together. With the gentlest of tugs, she led him out through the hole in the wall.

"This way," she whispered.

They wove through the dark foliage, but Gwendolyn remained certain and surefooted.

"Here it is." She placed her free hand on a thick, gnarled trunk which split into a V. "'Tis easy to climb. I shall go first."

He followed her as she scrambled lightly up the tree. About eight feet up, Gwendolyn scurried onto a thick branch and sat upon it with her legs dangling free.

"What of the guards?" Allen whispered.

"I can take care of them."

At that very moment a loud, "Halt, who goes there?" came from the castle wall.

Allen froze, but Gwendolyn just smiled. "Trust me."

She scooched farther down the branch and poked her head out from the dense section of evergreen boughs. "'Tis just me, Sir Jasper. Lady Gwendolyn. I came to fetch something from home, but please do not tell my father."

"Tsk, tsk." The guard's voice sounded friendly and playful, though Allen could not spy him through the thick tree. "Lady Gwendolyn, always into some mischief. But I shall not be the one to tell tales, not after the way your father locked you up and left you to go hungry the last time you crossed him. 'Twas not right."

Allen's heart twisted to hear this, but he remained still and quiet as he listened to their conversation from his dark hiding place.

"I say, do you know where my pups might be? I would like to fetch them as well if I can."

"Not in secret, you shan't. They've been sleeping with your mother since she returned without you."

It took a rare woman to battle like a soldier one moment and worry about her pups the next. After all this time, Allen still found Gwendolyn utterly charming.

"That is too bad. But thank you for your help. I shall owe you a favor for this," Gwendolyn said.

"Did you bring your pipe along?" the guard asked.

"Indeed, I never go anywhere without it. Shall I play for you?"

"I would love that."

"But what of my father?"

"There's a rowdy bunch of his men in the great hall. They shall not hear a thing. And I will keep a close watch for them from the gatehouse."

290

"Excellent. Just give me a moment, then," she said.

Her pipe. That awful, wonderful, mesmerizing pipe. Allen did not wish to hear it now. Not in this tree where he had once imagined he might kiss her.

After the guard walked away, Gwendolyn moved back down the branch and settled herself so close that her thighs and shoulders grazed his. She opened the sack that hung from her belt and pulled out the pipe. Then she began her haunting tune.

It reached out to Allen and wrapped about him, much like her hand had done earlier. Though he could see only the barest shadow of profile, he had studied her often during the past weeks, and he knew every slope of her cheek, every nuance of her skin.

His hands trembled to reach out and touch her. His lips pulsed with the desire to brush against hers. But beyond any of that, he felt God's presence swathing about him more keenly than he had in these many weeks—which made no sense at all!

Gwendolyn appeared to be every bit as caught up in the music, in the wonder of the moment, as he was. Then something in her demeanor seemed to shift. She abruptly halted her performance and slapped the pipe down upon her lap. "I cannot argue with you whilst playing."

Yes, better that they should focus on the issue at hand, even spend their time bickering, than risk being overcome by this magical spell. But as he could no longer remember what they had been fighting about, he waited for her to continue.

She shoved the pipe into her sack. "You must leave this castle tonight. You believed I would know my own home. Now believe that I know my own father. He is a ruthless man. I do not trust him, and he quite hates you."

Allen had suspected as much, yet his blood went cold at the words.

Turning to face him, she continued. "Do not leave your fate in his hands. I think he will remain faithful to the duchess and return you, but I am just not sure. No doubt he will make you suffer along the way. And I suspect he will leave Randel here to rot, for he will not risk setting him free to fight in the tournament for me. Father is still determined that I marry that cruel Gawain."

His heart mirrored the hurt, even the anger within her words. How he wished he could save her from it all, but he knew only one way to help her now. "You are right. You know your father better than I do. But might I suggest that I likewise know my Father, my heavenly Father, better than you, who have not claimed Him as your own? My Father is faithful and true. You can . . . No—you *must* put your trust in Him."

He gripped her by the forearms in his need to convince her. "Circumstances might look grim for a time, but God can turn matters for the good. He alone can sustain your soul through whatever adversity you might face."

"So if I will trust in God, you will take your men and flee?" She chuckled, and he realized the absurdity of what he seemed to suggest.

"I do not wish to strike a bargain. I only wish to know you are safe in God's love, and only because I care for you so much." He dropped her arms and gently took her hand instead. He traced his finger across her palm. A strong hand with callouses aplenty, yet tender and soft in the center, just like her.

"I confess that your devotion to God has inspired and challenged me," she said. "And I want you to know that I do trust you."

Those words warmed him like no others could. Gwendolyn had been wounded by this world. She did not trust easily. "I trust you as well, Gwendolyn. Everything about this situation has confused me, but I know you wish only the best for me and my men."

He turned and rested his forehead against hers, drinking in her perfume of wild herbs and fresh air.

"Then go," she whispered. Yet she placed her free palm against his cheek and held him in place.

What had made him think that he could abandon Gwendolyn? How did he imagine he might ever marry another?

His body drifted like a lodestone toward her, but more than that, his heart and soul and spirit cried out to unite with hers. He needed to be closer to her. To breathe in her very presence. No longer moving from any conscious sort of decision, he wrapped her in his arms.

Pressing close, she leaned her head upon his shoulder and sighed. She ran her hands over his chest. All of his senses spiked to high alert. She felt like Eve, come home against Adam's rib. Needing to drink of her essence, he lowered his lips to hers.

She met him, shy and hesitant at first, and then with more fervor.

But as he shifted his position to draw her yet closer to his heart, he lost his balance. The branch slipped from beneath his legs. The air rose up to meet him, the tree swirled about him, and they both crashed with a hard *thump* upon the ground.

Good heavens, not again!

He managed to take the brunt of the fall, as she landed atop him. Then he rolled over, placing her solidly on the ground. In truth, he must find a better place than precarious tree branches for kissing young maidens.

Once he found his breath, he asked. "Are you well?"

"I am fine." There she lay, for the briefest moment, staring up at him in the moonlight. Lips parted and seeking. She raised her hand to graze his cheek.

In that moment, a memory pierced through him, and that is when he recognized her! She—

"Lady Gwendolyn! Lady Gwendolyn!" called the guard upon the castle wall from a distance. "Are you well? Should I fetch help?"

Gwendolyn gave Allen a little shove. On instinct, he leapt to his feet and dashed into the trees, but his conscious mind still grappled with what he had just seen.

Lady Gwendolyn Barnes and Sir Geoffrey Lachapelle were one and the same.

He had never realized it until she lay beneath him on the ground as Lachapelle had when his visor flipped open. No wonder she had fared so well in battle this day, no wonder her moves had struck him as familiar. She had stood her own against Allen in the tournament not long ago.

Perhaps he did not know this Gwendolyn at all.

◇◇◇

Gwendolyn stood and brushed herself off. She wondered at the odd expression that had crossed Allen's face before he tore into the woods, but she could not waste time thinking about that now.

Waving to the guard who ran her way, she called, "I am fine, Sir Jasper. I must have fallen asleep. So sorry to have startled you."

She could only hope Allen had faded out of sight before Jasper had spotted him.

"Ah." Jasper jogged the rest of the way along the parapet to her and leaned over the edge of the wall. "I wondered why my lovely tune ended so soon. Truly, you must take care."

Her tensed muscles relaxed. He seemed to suspect nothing. "You know me better than that."

"Well, your father would have my hide if something happened to you and I might have prevented it. So be careful for me, if not for yourself."

"My apologies, I did not think to put you in any danger." She checked her sack and weapons to make sure all was in place. "I will return to Edendale straightaway."

"Not in the dark alone, you shan't. Go and stay the night in the village, and head back where you belong in the morning. Your good luck cannot hold out forever."

"Excellent advice. I will do as you bid."

"Be a good girl now."

"I shall try, although we both know the odds are not great."

He laughed and turned back to the gatehouse.

She lingered a moment, gazing up at the tree and reliving the wonder of her brief interlude with Allen. Her first kiss.

Running her finger across her tingling lip, she recalled that sweet moment when his mouth first touched hers. She had felt so attuned with him. So safe and right within his arms. So unified in spirit and in heart. Had he experienced those sensations as well? Dare she dream he might rethink his decision to marry the duchess?

Her path toward the village took her past the dungeon wall and the escape route she and her brothers had rigged years ago from both inside and out in case Father got overly zealous with his discipline. The stone was back in its place. She bent down and peered through the small barred window. The dungeon was empty. Sir Allen was gone.

Of course he was gone. Although her heart might cry otherwise, Allen did not belong to her. That one brief moment, that single ecstatic kiss might be all she could ever share with him. She must turn her mind to thoughts of Randel and hope she might grow to experience that same sort of love with him someday.

Though being held in Allen's arms had felt like coming home, though his lips had struck hers like flame to the tinder, he would never belong to her. The sooner she accepted that, the better.

She gathered her horse and meandered toward her old friends in the village. As she continued to replay her interlude with Allen in her mind, a realization washed over her. Only once had she ever experienced a love that overshadowed even the feelings that Allen awoke in her. That day in the cathedral, God's love had completely enveloped and overwhelmed her.

She had thought God abandoned her when she heard Mother's awful report. When she saw with her own eyes the abuse Mother had suffered for defending her. When Gwen herself lay rejected, crushed, and bleeding upon the ground.

Yet that very trauma had gotten her away from her father's clutches and into the duchess's care. God had turned that situation around, much as Allen suggested He might.

Perhaps God yet deserved her trust.

It was not as if she had anywhere else to turn. She had missed her chance to run away with Lady Merry. And given what had just transpired in the tree, she did not feel ready to flee North Britannia just yet.

She would return to Edendale on the morrow and see this matter through to the end.

Chapter 29

As the Edendale Castle dwellers gathered for their nooning meal the following day, everyone appeared to be back in their places.

Allen sat at the duchess's right side and Gwendolyn to her left. The castle guards Allen had brought along for his mission joked at their table across the room. And he was happy that somewhere far away Merry was safe with her newly espoused Timothy. Yet nothing was truly the same.

Council members glared at Allen from their various seats about the great hall. Randel's arm was secured in a splint. And the tension between Allen and Gwendolyn was so thick that one would need a well-sharpened sword to slice through it.

Fortunately, the duchess seemed not to notice. "How was your trip home, darling Gwendolyn?"

"Perfect," Gwendolyn muttered.

The duchess reached for a slice of fresh baked bread. "Although I hated to see your father chasing Sir Allen down, I did not waste breath dissuading the council, as I assumed matters would be easier for you at home with your father far away."

"Indeed," Gwendolyn said, apparently determined to stick to her one word answers. Smart—for to divulge details would require much fabrication.

Allen himself offered not a word. He did not wish to be a party to yet another deception by Gwendolyn Barnes. Gwendolyn and Sir Geoffrey Lachapelle, one and the same. He could still hardly fathom it. A part of him longed to speak with her about it. But a larger part dreaded any conversation between them.

Whatever could he say? Guilt draped over him like a heavy yoke, weighing him down. Why had he kissed her in that tree? He could never undo it. He could never un-know how it made him feel. He could never erase the fact that he had betrayed his intended.

The duchess swallowed down her bread with a sip of wine. "Gwendolyn, is everything well with you?"

Gwendolyn sat up straighter. "I am tired, that is all. I awoke early today."

"I hope you are not coming down with whatever your mother had."

"'Twas just a minor illness. Mother can be a bit dramatic."

Lies, lies, and more lies. Allen understood using subterfuge on a mission, but deception came so easily to Gwendolyn, even with the duchess, who was her close friend.

"Good to hear." The duchess shifted to include Allen in the conversation. "And I am glad you are back safe and sound and that your friend has escaped that unscrupulous Warner DeMontfort. But whatever shall we do about Sir Randel?"

Gwendolyn shrugged her shoulders. Strong shoulders that Allen should have recognized could wield a sword. "'Twas not as if he had much chance of winning."

"Have you heard from your brother?" the duchess asked Gwendolyn.

"Only that he has received word of the tournament and will try to come. I suppose we must continue to hope and pray."

Allen remained silent. How he wished he could be the one to rescue her.

"I have been thinking to suggest a change of rules for this tournament," the duchess said. "Since Gawain is the reigning champion as well as your father's choice, we could demand that he face all opponents one at a time. Then if only a single person could best him, you would escape your horrible fate. What think you, Sir Allen? You have fought him."

Unable to be so rude as to ignore her question outright, Allen considered the duchess's plan. He was careful not to meet Gwendolyn's gaze as he answered. "It might work. He tires quickly. Yes, I think it is the best course possible."

Indeed, the very best course would be for Allen to fight for Gwendolyn himself, but that would never be possible. The dukedom needed him, besides which, he was no longer so sure he trusted the girl.

He had thought he knew her, perhaps that he loved her, but he had not even recognized her as Sir Geoffrey. If she was capable of fighting in a tournament as a man, what other troublesome deception might this enticing woman be prone to? Might she have lured him into the tree for the sole purpose of that confusing kiss?

Following his duty, as he knew he should, he reached over and took Duchess Adela's hand, clutching it tight, as if it were an anchor that might rescue him from his soul-crushing guilt and moor him safely in place.

Adela smiled up at him with her dark, enchanting eyes. So hopeful, so trusting.

There, that was not so awful. Her silky hand fit nicely into his. It bore no callouses, and he had no fear she might live a double life.

Meanwhile Gwendolyn bit her lip and clutched tightly to her dagger. "I must excuse myself," she said, pushing away from the table. "I fear you are right, m'lady. I am not feeling well after all."

"I am so sorry, my dear. Go and rest." The duchess patted Gwendolyn's hand with her free one, for a brief moment linking them all in the oddest sort of charged triangle.

Gwendolyn's maid rushed to her from a different table, and the two of them disappeared through the archway.

Allen would grow to love the duchess in time. He was determined. For good or for ill, soon Gwendolyn would wed another and move away from this castle. His feelings for her would pass with time.

They simply must.

◇◇◇

Thankful to be leaving the noisy great hall, Rosalind escorted Gwendolyn up the stairs to her chamber. The two of them had barely had a chance to talk as Rosalind hurriedly prepared her wayward mistress for the meal.

To think that Gwendolyn had taken advantage of her absence to sneak off like that. Why, she should throttle the girl, except that Rosalind seemed to have no energy anymore. Nor even any real will to live left within her.

She was glad to leave her meal behind, for food, along with everything else in life, had lost its savor now and tasted of ashes in her mouth. Eating was just one more obligation to endure. Like moving . . . and breathing.

Once they reached the chamber, she directed Gwendolyn toward the bed. "Lie down. I will fetch a cool cloth for your head."

"I think you could use a rest as well. Come. You need it."

Rosalind dipped the cloth in the basin, wrung it out, and handed it to Gwendolyn.

"I should not."

"That is an order," Gwendolyn barked.

"Fine then." Rosalind curled up close to Gwendolyn, truly, her best friend in the world.

"And take this." Gwendolyn pressed the cloth to Rosalind's forehead. "You need it more than I do."

For a moment they lay side by side, each lost in their own thoughts. It had all sounded so easy when Rosalind's mother suggested it. Visit the herbalist. Take the potion. Save the family. No one would ever need to know. The problem would be solved. Only Mother's plan had solved nothing.

Rosalind felt worse than ever. Her illness had extended from her body alone to consume her very soul. Had she not so recently come to the conclusion that sometimes one must do right and trust God with the outcome? Yet in this situation, she had failed so miserably.

"Did things not go well with your mother?" Gwendolyn finally asked.

"I do not wish to talk about it."

"I am sorry." Gwendolyn laid her hand upon Rosalind's shoulder.

"I take it something went amiss on your trip as well."

Gwendolyn rolled on her back to gaze at the ceiling. "He kissed me."

That simple statement roused Rosalind's curiosity, if not her spirit. She sat straight up and stared at Gwendolyn. "Sir Allen or Sir Randel?"

"If only it had been Sir Randel, all might be well. No, Sir Allen, and it was the most terribly wonderful thing I have ever experienced. After sitting next to him and the duchess at today's meal, I am almost glad that I shall soon be married and moving away."

"Oh, Gwennie!" In her own recent heart sickness, Rosalind had almost forgotten about Gwendolyn's trouble. But perhaps it was indeed a good thing that Gwendolyn would soon be married and would never experience the horror that Rosalind had this week. Surely even marriage to Gawain must be better than the agony she suffered. "I know not what to say."

And so neither of them said anything for a time. Gwendolyn sat up, and they shared a tearful embrace. Both wounded, both hurting, and yet somehow able to support one another in their grief.

"I know." Rosalind swiped at her eyes. "Your book. We should return to it. It always brings us comfort, yet we do not read it nearly enough."

"I have given much thought to God recently. And I do believe I felt His touch that day in the cathedral. Tell me, Rosalind, do you truly believe in Him, or do you simply say so because everyone does?"

Rosalind pondered the question, and felt the answer stirring deep in her soul. "I truly believe. There has to be more than just what we can see and hear and touch. More than just the pain of this world. I find God all around me. In the beauty of the clouds and the sunshine and the birdsong. I catch a glimpse of Him in the loving eyes of friends like you."

Clenching her eyes shut against the awful words she must speak next, Rosalind said, "Only I have not lived a holy life worthy of His child. I fear I have let Him down too badly this time, and that He might never love me again."

"Rosalind. Whatever do you mean?"

"Never mind. I have said too much."

"But that is not what our book says. It says that Christ paid the price for our sin. That none of us are good enough on our own." Gwendolyn picked up the beloved manuscript from the side table and commenced reading.

But this time the words did not reach Rosalind's heart. She felt herself shrinking away from them. She was too ugly, too filthy to stand before God and claim to be His daughter. She was not a princess in the kingdom of heaven.

She was a sinner, the greatest sinner of them all.

◇◇◇

After Rosalind fell asleep against her shoulder, Gwen slipped away and headed to the castle chapel. The time had come. She would put it off no longer, not allow the enemy of her soul to offer another distraction that might lead her down a deadly path.

And the good Lord knew better than anyone how badly she needed His assistance right now. In just a handful of days, the tournament would be fought and her fate would be sealed.

She tiptoed into the hushed and shadowy room and knelt down before the small altar. In a whispering voice, she poured out her petitions, her love, her new devotion in the general direction of the wooden cross. Tingles washed over her, and tears trickled down her cheeks. God's warm, soothing presence wafted about her. Touched her to her very core. And she did feel it. His love. Better, deeper than any earthly love could ever be.

"Lord, please sustain me over these next days. Take this situation that seems impossible and turn it for good. I pray that you will somehow deliver me to a bright future. Brighter than my frail human mind can even imagine."

She sensed His eternal arms wrapping about her. Recalled the shimmering love she had witnessed in His eyes. Despite her troubling circumstances, she would leave her future in His hands, for no safer place could it ever rest.

Then the memory of Rosalind, so wan and discouraged, rose to the surface in her mind. She must pray for Rosalind as well, for something was terribly wrong. And just as soon as she had finished, she would head off to find the duchess. She owed the gracious woman a most sincere apology for her lies.

◇◇◇

Anger surged through Warner DeMontfort, and he slashed his hand across the table, sending Morgaine's basin of water and herbs crashing to the floor of his chamber. "I have missed my chance! How dare you speak such drivel? How dare you mock me? I know not why I ever believed you."

Morgaine raised a haughty brow at him. "Do you think angering the evil spirits shall help your cause? They alone have sustained you thus far."

"I do not need you or your blasted spirits. I have an entire squadron at my disposal, and North Britannia shall yet be mine!"

She snickered at him. "Imbecile. You shall fail."

"Get out." He snatched her sack from the table and pelted it at her head. "And do not return to me!"

"You have made a deadly mistake this day." Her words flew his way like daggers of ice and pierced his chest.

But he would not give in to the pain.

She picked up her sack from the floor and turned to leave. With her hand upon the latch she paused and glared at him with a pure hatred. "On second thought, you should attack. What have you got to lose?"

He would no longer allow that witch to control his life. And he would no longer suffer his hoyden of a cousin, Adela, to steal the power and riches that should rightly be his.

He still did not understand why the North Britannian army

had slighted him by sending a troop his way, then turning back without even a single word. Had they come to offer support to Lady Merry, then heard of her escape? Had they in fact aided her? And when he heard word that it was led by the Lord Barnes, he had experienced a moment of hope that he might finally be coming over to his side.

But nothing.

Did the man simply wish to poke at his pride? Did the entire dukedom?

If so, it had worked. He would suffer them no longer. With the duchess's nuptials looming and the new young king headed to North Britannia, he must secure the dukedom now.

Mentally, he flagellated himself yet again for letting Merry Ellison slip through his fingers. Perhaps Morgaine was right, he had been an imbecile, but he would remain one no longer. No longer would he hide away, vanquished and dispossessed. He would go for everything or nothing at all. In two days' time, while the entire region was distracted by the tournament, he would attack.

Nothing could stop him now!

Chapter  30

"No!" Gwen whispered, clutching her hands to her heart as Gawain's eighth opponent of the day crashed to the ground.

The sun beamed bright and joyful overhead, as if mocking the travesty of this tournament that would decide her fate. Her father cheered at her side, as if Gawain's unmitigated dominion over Gwen was something to be celebrated. Even her mother, seated to the other side of Gwen, faked a pleasant smile at Gawain's easy victory to placate her husband.

Rosalind slipped into the small space between Gwen and her mother to offer a sympathetic squeeze of her hand. "Do not lose hope. Our prayers shall not be in vain."

Gwen, Rosalind, and the duchess had spent many hours on their knees over the past few days. But over the same duration, Gawain had established his reign of terror, declaring Gwendolyn his by right and threatening anyone who might oppose him.

While tournaments often featured thirty to forty contenders, today only nine men had dared register to fight Gawain. Eight down upon the ground. One to go.

As Gawain in the Ethelbaum's blue and green colors pranced and strutted, the crowd booed and hissed. He waved his hands toward himself, as if he welcomed their disdain. "Come! Will no one make me sweat this day? This is too easy. You send me pups when I wish to slay a wolf." He cackled at his own pompous jest, at which the crowd booed and hissed all the louder.

Gwen craned forward to better view the duchess next to Allen. Both looked as miserable as she felt. She had chosen to sit away from them today, knowing that Allen's presence at her side could only make this experience that much more awful.

But she broke into a small grin at the more welcome sight of Randel standing near the duchess, leaning over the rail and clutching it with his good hand. He let go and swiped at Gawain in disgust. Randel appeared to be pleading with the duchess and several of the high-ranking councilmen who sat near her.

But the duchess only shrugged her delicate shoulders in defeat, for she had done all she could.

The herald announced the final contender, one Sir Wilbur of Whichester. Gwen did not recall the name, but as he came to bow before the duchess, she indeed remembered him, for she had met him briefly at the most recent feast.

A man of few words and slightly awkward in social settings. A second son who was late into his twenties, with a crooked overlarge nose and a scar cutting through his left brow. But if his reputation held true, a good and honest man.

Certainly preferable to Gawain.

Sir Wilbur looked to be several inches shorter, but nearly as wide as his opponent. The largest fellow to face Gawain so far this day. Perhaps all was not yet lost.

If only Hugh would make an appearance, she might not have to rely upon this virtual stranger to rescue her. As the two men faced off upon their steeds and lifted their lances, she hollered, "Go, Sir Wilbur! Garnet and grey! Garnet and grey!"

Her champion offered her a shy smile before pulling his visor down over his eyes, and she tossed her kerchief his way.

"Stop that this instant," Father ground out at a whisper. He reached over to pinch her arm hard beneath the flowing sleeve of her amber gown in a way that no one would notice but that would surely leave a bruise.

"Ouch!" she yelped.

He shot her a glare. "Do not cross me further. The Barnes family is cheering for Sir Gawain this day."

But in her heart she continued to chant. *"Wil-bur. Wil-bur. Wil-bur."*

She studied the two men and their individual techniques. They flew directly toward one another, both fearless and bold. Sir Wilbur remained straight and true. But precisely as he had done each time she watched, Gawain lifted his lance for a brief moment just before he struck.

Then right as they might have clashed, both dodged to the outside and sped past one another unscathed.

Gwen sighed and shook Rosalind's hand in her excitement. Rosalind patted her shoulder with her free hand.

After circling about, the two men galloped at each other again. Again, Gawain lifted his lance for the briefest moment, but then he brought it back dead center. Within an explosion of shattering lances, both men tumbled off their horses.

Rosalind bounced on her toes and raised her brows to Gwen.

Gwen's heart raced even as Sir Wilbur's must at that moment, joining them in that simple manner.

The combatants found their feet and drew their swords. They slashed and ducked, dodged and parried. It looked for a moment as if Sir Wilbur might stand a chance, but then Gawain surged at him with a piercing howl and such fierce determination that Sir Wilbur stumbled backward.

In a flash, Gawain had him pinned to the ground by the point of his sword.

And all seemed lost.

But no. Gwen could not despair. She squeezed her eyes closed and steadied her breathing as Rosalind clutched tightly to her hand.

Gawain commenced to preening and strutting once again. "That is all of them. I have won. Lady Gwendolyn is mine. And I now shall claim my prize!"

He thrust his hips forward in a most threatening and unchivalrous display. Gwen felt faint at the thought of what the vulgar gesture forewarned. For a moment her faith faltered like Saint Peter struggling as he walked upon the water, but she could not afford to sink.

Her future, her life, and her happiness were all at stake.

The duchess stepped forward and held up a steadying hand. "This tournament has not ended yet. It is still early in the day." She appealed to the audience. "Will no one else offer to fight for Lady Gwendolyn's hand?"

Gwen bit her lip and awaited her miracle.

That is when she spied him. A handsome knight thundering upon a noble steed toward the arena. Two attendants swung the gate wide and let him enter. Gwen's spirits soared. So much so that she rose from her chair and thought she might float away.

Her beloved brother Hugh pulled to a stop next to Gawain. "Do not celebrate yet, you arrogant coxcomb! I intend to put you in your place and choose a husband for my sister myself."

He leapt down from his horse and spoke directly to the duchess. "I would like to challenge Sir Gawain."

"Sir Hugh, you are just in time," the duchess said.

"This is not fair!" Gawain whined like an overgrown child. "He cannot fight for his own sister's hand. And he did not register for the tournament in an official manner."

As the two hulking knights stood side by side, Gwen smiled to note her brother's even taller stature and even broader shoulders. Gawain had already endured nine matches. Although he had by some mishap managed to best Hugh once, it would not happen today.

The duchess raised her chin and shot Gawain a quelling glare. "I say he can fight for his sister's hand. We declared that you must face *all* challengers. What is the trouble? Are you afraid, Sir Gawain?"

"I . . . no . . . but . . ."

Just then Gwen's father hopped over the railing and down a good six feet, as if he were still a fit young knight himself.

He dashed onto the field and stood between Gawain and Hugh, waving his hands high over his head. "Wait! I must speak with my son before you commence with this farce."

Lord Barnes, every bit as tall and broad as his champion son, grabbed the younger man roughly by the arm and pulled him back toward the gate, where they might speak more privately. He flailed his arms in the air as he chastised his son.

Hugh stood firm, feet planted in the ground, staring down his father, angrily pointing to Gwen, then Gawain and back again.

Father's face turned bright red. Even at a distance, Gwen spied the throbbing vein. He clenched the collar of Hugh's purple surcoat in his meaty fist. Whatever he said next quelled Hugh. Hugh ripped himself away and took a few steps back with his jaw gaping.

He rubbed his hands over his face, concealing it for just a moment. But when he dropped them to his sides, Gwen knew his decision had been made. Across his pale face he wore an expression of defeat, which melted into raw fear as her father continued his tirade.

She sunk back to her chair. Her spirit, which had soared so high a moment ago, threatened to bury itself deep within the earth, never to rise again. But still, somehow she must cling to her faith.

Randel leapt over the rail much as her father had. He ran to the men and pleaded with Hugh. No doubt ensuring him that he wished to marry Gwen and entreating Hugh to reconsider. But it was too late. Due to whatever threats her brutal father had made, her brother would not fight for her.

Hugh trudged back toward the duchess with his head hanging low. He did not bellow with confidence as he had the last time. But Gwen heard him all too well nonetheless.

"It seems I have made an error. I did not rightly consider all the consequences my actions might evoke. I withdraw my bid to battle Sir Gawain, and I declare him victor of my sister's hand."

The duchess clenched her jaw. She looked to Allen, then to the council. Then she turned and caught Gwen's gaze.

After taking a deep breath, finally the duchess spoke. "Concede if you must, Sir Hugh, but I will not decree this contest over. Today is a day of celebration, and I shall not have the fun end so soon. The sun has barely reached its zenith in the sky. We shall wait and see who else might offer to fight."

The duchess glanced about, no doubt noting the lack of potential candidates.

"In fact," she said with a forced smile, "let us bolster the game and increase the merriment. I declare that even the common folk may enter for the prize of the noble Lady Gwendolyn and her dower lands. I will provide the needed battle gear. Let us take a break for our midday repast so that all in attendance might consider this offer. I open the field to all contenders."

As those words, *"I open the field to all,"* echoed in Gwen's head, an idea burst to life in her mind.

This battle was not over yet.

◇◇◇

Rosalind dashed down the lane after the retreating Sir Hugh as he led his horse away from the tournament grounds. She had never been so disappointed with another human being in her entire life. Well, except perhaps with herself. He was nearly to the city gates, but Gwendolyn had trained Rosalind well, and she ran to catch him.

"Hugh! Hugh! Please wait."

He turned and, upon spotting her, froze in his place.

A portion of Rosalind longed to throw herself into those strong arms. But a mountain of hindrances now stood between them. She pulled to a stop before him and took a moment to catch her breath. "How . . . how could you?"

A defeated Hugh hung his head low. "Do not judge me, Rosalind, for you know not what he threatened."

"To take away your inheritance? So what? You are only a third son, and you are a valiant soldier. You can earn your own way in the world."

"To disinherit me? You would like that, would you not? Perhaps you fancy I would settle down and marry you then. But no, it was nothing so benign as that. He threatened to declare me illegitimate and my mother an adulteress. He would shame us all to get his way. Mother has her faults, but she has always been a faithful wife. I cannot win against my father."

Those words stole the fight right out of Rosalind. Yet he had mentioned marriage. Perhaps if she had waited. . . . Perhaps if she had chosen differently. . . .

"Can I go now?" Hugh collected the reins of his horse.

She watched him preparing to leave through tear-filled eyes. "But what of us?"

"Is there an *us*? I thought we agreed this was only a dalliance. I will marry whomever my father declares, just like my poor sister must."

"I realize we could never marry." She glanced about at the once-pretty street, but it had lost all its color, all of its vibrancy, all of its charm, taking on a grey sort of haze, as had her entire life.

And so she turned her gaze down to her hands as she wrung them together. "There is something I feel you deserve to know before you leave."

He tilted his head and waited for her to continue.

"I . . . we . . . that is . . ." She took a deep breath for strength. Rosalind pleaded with him with her eyes. From the core of her being. He simply must forgive her. Offer her the absolution she so desperately needed. Elsewise, how could she ever go on living?

"I've been sick these last weeks. And I discovered that . . . I was with child."

Now she dared not look up at him, but rather focused upon her hands and rushed on with her tale. "I knew it would cause too many problems, for both of us. So I borrowed some coins from the stash you mentioned you keep hidden at the townhouse, and I went home to my village for a few days. I paid . . . the herbalist . . . and . . . well . . . 'tis taken care of now."

Finally she lifted her gaze to his, but those playful blue eyes she so adored had turned hard and cold.

"*It* has been *taken care of*?" he repeated with ice dripping from each of the words.

"Yes. It h-has. You were . . . were gone. I knew not when you might return, and I did not wish to-to trouble you," she managed to stutter.

"You mean my *child* has been *killed*."

The words struck like a blow to her gut, and she gasped at the pain they inflicted.

Hugh stared straight down at her now with disgust emblazoned across his face. "I am the man. I am the noble. You should have waited for my return."

He tore his fingers through his blond curls, then swiped his hand through the air. "'Tis not right! 'Tis not fair! You stole this decision away from me just like my tyrant of a father."

Rosalind tried to think of any sentiment that might soothe him, any words that might defend her actions. But none existed. She buried her face in her hands and braced herself for whatever he might deservedly hurl her way.

"You are right, we could never marry. But we could have worked out some arrangement. I came near to loving you once. I would have provided for you. But you killed my child. I cannot believe this!"

Her heart shattered to a million pieces in her chest, leaving naught but a cold, gaping hole in its place. She would have sacrificed anything, even her position, even her reputation, to bring back her baby. Only she could not.

Clutching Hugh's arm, she begged him. "Please forgive me. You must—otherwise I shall never forgive myself."

He ripped his arm from her grasp. His hands trembled, then fisted with resolve. "You thief! You harlot! You murderess! I shall never forgive you."

With that awful pronouncement, he turned and stalked out of her life.

Yet Rosalind could hardly bring herself to care. She sank to the dirt road. Her chest throbbed with pain—but not at his rejection. Only at his harsh indictment. *Thief! Harlot! Murderess!* Those words would resound in her head for as long as she lived.

She'd had her fill of men. More than enough to last her a

lifetime. From now on she would seek only one thing—redemption from her heinous sin. Perhaps if she worked hard enough, gave her all for God, someday He might see fit to forgive her. Even if her baby's father never would.

Rosalind managed to scramble back to her feet. Clutching her aching chest and hunching low, she headed toward the cathedral.

She would begin her quest straightaway, lighting candles and whispering prayers for the eternal soul of her child who would never know life on earth.

◇◇◇

Warner DeMontfort led his squadron of more than a hundred soldiers as they charged up the next hill. They had lain in wait until dawn just beyond the borders of the dukedom. Now they galloped straight east toward Edendale with great haste, so that they might beat any word of their attack.

Only at the border had they clashed with a small contingent, leaving none alive to tell their tales. If his intelligence served correct, soon they would meet a second line of defense, which they would likewise leave to soak the ground with their blood.

Then onward to Edendale and victory!

His cold heart nearly warmed at the thought.

Chapter 31

"Who will fight for the grand prize of the fair Lady Gwendolyn and her dower lands?" the duchess called out once again following their recess from the tournament.

Allen clenched the arms of his carved chair tight, stopping himself from jumping to his feet. Desperately hoping that someone, anyone, might come to Gwendolyn's rescue.

The hulking Gawain paced the arena, staring down the common people in the stands. He raised his fists over his head to remind them all of his superior might—then cackled at their collective cowardice.

Would no David stand against this jackanapes of a Goliath? Would no one at all come to Gwendolyn's rescue?

This day had pulled Allen's nerves taut to the snapping point. How his heart ached to defend her. How his muscles strained to fight for her. Just when he thought he could not take it another moment, a lone figure dressed in chain mail entered the arena.

His hands loosened their grip on the chair as he awaited the arrival of this new champion. He surged forward as he realized the figure was Gwendolyn herself.

Gwendolyn Barnes, holding her helmet under her arm and dressed once again as a valiant knight, took a knee before the duchess. She wore no surcoat, no colors at all, only her armor. Allen understood the message. This time, she fought for no one but herself.

"Arise, Lady Gwendolyn Barnes!" the duchess called with a regal shout.

"Your Grace, you said the contest is open to all. I ask for the honor of fighting for my own hand. I ask for the chance to choose my own husband, or even none at all."

The duchess smiled to Allen and took a deep breath as she pressed her hands to her heart.

Relief rushed through Allen. Although he still feared Gwendolyn could not best Gawain, at least she had this one last chance of escaping him. Had he not wondered if a David might arrive on the scene? Gwendolyn herself, who had spent these last days praying fervently in the chapel, certainly fit that role. A woman of outstanding character who now sought God with all her heart. Courageous, faithful, a protector of the innocent.

A chivalrous knight by anyone's standards. It must have been his own confusion, his own guilt, that had ever caused him to doubt her.

He nodded his assent to the duchess.

"Absolutely you may fight for your own hand." The duchess's gleeful voice echoed throughout the stadium.

Gawain just laughed. "You wish me to fight a girl now?"

"Absolutely not!" came a disgruntled bellow from the grand-stands.

For the second time that day, Lord Barnes leapt onto the

field. He stormed toward Gwendolyn, yet the brave woman never cowered.

The baron grabbed her by the arm. "This girl is under my complete and utter authority. As both her father and her baron, I say she cannot fight."

"That seems rather unfair, Lord Barnes. Can you offer any reason why she should not?" The duchess raised her quelling brow his way.

But the man did not waver. "Indeed I can. If she fights in this battle, who is to say that her valuable reproductive organs might not be injured. Is this not why we guard our women so carefully? Keep them in castles and away from . . ." He paused and shot an especially venomous glare the duchess's way. "Horses! Gwendolyn is an asset to my family and my name. I will not allow her to jeopardize herself nor our futures in such a ludicrous manner."

He turned in entreaty to the stadium at large now. "The Ethelbaums are a fine, upstanding family. I would be honored to link my line to theirs. Do not rob me of this right!"

A general hum of assent filled the stands, although a few feisty females shouted their disapproval.

Allen turned to the duchess and the handful of council members seated behind her. "Is this horrid fellow correct? We pride ourselves in being so progressive." But then he recalled his study of the extensive legal code and winced.

"I am afraid so," Hemsley said. "The duke wished to change the law, but he was never able to gain enough support."

"A man has the right to rule over his own home," Fulton added, "including his wife, daughters, and sons who have not reached their majority. It has always been so, both here and throughout Europe. Although, to hear such a just statute twisted in this manner certainly does rankle."

"It is neither just nor right," the duchess grumbled for their ears only.

"Perhaps not," the bishop said, "but I am afraid the time has come to concede defeat. We cannot strip a man—a baron, no less—of his right to rule his own daughter simply because we do not like his attitude."

The baron, clearly growing impatient, hollered out again. "Your Grace, have I misplaced my trust in you? In the council? Have we all?" He swept a hand across the stadium.

The inherent threat in his words was clear. They could not afford to lose a strong leader like the baron to DeMontfort's side. Nor could they have him stirring up trouble among the common folks.

Duchess Adela bit her lip and lowered her chin in defeat. "How can I ever bring myself to utter the awful words?"

In that moment, a certainty surged through Allen, the likes of which he could no longer resist. "You shall not!"

Consequences be hanged! Allen would do what he knew in his own heart to be right and deal with the aftermath later. He leapt over the rail and ran to stand at Gwendolyn's side. "I will battle for her! She does not need to fight for herself. I will be Lady Gwendolyn's champion and choose her mate."

Fulton and Hemsley jumped to their feet. The bishop just dropped his head in dismay, his conical hat falling forward to shield his face.

"You shall not!" Fulton hollered. "We cannot risk your safety at such a vulnerable time for our dukedom."

"Allow me to fight, or I swear I shall get on my horse and storm out of this place. You do not own me. I stay here only of my free accord. Someone must champion the Lady Gwendolyn, and it shall be me!"

At that the people stood and roared their support.

The duchess smirked to the council members. Fulton and Hemsley slowly retook their seats.

Gawain strode Allen's way with his jaw clenched tight. "I have bested you before, and I shall prove myself the better man once and for all. Let us not waste time. I long to see you lying beneath the tip of my sword."

"And what of you, Lord Barnes?" the duchess asked.

"I . . ." The man trembled and a pulsing vein protruded from his red face. "If Gawain wishes to fight him, I will not stand in the way." Although the gleam in his eye said he would gladly murder Allen with his own two hands.

"Sir Allen of Ellsworth, it seems you shall have your way." The duchess offered her most grateful smile.

Joy burst forth in Allen's heart. This was right. He knew it. He would be no man's puppet, and he would finally have his chance to thrash Gawain!

Gwendolyn offered Allen a quick kiss on the cheek, but her father dragged her away just as she began to whisper something in Allen's ear. She wrenched herself from her father's rough grip and departed of her own volition.

In a flash, attendants scurried at Allen with the armor that had been readied for the common folk and topped it off with the North Britannian regalia of crimson, ivory, and black. As they strapped the blunted sword about his waist, a groomsman delivered Thunder to Allen. Once astride, he was handed a lance. The announcement was made, and he turned his horse to head to his appointed starting place.

Here he was, again, staring down the point of his lance at Gawain. This time he must win, not only to acquit himself, but to save Gwendolyn as well.

Gawain roared toward him with a new determination, a new ferocity, Allen had not seen before. Allen thrust his own horse into action. They flew at each other. In the blink of an eye, their lances tangled and shattered. Allen held tight, praying with all his might that Gawain had fallen. But as he turned Thunder, he saw the man still sat astride.

With his typical preening swagger, Gawain taunted, "Come, Sir Allen. Enough playing about. Joust me in truth this time."

Allen's attendant brought him a new lance, and he tucked it tightly to his side. This time he spurred Thunder first, and sped toward the arrogant knave.

But Gawain was ready. Their lances clashed again. Allen's flew from his hand and flipped through the air. But Gawain retained his weapon.

"Aw . . . do you not wish to joust at all?" Gawain called.

But Allen would not be roused to anger. No, he must maintain his focus and bring this fool down. He had not remembered just how skilled Sir Gawain was. His confidence wavered, but he could not leave Gwendolyn victim to this fiend.

From the side of his eye, he noticed a splash of lavender kerchief waving in the breeze.

"Wait!" Gwendolyn's beloved voice called from his previous seat next to the Duchess Adela. "Sir Allen, please wait."

The duchess held up a hand to pause the proceedings.

He trotted her direction.

Then Gwendolyn, clinking in her chain mail, leaned over the rail to offer it to him.

As he reached to take it, she caught his eye, and he gave her his full attention.

"Gawain always lifts his lance too high just before he strikes," Gwendolyn whispered. "Lean in low and take him out before he has a chance to right it. And do it on the very next pass. He must not have time to adjust to your correction."

"Are you certain?" The strategy would not be the wisest in

normal circumstances. But he had barely been able to watch throughout the morning as Gawain defeated knight after knight. Gwendolyn might well be correct.

"Yes, I am certain. I have studied him closely, as if my life depended on it." She shot him a significant glance.

Her life indeed depended on it. And of course he must trust her judgment in this matter.

He saw in her eyes that he could trust her in all matters.

"Enough flirtation! You shall be my wife soon, and I shall tolerate none of it!" Gawain bellowed. "Let this match resume!"

Allen nodded his affirmation to Gwendolyn. She squeezed her hands together and nodded as well. He spied the trust, the hope, the faith shining in her eyes. He tucked the kerchief into his sleeve, and then he trotted to his spot and prepared to battle Gawain.

As he leveled his lance and lowered his visor, time slowed. The roaring crowds dimmed. The broad expanse about him pulled in to a single target. Until only he, only Gawain, existed.

Spurring his horse, he clamped the lance tight to his side, aiming it straight for Gawain's stone-hard heart. The horse leapt forward, step by step, in rhythm with the pounding of Allen's own heart that echoed in his helmet. Forward, always, one hoof and then the other.

As he reached a point only several yards off, Allen noted the precise anomaly Gwen had predicted. Gawain lifted his lance just a touch. Allen crouched low and dug his heels into his horse's side to command an extra burst of speed.

Before Gawain could right his hold, Allen's lance pierced straight into the inch of space to the side of his shield, slamming into his chest and splintering upon the impact.

Gawain howled even as he flew backward, flipped through the air, and landed with a clash like cymbals upon the ground.

It was over. Allen had won. And Gwendolyn had showed him the way. They had done it.

Together.

He dragged air into his lungs and circled about pumping the remnants of his lance overhead as the crowd went wild.

Gawain staggered to his feet and drew his sword. He tossed off his helmet and looked about with blood trickling down his cheek. When he spotted Allen safe upon his horse, he howled yet again, fell to his knees, and beat the ground with his gloved fist.

Swept upon the glorious tide of victory, Allen approached the duchess and Gwendolyn, both beaming at him with sheer, unadulterated joy.

"Sir Allen," the duchess called, "I declare you the victor."

His chest swelled to twice its normal size and pressed against his hauberk. This was the moment he had dreamed of.

The duchess took Lady Gwendolyn's hand in her own and raised it over their heads.

"And this is your prize."

Never such a glorious, perfect, enchanting prize had Allen ever dared imagine. A tall, fair woman dressed in chain mail with a golden braid hanging down her shoulder. His heart sped even more than it had during the joust. His mind flashed to that wondrous kiss in the yew tree outside her castle wall. To the perfect fit of her lips against his.

"Whom shall you choose to wed the Lady Gwendolyn Barnes?" The duchess smiled down sweetly to him.

Of course she expected him to speak Sir Randel Penigree's name. He had been their agreed-upon choice all along.

But Allen's heart clutched. His throat went dry. His lips tightened and refused to speak the words.

The duchess awaited, looking at him with anticipation. Sir

Randel grinned with excitement. Randel, who admired Gwendolyn but admitted he did not quite love her.

Gwendolyn pressed a hand to her mouth. She alone understood what this next utterance would cost Sir Allen of Ellsworth, who knew himself to be the best possible match in all creation for one Lady Gwendolyn Barnes, yet was being forced by fate to wed another.

He could not bring himself to call Randel's name. Not yet. Perhaps not ever.

Allen sighed. "Allow me a moment of respite. This all came about suddenly. I would consider my options first."

Though he could imagine no option that might provide a balm for his throbbing soul.

◇◇◇

Since the castle lay so nearby the tournament grounds, Allen had returned to his own chamber to collect himself. He splashed cool water upon his face and stared into the mirror as the liquid dripped into the basin. Studying his reflection, he was not at all certain he liked what he saw.

A man of duty. A man of honor. Yet a man who too often refused to follow the guidance of his own heart. A man who for this past month had chosen to drown out the whispers of that still, small voice of the Holy Spirit deep within.

Was it more courageous, more true, more just to protect the dukedom—or would exhibiting true courage mean following his own convictions? And would his marriage to the duchess even protect the people of North Britannia? The entire supposition was built upon a suspect prophecy. Shaky ground compared to the solid rock of God's Word.

But the Bible contained no instruction concerning whom Allen should marry. And what did God himself have to say on this matter? Allen heard Him shouting now, no longer whispering but bellowing His warning loud and clear. *Gwendolyn belongs with you! Do not wed her to another! Marry her yourself!*

So why did Allen yet doubt?

Checking himself in the mirror again, he noted that his North Britannian crimson and black surcoat remained pristine. He had barely broken into a sweat during today's tourney. Yet this daunting decision might cause him to perspire agonizing drops of blood. And so he headed to the one place where he might find an answer.

The castle chapel.

Not surprisingly, Father Marcus meandered through the place, chanting his prayers. "There you are, my boy! Whatever took you so long?"

Allen rushed to him and clutched his hands. "I desperately need your guidance. Tell me of the prophecy. Do you believe it is true?"

The old priest clucked his tongue. "I do not. Not that I do not believe that God can and will speak to His people. But this supposed prophet dabbled in the black arts as well. I remember. I was there."

Allen's mind spun with confusion. He wanted to believe the old man, but even if what he said were true, that did not diminish the fact that the people of this dukedom were relying upon Allen. They needed this wedding for encouragement and morale.

"However," the priest said, "I do not believe that is the most pressing issue here."

He gave Allen's hands a shake. "Although your respect for the ruling authorities is admirable, you must let no man dictate your path. You alone must endure the consequences of your choices. You alone must answer for them on the Day of Judgment. And you alone must decide what course you will take this day."

Most excellent advice. In his own odd but wise way, Father Marcus had shed new light on this subject. Allen should not cave to the whims of the council. He must make his own decision in this matter.

Only Allen was still not fully convinced what decision that should be. The people needed him—Sir Allen of Ellsworth, heir to Arthur, savior of North Britannia.

"Remember that haze of pride, my son. Do not let it cloud your vision."

Allen's jaw gaped as the priest's words pierced through him.

Chapter 32

The crowd grew raucous as they awaited Sir Allen's decree, yet no one seemed willing to leave the stands.

Gwen, still dressed in her chain mail, emitted a rhythmic clink as she paced back and forth across the front of the duchess's box, and no one bothered to chide her for her unladylike behavior. She wrung her hands together. Wherever was Rosalind? How she needed her maid's strength and clear thinking.

The duchess took Gwen's hand and offered a quick squeeze as Gwen marched past. "Do not despair, Sir Geoffrey," she whispered with a wink.

Gwen responded with a wry grin, glad the duchess finally knew the truth.

Meanwhile, Randel stood to one side, nervously tapping his foot.

Of course Allen would choose Randel. The path had been decided weeks ago. He was the only sound option. Randel would treat Gwen well, and out of her gratitude, she would grow to love him.

So why did Allen delay?

As she pivoted and strode away from Randel, she wondered just how settled this matter was in her own heart. She yet loved Allen. Yet longed for him. Yet relived the wonder of his kiss with every moment she did not keep her mind under tightest rein.

She still dreamed of him at night while she slept. Still turned her thoughts to him even as she knelt and prayed.

How could she in all fairness marry Sir Randel? But what choice was left?

In that moment her gaze scraped the sky and landed on the cross atop the spire of the cathedral.

Gwen stopped to stare at it as an idea struck her. She need not marry Randel, for she could yet be wed to Christ. Only God had ever loved her with a love that overshadowed her feelings for Allen, and she would gladly spend her life in devotion to Him. Her father would not relish the idea, but what professing Christian parent would publicly refuse his daughter the right to offer her life to Christ?

Her mind reeled at the thought. Gwendolyn Barnes, a nun. She chuckled. A mere month ago it had not seemed possible, and now it was the only course that made one whit of sense.

She must speak to Allen. She must let him know.

The mood of the crowd shifted. A number of people stood to their feet and pointed. They began to chant. "Sir Al-len. Sir Al-len."

And most assuredly, he marched directly toward them from the castle.

He entered the tournament ground, crossed the field, and stood before the duchess and the council with a new confidence—a greater authority than Gwendolyn had ever seen him wield. The crowd fell silent.

"Sir Allen," the duchess said, rising to her feet. "Have you made your choice?"

"Nearly. Would Lady Gwendolyn Barnes please join me on the field?"

Thank the good Lord. She would have her chance to speak with him. Though she longed to leap over the rail—as had become everyone's habit this day—she exited through the back of the duchess's box as a lady should. A guard escorted her around the perimeter of the tourney field and through the gate. In short order, she stood at Allen's side. Precisely as she'd always wished.

He turned and captured her hands in his. Energy pulsed and snapped between them.

She drank from the depths of his eyes.

Bending close, he whispered, "I need to know, Gwendolyn. What is your choice?"

Even as her mind prepared to speak the words she had planned, prepared to tell him that she would be wed to Christ, completely different ones rushed from her heart and poured from her lips. "You, Allen," she whispered. "I choose you. There is no one else for me."

Appalled by her own lack of self-control, she ripped a hand from his grip and slapped it over her mouth. Through her fingers she said, "I am so sorry. Forgive me. I did not intend to speak the words. Please instruct the council that I will enter a convent."

But Allen just smiled down at her, eternal love shining from his gentle hazel eyes.

He turned to the duchess, to the council, and swept his chin from side to side to include the entire audience in his announcement. "My wish is that the Duchess Adela be allowed to rule alone, as I know she desires. As we all know she can."

Gasps went up around the place.

"My wish is that a new law be decreed to allow her to do so

and to choose her own husband in her own time. And my wish is that I might marry Lady Gwendolyn myself."

"Treason!"

"Dishonor!"

"Travesty!" the cries rang forth.

Gwen could not so much as breathe. She dared not think. Dared not plan. All thoughts drained from her mind. All she could do was watch and wait and hope. Randel smiled his approval. She spied her father standing with arms folded across his broad chest and a smirk pasted across his face, as if he knew this would not turn out well.

"Halt!" the duchess hollered with that authority that never faltered. "Do not cry out on my account. I yet love and mourn my husband. I agree with Sir Allen, and I wish that the council would make it so. Place your trust in God, not in some superstitious prophecy. God alone is our deliverer. We do not need this wedding to defeat DeMontfort."

Fulton and Hemsley surrounded her on either side, and Fulton addressed the riotous crowd. "The duchess speaks from grief. But we will exert reason in her place. As the entire region knows, this marriage must occur to fulfill the prophecy and save us all from sure destruction. Take Sir Allen into custody! The wedding will take place upon the morrow."

Guards shoving Gwen away from Allen's side woke her from her trance-like state. She gasped for breath. But as they prepared to lead him away, four horsemen galloped onto the field.

"'Tis Warner DeMontfort!" one of them shouted. "He is on his way! Just a few miles from here! With a hundred mounted men at least!"

"You see," the bishop yelled, his voice shaking. "We have tested the wrath of God. Destruction has come upon us. We must hold the wedding immediately!"

◇◇◇

Allen searched for Gwendolyn through the screaming mob that jostled him toward the cathedral steps. He found her just behind him, secured between two guards. To his greater surprise, he saw the duchess also held captive and swept along with the tide.

He stumbled up the stairs as a number of armed men dragged him along. Someone thrust the duchess to face him. Then both he and the gracious Duchess Adela, most beloved lady of North Britannia, stood held fast with their arms pinned behind their backs before the desperate crowd.

Needing every advantage he might find, Allen scanned the area. Gwendolyn was being held behind him, likewise on the portico of the cathedral, but she retained her weapons. Nearby he spotted Sir Randel along with Durand and the other knights who had helped on his mission. All were dressed in armor, along with North Britannian surcoats, and must have been guarding the arena nearby.

Randel caught his gaze and nodded. They would support Allen if needed. Though Randel's right arm remained in the sling, he drew his sword with his left hand and stood at the ready.

A pathway parted, and the bishop passed through like Moses crossing the Red Sea. He glared at Allen and the duchess as he made his way up the steps and stood before them.

"Do you, Allen of Ellsworth take Duchess Adela to be your wife?"

"I will not!" he hollered.

"Would you leave our city to be ransacked? Our people to be raped and looted? Our dukedom to be overcome by this usurper?" The bishop shook his hands high over his head.

The man was being ridiculous now, but Allen's mind yet knew

reason. "I would most assuredly not. I would send out our own troops against DeMontfort. I would call for reinforcements from the countryside. I would alert the king in England. Do not hole up in this city like a bunch of cowards. Go out and fight him!"

"The prophecy!"

"Destiny!"

"Marry her now!" came the cries of the panicked mob. Hands reached toward them, fists pounded in their direction.

Allen feared they might be trampled completely. But he did not intend to back down. Gwendolyn, the duchess, Randel, all the people he cared about the most—and far more importantly, the God of the very universe—were on his side. Nothing else mattered. He must hold firm in his resolve.

The bishop turned to the duchess. "Duchess Adela, think clearly. Do what you must! Will you take Sir Allen as your husband?"

"I will not. Send out the troops. I am yet your leader!"

At that the people went completely insane. Screaming and thrashing.

"Just call them wed and be done with it!" Hemsley said.

"I cannot." The bishop lifted his palms in defeat. "They must agree. They must speak the words."

"We will swear that they did," called a man from the crowd. "We will be your witnesses."

The bishop dropped both his arms and his head. "I will not be party to perjury."

"Then seize them!" Lord Fulton shouted. "In the name of the council. Perhaps a night in prison shall change their minds."

"Wait." Allen pulled away from his guards. "If you will not hear reason, I have no choice but to concede. I cannot leave the dukedom to be destroyed."

The duchess shot a wild-eyed look his way.

He raised his brows and sent her a pointed gaze in return. "We must do this. For the people."

Catching the silent message that belied his words, the duchess took a step toward him. "We must, and we will."

Allen let out the low call of the barn owl, which sounded to any untrained ear like a dramatic sigh. Then he began the backward count.

Ten, nine. He took the duchess's hand.

Six, five. They knelt before the bishop.

Three, two. He put his hand to the hilt of his sword.

◇◇◇

On the appointed count, Gwen kicked her feet high, sending her full weight crashing to her back upon the stone floor and the unsuspecting guards slamming into one another. Once they lost their grips on her, she swung around, slicing her foot their way, and knocking them both to the ground. With a bound, she sprang to standing and drew her sword.

Allen had already knocked his captors unconscious, while Randel and his men fended off the crowd. The remaining guards protected Duchess Adela from the fray.

With the element of surprise still in their favor, Allen shouted, "To the horses. Come with us if you would defend our dukedom."

As they surged forward, the people scrambled out of their way. Only a small contingent of knights followed.

"Stop them. Close the gates! Line the walls!" Fulton shouted behind Gwen, but already his voice grew faint.

Slashing their swords toward the crowd to create yet more space, Allen, Gwen, and their comrades dashed toward the nearby clearing to the rear of the tournament grounds, where horses and weapons stood unprotected. Theirs for the taking.

They grabbed up sharp lances and steeds in a matter of seconds. Gwen found her own Andromache with ease and leapt upon her back.

"To the gates!" Allen called, pointing that way. A troop of about fifteen mounted horsemen followed.

Though the crowd now surged toward them again, those blocking their path ran away screaming as the armed knights thundered toward them.

While Gwen and the others approached the city walls, the gate slowly descended. The valiant knights pounded through the opening nonetheless. The spikes fell closer and closer. Gwen and Allen, bringing up the rear, ducked low to avoid being crushed.

They were through!

Allen led the charge up the hill. Only then did Gwen's thoughts clear enough for her to fully digest the hopelessness of their cause. Fifteen knights against a hundred men. What had Allen been thinking? But she would not turn back. She must remain strong and stand for right.

Near the top of the rise, Allen called for their troop to form a line. Before them spread a narrow passage through rocky cliffs. No one would enter the city from the west without passing this way. Gwendolyn fearlessly took her place between Allen and Randel in the row of horses and lifted her lance.

She surveyed their makeshift unit. Most of them lacked their helmets. Randel held his lance in his left arm. She did not even wear the uniform of a soldier, merely her chain mail. Unless someone came to support them soon, it would be David versus Goliath all over again.

Chapter 33

Just one more furlong now.

Galloping along the curving mountain ridge, Warner saw Edendale spread below him to his left like a treasure for the taking. He could barely believe his eyes; the gates were closed and all the soldiers within the walls. Would they give up so easily? The idiots! The fools!

He and his men could besiege the place and wait. Wait for Marshall and the king to take one look at this city in disarray with its incompetent council and declare him the new duke.

Snickering with delight, Warner leaned farther over his horse's whipping mane. He settled into the exuberant rhythm. He would savor the wind rushing against him, the leather reins biting into his palm, each and every hoofbeat. He wished to recall this, his most triumphant moment yet, long into the future. With great anticipation he galloped around yet another curve in the winding road that would lead him to his prize.

They entered a final passage surrounded by cliffs, and no one stood in their way. They rumbled through without a single obstacle. But as they exited the other side, a pathetic collection of North Britannian knights blocked the path.

Ha! The imbeciles.

◇◇◇

Gwen tucked her lance firmly to her side and prepared for battle. Their line held tight as DeMontfort's men swarmed through the fissure in the rock and filed into place before them. At least fifty men filled the clearing with as many or more pressing at their backs. Warner DeMontfort, surrounded by swaying banners in black and green, stopped thirty yards away. Even over the distance, Gwen detected his smug satisfaction as he took stock of their motley collection.

With the lift of a single finger, DeMontfort sent a troop twice their size crashing their way. Allen likewise signaled for them to charge. She surged forward upon Andromache. Much as she had always dreamed of battle, suddenly faced with life and death, all glory faded away. Only the horror, the seriousness of the moment, remained.

She tangled lances with her first opponent, but both weapons flipped through the air. As she moved closer and began to swing her sword, she realized one of them would likely die on this field. Still atop Andromache, she blocked and parried. She pulled on the reins to skitter sideways and attack from a different angle. But she could see her foe's eyes through the slit of his helmet and did not relish watching the light go out in them.

Even if she could kill one, two, perhaps three men, they could not win.

She would meet her Maker this day, but she was ready now, and she would go out fighting for something she believed in. Steeling her courage, she pressed on.

◇ ◇ ◇

Allen's opponent struck his sword hard upon Allen's thigh, but his chain mail held firm against the long side of the blade. Still, his leg throbbed with pain, along with his heart. He had led these men, not to mention his beloved Gwendolyn, to sure destruction.

As he battled off yet another onslaught of blows, he caught sight of two North Britannians falling from their horses, although he could not say which ones. Several of DeMontfort's men had fallen, as well, but were quickly replaced.

Valiant though his group might be, this fight could not last long. How he hated that DeMontfort would win and ride on to blockade the city. Allen had felt so sure his decisions were sound, yet they had led to disaster upon disaster. At least Gwendolyn could not be forced to wed Gawain from the grave.

His arm faltered at the thought, but he caught himself in time to fend off a blow from his right.

And that is when he saw them.

◇ ◇ ◇

Warner cackled as yet another member of the miniscule North Britannian contingent crashed to the ground. Too easy! Almost no fun at all.

Then, seemingly out of nowhere, the king's blue-and-red army streamed down a hillside from the south. Rushing to support the North Britannians.

Warner braced himself against the awful sight. They could not give up. "Attack!" he shouted.

All around him soldiers thrust their horses forward . . . and then slowed and faltered as they realized the king's own troops stood in their path. The very army that Warner had believed would support them in the end. The very king whom his men hoped to please. Now standing against them in a shocking turn of events.

"Onward, you fools!" he screamed. "Never surrender! Never retreat!"

That darkness he had come to embrace enshrouded him, wrapped about his heart.

Even the soldiers already on the battlefield dropped their weapons and pulled back.

One by one his men fell behind him, but he pressed onward. A frenzied drive overtook him. He could not go back, could never be a poor vanquished knight again. Never face Morgaine's haughty disdain. He had nothing to lose.

The remaining North Britannians snatched up lances from the ground and re-formed their line before him.

Though his horse balked, he kicked it hard in the sides and continued forward. The king's men closed ranks, while the North Britannians blocked the road.

He would strive for everything or for nothing at all.

Spotting a single knight not wearing the hated crimson and black, Warner veered in that direction.

Completely alone, Warner met his foe.

He looked down in both wonder and awe as the pointed lance of the unmarked knight found its way through the loops of his chain mail and sliced into his chest. He gasped as he felt it drive through and exit the other side. He screamed as his horse galloped away leaving him pinioned in the air.

And then he felt nothing at all.

◇◇◇

Gwen held tight to her lance with all of her strength, but after the briefest moment, the weight of her foe ripped it from her arm and he slammed to the ground.

His visor flipped open upon impact. Warner DeMontfort would trouble them no more. Though not long ago she had hated the man for murdering the duke, ruining her chances with Allen, and kidnapping Merry, all she experienced at the sight of him lying dead upon the ground was sadness for such a robust life wasted over envy and selfish ambition.

The rest of his traitorous soldiers had halted at the sight of the king's army surrounding them.

Gwen had not thought they could ever survive, though she had battled on until the very end. But the king's men must have been there, ready and waiting to deliver them all along. She spotted Allen, then Randel, safe upon their horses, though some from the group lay scattered upon the ground.

From behind her came a call, "Seize them!"

Gwen turned and spied Fulton, along with her father and a few soldiers heading their way.

"Would you imprison the men who saved your dukedom?" Allen asked.

"No, but I will most certainly seize you and Lady Gwendolyn, who caused this debacle," Fulton said.

"You have gone too far this time, Gwendolyn," her father added with a snarl.

She gripped tight to her reins. She had followed her convictions, and she would allow the man to bully her no longer.

All around them, the king's troops rounded up Warner's followers, yet Fulton stayed focused upon his mission to imprison his own faithful citizens.

Gwen turned to Allen. "Should we fight?"

"No." He lowered his lance. "This time we must face our consequences."

As the North Britannian soldiers circled around them, Allen

reached into a small sack at his waist and removed a piece of paper. "For you," he said, "in case I never see you again."

Gwen took the offered gift and pressed it to her heart. She would treasure it until the end of her days. Which might yet come sooner rather than later.

◇◇◇

"In you go, wench." Gwen's captor chuckled. "I would not wish to be you this day. Young ladies should stay in their place. You brought this upon yourself, you know."

The hand digging into her arm shoved her into the gaol cell. She slammed to the floor and caught herself on her forearms. The links of her chain mail pressed into her flesh.

"Mind your own business, you brute," Gwen said, even as he slammed the bars shut.

This could not be happening. Her mind still could not grasp that she was being imprisoned for saving the dukedom. For doing what any chivalrous knight would. But the whole of North Britannia had lost their collective minds this day.

Longing for any respite, she opened the note Allen had given to her in the battlefield. It looked to be a poem, written in his own hand.

> Flowing curves rush my senses,
> Like waves in a sea.
> Golden hair, streaming waterfall,
> How it beckons to me.
> Those eyes, pools so blue quench—
> Intoxicate, such bliss.
> While lips, seashell's fairest pink,
> Beg a lover's tender kiss.
>
> So bold, so true you stand,
> Athena in splendor arrayed.

Bedecked in steel or finest silk,
Your essence still aptly displayed.
A valorous woman who can find,
A tower of virtue and might?
Such a wonder at my side,
Would be my heart's greatest delight.

My soul in your hands for all of my days,
Guard well with your own sweet, fierce care.
Though fate be determined to keep us apart,
I surrender our future to prayer.

Surrender our future to prayer. Allen was correct, she must not despair. Gathering her fighting spirit, she crawled to the corner, rose to her knees, and pressed her hands together in desperate petition.

◇◇◇

Allen leaned against the bars of his cell listening for any cries. Gwen was somewhere in this prison as well. But hearing nothing amiss, he turned his attention to the nearby Duchess Adela. "So what do we do now?"

"I do not know. I never dreamed that I might see a day like today." The duchess sighed and shifted to a new position upon the hard stone floor. "I feel as if I know nothing anymore. To think that my own people could treat me this way over a legend, a superstition. . . ."

"I am sorry." Allen spoke the words that had been plaguing him. "I only tried to do as I felt God leading me, but I fear I made a mistake. The English army would have routed DeMont-fort either way."

The duchess sent him a hard look. "Never apologize for doing what you believe is right. Apologize only for compromising your convictions. If we had succumbed to their demands, they would have credited that blasted prophecy, and we would be wed, which neither of us wanted. Now they must face the truth."

Allen peered at her in the dim light and realized that the courageous woman meant every word. "But your dukedom. I might have ruined everything."

"If my dukedom has in fact been reduced to that crazed mob I watched outside, I know not if I wish to lead any longer."

Allen turned his heart back to prayer and felt God's soothing balm envelop him. Perhaps he had not made a mistake, for that holy presence was more acute than ever before. Time slipped away as he focused his heart and mind upon that other realm, that spiritual kingdom that always surrounded them, yet so often slipped from view. He had only spoken true. Only done what he believed to be right.

He must trust that God would somehow deliver him to his true destiny.

◇◇◇

Allen knew not how many minutes, or hours, had passed before the cell door creaked open.

"You can come out now," said a kindly guard Allen knew from the barracks. "Promise to cooperate and you will not be restrained."

"Of course," the duchess said, standing to her feet and lifting her chin high.

They followed the guard through the dim passageways, up the stairs, and through the stately halls of the castle. Finally they entered the council chamber with its marble floors and its walls festooned with billowing strips of fabric in ivory, crimson, and black. The entire council crowded about the large circular table. Lord Fulton sat in the head chair that rightly belonged to the duchess.

Duchess Adela took Allen's hand in her own. They stood side by side, unwavering before the council.

Fulton peered at their joint hands. "What is this? Will you mock us yet again by starting a liaison now?"

"Do not be a fool," the regal Adela said. "But we will support one another against your tyranny."

Fulton huffed. "We yet await more arrivals before we can discuss our decisions."

The duchess squeezed Allen's hand. They stood still and quiet, awaiting their destinies.

Then the chamber door swung open, and Gwendolyn entered, likewise of her own volition.

She came forth and stood at Allen's other side.

Her father entered behind her and took a seat to the rear of the chamber.

All that remained was for the council to issue their decree.

Lord Fulton stood and surveyed the gathering. "As most of you are already aware, William Marshall and the king have grown tired of Warner DeMontfort's scheming. They sent an army of their own soldiers to route the dissidents. And I have it upon good authority that DeMontfort is dead."

Allen was glad that justice had been served. Thankful that North Britannia was now safe. But that did not erase the fact that he had been a party to treason this day.

Fulton took a deep breath. "Despite the travesty that took place this afternoon, the council has decided that the Duchess Adela is yet the best candidate to lead our people."

The duchess appeared conflicted. "I will do so only if the council decrees an official apology and implements a number of serious changes."

Fulton nodded with a surprising degree of humility. "We never wished to dishonor you, Your Grace. I think we all lost our heads a bit in the madness of the moment."

"In that case, I will continue in my role as your leader. And the first change shall be to institute the law, which Sir Allen suggested, allowing me to rule alone and choose my own spouse in my own time."

"Of course," Fulton said.

"And what of Sir Allen?" the duchess demanded.

Fulton adjusted his tunic and pressed his lips together. "You are our duchess, thus you had the right to stand against us in our clash of wills this day. However, Sir Allen was not yet established as duke. We fear we would set a dangerous precedent by allowing his rebellion against the council to go unchecked."

"But Sir Allen is new to our region." The duchess let go of his hand and approached the large round table. "And he only supported my wishes. I will not consent to see him imprisoned."

Allen braced himself as he awaited their judgment. He had lived out his convictions, now he would bear his consequences with dignity.

"We considered his unfamiliarity with our customs," Fulton said. "We believe the best course of action is to strip him of his seat upon the council and send him back to Lindy from whence he came. Likewise, the guards who supported him will be dismissed from Edendale Castle and sent home to their families."

Allen's stomach churned. He would be a man without a purpose, without power or wealth once again. But his pride mattered little. He could survive any fate with God directing his path. At least he would leave with his honor and integrity firmly intact. Lord Linden would welcome him back, and he could start over again.

Only the thought of losing Gwendolyn hit him like a mace to his chest.

◇◇◇

Gwen yet tingled from her time spent in prayer. Peeking down at her hands, she would have sworn that she still glowed with God's holy presence. No matter what the council decided, with God's love surrounding her, she would stand strong. With or without Allen by her side, she would press forward, despite how badly her heart might beg for him.

"I agree that your recommendation is fair," Allen said at long last. "I accept the consequences of my actions. I shall leave the region as the council wishes."

The duchess pressed her lips tight together for a moment but maintained her regal stance. "If Allen is in agreement, I will not argue."

Though sadness washed over Gwen at the thought of losing Allen, she maintained her composure and her steadfast faith—until her father stepped forward and clasped her arm in his rough grip. From long-held habit, her muscles clenched with fear. But she bid herself to yet trust in God.

"And what of my daughter?" he asked the council. "I think we can all agree that this day proved a ridiculous mockery. I ask that you give Gwendolyn back into my care and allow me to choose her husband, as should have been my right this entire time."

Tears glistened in the duchess's eyes, but she dared not cause any more trouble. She had pushed matters to the limit with her bid to save Allen from prison.

Allen lurched forward as if he might argue for Gwen, but he no longer held authority in this place.

"Yes, Lord Barnes, you may take your daughter home now.

This matter is concluded," Lord Fulton dispassionately announced Gwen's fate.

As her father jerked her roughly, Gwen continued with her silent petitions. *Save me, Father God. Redeem me. Rescue me. Empower me to stand strong.*

Pushed along by her earthly sire, she took several steps toward the door.

Until something deep within bid her to dig in her heels and slow their progress.

Chapter 34

I am a knight.
Strong like steel.
Ready to conquer any foe.

Gwen recalled her battle chant. She knew her opponent—not her father, nor even the council—but rather the enemy of her soul who sought to devour her. Who fought with lies and tricks because, in truth, he had no power against her God. She would not concede to the enemy. She would not fear, never give way to despair. She would cling tight to her shield of faith. God would be her defense.

And victory would be hers.

Of a sudden, the doors burst open, and Timothy Grey with his familiar thatch of white-blond hair strode through. At the sight of him, something settled in Gwen's spirit.

"What is this?" Fulton asked, jumping to his feet.

A herald stepped through next. "Council of North Britannia, forgive our interruption, but I present to you Lord Timothy

Grey, the new Baron of Ellsworth, here with an urgent message from King Henry III."

A high-ranking North Britannian soldier spoke up. "He is the very one who led the king's troops to this place."

"Is this true?" Fulton asked.

"Yes." Timothy stepped forward. "I was at Warner DeMontfort's castle to save Lady Merry Ellison, whom I married just a few days past. While there, I noted that DeMontfort had gathered a large rebel army. Sir Allen recommended that I hurry back to warn the king. It seems that although William Marshall was once friends with DeMontfort, his mounting aggression did not sit well with the regent, and Marshall decided that he had best get the situation under control."

"Of course." Fulton stretched out his hand. "And we are forever grateful to our beneficent new ruler. We look forward to being an integral part of his reign. Long live King Henry!"

The assemblage echoed his cheer. "Long live King Henry!"

Timothy nodded his approval. "We have been interrogating DeMontfort's soldiers. I think we shall be able to gather ample proof that he murdered the duke, as well as the names of his supporters."

At that, a few of the council members shifted uncomfortably in their seats, but Gwen still did not understand what any of this might mean for her.

"Is that all the news you have brought us?" Fulton asked.

"In fact, it is not. The king would like to thank Sir Allen of Ellsworth for the role he played in rescuing Lady Merry and in foiling DeMontfort's plan. He has offered him a boon of his choice. Land. Marriage. Title. Perhaps Warner DeMontfort's own holdings, which will now be placed in new and faithful hands. Whatever he might desire."

Allen stepped forward, his sunshine grin returned to his face.

"I was willing to give up everything, yet God has returned it all to me."

Gwen's heart blossomed with hope.

Allen paused and tipped his face to heaven, seeming to bask in the wonder of it all. "I ask for the hand of Lady Gwendolyn Barnes along with her dower lands, which I rightfully won this day, and for the pleasure of staying in North Britannia with my new wife."

Wife. The word washed over Gwendolyn like warm rain. This could not possibly be happening, and yet it was.

"Well, given the mood I left him in, I dare say the king shall offer you more than mere dower lands, but it shall suffice for a start." Timothy winked.

Gwen wrenched free of her father's clutches. Even he could not stand against the king of England. She ran to Allen, threw herself into his awaiting arms, and hid her face against his strong chest.

"If, that is," he whispered in her ear, "the plan meets with your agreement."

She tipped back her head and cried for all to hear. "Oh, Allen, I love you, and I long to be your wife!"

Her lips melded to his as if by magic. He kissed her in front of the duchess, the council, and her father—in front of God and all the angels, and nothing had ever felt so right. At long last Allen would be hers, for now and eternity.

"I suppose we can say nothing against this," Fulton said, standing and offering the large throne-like chair back to the duchess.

"No, you cannot." She took her rightful place. "Lord Barnes, it seems your daughter will bring you honor in a new and unexpected manner."

"It seems she shall." Father huffed out the door. He was finally beaten.

Gwen tucked herself in tight at Allen's side, and he squeezed her against his heart.

The duchess beamed their way. "I think when the king comes to visit, we shall have a wedding to celebrate."

"Ho!" Timothy cheered. "Perfect. Our young King Henry does love a celebration."

"Perfect," Allen whispered in her ear.

And Gwen could not have agreed more.

"Your Grace, if you do not mind, might I be excused to speak with my betrothed in private for a moment?" Allen asked.

"By all means." The Duchess Adela, back in charge as she was always meant to be, swept her hand regally toward the exit.

Allen led Gwen to the door. Timothy offered them both an embrace on their way out, and several of the nobles took the opportunity to offer words and gestures of support as well.

At long last they found themselves alone in the corridor.

Allen pulled her into a shaded alcove and wrapped her in a warm embrace. He trailed a finger along the side of her cheek. "So, Sir Geoffrey, we meet again."

Gwen threw back her head and laughed. A hearty, solid laugh, the likes of which had not escaped her in some time. "Guilty as charged. I would say 'tis high time for a rematch. I came ever so close to thrashing you."

He shook his head in wonder. "That you did. I look forward to learning your strategies."

"So"—she barely dared to give voice to her fondest dream—"you shall let me continue to train?"

Allen pressed a hand to Gwen's flat stomach. "For as long as it is safe."

Torrents of joy washed over Gwen as images of their life together flashed through her mind. Family, future, children.

"But before we settle down for good, perhaps we should go on one last grand adventure."

He smiled and kissed the tip of her nose. "Perhaps we can join Duchess Adela and her cousin on that crusade they long to lead. But never fear, my love, one way or another, our lives shall be full of excitement."

She looked into Allen's warm hazel eyes and knew she had at last found her home. The distance between them faded, and they melted into another kiss so idyllic, her heart could hardly bear it. She longed to start their lives together. To witness the wondrous plans God had in store and discover what marvelous adventures might yet await.

Author's Notes

I am first and foremost a creator. Stories pop to life in my head, and then I look for a time and place to put them. For *Chivalrous*, I knew my time, since it was a spin-off of *Dauntless*. So I created a fictional dukedom where my idea of a new Camelot might make sense.

Although North Britannia is my own creation, the Norman rulers of England did hold several dukedoms—also known as duchies—around this time, mostly on the continent in the area that is now France. I placed my dukedom generally in the northern, mountainous area of England, close to the Scottish border.

King Arthur was a legendary figure who supposedly ruled somewhere in Britain during the fifth or sixth century. Scholars still debate whether or not this king and these stories were based on a real person, but if Arthur did live, his kingdom stood out during that dark time as a shining light. Similarly, I wanted my North Britannia to stand out during a time of corruption in both the nation and the church.

There was not a single "code of chivalry" during the Middle Ages, but rather these codes varied by time and place. I created my own code for North Britannia, drawing from other codes the standards that I felt best fit the character of this region. Likewise, I developed my own tournament rules based on the character of the dukedom.

The Christian principles in this story might appear at first glance to have more in common with modern-day Christianity than typical Christianity in my chosen time of 1217, but I did try to contrast the beliefs of the North Britannians with the more typical beliefs surrounding them.

In addition, Christianity at that time had many schools of thought, just as it does today. Despite the corruption in the church as a political entity, there were many devout believers who did their best to understand Scripture and live godly lives. For example, the well-respected historical church figure St. Francis of Assisi was alive during this time in Italy, and the book that Gwendolyn read in many ways reflects his teachings.

The language system of this time is complicated, involving the use of French, Latin, and Middle English. Although I explain that the characters would have read the Scriptures in Latin, the verses I use are from the King James Version, since it is the oldest settled translation we have access to today. The language I employ for the book as a whole is a slightly archaic, slightly British version of English for ease of reading.

Sadly, I believe that the marriage between Gwendolyn's parents was far more typical of that time period than many of the other relationships depicted in the book, particularly for nobles. Peasants had much more freedom in choosing mates, since power and money did not come into play, although they faced many other hardships in life.

On the other hand, women of the 1200s were a feisty lot.

Some held land and titles in their own rights, and many defended and ran their holdings while their husbands were off to war. I hope you've enjoyed this glimpse into their world, and enjoyed imagining what it might have been like for a lady who would rather have been a knight.

Acknowledgments

I have been blessed with so many partners who have helped me along my writing journey: the ladies of Inkwell Inspirations and Wenches Writing for Christ (Oh yes, you read that right), my local ACFW group, a supportive family and church, and many wonderful friends. Thank you to all of you! I would also like to take this opportunity to express my gratitude to all the members of my *Dauntless* launch group, who helped get this series off the ground. Just in time for *Chivalrous*, I also discovered the added blessing of the British Medieval History Facebook group, which is always ready to answer, and debate at length, any historical questions I might have.

A special thanks to my agent, Tamela Hancock Murray, who stuck with me through the challenging early years. Also to my editor Karen Schurrer, who played a huge part in keeping this book on track. And, of course, to the whole Bethany team, who has done such a great job with everything from cover design to marketing and publicity. Thank you also to Niki

Turner, Suzie Johnson, and Angela Andrews, who critiqued this book.

My final and most heartfelt thanks to my writing partner, the Holy Spirit. In God I live and move and have my being. I could never do this alone!

Dina Sleiman holds an MA in professional writing from Regent University and a BA in communications with a minor in English from Oral Roberts University. Over the past twenty years, she has had opportunities to teach college writing and literature, as well as high-school and elementary classes in English, humanities, and fine arts. She lives in Virginia with her husband and three children.

She can be found online at www.dinasleiman.com.

More Fiction You May Enjoy

Born a baron's daughter, Merry Ellison is now an enemy of the throne. Bold and uniquely skilled, she fiercely protects a band of orphans that must steal to survive. Timothy Grey plans to earn a title by capturing "The Ghosts of Farthingale Forest," but will he carry out his mission when he meets their dauntless leader face-to-face?

Dauntless by Dina L. Sleiman
VALIANT HEARTS #1
valiantheartsseries.blogspot.com

Journey to an Old Testament–style world full of action and intrigue! An unlikely prophet, a headstrong judge, and a reluctant king are called by their Creator to fulfill divine destinies akin to those of their biblical counterparts. All three face unforeseen challenges as they attempt to follow the Infinite's leading.

BOOKS OF THE INFINITE: *Prophet, Judge, King*
by R. J. Larson
rjlarsonbooks.com